THE WINEMAKERS TRILOGY
BOOK 3

Return to the Vineyards

Books by Laura Bradbury

Grape Series
My Grape Year
My Grape Québec
My Grape Christmas
My Grape Paris
My Grape Wedding
My Grape Escape
My Grape Village
My Grape Cellar

The cookbook based on the Grape Series memoirs that readers have been asking for!

Bisous & Brioche: Classic French Recipes and
Family Favorites from a Life in France
by Laura Bradbury and Rebecca Wellman
Bisous & Brioche

The Winemakers Trilogy
A Vineyard for Two
Love in the Vineyards
Return to the Vineyards

Published by Grape Books

Paperback ISBN: 978-1-989784-18-1
eBook ISBN: 978-1-989784-17-4

Visit: www.laurabradbury.com

This one is for all those brilliant scientists who performed the impossible and created a COVID vaccine within a year. Science saved my life with my transplant, and I never take it, or the people who devote their lives to it, for granted. They are the modern-day miracle workers.

Ce n'est pas l'amour qui est compliqué, c'est nous.
—Jean-Michel Guenassia

Chapter One

The phone call came when they were digesting amongst the detritus of an epic Burgundian lunch.

The May evening felt soft, with a pink sky and the gentle scent of freshly turned soil from the surrounding vineyards wafting over the long table set up in the winery's courtyard.

The table was littered with empty wine bottles and espresso cups, as well as a half-empty bottle of brilliant-green Chartreuse liqueur standing to attention beside a jug of homemade Pear Williams with an intact pear resting at the bottom.

Amandine fiddled with her espresso spoon. The glass of Chartreuse Gaspard had served her should have mellowed her out, but instead restless energy made her feet twitch, even though she was enjoying chatting with her friend, Cerise, about their favorite barrel-makers.

She sighed. She should be relishing a break like this from the punishing schedule of spring in the vineyards. There was always so much to do: weeding, aerating the roots, replanting, training the new shoots of the vines, de-budding … it never ended.

Maybe the fact that Cerise seemed so serene and in love with her partner, Clovis, was the problem. It was off-putting that amongst her three childhood best friends, only she and Gaspard were still single, and that they'd once—not that long ago, actually—been engaged to each other. Now they were … Amandine couldn't decide what exactly. Ex-fiancés? Frenemies? Awkward and distant, in any case.

Her glance meandered over to him; this man she no longer knew how to define. He leaned back in his chair, a faraway look in his dark eyes, sipping a glass of Chartreuse like her. He didn't look restless, damn him. He didn't look like he was doubting anything, and he definitely didn't seem to be thinking about her.

Amandine was still watching him when the hostess of the afternoon called out her name from the front door of the main house. Amandine looked up to see Sophie beckoning her inside with an urgent gesture of her arm, announcing there was a phone call for her.

Cerise nodded in Sophie's direction. "You'd better go. Sounds urgent. *Vas-y.*"

"Yeah," Amandine muttered, trying to hide from her friend how badly her hands were shaking.

When she was twelve, she'd received the news of her mother's death in the hospital by a phone call. Since then, she avoided them as much as possible. She owned a cell phone, but she was notorious for leaving it at home like she had that morning.

Almost everyone she knew and loved was at the lunch with her. Who could it possibly be, except maybe her younger sister, Éloise. *Please, not her.*

Cerise reached over and squeezed Amandine's arm, a warm gesture that was natural for someone like Cerise but caught Amandine by surprise all the same.

Amandine walked quickly across the courtyard to the house and took the old-fashioned receiver from Sophie.

"*Âllo?*" she said, registering that Sophie's face was unusually pale.

"Amandine?" Her younger sister Éloise's voice was strained. *Merci Dieu. Her little sister was alive.* "Something terrible has happened."

"Tell me." If Amandine hadn't been off relaxing with friends, Éloise wouldn't have had to deal with it herself, poor thing.

"It's Papa. He collapsed in the cellar and the ambulance has taken him to Beaune. He looked dead, Amandine." Éloise's voice broke. "I don't know what happened." Her shock vibrated through every word.

Amandine had to get to her. That was even more important than getting to her father, if he was still alive. "Where are you now?"

"At home. The paramedics wouldn't let me go in the ambulance with them." A sob crackled through the receiver.

"I'm coming right now to pick you up and we'll go together. Stay calm, Éloise. I'll be there before you know it—"

"I'm already watching for you."

"On my way." A hurricane of emotions began beating at the door to her mind, but she had to hold it at bay. She needed to get to Éloise, and even then she needed to stay strong for her sister. She knew she had to hand the phone receiver back to Sophie, who she now realized had been standing beside her the entire time.

"What can I do?" Sophie whispered, her fine eyebrows almost up to her hairline.

"It's Papa. He collapsed. They've taken him to the hospital."

"What do you need?" Sophie asked.

"A drive down there. I didn't bring my car."

"I'll take you," said Sophie. "Let me just go get my keys."

But then Gaspard appeared behind Sophie. "No, I'll take her," he said, in that dictatorial way of his that had been one of the reasons for their explosive break-up. "You have your guests to attend to, Sophie. I'll drive Amandine down."

Amandine's first instinct was to protest. That was always her knee-jerk reaction to Gaspard's tendency to manage everything and everyone, but ... no, not now. Her priority was getting to Éloise as fast as possible.

"Fine," she said. "Let's go."

Chapter Two

Gaspard was hurrying her across the edges of the courtyard after prying the phone receiver from her fingers and placing it on its cradle. "Did I overhear correctly?" he said to Amandine, as they half-walked, half-ran out towards the road. "Your father?"

His voice was perfectly calm and strangely it was exactly what she needed to center herself.

"Yes."

He looked over his shoulder at her long enough to send her a speaking glance that showed his understanding of the feelings warring in her chest—her hatred for her father and her brother and yet her acceptance of the fact they were still her family despite all that. In Burgundy, family still meant something.

"We need to pick up Éloise first in Pernand," she added. "Before going to the hospital."

"Fine. Where is your wallet? Did you bring a bag with you?"

Practicalities. Thank God for practicalities. They always grounded her. Despite everything, perhaps Gaspard remembered that.

Amandine shook her head. "No bag. My wallet is in my back pocket."

They reached his bright yellow Citroen Deux Chevaux. It usually made Amandine chuckle that such an autocratic man drove such an incongruously cheerful car, but there was no space in her mind for whimsy.

She got in and slammed the door hard. She had to or else have it fly open when Gaspard was hurtling down the road—she remembered that. She remembered far too much.

He revved up the engine, not wasting a single unnecessary movement. As he sped out of Savigny-les-Beaune, doubt began to creep in as shock receded. Even though he wasn't showing it, Gaspard must have found it strange to be alone with her for the first time since their final, cataclysmic fight. He must be surprised she'd accepted his offer so easily.

"You must be wondering—" she began.

"I never waste time wondering," he said in that abrupt way of his.

Why was it so comforting that Gaspard was as blunt as ever? As much as those qualities drove her crazy in day-to-day life, right then they were an anchor that steadied her.

He drove at his usual breakneck speed until they screeched to a stop in front of Amandine's house in the picturesque village of Pernand-Vergelesses.

Éloise, at sixteen a full ten years younger than Amandine, was blonder, prettier, and altogether more amenable than her older sister. She stood under the oak beams of the stone porch, chewing her thumbnail.

When she scrambled into the back seat, Amandine turned around and examined her. Éloise's normally creamy skin was pale white.

"It's going to be okay," Amandine told her.

"How? How is it going to be okay?" Éloise demanded, frantic, as Gaspard took off again, gunning it down the narrow, winding rue de Fretille in the direction of Beaune. "I don't know if Papa is dead or alive."

"Even if … even if something has happened, you know I'll always look after you." Amandine reached between the seats to clasp Éloise's trembling hand.

"It's not the same!" Éloise started to cry. "He's my father. Mother is gone. I'll be an orphan."

Her father had been so unsupportive that Amandine had felt like an orphan since her mother died, but he'd been different with Éloise—more fatherly somehow. She tried to find the words to reassure her sister. "No. You'll never be that." Honesty forced her to clarify. "I mean, technically you might be an orphan, but what I mean is you'll never be alone."

Gaspard cast her a warning look with his dark eyes, telegraphing that she was digging herself into a pit with her incurable honesty. Oh, so despite barely talking to her for months he still felt entitled to send her those intimate, wordless communications, did he?

Amandine shrugged back at him, annoyed. Besides, who was he to judge? Gaspard did the same thing all the time, which is one of the many reasons they'd been an unmitigated disaster as a couple.

Gaspard merely rolled his eyes. "Are you sure they took him to Beaune, not to Dijon?" he asked Éloise.

"No. I mean, yes. I'm sure they've taken him to Beaune. Jean-Marc called."

Rage flared up in Amandine at the mere mention of her brother's name. That was what her father had done to her since her mother died—pitted Amandine against her brother, Jean-Marc, creating a living hell for both of them in the process.

No, she wasn't at all certain she'd grieve him.

Jean-Marc was almost certainly already hovering solicitously at her father's bedside, doing everything in his power to ensure the family vineyards—the ones she single-handedly kept afloat—would pass on to him as the only son.

She let go of Éloise's hand and balled her fists tightly in her lap. Gaspard glanced over at her and arched an eyebrow that showed just how well he understood the anger brewing under her sternum. Damn him. She unclenched her hands.

"That's better," Gaspard said in a quiet voice meant only for her ears. "I wouldn't think the hospital is an ideal locale for a boxing match."

She was both incensed and relieved that she didn't need to explain the situation to Gaspard. He knew all of it—her frustration at being overlooked and undervalued because she wasn't a man, her need to fight for what was rightfully hers and Éloise's, the fact that her father and brother acted like enemies of hers instead of allies ... Gaspard knew the blackest emotions of her heart. More amazingly still, he'd never seemed at all unnerved by them. She had to give him credit for that, at least.

Despite what many people believed, her ongoing family drama wasn't why they had broken off their engagement. It had started with something so stupid—an argument about a parcel of vines for sale that Gaspard wanted to buy for her.

An few innocent rows of vines were the fuse that had ignited that fatal fight, through which she realized that the domineering nature of Gaspard's personality and her own refusal to be controlled in any way, shape, or form, could never work in a marriage.

She'd broken their engagement off right then and there, standing in the vineyard he proposed to buy for her. He'd agreed with alacrity—so fast and definitive that her knee-jerk reaction was to feel insulted. They were both absolutely the type of people to hold a grudge—hence the icy civility that had developed between them ever since.

Gaspard screeched up to the entrance to the ER of the Beaune hospital. "*Allez.*" He gestured them out of the car. "Go."

Éloise grabbed her hand and Gaspard sped off. She didn't even have time to thank him, but then again he didn't go in much for civilities like that.

She needed to locate her father and her brother … for Éloise. For herself it was quite a different situation. What she might find could jeopardize all her future plans and dreams of taking over the family winery and preserving her mother's last remaining legacy.

It didn't take long for the nurse to locate her father. He was in the OR, she told them, being operated on for what they suspected was a brain aneurysm. The nurse talked about a clipping procedure and gave the name of the neurosurgeon who was conducting the surgery, but Amandine heard all of that as though she was underwater, not fully absorbing the meaning. The place reeked of antiseptic and unpleasantness. She tried to keep the memories of visiting her mother here under lock and key.

Éloise remained tethered to her hand. She'd begun to cry when the nurse said "aneurysm". All Amandine could do was pull her close and offer her empty assurances.

The nurse led them to a family waiting area off the OR, where their brother, Jean-Marc, sat splayed on a plastic chair, scrolling mindlessly on his phone. Everything about him annoyed Amandine even now—his burly shoulders, the bitterness in his eyes, how he pinched his mouth together when he was feeling vindictive, which was basically every time they were together.

Éloise threw herself into his arms while Amandine kept her distance. Jean-Marc patted Éloise's back.

"Now, now," he said, murmuring platitudes. "They have the best surgeon working on him. You did the right thing to call the ambulance, Éloise. You may have saved his life." Of course Éloise loved him. He was a completely different person with her than he was with Amandine.

"Amandine." He nodded his head grimly over Éloise's shoulder. "Where were you when Éloise was home alone?"

How dare he. "She's sixteen. I think under normal circumstances she can be alone at home by herself. Besides, I could ask you the same question."

"I was meeting a new sales representative from New York."

Amandine snorted. Jean-Marc was a born sucker. He was ripe pickings for any huckster looking to make some quick money. He was like a homing beacon for people who were too uneducated—or just plain dumb—to realize that he was a terrible, negligent winemaker with no palate.

"He can do great things for us," Jean-Marc added with a scowl.

"It's tragic how gullible you are. I might consider lending you half an ear if you could tell the difference between a white and a red wine, but seeing as that's not the case—"

"*Non!*" Éloise shouted, tears rolling down her cheeks. "Not today."

Amandine glared at Jean-Marc and he glared back. Surely it was not right to loathe one's brother so profoundly.

"Fine!" she said, the word coming out like a gunshot.

Jean-Marc shrugged. "Whatever."

Just then Gaspard came around the corner and Amandine's head swam with relief. She had to concentrate on planting her feet firmly on the ground so she didn't follow her instincts and fling herself into his arms. *Under no circumstances was she going to do that.* "I thought you left."

"No," he said. "I figured that you could use another calm head up here, besides Éloise of course."

Gaspard winked at her and Éloise's eyes widened. Gaspard wasn't exactly known for his sense of humor, and Éloise had confessed to Amandine several times before that she never knew what to say to him.

But that was because Éloise didn't really know him. His dry wit and ironic observations never failed to make Amandine roar with laughter, even when she was angry with him and tried not to be entertained. Éloise couldn't possibly know how much he bottled up behind that brooding exterior and harsh-featured face. No matter how badly it had ended between them, she felt privileged she had seen a glimpse of that. She hadn't wanted to admit it to herself, but she missed him terribly as a friend.

Gaspard couldn't respect anybody who didn't stand up to him. They had certainly had their problems, but that had never been one of them.

Jean-Marc narrowed his eyes at Gaspard. "This is a family matter. Last I heard, my shrew of a sister drove you off and you're no longer engaged."

"What did you just call Amandine?" Gaspard reached up and rubbed the bridge of his nose slowly, a seemingly casual gesture that he nevertheless made ripe with menace. "I must not have heard correctly."

Jean-Marc became fascinated with his phone again. "Nothing," he grunted.

"That's better." Gaspard had never been the least bit intimidated by Jean-Marc despite his burly build. As far as Amandine knew, Gaspard had never been intimidated by anybody. Amandine's fingers tingled with warmth. *Had he actually just defended her?*

Gaspard turned to Amandine, ignoring Jean-Marc completely. "I talked to a nurse who just came out of the OR. She said things are still precarious but that your father is hanging on, and to expect the surgery to last another hour at least."

Jean-Marc opened his mouth to say something, but must have thought the better of it when Gaspard cast him a blighting look. "Can I get anyone a coffee or anything from the cafeteria?" Gaspard asked.

"Café," Jean-Marc said without looking at him.

"Me too," Éloise said, her voice tremulous.

"I'll come with you." Amandine followed Gaspard out of the waiting room, grateful for a chance to escape.

Was it possible that maybe they could strike up some sort of friendship again? She realized with a tug of longing how much she'd like that, but she wasn't about to beg for it either.

Amandine followed Gaspard down the corridors and into an elevator. Something in the rigidness of his shoulders anchored her to the present and dissipated the anger toward her brother.

"How do you know where you're going so well?" she

asked, when they stepped inside the elevator doors.

"Don't forget I have four younger sisters," he said. "I was expected to come and admire my new siblings as they arrived, so I figured out the hospital layout rather quickly."

Amandine nodded. Of course. Like a rutting stag, Gaspard's father had sired four daughters after Gaspard was born, to three different wives. He'd been far more interested in the impregnating part than the parenting part, and the women he'd chosen seemed to share his disinclination for responsibility, so they all ended up leaving—including his father. This left Gaspard in the role of a de facto parent for his sisters. Before they grew older and more independent, Gaspard was rarely ever seen without a gaggle of his sisters trailing after him.

"Right." She began to search for how to thank him for going well above the requirements of a dumped fiancé and being there for her. As always, though, words of gratitude came far less naturally to her than words of anger.

"If you're torturing yourself about how to thank me, don't bother," Gaspard said.

Amandine stared at his striking profile in disbelief. "I hate it when you read my mind."

"It's because we're so much alike."

"Too much alike." She let out a sigh. "Which is why we broke up."

Gaspard grimaced. Just for a moment, as they were suspended in that cube together, Gaspard felt so familiar—like he was a part of her—yet also a complete mystery. It was so unsettling the tiny hairs on the nape of Amandine's neck stood on end.

Thankfully, the elevator stopped and disgorged them on the ground floor. Either *boeuf bourgignon* or *coq au vin* was bubbling in the cafeteria kitchen—the scent of cooked wine and garlic provided a welcome break from the usual hospital smell of antiseptic.

Beaune's hospital—set in the midst of some of the world's most prestigious vineyards and in the culinary mecca of the Côte D'Or—served incredible food, including glasses of world-class wine to the patients whose medical conditions allowed it. It might be a hospital, but this was Burgundy, where bad food was tolerated under no circumstances.

They got in line for the *à emporter* food and drinks. Gaspard turned to study her—one of those long, lingering looks from head to foot. A familiar heat fizzled in her veins, even now. *Memories, damn them.*

"I was shocked you didn't have Jean-Marc in a chokehold by the time I parked the car and got in there."

Amandine clicked her tongue. "You got there just in time."

"I figured as much." Gaspard didn't smile so much as raise the right side of his lips by a few millimeters.

Why was such a small movement so gratifying, even now? She sighed. "I just can't understand why Éloise doesn't see him for the bully he is. How can she love him?"

"Jean-Marc is a very different person with Éloise than he is with you. Besides, I see it with my sisters too. My father is one of the most neglectful parents on the planet, as are their mothers, but still … they need to love them."

Gaspard's sisters owed far more to their brother—who filled in for all their careless parents—but maybe he was right. "I guess," she admitted, grudgingly.

This felt nice … this friendly conversation. So nice it scared her.

After they'd shuffled forward a bit in line, he waved his hand, impatient. "Forget all that," he said. "How are you?"

She tilted her head. He was trying to break the ice between them, so it was only fair she met him halfway. It probably said something that she was far more preoccupied with Éloise, Jean-Marc, and especially Gaspard himself than her ailing father. "I honestly don't know what to feel. I mean, I know I should be more ... sad? Shocked? Scared? But—"

"Why would you be after all he's put you through?" He passed her two coffees to carry and then took out his wallet to pay.

"Let me get these at least." She put the coffees down to dig out a few bills from her back pocket.

He arched his eyebrows. "You can take one day off from being ferociously self-reliant, Amandine."

She could glower and throw back a comment that would dredge up their old argument, but ... no ... she was too curious where these tentative overtures of friendship might lead. That was worth controlling her temper. It might come to nothing, but anything would be preferable to the stalemate they'd been maintaining since their break-up.

"Maybe," she said airily.

His eyes widened with shock. "I can't believe you didn't fight me on that."

She took a sip of her coffee. "Never give up on miracles, Gaspard."

Chapter Three

Five days later, in the middle of a family lunch—an extremely noisy family lunch which was always the case with four obstreperous sisters—Amandine called Gaspard from the hospital. His first reaction was to be stunned she'd remembered her phone for once.

"Yes. What is it?" If she was calling him, he would need to go to her. She never reached out otherwise, but he wasn't going to indulge in brooding over that.

His sister, Margaux, dangled the set of car keys in front of his face with one hand while she ate a fresh apricot he'd picked up at the market in Beaune. That had been their dessert at lunch, which had been perfection after the rather heavy *blanquette de veau* he'd made the night before.

He frowned and shook his head at her. From the sound of Amandine's voice, he'd be needing the car.

"My father woke up," Amandine said. If she wasn't shocked when he'd had his aneurysm, she sounded shocked now.

Margaux stamped her foot. She'd just gotten her license and wanted to take the car out all the time. *His* car. She even had the temerity to complain that it was old and rusted and not something that she liked being seen in.

Sisters. He turned his back to her so he could listen as closely as possible to Amandine. Her voice was thin and panicked.

"Is he coherent?" He knew that was the big question that had hovered in Amandine's mind the past several days. The doctors weren't willing to guess how much brain damage had occurred due to the bleed, and whether he would be able to regain any of his faculties when ... or if ... he woke up.

"I guess ... I don't know, because what he's saying is crazy."

A week before, Gaspard would have been stunned if Amandine called him out of the blue, but now they'd become ... well, not exactly friends again—it was doubtful they could ever be something that simple with their history—but friend-ish.

"So, he's his usual self then." Gaspard harbored true hatred for very few people, despite his lack of social graces. Amandine's father and Jean-Marc had earned top slots on that short list.

Besides bringing his four younger sisters up almost single-handedly when his father and their mothers bailed on parenthood, one of the hardest things in Gaspard's life had been to stand by, impotent, as Amandine was constantly belittled by her father and her brother. It almost killed him to resist the overwhelming urge to rush in and rescue her from her impossible situation. When he'd finally given in to his need to help her and surprised Amandine with a small vineyard of her own as respite from her ongoing family dramas, Amandine had gotten furious and broke off their engagement.

"No," Amandine answered. "This is a new kind of crazy. My father said—"

"Wait." Gaspard waved his finger at Margaux who had begun poking him in the back to get his attention.

"*Non!*" He mouthed to her, shaking his head to underline his answer. She was the third sister in descending age and since she'd gotten her first taste of independence with her license, she'd become an incorrigible pest about borrowing his car.

"Look, I was heading down to Beaune anyway, so I'll swing by the hospital right now," he said to Amandine. "I get the feeling this may be a conversation that is better to have in person."

"Maybe you're right."

"Besides," Gaspard added. "I can't think straight with all my sisters here."

Margaux gasped, affronted.

Normally Amandine would have chuckled at this. Nothing amused her like seeing his sisters giving him a hard time. The silence on her end of the phone line told its own story.

"I'm leaving now." He hopped up from his chair.

"Come to my father's room," she said. "I'll be here."

"*Oui.*" He slid his phone into his back pocket and plucked the keys from Margaux's fingers.

"Gaspard!" she yelped.

"It's my car and I need it." He knew an argument he didn't have time for was brewing.

"It's the Domaine's car!" she countered.

"And I work very hard to run the Domaine," he reminded her. "So I can pay for things like driving lessons so you could get your license in the first place."

This provoked a roar of disapproval from his other sisters who were still sitting around the table.

"You're not even sorry!" Margaux yelled after him, as he made his escape from the dining room.

"I know," he said, over his shoulder. "I'm the worst."

At the hospital, Gaspard found Amandine outside her father's room, pacing up and down the hall while wringing her hands. Her cheeks had no color in them at all and she was biting her lip. None of these were good signs, and Amandine was not the sort of person to fret over nothing.

"Amandine. *Je suis là.*" He snapped his fingers to bring her back from wherever she'd gone in her mind. It was not exactly gentle, but it was effective.

She stopped and turned her face to his. There was a distinctly hunted look on her delicate features. He'd never understood why seeing Amandine hurt made him hurt too, but it did even now. It shouldn't—not after she'd unceremoniously dumped him, humiliating him to his core.

She shoved her hands in her jean pockets as she leaned forward to give him a quick, distracted *bisous*, but not before he noticed her hands were shaking. From what, was his question. Fear? Rage?

"What did he say?" he asked. There was no way Amandine would be this distressed if her father was muttering mumbo-jumbo.

"He's lost his mind." Her clear green eyes were huge in her elfin face. "He said that the entire family Domaine will go to the first one of us to get married. Me or Jean-Marc," she clarified. "He didn't mention Éloise." She shook her blunt, chin-length blond bob in consternation.

It seemed Amandine's father was determined to be dreadful right until the end. "Amandine." He took a firm hold of her arm and felt that electric energy, unique to her, coursing through her. Like it always did, it echoed in his blood—ignoring it was the only option. "It's too early in his recovery to take anything he says seriously."

She scoffed and resumed her pacing. "I'm sure Jean-Marc is taking it seriously."

"What do you mean?"

But before Amandine could explain, her brother came striding down the hospital corridor towards them, his girlfriend, Julie, twittering on his arm.

They'd been an on-again, off-again couple since lycée, and Julie was an easy choice for Jean-Marc—an amenable village girl from Pernand-Vergelesses, as well.

Julie's round face was flushed, and she was holding up her hand in front of her with her palm facing in. She twiddled her fingers. What was the inane woman doing?

The diamond on her finger flashed under the fluorescent light in the hospital corridor, providing the answer.

"You bastard," Amandine growled at her brother.

Julie, oblivious, grabbed Amandine in a tight embrace. "Your brother and I are engaged! Can you believe it, Amandine? We're going to be sisters! Isn't that *fantastique*?"

Amandine remained stiff as a board and quickly extracted herself from Julie's arms. "You know why Jean-Marc asked for your hand now, after all these years, *n'est-ce-pas*?" she demanded.

Gaspard pulled Amandine backwards towards him. Instinct told him that, from the look on her face, she was going to regret what she was opening her mouth to say next. Yes, Julie needed to be warned, but there was a certain way to go about it, and he could tell from the snake-like stillness in Amandine's green eyes that she was out for the kill.

"We love each other!" Julie said brightly. Good God, but the woman was dim. He suppressed the urge to give her some blunt words of his own, but at the same time he knew, deep down, that Julie was no match for him. Not like Amandine.

"Jean-Marc asked you to marry him because not even three hours ago my father told us he was giving the entire Domaine to the first one of us to get married," Amandine said to Julie.

"Amandine," Gaspard hissed in her ear. "Go gentle."

But as usual she wasn't listening. "You sure bought that ring fast." She glowered at Jean-Marc.

"I had it already," Jean-Marc's face flushed ruddier.

"I doubt that."

"Jean-Marc already told me about your father's will!" Julie spluttered. "But he also told me that he's been planning on proposing for years, and that this just spurred him on. It doesn't change our love for one another one bit, and now we can plan a wedding!"

Amandine snorted. "And you actually believed him?"

"Of course!" Julie grabbed on to Jean-Marc's arm and went up on tiptoe to give him a kiss. "He loves me."

"Julie's right. I do," Jean-Marc said, but he was looking at Amandine instead of down at his betrothed. "I'd better practice saying that ... 'I do', *n'est-ce pas?*"

Gaspard wanted nothing more than to knock the smug expression off Jean-Marc's stupid face.

Amandine pressed her lips together. A livid splotch of red bloomed high on each cheekbone. Gaspard was aware of a tug of sympathy for her. She always had to fight so hard for what she'd already earned through her hard work and talent.

"When's the wedding?" she demanded. "I imagine it's going to take months, if not a whole year, to pull together your dream wedding, Julie." She arched a defiant brow at her brother.

"We don't want to wait that long, do we *ma puce*?" Jean-Marc engulphed Julie's tiny hand in his huge one. "We're going to do it six weeks from now."

"I wouldn't put too much stock in what your father said this morning if I were you," Gaspard said to Jean-Marc, keeping his words on a tight leash. "He's surely on high doses of morphine, not to mention the potential brain damage he might have suffered. There's not a court in all of France that would abide by such hospital bed rantings."

"I went to check in with the Notary before going to Julie's house." A self-satisfied smile grew on Jean-Marc's face. "As it happens, he added that stipulation in his will well before the aneurysm."

Out of the corner of his eye, Gaspard could see Amandine vibrating with fury. How he longed to fight Jean-Marc, the way they used to when they were schoolboys.

"Doesn't it bother you that my brother confirmed the inheritance with the notary before proposing to you?" Amandine narrowed her eyes at her future sister-in-law. Gaspard pulled her back again. Julie might be naïve, but she didn't deserve Amandine's wrath.

"No," said Julie, blinking up adoringly at Jean-Marc. "I know what's in his heart."

"Where's your pride?" Amandine's lip curled in disgust.

"We love each other," Julie said.

"How about the fact that he's trying to rush you to

plan the wedding of your dreams in six weeks?"

"It doesn't matter."

Amandine let out an incoherent sound of disbelief and turned to Gaspard, her eyes round. "Of all the idiots …" she muttered.

"It's not as though the amount of time makes any difference to you," Jean-Marc said. "You scared off the only man who was fool enough to offer for you." He jutted his chin out at Gaspard.

Enough! Gaspard swung his arm back to punch him, maturity be damned, but a nurse grabbed his elbow from behind before he could complete the deed.

"There will be no brawling on my ward! Take this outside."

Gaspard clenched his teeth but dropped his arm.

"No need, we're going." Jean-Marc winked at them. "Julie and I have a lot of planning to do in very little time. You can expect your invitation in the mail soon. No hard feelings and all that."

Amandine watched the two of them stroll down the hallway and then snarled—she actually *snarled*—a ferocious animal sound Gaspard had never heard her make before. Was it wrong that he didn't completely dislike it? The same went for the fire in her green eyes. He'd missed her, goddammit.

"Hey." Gaspard took her by the arm. "Let's get out of here."

"I should be here if my father wakes up again. Maybe I can talk some sense into him—"

"No," he said, that familiar exasperation about her blind spots rushing in. When would Amandine finally realize that she was never going to get her father or her brother to act honorably or justly? How could such a pragmatic person have one area of her life where she was so impractical? "That's not going to happen," he said.

Amandine's normally generous mouth clamped to-gether. "Can you believe he put that in his will? The bastard—"

"Yes." Gaspard dragged her down the corridor. "I know, but let's wait until we get outside at least."

Chapter Four

Gaspard was driving her home—or what would be her home for perhaps only a short time if her father died. Jean-Marc would drive the Domaine into the ground in less than a year with his incompetence. Amandine's stomach clenched. For a few seconds she wondered if she needed to ask Gaspard to stop his car so she could lean out on the road and throw up.

She stuck her head out the window as the entrance to Savigny sped by, taking in huge gulps of fresh air. How could she lose her vineyards? She had winemaking running through her veins—the only one of her family who did.

Her sense of failure was more than that though. It went far deeper than she had ever told anyone, even Gaspard.

She glanced up now at the vineyards looming above them as they passed the entrance sign to her village of Pernand-Vergelesses. The precious parcel of vines at the very top had been her mother's—those vineyards on the highest slope of the village—just below the statue of the Virgin Mary that guarded the whole valley. She'd brought them into the marriage with Amandine's father, as well as most of the other ones that now made up the holdings of the family winery.

When a woman brought vineyards into a marriage in Burgundy, they were automatically absorbed into the family holdings. It was slowly changing, but that was how it had been for centuries—a woman's vines were taken away in the same way she was expected to disappear into the traditional roles of wife and mother.

Amandine's mother, though, had bucked the trend. She couldn't do much about the ownership issue, but she'd remained a devoted winemaker, at least until she got sick when Amandine was eleven.

Her favorite memories of their time spent together were working side-by-side in the vines, particularly those high on the hill, with the whole valley of vineyards flowing out at their feet like a patchwork quilt.

Her mother taught her how to prune and train the vines in the old tradition, and to never bottle wine during a new moon cycle. Her mother had started Amandine tasting from the barrel at a young age so she could learn how to decipher the maturation process and get a sense of how a wine might unfold. Amandine gave her mother credit for her finely tuned palate—one of the most powerful weapons a winemaker possessed.

She'd been twelve the day they'd received the phone call that her mother had died in the same hospital where her father now was. The mid-January landscape out the window of her bedroom had been bleak, full of frozen rain and black ice. She couldn't breathe in their house, which was fast filling with mourners, so she ran up to the vines at the top of the hill—her mother's favorites.

At the top, she'd faced into the blustery wind rushing up the hillside. It was nothing compared to the desolation raging inside her. She reached down and touched the vines closest to her. Even in their winter hibernation, bare of leaves and grapes and anything resembling potential, the vine filled her with a rush of warmth. A wave of love almost knocked her off her feet. That was when she'd known her mother wasn't going to be in that cold grave in the Pernand-Vergelesses cemetery at the bottom of the hill—she would live on in her vines.

She made a vow right then to fulfill her mother's destiny in a way that her mother couldn't. The idea that Jean-Marc would ruin that legacy and her vow … bile rose in her throat again.

"Jean-Marc is going to ruin everything," Amandine said, to herself or Gaspard she didn't know, or particularly care.

Gaspard shook his head, his forehead wrinkled with patent disgust. "You don't have to argue that point to me."

She had to find a way to fix this. Jean-Marc would desecrate the place where her mother's soul resided.

And then, with a blinding flash, she knew.

It was a horrible, selfish idea, yet it was the only way she could think of to save the Domaine from the men in her family. It was … well … awful that she had to ask Gaspard, of all people, after dumping him so spectacularly, but she literally could not think of anyone, or anything else. She would lose everything if she didn't at least try.

"What if we got married?" she said in a rush.

Gaspard's Citroen screeched to a stop in the middle of the small road through the vineyards. He turned and stared at her, disbelief writ on every feature.

Merde. So it sounded just as bad out loud as it had in her head. "You shouldn't stop here," she said, trying to break this awkward silence. "It's dangerous. Someone might come up fast behind us." Everyone whipped through the vineyard roads at breakneck speed. This was France, after all.

With a clenched jaw, he pulled over to the side of the road and got out of the car, slamming the door behind him. Then he just … took off. She watched, confused, as he stalked up into the vineyards—vineyards that happened to belong to their friend, Luc—but in the context of Gaspard's reaction that was neither here nor there.

So … not going well so far. She hadn't exactly expected him to agree immediately, but she hadn't expected the whole stopping the car and stalking into the vineyards thing.

Gaspard was as pragmatic as she was. Surely, it wasn't too much of a leap for him to come to the same conclusion as she had.

She scrambled out of the car and followed him up the same row where he'd gone, her feet sinking in the soft, freshly overturned dirt. She spared a moment of appreciation for the fact Luc never neglected his Spring plowing.

"I don't think Luc will appreciate us tramping through his vineyards," she yelled at Gaspard's back.

He froze and after a few beats whipped around. The fury in his flared nostrils and heaving chest almost made Amandine take a step back, but she held her ground. Obstinacy rose in her, as well as her nerve. Gaspard's temper might be an inferno, but so was hers. They were made of the same combustible stuff. At one time she'd held high hopes these sparks would translate to their more intimate moments, but somehow it never had. They'd both held themselves back in bed in a way they never did in the rest of their lives … like in this moment.

His dark eyes flashed. "I cannot *believe* you, Amandine."

The light spring breeze blew hair into her eyes, and

she brushed it away, impatient. "I don't see why not. You're the only one who has ever even considered marrying me. Think about it, you're the only one I can ask. I know things have been well … weird between us since we broke our engagement, but Jean-Marc was right about one thing—there is not exactly a rush of contenders falling over themselves to ask me out."

"Amandine," Gaspard groaned, his voice low and strained. "I've only ever asked one person to marry me."

Amandine pointed to herself. "You mean me?"

He ran his hand through his dark thatch of hair, clearly trying to get his temper under control. "Of course I mean you!"

"So? What has that got to do with it?"

He scowled at her, emanating wrath. He looked rather magnificent with Luc's vineyards rising behind him and white clouds racing in the sky above. Dark. Brooding. A man of uncontrollable passions—sort of like Heathcliff from that novel they'd had to read in English class at lycée. She'd had a bit of a thing for Heathcliff. He seemed like the sort of man she would actually consider getting married to, and not only for practical reasons.

As attractive as she found Gaspard, the fact was that when they had at long last got together it had been disappointing. It had all happened so fast. She'd come to Gaspard in distress after finding out (mistakenly, as it turned out in the end) that their friend Clovis had done something terrible.

She'd needed reassurance that all men were not vile, and somehow she and Gaspard had fallen into bed together—the upshot of years of simmering sexual tension that both of them were too proud, and scared, to act on—except for their frequent squabbles of course.

That night, Amandine had been more vulnerable, and in need of reassurance.

Still, even then, she'd held something back from him—unsure what exactly this thing between them was, and not wanting to expect more than he wanted to give. He was the same, guarding a piece of himself under lock and key.

Nevertheless, the next morning, Gaspard had shocked her by proposing. Stunned, and cognizant that she'd been more or less waiting for him since she was a teenager, she'd accepted. Gaspard seemed like the only person who could fix the damage of her brother and father's treatment of her. In the end though, they were never brave enough to share those parts of themselves they'd been holding back. She still had a hard time—especially in crackling moments between them like this—understanding how that could be.

"You broke up with *me*," he reminded her.

"I remember, but if *you* remember, you immediately and whole-heartedly agreed. Anyway, wouldn't you say that we broke up with each other?"

He swore softly under his breath. "No. I would not."

"Does it really matter who broke up with who?"

"*Oui*! Of course it does."

"Why?"

"I asked you once to marry me, Amandine," he bit off. "I will not do it a second time."

"But that's exactly what I *am* asking you, so I don't think now is the time for a sweeping declaration like that."

He arched a haughty eyebrow. It was effective, but not on her. Not the way he intended, in any case.

"Don't try your eyebrow thing on me," scoffed Amandine. "I'm not so easily intimidated."

The intensity between them felt like it ratcheted down one small notch. Gaspard crossed his arms. "You can put the idea of us getting married out of your mind at once, Amandine. Listen to the message I'm trying to get into that thick skull of yours. It … will … not … happen."

"I think you don't understand what I'm asking." Frustration was building in her chest—a scratchy, prickly ball of it. She just had to explain better, then he would understand.

"Oh, I do, and it's degrading to both of us."

She shook her head. *If he would only listen.* "We'll have a wedding, but it doesn't have to be an actual *marriage.*"

He let out a strangled sound of disbelief.

"We can get divorced as soon as I get possession of the vineyards."

Gaspard's mouth dropped open. He was a hard man to shock, but it seemed as though she'd managed it. Maybe she shouldn't have approached this like a bulldozer. Oh well … it was a bit late for that.

"I want to hear no more of this," he said, his voice strained and, she could tell, on an extremely short leash. "I can't believe you haven't understood this by now, but marriage is something I take seriously. I refuse to be like my father and marry and divorce like it's nothing more than buying and returning a series of unsatisfactory washing machines."

"But Gaspard," she pleaded. "I wouldn't ask you if I had any other choice."

"I think I know how to take that!" His eyes were flint.

Yes, he owed her nothing, but would he really leave her stranded in her present predicament? Had she misjudged him so badly? "But—"

"Amandine." He strode forward and caught her upper arms in his hands before she realized what was happening. "Stop this."

It was the first time they'd been this close, face-to-face, since they'd broken up. Her breath quickened and her heart was leaping all over the place in her chest. *Dammit.* She hadn't realized he still had this effect on her. *Inconvenient, but it meant nothing.* Gaspard was many things, but he was not a man to be trifled with.

"You would let Jean-Marc steal the vines out from under me?" Her voice sounded too close to begging for her own comfort. She wouldn't lower herself like this to anyone—especially not Gaspard—for anything less than the vineyards—her mother's vineyards, not to mention the only way Amandine had of ensuring a viable future for her and Éloise.

Did Gaspard not understand how much the Domaine meant to her? The land was her mother's legacy. It was part of her as much as her arm or her leg ... even more so ... it was part of her soul. Maybe Gaspard had never understood that, and never would. That possibility only dawned on her now. It was ultimately the reason they'd broken up in the first place—he had thought new vines and her mother's vines were interchangeable somehow. He'd never understood the most important part of her.

"I will help you in any way I can except marrying you," Gaspard said.

"But that's the only help I need."

"Then I'm sorry." He dropped his hands from his hips and walked back to the car, staring straight ahead as Amandine followed. She slid into the passenger seat.

They didn't say another word, not even to say goodbye when he dropped her off at her house. But then again, she was not the type of person to give up so easily.

Chapter Five

Gaspard ordered a glass of Pernand-Vergelesses at the bar and then joined his friends at their usual table. They had an informal get-together every Tuesday night at the combination café and bistro sitting right on the main village square of Savigny-les-Beaune.

Whoever could come, came, and it was a moment where they could relax, catch up, and share what was going on with their lives. He still hadn't decided if he was going to tell them about Amandine's insane wedding scheme, but he knew he needed to get out of his house. He didn't expect Amandine to show up—she'd be far too busy with her Machiavellian plotting to socialize.

Out of spite, he purposely didn't choose one of Amandine's wines when he ordered, but one from her neighbor across the street who her family had never gotten along with. He wasn't proud of himself for still smarting from her insult but choosing her neighbor's wine was a way of indulging his pettiness without hurting anyone.

His friend, Clovis, was already sitting at their table and studied Gaspard's face as he joined them. "What's wrong with you?"

Gaspard still didn't know where to begin, or even if

he wanted to. To add insult to … well … insult, Clovis was looking so goddamn happy across the table with his fiancée, Cerise, by his side. She was drinking tea and her pregnant stomach had grown so much it now touched the edge of the café table. He'd never in his life seen Clovis so contented.

Theoretically, of course, Gaspard was thrilled for his friend. Still, he couldn't shake the feeling that the fact his childhood friends, Luc—ensconced at the table beside his girlfriend, Sadie—and Clovis had recently discovered domestic bliss made his own solitude that must heavier to bear.

"Who's looking after the boys?" Gaspard tried to change the subject by asking about Cerise's sons from her first marriage.

"Jean is spending the evening with them." Clovis smiled.

Gaspard glanced over at Luc. It had recently come to light that Jean, Clovis's *régisseur* who managed his extensive wine Domaine, was Luc's biological father. It was all insanely complicated, but this was Burgundy, where family dramas and scandals were as much a part of the region as Pinot Noir. Everyone knew and loved Jean, but Gaspard still wasn't sure if Luc had come to terms with this shocking revelation.

Gaspard cleared his throat. "That's nice. Jean always enjoyed children. He was wonderful with my sisters and me. How are things between you two?" he asked Luc. *What good could come from dancing around the topic?*

"Surprisingly well." Luc nodded. "The fact that he's my father … it's one of those things that seems like it should feel completely bizarre, but in fact feels … I don't know … almost natural."

Cerise pointed the spoon she'd been using to stir her

tea at Luc. "That right there is *exactly* how pregnancy feels. Logically should feel weird yet doesn't."

Gaspard felt a stab of envy as Clovis gazed down at Cerise adoringly.

"We went to Jean's place for dinner last night," Sadie said, and Luc pulled her closer to his side. *Mon dieu.* Those two were sickeningly happy too. How was it that all his friends were now coupled up and he and Amandine had made such a monumental mess of everything?

"What did he make you?" asked Clovis. "Was it his—"

"*Saucisses de Morteau,*" both Clovis and Sadie said it at the same time, then laughed. That was indeed one of Jean's favorite meals—one large *appellation controllé saucisse de morteau* per person, boiled potatoes, excellent quality heated *cancoillote* cheese poured over it all, chopped fresh parsley sprinkled on top, and a large tossed green salad with a light vinaigrette.

Luc chuckled. "Did you know he buys the sausages directly from the Jura every month?"

"Do I? He never shuts up about it." Clovis's eyes danced. "He has a sausage guy, just like he has a *cancoillote* guy in Franche-Comté and a comté cheese guy and a Calvados guy up in Normandy."

Gaspard was, of course, glad things were going well between Luc and his newfound father, and of course for all his friends' love lives, so why did the reigning harmony at the table make him feel ten times worse? Maybe it was a mistake coming to the bistro.

"What's up?" Luc asked, his bright-blue eyes perceptive. "You look … disgruntled."

"Now that's unfair." Clovis chuckled. "Gaspard always looks disgruntled."

Everyone grinned and Gaspard rolled his eyes. Still … they weren't entirely wrong.

"Okay. Okay. More disgruntled than usual," Luc said. "Hey, where's Amandine? She texted us yesterday that her father woke up. Not to be callous or anything, but we couldn't figure out if that was good news or bad news."

Gaspard blew air through his lips, his limbs heavy with exhaustion from all of that anger since Amandine had proposed her outrageous scheme. "Apparently he's bad news regardless of whether he's alive or dead."

"Well, I can't say I'm surprised to hear that." Luc took a sip of his wine. "But how is Amandine coping?"

Gaspard peered down into his glass of wine, but there were no answers there. Where to even begin? "I think she's gone crazy. You are not going to believe what she suggested when I drove her home from the hospital yesterday."

"What?" Sadie asked, her red curls bouncing as she leaned forward in her chair.

The coil of frustration in Amandine's chest hadn't loosened since Gaspard had dropped her off at home—in monastic silence—the day before.

Right after lunch, Éloise had begged Amandine to take her to Gaspard's house in Volnay to hang out with her best friend who was—inconveniently in this instance—Gaspard's youngest sister, Bertille.

Amandine, of course, remained in her car while

Éloise got out. She couldn't see Gaspard until she'd figured out a way to convince him that this marriage need only be a blip in his life, and that they could divorce in a matter of months. It didn't need to be the big deal and moral compromise he seemed to think it was.

Still, after a day of trying, and failing, to come up with a new approach—while weeding and plowing her mother's vines on the top of the hill until every muscle in her body ached—she still came up short. One thing that being in those particular vines reinforced for her was that no matter what, she had to find a way to save them from Jean-Marc.

The only silver lining was that she'd been spared any visits by her brother or Julie. Jean-Marc probably figured he'd defeated her, so didn't consider rubbing it in worth the bother. While their father was still alive, he most likely reasoned there was no rush to torment her any further—for the time being anyway.

Jean-Marc had always been short-sighted.

After a shower and a wedge of Camembert and a chunk of baguette for dinner, Amandine couldn't sit still as her mind pinged in all directions. She needed to move. She needed noise and people and distraction.

Gaspard's reaction had insidiously begun to weave doubt through her heart. A reliable sounding-board would provide a much-needed dose of objectivity and she knew where to get it. It was Tuesday night, her friends would be at their café in Savigny. If she brought up her dilemma to the group, surely their friends would see her side and help her de-dramatize the whole thing for Gaspard.

She wasn't certain Gaspard would be there—he might still be too outraged for socializing—but either way getting their friends onside was the first step.

She hopped in her rusty old Renault and sped past the beautiful stone washing house and the village church that dated back to Roman times with its brightly tiled black and yellow steeple. Pernand-Vergelesses was routinely voted one of the most beautiful villages in all of France, but it was more than that to Amandine. It was her home.

She sped through the tiny vineyard lanes that connected Pernand-Vergelesses and neighboring Savigny-les-Beaune, past the round little stone huts called *cabottes* that dotted the rolling vineyards, and into the narrow roads of Savigny-les-Beaune.

She parked right beside the huge chateau with its four chubby turrets. Such sights were part of her everyday life, but tourists came from far and wide to marvel over them, just like the wines of the region. She breathed in the sweet air that smelled of freshly growing leaves and the sharp scent of the newly overturned, limestone-rich soil. She was knitted into the fabric of Burgundy in the same way as the *cabottes* and the vines and even the thirteenth century castle across the square. She just needed to get Gaspard to marry her, so she could cement her belonging with official ownership.

When she opened the door to the café, she spotted Cerise, Clovis, Sadie and Luc already sitting at their usual table. No Gaspard, although it was too crowded to see perfectly. The spring air outside gave way to the familiar smell of spilled wine, coffee, and nicotine that greeted her like a hug.

She released a breath she hadn't realized she'd been holding. The owner, who also tended the bar, shouted her name and raised his hand in greeting. She smiled back. She wasn't done with Gaspard yet—far from it.

Even though Gaspard's back was turned to the door of the café, he could hear a chorus of voices shouting, "*Salut Amandine! Bonsoir ma belle. Comment va ton père?*"

Eh merde. Amandine certainly had a sense of timing. He'd just been about to start telling their friends what she'd asked of him, and he would have appreciated a chance to tell his side of the story without her around.

He cleared his throat, unsure how to act around her all of a sudden. *Stop it Gaspard. You're being ridiculous. You, at least, have nothing to be ashamed of. Amandine on the other hand …* He kept telling himself that, yet at the same time guilt nipped him like an annoying mosquito. Amandine needed him, and he had refused to help her.

She shouted her order of a glass of Gevrey-Chambertin to the bartender and, still standing at the bar, turned around to wave at their table. Her green eyes went wide as she caught sight of Gaspard. Ah. *So she hadn't seen him at first.*

Gaspard watched as she accepted her glass of wine, stiffened her spine, and walked over to sit down at the empty chair across from him. Even though she was shameless, he had to grudgingly admire how she didn't back down.

She arched a blonde eyebrow in his direction. "Still furious with me?"

Well, as it happened, Gaspard could arch his eyebrow too. "What do you think?"

"He was just about to tell us what happened between the two of you," Sadie said, her golden eyes ping-ponging back and forth between the two of them. "Though you two being at odds is hardly news."

"I asked Gaspard to marry me," Amandine said in an off-hand way as she slipped off her cardigan.

Jaws dropped all around the table.

"What did you say?" Luc asked Gaspard.

Gaspard scowled. "I said no *bien sûr!*"

"But … why?" Clovis asked in bewilderment. Both Clovis and Luc had recently made it clear to Gaspard that they thought he and Amandine belonged together. Of course they did—it would finish off their little friendship group so neatly, after all. They had no idea.

"What Amandine has neglected to explain is *why* she asked me to marry her."

Amandine tossed her head, defiant as ever, but didn't fill in the blanks.

"*Allez!* Don't keep us in suspense," Cerise cried. "That's cruel. You have a pregnant lady here."

Gaspard sighed. He was going to have to do it, even though his heart still smarted from the insult. "Apparently Amandine's father has put some sort of archaic stipulation in his will that the first of his children to marry will inherit the entire Domaine. Don't delude yourselves, that's the only reason why Amandine asked me, not because of any tenderer feelings. Amandine doesn't *have* tenderer feelings."

Amandine's head jerked back, and her throat contracted as she swallowed hard.

"Don't be malicious, Gaspard," Luc said, his azure gaze understanding, but reproachful. "I know you. You'll regret it later."

"Luc's right," Amandine said. "Can you blame me

for asking?" She lifted her palms in the air. "At least I was completely honest with you and didn't try to pretend it was for any reasons besides the inheritance."

Cerise reached out and touched the top of Amandine's hand with her own. "Fill us in with the details. I think we're missing some pertinent information."

Amandine rubbed her eyes with her thumbs. Now he studied her closer, he noticed the dark circles under her eyes and how her skin was pulled tighter than usual over that stubborn chin of hers. Gaspard fought the absurd urge to take her home and tuck her into bed.

"When my father woke up from his … well, coma or wherever he was," Amandine began. "He mentioned the marriage stipulation in his will and told me I'd better hurry up as he'd told Jean-Marc just before I got there."

"Good God. He's still pitting you two against each other even from his death bed." Clovis's mouth twisted in disgust.

Amandine nodded, equally grim. "He'd never mentioned it before, so he must have been keeping this piece of information in reserve to deploy for maximum impact. Anyway, I called Gaspard because I needed to talk to someone after finding out, and then Jean-Marc arrived at the hospital with Julie on his arm, wearing her brand-new engagement ring."

Luc whistled. "And you're sure it was your father talking, not the morphine or the brain injury?"

Amandine shook her head. "Jean-Marc didn't wait to find out. He went to the notary to confirm that stipulation before going to propose to Julie."

"The nerve!" Sadie gasped. Gaspard didn't miss that Luc slid his arm around her shoulders and pulled her even tighter against him. "Julie didn't mind being proposed to under those circumstances?"

Amandine rolled her eyes. "Unbelievably, no, not at all, but she's never been the brightest bulb in the pack."

"From what I could see, I think she truly loves Jean-Marc," Gaspard observed, not wanting to drag Julie into the mess any further than necessary. From what he knew of her, she was naïve, but she didn't deserve anyone's hate. "As unbelievable as that sounds. I can vouch for the fact that she seemed completely happy with the circumstances of Jean-Marc's proposal."

"Of course, that got me thinking," Amandine continued. "Gaspard was there, and it occurred to me that perhaps he was my only way of getting the Domaine from Jean-Marc." Two bright spots of red appeared on Amandine's pale cheeks. Was it possible she was actually feeling a smidgen of shame? "If a marriage was what my father needed why can't Gaspard and I get married … in name only, of course," she added hastily.

Gaspard ground his teeth together. He was over her, so why did that hurt far more than it should?

Cerise whistled. "This has a lot of components."

"I said no," Gaspard clarified this point, in case there was any doubt. "I refuse to take part in a sham marriage. I will not be planning my divorce when I'm still standing at the altar. I won't repeat my father's pattern. The whole thing is grotesque."

Clovis tilted his head. "Amandine, I know what the Domaine and the vines mean to you. I think all of us here can understand that, but you can hardly blame Gaspard for his refusal, can you?"

"Hang on a second." Cerise put out her arm in front of Clovis. "Not so fast. I know first-hand how frustrating and impossible it can be to be a woman in the winemaking world here. The way I see it, Amandine was put in an intolerable position. What other options did she have than to ask for a friend's help?"

"Maybe you haven't noticed," Gaspard snapped. "But since our break-up we haven't exactly been friends. Civil, but not friends."

"*Merci* Cerise," Amandine said, pointedly ignoring Gaspard. "That's it exactly—I wouldn't have asked him otherwise."

"Flattering," Gaspard muttered, his jaw aching from clenching it so hard.

Amandine bit her thumbnail. "You know that's not what I meant."

"Oh?" Gaspard bristled.

She inhaled deeply. "No. What I meant is I hated having to ask you because of our history."

Everyone around the table nodded—they all knew about the engagement and break-up.

"As you see." Gaspard took a sip of his wine, which he hated to admit to himself, wasn't as good as the white wine that Amandine made—when she could prevent her brother from interfering. "We are at an impasse."

Several beats of silence passed, filled up with the clatter of conversation and wine glasses being washed and filled and the soft pop of a wine cork being drawn. Surely, they would take his side. Amandine's proposal defied belief.

Finally, Cerise spoke. "I'm wondering to what lengths I would go to save Domaine du Cerisier." Her eyes slid over to Clovis. Gaspard remembered the now-happy couple had almost broken up for good because of that.

"And?" Clovis asked.

"I really don't know."

"Same with me and archaeology." Sadie tilted her

head. "If someone threatened to take my dig away from me before I'm finished … I don't know how far I would go to save it … pretty far, I would imagine."

"But there are other vineyards!" Gaspard argued for what felt like the umpteenth time. He'd never understood Amandine's obsession. He'd tried, but his role of head winemaker at his family's Domaine had always felt like a burden rather than a gift. "And other jobs in the wine world."

"Said like someone who has never known what it feels like to risk losing their winery." Cerise's dark eyes were challenging.

"He's never understood that." Amandine shook her head at Cerise. "It's his blind spot."

"Excuse me, but I'm right here!" Gaspard protested. Maybe he wasn't particularly gifted at seeing things from other people's perspectives—after all, his sisters were constantly accusing him of this shortcoming. Still, how could a bunch of vines take precedence over people and important relationships? Amandine was right about one thing—he didn't think he would ever understand her absolute determination to control her family's winery.

Gaspard did an excellent job as a winemaker—that was a point of pride with him—but his heart had never been in it in the same way as his friends. Ever since he was a young boy, he wanted a job that was more dangerous and more exciting than doing the same routines in the vineyards and the cellar, year after year. He'd always longed for a career where he could help people in a more tangible way than just making them something good to drink.

He'd never told anyone this, not even these best friends, but his dream had always been to be a firefighter. It was impossible, of course, but that wild fantasy still intruded into his thoughts, despite the fact he'd long ago left childish things behind.

He'd been thrust into the role of running the Domaine to continue the family legacy and to provide for his four sisters. He'd never been asked his opinion in the matter. It was just like looking after his sisters—it was simply expected of him.

He often felt like the odd person out in this regard, well … except for Sadie, but she was new to the group and she had her archaeology. He'd never had a choice. Here, Amandine did, and yet she kept choosing the most impossible option. He'd tried to get her to explain her connection to the vines in the past, but she'd never been able to articulate it. Or maybe, he thought now, she'd simply never trusted him enough. "Amandine," he said. "I can try to put myself in your shoes, but it still doesn't change my opinion."

"And what is that exactly?" Amandine demanded with a sharp thrust of her mulish chin towards him.

"That you need to deal with reality instead of how you wish things to be in an ideal world. Did it ever occur to you to just accept the situation? Your father—even beyond the grave it would seem, although he's still of this world … for the moment—and your brother will always stand between you and the Domaine. Nothing but frustration can come from banging your head against that wall over and over again. Why would you willingly choose that?"

After all, Gaspard's family's Domaine stood between him and his dream, but what good would have come from resisting that reality? Nothing, and his sisters would have paid the price. Intolerable.

"Yes, why *would* I choose that?" Amandine said, each word distinct and ripe with meaning. "Especially when another option displays itself so clearly."

He had to extinguish that dangerous glitter in her eyes that told him she wasn't giving up. "Despite what you may think, marrying me is not an option. I said no, and I stand by it ... unless you plan on knocking me unconscious and dragging me to the altar?"

Amandine chewed her lip.

"You're terrifying. I was *joking*."

"Minds can be changed." She lifted up her right shoulder in a tiny shrug.

"Not mine. You have met me, haven't you?"

She just shrugged again, damn her.

"Enough of this." He got up, grabbed his coat, and threw a few euro coins on the table. "I have things to do tomorrow. *Bonne nuit*," he said over his shoulder, as he walked away. But he knew for him, at least, it wouldn't be *bonne nuit* at all.

Chapter Six

A week passed, and her father had lapsed back into unconsciousness. She hadn't seen Gaspard since that evening at the café, and her anger and determination to bring him around had begun to splinter a bit.

At the time, asking Gaspard to marry her to thwart Jean-Marc had seemed like such an obvious solution to an otherwise unsolvable problem. How could she have known that he had such definite and traditional thoughts about the sanctity of marriage? Despite their squabbles, he'd always been the type of person who helped others. She was still reeling with shock that he would refuse to help her with this.

Then again, he'd never fully understood this part of her—the part that would fight until the death for control of her mother's legacy. To be fair, she'd never been able to properly explain it either, so she'd never really tried. It felt impossible to trust anyone, even her fiancé at the time, with a part of herself that felt so sacred. Still, how could someone like Gaspard, who she'd always felt viscerally linked to on some level, not understand? That, she couldn't comprehend.

In any case, hard work in the vineyards—weeding, trimming, and plowing—filled every hour of her days when she wasn't at the hospital or tending to the needs of Éloise.

Jean-Marc was still nowhere to be seen. He was surely busy with the wedding preparations, but part of her was surprised that he hadn't taken to hanging around just to gloat and watch her squirm under his triumph. She wondered sometimes why she was working in the vineyards that, if she was as realistic as Gaspard thought she should be, would only benefit her brother in the future. She reminded herself that she still had time. Jean-Marc wasn't married yet, and her father might be in a coma, but he was still alive.

The thing was she could not be rational about the vineyards—not ever. She *had* to find a solution. She had no idea how, but that flame hadn't been extinguished inside her.

It was Saturday, and Bertille and Éloise were helping her out in the Pernand-Villages parcel. With the warm weather and the sporadic showers, the vines were growing like crazy and Amandine had decided de-leafing was needed to remove some of the new growth in the direction of the rising sun in the east and help the grapes ripen.

Luckily, both Éloise and Bertille at sixteen were old hands at such tasks, so Amandine could leave them to work. The girls knew that Amandine would surely slip them a few bills at the end of the afternoon to compensate them for their time.

When Amandine was de-leafing the vines in another row, she overheard the girls talking.

"It's no wonder why he's angry," Bertille said. "Do you know what your sister did to him?"

"What?" Éloise asked.

"She asked him to marry her, but not for real."

"What do you mean, not for real?"

"I mean a fake marriage so she can inherit the vineyards. But you can't tell her I told you. Gaspard told us because we were all after him for being in such a bad mood—or a worse mood than usual anyway—and we were worried."

Amandine stood up and cleared her throat. The two girls whirled around, caught in the act. Instead of looking chastised, however, Éloise narrowed her eyes at Amandine. "Why is this the first I'm hearing of this?"

Amandine hadn't wanted to upset her sister or involve her any more than necessary. Now though, Bertille had left her no choice. She apologized and gave her sister a brief rundown of the situation. Given her loyalty to their brother, she wasn't at all sure whose side Éloise would take, but she tried to present the facts as objectively as possible without bringing her many emotions into it.

"But ..." Éloise frowned. "That's so wrong of Papa after you've worked so hard."

A wave of relief rushed through Amandine. Despite their age gap, it was still important to Amandine what Éloise thought of her. "That's why I proposed the marriage idea to Gaspard. I didn't think he would react so badly."

Bertille stared at Amandine. "Are you serious?" Her words were clipped and indignant.

"What do you mean?"

"*Bon Dieu.* You have no idea, do you?"

What was Bertille talking about? "Apparently not."

"You hurt Gaspard's feelings ... badly."

Amandine snorted at this. "No, that wasn't it." He was mad, not sad.

Bertille looked beseechingly up at the azure sky, as if

asking for divine assistance. "He gets in a bad mood when he's feeling pain because he doesn't know how else to deal with it," Bertille explained finally. She talked to Amandine as though she were a child. "Don't you know that by now?"

Amandine thought back to him stalking away in Luc's vineyard. She hadn't seen any sign of hurt feelings. He'd been furious, that's all. "I think you're reading too much into it."

"I'm not." Bertille crossed her arms in front of her.

"But that makes no sense," Amandine continued to argue. "I can understand, even if I don't agree, with the fact that he was angry, but I can't understand why on earth he'd be hurt. I was just asking a friend … well … an ex-fiancé, for help. *C'est tout.*"

Bertille cocked a disbelieving brow at Amandine—it was disarmingly reminiscent of her brother. "Oh, really? That's what you think?"

"She just said it." Éloise gestured at Amandine. "So I think the answer is yes. Enough with the rhetorical questions, Bertille."

Bertille rolled her eyes heavenwards again. "I swear, you and my brother are equally hopeless."

"Explain yourself, please?" Amandine had taken quite enough grief from this particular sixteen-year-old. "This week has been trying enough."

"It's because Gaspard still loves you, *idiote*," Bertille said. "He probably never imagined in his wildest dreams that you would ask him to marry you—you know, after the disaster last time—but when you made the offer for the inheritance instead of …" Bertille tapped her chest. "What did you expect? It's your heart he wants, Amandine, not some business deal."

Amandine remained speechless for a good minute.

Was it possible Gaspard still had feelings for her? How could she have known when he showed no sign of anything besides … well, civility? She shook her head. Bertille was only sixteen, and girls that age often saw life with the pink tinge of romance around it. "I don't believe it. He doesn't act any different towards me than he does to any of our friends. Wait. Yes he does, actually. He's far more distant with me."

"Have you ever considered his reserve around you is because his emotions are *bigger* when it comes to you than your other friends? He's trying to protect himself."

Did Bertille know what she was talking about, or was she merely caught up in teenage sentimentality? "Get back to your work," Amandine said finally. "And stop playing with my head."

"Just think about it." Bertille crouched back down in the dirt again to continue the de-leafing.

Éloise remained standing. "What do you think of all this?" Amandine asked her.

"That Papa is very much in the wrong."

"I meant about Gaspard."

"I don't know him that well, but Bertille does. You should consider what she said."

Amandine went back to work then, trying to still a nagging sense of guilt that hadn't been there before by pushing her body at a punishing pace, but it wasn't working … her thoughts kept straying back to Bertille's reproaches. If what she said was true, Amandine had hurt Gaspard. She'd have rather done almost anything in the world than that—almost anything in the world, except lose her vineyard.

Gaspard's sister, Louise—the second oldest—had come home for the weekend from Paris, where she went to one of the country's top business schools. Gaspard was counting on her visit to take his mind off the whole Amandine debacle.

He felt a great deal of satisfaction about being able to pay for Louise to go to her prestigious school. She deserved full credit for getting high marks and being accepted, but it was a private school, and a grossly expensive one at that. His hard work and sacrifice at the Domaine allowed him to pay for it, as well as for Sophie's medical degree in Lyon.

Maybe he wasn't the fireman of his boyhood dreams, and maybe he set out to work every morning with a sense of obligation rather than inspiration like Amandine, but at least his efforts had opened up possibilities for his sisters. That made something warm and reassuring kindle in his chest.

When she'd arrived the night before, Louise had offered to help him in the cellars the next day. He'd accepted her offer gratefully, as he needed to bottle and label a shipment of wine bound for New York. It was much faster—not to mention more pleasant—with two people.

Of all his sisters, Louise had always been the one who was the most interested in winemaking. He never let her get too invested, however, and made sure that she never felt that he needed, or indeed wanted, help. He was determined that all his sisters felt free to choose their own paths. He hadn't had that freedom, but he could give it to them.

They were getting the machine set up with all the supplies, when Louise reached out and stopped him with a hand on his arm.

"Before we turn on the machine, I have something I need to talk to you about."

"Sure," he said, not liking the worried darkness in her blue eyes. Her mother was Moroccan, and the combination of Louise's blue eyes and her dark skin and hair had always drawn the kind of attention she didn't particularly want.

"You're going to get angry." She looked down at the box of corks she held in her hands.

He sighed. "I know I've been in a bad mood, like an injured fox wanting to just be left alone, but I promise to do my best to just … listen."

"It's about school." She set down the box of corks on the machine, pulled up a nearby chair, and sat down, twisting her hands together in her lap.

"Hey, don't look like that." Gaspard reached out and touched her shoulder. "I'm not an ogre."

She took a deep breath. "I quit my program."

Gaspard fought back a spurt of anger. It was midway through the year and half-way through her degree. How could she possibly give up now? Unlike him, she'd been able to make her own choice and she'd chosen the business school. He'd never had such a luxury. It was not in his nature to quit anything, even something he didn't enjoy. What could he say that wouldn't shut her down? His mind searched frantically for the best words.

"Why aren't you talking?" Louise demanded, finally. "It makes me nervous when you don't talk."

"I'm thinking," he said. "And I'm trying to listen."

He was aware his voice sounded strained, but he was doing his best. "Can you explain why you quit?"

She was chewing on a fingernail, a habit he'd struggled to help her break when she was little by painting her nails with some foul-tasting stuff. He had to listen to her with an open mind.

"Please," he said, keeping his voice as gentle as possible. "Just tell me."

She took another steadying breath. "I chose business because … well … I always dreamed of going into wine and I thought maybe if I got a business degree I could work in the International wine trade or something—importing or exporting. Maybe building a company around that."

"Those still sound like good ideas," he said carefully.

She sighed, still staring at her hands in her lap, not quite daring to meet his eyes. "Yes, but … the truth is I've been unhappy since I started the business degree."

Why was this the first time Gaspard was hearing of this? "What?"

"Don't get me wrong. I loved the experience of living in Paris for two years. I think everyone can benefit from that, but the degree itself … not so much. From my first day of classes, I knew it wasn't for me."

Gaspard tried very hard to not think of how much money those two years had cost. "Tell me more about that," he said instead.

"The business stuff … it was just so abstract—doing case studies for all these businesses—"

"That doesn't sound abstract."

She gnawed on her lower lip. "I realized all I cared about was wine."

Gaspard tried to take this in. His mind was already off and planning. If Louise was really focused on wine then there were other programs, after all. "There are programs that concentrate more on wine and commerce in Beaune, of course, but I'm sure they exist in Bordeaux too or even internationally—"

"No. That's not it." She shook her head, emphatically.

There was something he was missing here—some essential piece of information. "I don't understand."

"I'm sick of doing things that are peripheral to my true dream of working in the vineyards ... of *being* a winemaker like you. I realize now that nothing else will satisfy me. Surely you understand. You're living your dream, aren't you?"

Gaspard couldn't help but be impressed at the irony. She had been given all the choices, and she had chosen the one thing that Gaspard had never had a choice in.

For a moment he considered confessing his true feelings to her, but no. She couldn't know what was in his heart. None of his sisters could, otherwise they would feel guilty about the sacrifices he'd made for them. There was no point in that.

"I know Amandine would understand," Louise added with a sigh.

He probably should have said something instead of just remaining silent, which she clearly interpreted as disapproval. "Why are you bringing Amandine into this?"

He really didn't need to be reminded of her—not when he could barely think of anything else besides her and her insulting proposal, no matter how hard he tried.

"Because I know how passionate she is about her vineyards and winemaking, and I know as a woman the choice I'm making is ten times harder than it would be if I was a man."

"Things are changing," Gaspard reminded her. "It's not nearly as bad for women winemakers as it used to be."

Louise made a "tcha!" sound of disbelief. "They are still bad enough that Amandine was forced into a corner to propose a fake marriage to you in order to inherit the vineyards—vineyards she has *earned* ten times over. She would never have to do that if she had a penis."

There was a fury in Louise's voice that took Gaspard by surprise. "Are you mad at me?" he demanded. "Also, aren't we getting off-topic here?"

"We are, but I guess it just dawned on me now ... I *am* mad at you." She cast him a look of reproach.

"Why?" Gaspard was baffled by this quickly shifting conversation.

"Why couldn't you have helped out Amandine with this inheritance thing? You know she deserves it. It's what I would hope someone who cared about me would do."

"But Louise, don't you understand? This is marriage we're talking about, not some minor favor."

"So? What does marriage mean in this day and age anyway? Look at my mother, look at *all* of our mothers, not to mention our father."

"I don't want that, Louise. When I get married—if I get married—I want it to mean something. You can't possibly blame me for that." Still, his throat thickened with guilt. As far as he knew, Amandine hadn't found another solution.

"Doesn't Amandine mean something to you?"

"Of course she does. She's my ..." He blew out a gust of frustration. "To be honest, I don't know exactly what we are to each other anymore."

"Doesn't justice mean something to you?" Louise demanded.

Maybe the law was his sister's calling, specifically

litigation. He was feeling decidedly persecuted. "You know it does."

"Then I think you should have said yes to Amandine." She nodded once, as though her opinion was definitive.

Gaspard stared up at the stones that made up the vaulted cellar ceiling, searching for some patience that he definitely wasn't feeling, given the tightness in his chest. They'd strayed far off track. "Look," he said finally. "I don't know how we got on the subject of me and Amandine, but we still haven't finished talking about you quitting school."

"It's all related."

How was it that after all this time he still couldn't follow the mental gymnastics of his sisters? "Okay," he said, guardedly. Maybe if he just kept her talking he would figure her logic out.

"My point is I want to come and start working with you at the Domaine to learn the ropes. I'm sorry about the school thing and I'll pay you back, but you know I'm not a person who changes their mind easily. I'm not a flake."

"You don't need to pay me back anything," Gaspard said. "That's not at all what I meant."

"Then what did you mean?"

He sighed. "Are you sure you don't want to create your own life, independent of all of this?" He waved his arm around the cellar to include it all—everything that had weighed so heavily on his shoulders all these years.

"No. This is what I want. Winemaking. Will you take me on?"

A warm wave of relief rolled through him. It would be a godsend to share the work—especially with his sister—if that was what Louise truly wanted. "I don't understand exactly," he said. "But it would be an absolute pleasure to have you around. This Domaine is as much yours as mine, *tu sais.*"

"Wow." She stood up in her chair and resumed stocking the bottling machine. "I didn't expect this to go so well."

"Louise, despite how I may appear sometimes, I'm not unreasonable."

Louise examined him then, with her penetrating blue eyes. "No, you're not are you? Don't worry, I won't tell anyone."

"*Merci.*"

"But please rethink helping Amandine," she said. "For me … for all your sisters … hell, for womenkind."

Yet another burden … but Gaspard, for once, knew better than to say the first thing that popped into his head, so he just nodded.

Chapter Seven

Amandine collapsed in her bed that night, exhausted, but she couldn't fall asleep. Her body ached from going from crouching to standing about a million times with the de-leafing, but it was the idea that she'd unintentionally hurt Gaspard that gnawed at her like an aching tooth.

One moment she concluded that Bertille was making it all up thanks to an overactive imagination, the next she would find herself replaying her last few interactions with Gaspard, searching for any indication that he harbored any feelings for her beyond friendship.

There was certainly nothing obvious, but then again Gaspard was not the type to wear his heart on his sleeve. Even when they'd been romantically involved before, he whispered once between kisses that he'd been wanting to kiss her for years … but she'd truly had no idea. Even in private, he always held an important part of himself back. But if Bertille was completely off base, then how could Amandine explain away Gaspard's reaction when she suggested the fake marriage?

One thing was for certain—she'd never intended to hurt Gaspard. It wasn't easy to admit to herself, but she cared about him, despite all their ups and downs. She would never intentionally cause him pain.

When she finally drifted off into a fitful sleep, Gaspard even invaded her dreams.

He was leaning over her and she could smell his scent of coffee and peppermint shampoo and just ... *him*. She wanted to reach out and draw him closer, but her arms were frozen. Why had they broken up again? She couldn't remember exactly.

A familiar touch smoothed her bangs off her forehead. *There he was.* Had he been with her the whole time, in her bed? If this was a dream, she didn't want it to end. She murmured his name and reached out to get closer so she could feel his strong, unyielding body against her skin.

"Amandine!" Gaspard's shocked voice came from above her. The bulb of her bedside table lamp flicked on.

She flung her forearm over her eyes, temporarily blinded. Why was Gaspard—the real Gaspard—in her bedroom? Had he changed his mind about the marriage? Hope soared in her chest, and not only because of the inheritance. She was still disoriented, but the main lingering thought was that she wanted him *closer*.

"I've come to take you to the hospital." His dark brows were knitted as he stared down at her.

"Papa?" Amandine asked, her voice sounding like the young girl she had been, what felt like another lifetime ago, before her mother died and her father became a spiteful shell of his former self.

"No!" Gaspard said, sympathy in his dark eyes. "I'm sorry—I wasn't thinking—of course you would assume that. I would never scare you like that intentionally."

She sat up and crossed her legs, sleep quickly evaporating. "What then?"

"It's Cerise, she's in labor. Clovis texted all of us but I know how deeply you sleep. I figured you wouldn't have heard your phone, if you even knew where it was, that is."

She hadn't closed her shutters against the short June night, and she blinked at the dark sky outside. "What time is it?"

"Two o'clock in the morning ... ish. Do you know where your phone is, incidentally?"

Amandine tried to trace back to the last time she'd seen it and couldn't. "No."

"I was right," he murmured to himself.

Amandine remembered why she'd struggled to fall asleep in the first place, but examining his face she could detect no signs that he was emotionally devastated by her mercenary marriage proposal. A stab of disappointment took her by surprise. Wait, she didn't want Gaspard to still have feelings for her. That would complicate everything.

"No need to be a know-it-all," Amandine chided. She climbed out of bed, forgetting that she was only wearing a tank top and her underwear, and that now they were broken up she was supposed to wear more clothes in front of Gaspard.

His dark eyes went fathomless for a split second, and she caught a flash of ... something. He blinked and it vanished.

She was becoming just as bad as Bertille, but in her defense she wasn't used to being woken up in the middle of the night. Anyway, even if Gaspard *had* felt a brief pull of attraction, she knew him well enough to be certain that lust would never be enough to change Gaspard's mind once it was made.

"I should let Éloise know that I'll be at the hospital so she doesn't worry." Amandine pulled on the jeans she'd shed just before climbing under her duvet. They were a bit muddy, but she didn't think a woman in labor and a newborn would care about that.

"I already left her a note downstairs telling her where I've taken you and why."

She pulled on a T-shirt over her tank top. "Look at you thinking ahead."

Gaspard shrugged. "I have four sisters of my own. I've learned a thing or two."

Amandine snorted. "I'll bet." She'd always found the care—even though it could sometimes err on being a tad dictatorial when he was tired or frustrated—that Gaspard gave his sisters was one of the most appealing things about him. Whether he would admit it or not, and he probably wouldn't, his sisters softened him. There were few things that tugged on Amandine's heartstrings like seeing him interact with them. Amandine knew what it was like having a poor excuse for a brother, and she never stopped being amazed at what a thoughtful, responsible, and loyal brother Gaspard was, day in and day out.

Amandine pulled on a sweater. Despite being early June, the nights still had a bit of a chill and the hospital was always either freezing or boiling.

She passed by Gaspard, close enough that she could smell the licorice Flavigny mints he liked to suck on throughout the day. Her mind was wiped blank all of a sudden. She remembered snuggling up against him just after he shaved when they were briefly together. She used to trace the smooth, dramatic contours of his face with her finger. Her index finger twitched. *No. Everything about that would be inappropriate. This wasn't a dream; it was reality.*

"You shaved?" she noticed.

"I wanted to look nice to meet the newest member of

our gang." His smile was sheepish. She couldn't stop staring … and remembering. Had she forgotten how adorable he could be, or had she just blocked it out?

"Ready?" He stood up from the edge of her bed. "This is Cerise's third baby. It could go fast, you know."

"Right." She hurried down the stairs to the front hall and Gaspard followed her. She found her sneakers in the middle of the kitchen floor and tugged them on. "Did Clovis give any more details?"

Gaspard chuckled. "What do you think?"

"He could barely string two words together?"

"Precisely. His text was pretty much incoherent. I just got the gist it was happening."

Amandine chuckled, enjoying how much their previously unflappable friend had changed now he'd found a family to care deeply about. "I think he's far more anxious than Cerise."

From Gaspard's face, it was clear he shared her amusement. "By a long shot."

God, she'd missed this complicity they'd always shared. She spotted her phone on the table near the back door and picked it up. "Look what I found!" As expected, there were several group texts from Clovis and their friends. She slipped it into her back pocket.

It felt good, this temporary truce with Gaspard, like she'd rediscovered her bearings after being lost. She tried very hard not to think about Bertille's opinion.

They left the house like a pair of thieves and hopped into Gaspard's car. An almost full moon sailed high in the sky, casting a silver light over the rows upon rows of vines they whipped past. It was insanely romantic but they didn't do romance any longer … did they?

Breaking her engagement with Gaspard the first time around had really seemed like the right—the only—

action she could have taken. Questioning her certainty around that was a futile exercise, yet now, in the middle of the night, everything seemed open to doubt. It wasn't even three o'clock in the morning, she reminded herself. She wasn't thinking straight. Everything would be clearer when the sun rose.

She strong-armed her thoughts back to Cerise and Clovis and their soon-to-be born baby. "I can't believe I almost broke them up when I showed Cerise that stupid magazine article about Clovis."

Gaspard's profile remained impassive in the moonlight. "Me neither."

She snorted. "Thanks for the comfort."

"Providing comfort is not really my forté. Providing the unvarnished truth, however ..."

There it was. One of the reasons they'd broken up— Gaspard's bluntness. Somehow Amandine felt grounded by this, rather than disappointed.

Gaspard shook his head. "I still can't believe that you thought so badly of Clovis you believed he would do such a thing."

She opened her window to let in the sweet night air and breathed deep to fill her lungs with it. He had a point. Her accusations had been short-sighted and unnecessarily suspicious, yet it had truly seemed like the right thing to do at the time. "It's not exactly like the men in my life have built up my trust of the male species." Yet, when she'd gone to Gaspard that night and they'd slept together for the first time, he'd been there for her.

"I know that, but your friends have never let you down."

She lowered her head, smarting with the knowledge he was right. "It was wrong of me," she admitted finally.

"I cannot even tell you how much I regretted it since." She also regretted how she'd accepted Gaspard's sudden proposal the next morning. It was too much, too quick. What sort of madness had possessed them? "You don't need to kick me when I'm already on the ground, *tu sais*."

Gaspard made an odd, strangled noise of frustration. "I'm being too harsh again, aren't I? Damn my sharp tongue. I know you thought you were doing what was right, Amandine. It was misguided, definitely, but anyone who knows you would know you weren't trying to be malicious."

Amandine nodded in the moonlight, trying to hide her shock. Gaspard almost never apologized.

"What about Luc and Sadie?" Amandine said, after a while, trying to change the topic of conversation. "Do you want to make a bet how long it's going to take them to have a baby?"

The right side of his mouth twitched. "The way they keep disappearing together, I would wager on sooner rather than later."

She sighed. "We're going to be the odd ones out. Single, childless …"

Gaspard parked the car in the almost empty lot. He took his key out of the ignition and turned to her. "Who would have us? We're both impossible."

The unspoken answer lingered in the air between them as they entered the bright lights of the hospital. The only solution was each other. Shame they'd already wrecked it.

Luc and Sadie were already in the maternity waiting room. Sadie was cozied up on Luc's lap on a truly hideous green vinyl couch, her red curls resting against Luc's shoulder.

Amandine's stomach burned when she saw how protected Sadie looked, how in love. Like Clovis and Cerise, they were just so *happy* together. Surely she and Gaspard, with their prickly personalities, could never achieve such harmony.

"Is Clovis in with Cerise?" Gaspard asked, as he sat down on the opposite couch.

Luc rolled his eyes. "Do you really think he'd be anywhere else?"

"Of course not," Gaspard said. "How did he seem?"

Sadie grinned. "Did you read his text? Or try to read it, anyway? I've translated ancient manuscripts written in obscure dialects of Gaulois that were less complicated to decipher."

They all laughed.

"Poor Clovis." Gaspard shook his head.

"What are you talking about?" Luc said. "Poor Clovis? *N'importe quoi.* I've never seen him happier. Hey, how is your father, Amandine?" he asked. Luc was one of the most thoughtful, loyal people she knew. He was truly a wonderful friend—Gaspard was right—she shouldn't judge all men based on the two related to her.

Amandine pointed at the ceiling. "He's two floors up. He's slipped back into unconsciousness as you probably know, but nothing much has changed really. He's stable.

According to the doctors, it could go on like this for a long time. They said it might be a coma, or it might just be a necessary step for the brain to heal itself."

Sadie watched Amandine closely with her perceptive amber eyes. "What do you think?"

Amandine thought about this for a second. "Somehow, he's so annoyingly consistent with his tormenting of me that I just can't imagine him dying. I just can't ever imagine him ... not existing," she admitted. "I think he'll probably pull through." Her stomach dipped with dread. Despite the whole will thing, day-to-day operations at the Domaine had been so much more peaceful without her father stalking around on the prowl for a fight.

"That's good," said Luc. "Then you can put his whole ridiculous matter of the inheritance on the back burner."

"For a while, yes," she said. The truth was, however, that the days until Jean-Marc and Julie's wedding were slipping by quickly and after that ... well, it was game over, regardless of whether her father lived or died.

Sadie cleared her throat. "I had a different ... a better relationship, I think, with my father than you have with yours, but when he died my whole world changed overnight. Good or bad, our fathers take up a huge space in our lives. Without them there is a vacuum and it takes time to figure out how to come to terms with that."

Just then Clovis burst into the waiting room. He was dressed from head to toe in yellow disposable scrubs, including booties over his shoes. He was shaking from excitement, his dark-blue eyes wide and full of wonder. "Good!" He clapped his hands together. "You're all here. Cerise's aunt Geneviève should be arriving soon, and she'll be bringing Marc and Yves. Can you make sure they're comfortable?"

They all answered with a chorus of "*ouis.*"

"How is Cerise doing?" Gaspard asked.

"Wonderful! She's six centimeters dilated!" Clovis exclaimed. "She's amazing. I should go back to her!"

He hurried away, leaving them all highly amused with this transformation from the suave, urbane Clovis of a year before. He was living proof just how fast and completely a person, and a life, could change.

Shortly after, just as Clovis had predicted, Cerise's Aunt Geneviève, her uncle, and Cerise's boys arrived.

Geneviève—almost as beside herself with emotion as Clovis and never one to miss an opportunity to celebrate—had brought along four bottles of chilled *crémant* in a cooler. She had tasked her quiet husband with carrying another tote full of champagne flutes carefully wrapped in paper towels.

Amandine assumed she brought them to celebrate the baby's actual birth, but no such thing. Geneviève immediately instructed her husband to pass everyone a champagne flute, even young Marc and Yves. She uncorked the first bottle of crémant with a cry of joy that coincided with the loud 'pop' as the cork flew out of the bottle neck.

"Hurry up with those glasses," she commanded her husband, as she began pouring.

"I thought the tradition in France was to drink champagne *after* the baby was born," Sadie said.

Geneviève made a dismissive noise. "Dear girl, this is Burgundy. First of all, we're celebrating with Burgundy *crémant*, not champagne, and there is no better way to ease a new life into the world than by drinking. *Bien sûr* we will have some after too. That's why I brought four bottles, after all. *L'un n'empêche pas l'autre.*"

"If we have a baby," Sadie said to Luc. "I think I

definitely want to do it here and not back in New York."

Luc cocked an eyebrow. "That can be arranged."

Time sped by faster and faster with each flute of *crémant* consumed.

"Won't the nurses mind?" Sadie asked, making inroads on her third flute. Her eyes darted this way and that.

Everyone stared at her. "Only if we don't offer them some," Geneviève said.

Amandine stifled a chuckle. It'd been years since she'd had this much fun at four o'clock in the morning.

After quite some time, a flushed Clovis burst out into the hallway. "It's a girl! A beautiful, gorgeous, perfect girl! You have a new sister!" He rushed over to Marc and Yves and scooped them up, one in each arm. "Do you want to come and meet her?"

Everyone cheered and broke out into a spontaneous *ban bourgignon* and, before it was even finished, Clovis had whisked the boys away.

"Damn, we should have asked for more details," Amandine said.

"Don't worry." Gaspard touched her back. It was a brief, casual gesture, but they hadn't done anything like that since they'd broken up. Shocks from his touch spread everywhere inside Amandine. "He won't be able to resist sharing more details. Did you see how proud he looked?"

It was true. Clovis's eyes had been glistening with wonder and pride, but Amandine's thoughts were caught on Gaspard.

During their brief engagement, Amandine had daydreamed about what kind of children she and Gaspard would have, if they were lucky enough to have them. They'd surely be strong-willed and stubborn like their parents. How could the mixture of the two of them be any other way? But would they be blonde like her or dark like him? She wondered if she and Gaspard would perhaps meet their match in their children, in a similar way to how they met their match with each other.

Amandine shook her head. That was the past. It was over, for good. Gaspard had made that very clear, no matter what Bertille imagined.

About a half an hour later, the friends were ushered into Cerise's room. Geneviève and her husband were already in there, and it was hard to find room around Cerise's hospital bed, but she looked elated. A bit tired, maybe, but wreathed in smiles. Clovis was fussing around between the baby and Cerise and the boys.

Clovis brought over the baby in his arms to show his friends. "Thanks for being here you guys," he said. "I hope you know how much it means to me."

"We wouldn't miss it." Gaspard patted him lustily on the back. Everyone nodded and echoed the sentiment.

"Four children!" Luc exclaimed. "You're officially a family man now, Clovis."

"Aren't I the luckiest man alive?" Clovis said. "Meet Myrtille."

"Myrtille?" Sadie asked. "Oh, that's adorable. Doesn't that mean "blueberry" in French?"

"Well, Cerise means "cherry," Luc said. "Continuing with the theme, *non*?"

"That's why I suggested it," Clovis said. "Isn't she a beautiful baby? Just like her mother."

Indeed she was, and Myrtille was a beautiful name— a little old fashioned but chic in a retro way. When she got closer to the bundle in Clovis's arms, Amandine took in her perfect little fingers kneading at the edge of the blanket wrapped around her and a swath of black hair.

Myrtille's eyes were shut tight against the world. She was perfect. She was beautiful. She was *here*. How could such a tiny thing have so much power?

"*Félicitations*," Gaspard's voice, coming from behind her, was reverent too. "She's sublime."

Her back pocket began to vibrate. Who would be calling her now? It was still dark outside. Had Éloise woken up and not found Gaspard's note? She pulled it out and frowned at it.

"Who is it?" Gaspard said, stepping back from the crowd around Myrtille to stand by Amandine's side.

"The hospital," Amandine read the call display, confused. "But I'm *at* the hospital."

Her eyes flew to Gaspard's.

"Did they leave a message?" he asked.

She checked. "No." It had to be something with her father, and she knew from the intent look in Gaspard's eyes that he'd come to the same conclusion. "I'll go up there now."

"I'm coming with you."

Amandine nodded once, sharply. The blood in her veins turned to ice. It wasn't as if her and her father had a good relationship—it had been downright awful to be blunt—but he'd been someone different before her mother had died. The hope that he could somehow become that earlier, better, kinder version of himself had never completely been extinguished for Amandine, she realized only now. Was it too late?

Gaspard had a quick word with Clovis, and they backed out of the room.

Chapter Eight

Gaspard was certain the news couldn't be good. The hospital was not in the habit of making calls before six o'clock in the morning without a serious reason. There was no way he was going to let Amandine deal with it on her own, especially as the hospital had undoubtedly already called in Jean-Marc as well.

He was consumed by a familiar and fierce desire to protect Amandine from any pain. He'd thought that had been kicked out of him with their break-up, but apparently it had merely been hibernating.

He followed her down the hallway to the nurses' desk, where she asked in a controlled voice that must have required a fair amount of self-mastery, what the phone call was about.

As they waited for the nurse to go and find out, Gaspard caught sight of a full crash cart being wheeled out of Amandine's father's hospital room down the hall. It looked well-used, with empty syringes and tubes and vials scattered messily all over it. One of the cardiac paddles had fallen over the side of the cart and swayed loosely a few inches above the linoleum floor.

His heart caught in his throat. He fought the urge to gather Amandine in his arms and shield her from all of it—the crash cart, her dead father, the mess of the inheritance that would now be enacted.

The doctors and nurses following the cart out were rubbing hands over their eyes and through their hair and shaking their heads.

Gaspard hesitated for a moment. Should he point out what he was seeing or wait? Neither option was good, but which would be the least painful for her?

He had to point it out. It would be better if she had some time to deal with it on her own before the rest of her family descended. This time here alone was precious—it couldn't be wasted.

He touched her palm with his forefinger, something that used to be a secret gesture between them to get each other's attention in a crowd.

Her pale face whipped around. He hadn't done that since their final fight. He tilted his head towards her father's room down the hall. Gaspard would have done anything to save her this pain but, seeing as it was unavoidable, at least he was there at her side.

Her eyes went round. "*Merde*," she breathed and rushed down the hallway.

She went into her father's room. Gaspard followed. A nurse was busy strapping up her father's jaw and closing his eyes. His body looked so small, so broken … it was hard not to pity what he had come to in the end despite all his bluster and bitterness.

The nurse's head snapped up. "Who are you? You shouldn't be in here."

"I'm his daughter," Amandine's voice broke on the last word. Pain lanced across Gaspard's chest when he heard that, and he reached out and grabbed her hand. Her fingers closed around his and she squeezed hard. He was just giving her comfort and support—that was all it was.

Death was rarely easy, but some deaths were simpler than others. If her father had been a loving, caring man, Amandine's grief would have been difficult, but it would eventually heal like a deep but clean wound. With her father, everything about his departure felt messy and dirty, infected with regret over all his shortcomings. He'd run out of chances to become the father Amandine deserved. His was the type of death that could leave debilitating scars in its wake.

"But how did you get here so fast?" the nurse demanded.

"A friend just had her baby downstairs in the maternity ward. The hospital called me so I just—"

"I see. We just called time of death less than five minutes ago. They must have called you when he coded." The nurse was brisk and competent, but her jutted bottom lip indicated she was put out that they had descended on her without giving her time to prepare things to her satisfaction.

Amandine's shoulders dropped. Gaspard knew why—despite the difficulty of the situation, she was calmed by other people acting competently and unemotionally. "What happened exactly?" she asked, her voice steadier. "I was here this morning and although he was still unconscious, the doctors told me he was stable."

The nurse shrugged, looking down at Amandine's father dispassionately. This clinical detachment would probably bother most people at such a moment, but Amandine wasn't most people. "We won't know for certain unless we do an autopsy, but he most likely suffered from another aneurysm or bleed. It's not uncommon."

"Right." Amandine nodded. "That makes sense."

The nurse watched Amandine closely. "Would you

like a moment alone with your father?"

Amandine looked down at her father's bruised, tortured face. It was as if, Gaspard thought, the twisted nature of his personality had physically manifested in his death. "Yes. Thank you."

"I'll leave you then." The soft suck of the nurse's plastic-soled shoes signaled her quiet departure from the room.

Gaspard hesitated, then let go of Amandine's hand and turned to leave her alone as well.

Her hand flew out and grabbed his forearm. "Stay."

"You sure?" He would do anything, it dawned on him in that moment, to take away even a gram of her pain.

"Please. I don't think I want to be alone with him. I just can't … I just can't get over the fact that that's him, and he's *dead*. He's been such a thorn in my side, and yet I can't forget how he was before my mother died. He was someone different. I think he was almost a good father back then. I just wish—" She covered her mouth with her hand.

He slid his arm around her and pulled her close against his side, wishing he was still in a position to actually hold her in his arms like he used to. But no … the last thing Amandine needed was extra confusion.

He half expected her to say something about how unfair and unjust her father had left things, but she didn't. At that moment, if she asked him to marry her again to get the vineyards, he probably wouldn't say no. Louise's words still rung in his mind, about doing it for his sisters and womankind and all that … but really, he'd be prepared to do just about anything to take that stricken look from Amandine's face.

Amandine clearly hadn't realized that so much of his

anger around her proposal wasn't so much that he couldn't bear the idea of a sham relationship if there was a good justification. It was that he couldn't stand the thought of a sham relationship with *her*. He couldn't see a way in which it wouldn't tear him apart.

They remained standing side by side like that for a long time. Finally, Amandine shook her head. "I'm sure the hospital called Jean-Marc too, and now that I think about it, he'll surely bring Éloise. We need to fix him up as well as we can. Do you mind? I don't want Éloise to have to see her father like this."

Gaspard recoiled at the idea of touching this man who had caused Amandine so much torment when he was alive, let alone dead, but he would do it so that Amandine didn't have to.

Gaspard moved Amandine's father's head—which was surprisingly heavy—and adjusted the pillow so that he lay peacefully on it, like he was sleeping. His skin was still slightly warm, but it was cooling fast.

Gaspard straightened out the sheets and tucked him back in tightly, so no rogue limbs could fall out of his origami-like sheet package. He even brushed out the hair on his forehead with his fingers, so it lay smooth.

Amandine just watched him. She probably couldn't bring herself to touch him—understandable.

Gaspard finished doing what he could and even though he wanted nothing more than to go and wash his hands—wash his whole body in fact—he took a step back to better survey his work. "What do you think?" he said. "Did I miss anything?"

She shook her head. "I don't think so," she said. "It's better. Much better."

"Good."

"Thank you." She took hold of his hand again. "I

don't know exactly why you being here helps, but it does."

Jean-Marc and Éloise burst through the door then, and Gaspard retreated to the corner of the room. He would stay there for Amandine, but far enough away so that he wasn't interfering more than necessary. He ducked into the bathroom to wash his hands quickly.

When he came out, Amandine was consoling her sister. Jean-Marc stood awkwardly apart, staring down at the dead body of his father with a shocked expression on his features. Gaspard sometimes forgot that their father had tormented Jean-Marc almost as much as Amandine. It wouldn't be clean grief for him either.

But he was only here for Amandine, and for her he would stay.

The next day, Gaspard went back to the hospital for a quick visit with Cerise and Clovis and little Myrtille. He'd stayed at the hospital until mid-morning with Amandine, until all the paperwork was done for her father and the undertakers had been called. He drove her and Éloise home to sleep, or try to, in any case, while Jean-Marc went back to Julie's. After that, he'd headed back to Volnay to crash in his own bed for a few short hours.

Gaspard could hear the joyous laughter coming from Cerise's hospital room as soon as he stepped off the elevator. Cerise's room in the maternity ward could not be a starker contrast to the recent scene two floors above with Amandine's father.

Geneviève had brought a magnum of Échezaux Grand Cru and it was flowing freely. Luc and Sadie were there, as well as Jean, Luc's biological father, and Clovis's *régissseur du domaine* who also served as a de facto father figure to him.

Geneviève thrust a glass of Échezaux in Gaspard's hand as soon as he came in the door, before he was even finished giving everyone *les bises*. He certainly wasn't about to refuse—it was one of his favorite wines, after all, and Cerise's uncle was a meticulous winemaker. Besides, he could use some cheering up. Witnessing Amandine's pain had left him with a crushing headache and his mind in a tangle of doubt.

Jean was ensconced on a chair with Myrtille in his arms and a beatific look in his bright blue eyes. "She's just beautiful," he said. "I can't decide who she looks like the most, but she's a rare vintage, this one. That much is certain."

Geneviève appeared in front of Gaspard with a pastry box from Patisserie Millot in Beaune. "Éclair?" she asked.

Although he wasn't much for sweets, Gaspard selected a coffee flavored one. He didn't feel like resisting the celebratory mood of the room—it was a balm to his aching soul.

"Now," Sadie said, frowning. "Tell us. How is Amandine?"

He'd texted his friends the night before to let them know what had happened.

He grimaced. "It wasn't easy, and I think it's going to be difficult for a while, especially with the whole matter of the inheritance—"

"You sure you can't marry her?" Luc burst out, and

Sadie slanted him a look. "I can understand why you wouldn't want to do that, of course, but it just seems so silly that Jean-Marc will be given the Domaine—which we all know he will ruin within months—because of that stupid marriage stipulation," Luc explained.

"But we're talking about *marriage*," Sadie reminded her boyfriend.

"I know, I know." Luc leaned down and kissed her, just in case she mistakenly thought he took marriage lightly. "It's just that the will is so ridiculous … it almost calls for an equally ridiculous way out."

"Like a fake marriage," Gaspard clarified.

"Like a fake marriage." Luc nodded.

"I sympathize with Amandine, of course," Cerise said, from her bed, as she nibbled on a raspberry éclair. "But the more I've thought about it, the more I realize I would have a hard time with a false marriage too, especially to someone I cared about. Marriage is something sacred, don't you think? Maybe it's my superstitious side, but I worry it invites bad karma to play fast and loose with it."

Clovis was sitting beside Cerise on the bed, savoring his glass of wine. "I see what you mean, but at the same time I know we've all been racking our brains for any other solutions and so far—"

"I know," Gaspard said. "None of us have come up with anything."

"In any case," Sadie said. "I'm glad you were able to be with her at the hospital last night. I know that must have helped her cope."

Gaspard ducked his head. He didn't think he deserved such praise, and whatever he'd done, it wasn't for accolades. "I didn't do much."

"You were there for her," Luc said. "Sometimes,

that's all we can do, even though we want to do more."

Gaspard's chest tightened again with guilt. That was the thing, wasn't it? He *could* do more.

When she first propositioned him with the idea, he'd been too angry to think straight, but now he realized that underneath his indignation was hurt. Her proposal showed him just how completely she'd exorcised him from her heart. He'd never quite been able to manage the same feat.

He could marry her and save the Domaine from her brother. He could give her everything she'd ever wanted. It would most likely destroy him to be a shadow of the husband he'd once wanted to be to her, but maybe … maybe her happiness would be worth his broken heart?

He popped the end of the éclair in his mouth and drained his wine glass. "I'm going to go up to Pernand and check on her now."

The visit would be much simpler, though, if he could only decide what he should do.

Chapter Nine

Gaspard didn't bother checking at Amandine's house or inside the vat room at her Domaine. He'd find her in the vineyards. Sure enough, after driving in the vineyard paths above the village for a few minutes he saw her solitary figure pushing a plow up the slope just under the Virgin Mary statue at the top of the hill.

Some people might judge her harshly for working the day after her father died. Others might find it insane that she was still working herself to the bone in a vineyard and for a Domaine that would officially become her brother's as soon as her father's will was read and enacted.

Then again, most people didn't understand Amandine.

She was working the vines because it was her greatest solace. She'd never said it directly, but it was clear that, for Amandine, the vineyards were something that had their own intrinsic value outside of any questions of ownership. They'd broken up over his inability to understand that part of her, after all. It was a concept that Gaspard—who'd had his vineyards thrust upon him—still struggled to grasp. He wasn't sure he ever would.

He parked his car, thrust his hands in his pockets and loped towards her. She was so engrossed in her work that she didn't see or hear him coming. Her blonde blunt cut was smudged with greyish-brown dirt and she wiped the sweat off her forehead with her forearm without stopping the plow.

"Amandine!" he said, raising his hand in greeting.

She looked up and set the machine upright, leaning against it. She watched him with those emerald eyes of hers. He leaned forward and gave her *les bises* in greeting, as was expected between friends. He was conscious of the heat of her skin underneath his, and the coiled strain that lay under her calm surface. Like the night before, he was struck with the need to hold her close and shelter her from her father's death, that stupid will … all of it.

"Have you come to check on me?" She arched one of her finely drawn blonde brows.

"There's no point in lying, is there? You'd see right through it."

That got a tiny quirk of her lips. "I would. I *do*."

"So … here I am, checking up on you. How did it go after I dropped you and Éloise off at home?"

She exhaled gustily. "It was wretched, which was to be expected, I guess. Éloise was inconsolable. This morning we had to go to the funeral home to do cheery tasks like pick a coffin. Luckily my father made it very clear that he wanted no funeral, just a simple burial, so that made things a bit easier, but still. Hey, do you remember Guillaume?"

"From high school?"

"*Oui*." She nodded.

"The one who was a grade below us or the one who was a grade above us?"

"The grade above us. Anyway, he was the person we met with at the casket place."

"Huh." Gaspard was having a difficult time reconciling the jolly older boy with the blond hair and round face selling caskets and tombstones. "Really? He's taken over from his father?"

"I guess so. It was nice to see a familiar face, even though the whole procedure was … well, horrible."

"Is he still as merry as he used to be? It seems a strange career choice for him." Or maybe he was like Gaspard and hadn't been given a choice.

"Yes, he's just the same. It's a weird juxtaposition, but somehow the way he pushed us along and that good-humored way of his helped. It definitely helped Éloise, in any case. I dropped her off at your house to be with Bertille on my way home."

"Good. That will distract her, at least."

Amandine nodded. "That's what I thought." She blinked up at the June sun, which was already taking on that merciless edge of heat that typified the Burgundian summers. "Don't get me wrong," she said finally. "None of it was fun. I never realized there was so much administration involved in death."

"I've heard the paperwork is atrocious," Gaspard said. "It seems so cruel to inflict that at such a time."

She nodded.

Both of them were skirting around more troublesome topics in a well-rehearsed dance. They'd done that a lot in the short time they'd been a couple—probably far too much.

"I just came from the hospital," he said. "I was visiting Cerise and Clovis and *petite* Myrtille.

"Is she just as gorgeous as yesterday?"

"Even more." She truly was a beautiful child. "Jean

was holding her. Sadie and Luc need to give him his own grandchild. He's way past ready."

Amandine smiled for real this time. Why did that give him such warm satisfaction in his gut? "I'll have to see that for myself. So what's going on over there? Is everyone well?"

"That's an understatement. It's a full-on party. Geneviève was there with a magnum of Échezeaux and éclairs from chez Millot."

Amandine chuckled. "I'm happy for them, and disappointed that I'm having to deal with death in the middle of all that joy ... and the whole inheritance thing ..." Pain darkened her eyes, like a cloud crossing the sun. *Pain he could do something about.* Louise's words echoed in his mind. "I just didn't feel ready to go and see them this morning. I felt like the grim reaper or something."

"They understand. They all sent you their love. So ... how are you feeling today?"

"Fine?"

Gaspard arched an eyebrow.

"Well ... of course not fine," she admitted. "But that's a stupid question of you to ask me right now, don't you think?"

Touché. Again, he felt that stab of urgency to remove the pain and uncertainty off her shoulders, but was the fake marriage truly the only way? How could he be married to her, and *not* fall back in love with her?

"You came out here to work in the vineyards." He was stalling now, and he was ashamed with himself. "I imagine you've gotten some strange looks from some of the people who've heard the news about your father."

"I guess so." Amandine said with a dismissive shrug. "Which is why I've been keeping my head down."

"So it helps, does it? Gaspard asked, surveying the view from where they stood, with the picturesque church spire of Pernand-Vergelesses and the whole bright-green valley full of vines unspooling out in front of them. "Being out here, working?"

Amandine's eyes followed his down the valley. "*Oui*. It's who I am. It's what I do."

Gaspard nodded, not expecting a lot more, but to his surprise Amandine continued.

"I came out here the day after my mother died, you know," she said. "That day was far worse than today, if one can even compare that sort of thing. I knew, deep down, that from that moment on my life would be different. I was right. Everything became so much harder almost instantly. My father was in no shape to be looking after us with his grief and rage that the world had taken my mother. I needed to protect Éloise and look out for her. Jean-Marc … well, Jean-Marc became the Jean-Marc we know today."

Gaspard took a while to say anything. He hadn't known that about Amandine coming to the vineyards for solace after her mother's death, but like a coward he decided to concentrate on the other, easier, part of what she had said. He needed time to *think*. "If I recall, Jean-Marc wasn't always the way he is now."

"Amandine frowned. "You're right, although I often doubt my own memories around that. I was grieving, after all. For a few months after Maman's death we'd been a team—looking after Éloise and acting as a united front against our father. Everything changed after that ski accident in the Jura when he hit his head."

"Brain injuries can change people." He was still stalling, his mind whirring as they talked about Jean-Marc.

"Make them vindictive and malevolent?"

"Hmmm. Have you ever asked him about it?"

"No. He became so angry and bitter towards me I never dared. And my father saw how Jean-Marc had changed, and it was as if … he liked it. He encouraged Jean-Marc to be awful … to milk that fundamentally broken thing inside him. He took perverse joy in fanning the flames of Jean-Marc's antagonism."

"It just seemed so sudden."

Amandine nodded. "I've turned it over in my mind hundreds of times, but I just can't figure it out. I mean, sure, a head injury can take a while to heal, but the injury wasn't even that bad. It was described as only a bump, and his concussion was classified as minor. It never seemed like enough to change him the way it did. I often wonder if there was something else that happened during that trip."

Amandine looked so perplexed that, without thinking, Gaspard reached up and stroked her cheekbone. Her skin was so soft … how had he forgotten the silky feel of it?

She froze. *Eh merde*. What had he just done?

"These vineyards were my solace," she rushed on, trying, he knew, to cover up the awkwardness. "They were my mother's and by taking care of them I was also taking care of her and Éloise and myself. When so much of my life was spinning out of control, it was my way of building something for myself that I loved."

"I see," he said. *How could he refuse to help her when she revealed herself like that to him?*

"This Domaine should be mine," she said, reaching out and touching a nearby leaf. "It would flourish under me. We both know what a terrible winemaker Jean-Marc is. I've earned these vineyards, Gaspard. I have worked for them, fretted over them, loved them … it's just so unfair."

"It is." It was going to be hell on earth, being married to this woman but not being able to truly be her husband, but he couldn't just leave her like this.

"It's just …" Amandine gazed around her. "I don't love anything in half-measures. If I do, it's with every fiber of my being." She turned her eyes to meet Gaspard's. He could feel every contraction of his heart. He was only aware of that and of the green of her eyes that matched the soft, new tendrils of the vines that waved in the warm breeze. "You remember?" she asked, her voice hushed.

The ground seemed to tilt with just how well he remembered. It had been so brief—only a handful of days really—that he'd glimpsed at the force and power of Amandine's love. It had been so fierce and all-encompassing that it had terrified him as much as it had thrilled him. It hadn't completely translated to the physical side of things—they'd both been too guarded for that—but he was certain that if they hadn't broken up so quickly, it would have.

"I remember." A buzzing sound filled his head. He turned and paced up and down the row of vines a few times, scrubbing his face with his hands. *He had to.* There was no other choice, but maybe there was a way …

"What's this all about?" Amandine waved the hand that wasn't supporting the plow at him and his pacing.

He drew to a stop in front of her. "All right."

"All right *what*?"

"All right, I'll marry you."

Her eyes went huge in her face, and for a moment it appeared as though she forgot how to breathe. "You mean it?" she said finally.

He sighed. If she only knew how much time he'd spent fighting with himself over this. "Do you seriously think I would joke about this?"

She leaned heavily on the plow, not quite steady on her feet. "I don't think so, but then again—"

He reached out and grasped her shoulders. They were warm and familiar under his hands. How he'd missed touching her. "Amandine, will you marry me?"

The words should have destroyed him and his hopes, but the look of relief on her face made all of that melt away.

She hopped on the balls of her feet. "*Oui*! *Oui*! Of course! Please, yes!" She flung her arms around him and oh … how *right* it felt to be this close to her again.

It broke a dam within him, to feel her in his arms, and unleashed a torrent of emotions that he could only handle experiencing alone. He released her like she was on fire. "I need to go now," he said, brusqueness hiding his sudden vulnerability. "But before we agree for good, I have stipulations. We need to sit down and discuss them."

"When and where?" she asked, all eagerness.

"Tomorrow morning. Let's go to a café for tourists so we won't bump into anyone we know."

"How about the Café Vingt-Et-Un? Only tourists go there."

"Fine." He jerked his head in agreement, avoiding her eyes. "Seven o'clock? Before we start work?"

"I'll be there."

Chapter Ten

Amandine was ready to leave for the café the next morning with plenty of time to spare, even though she'd barely slept a wink.

She'd tossed and turned with nightmares about Gaspard not showing up at the appointed hour despite the fact that in all the time she'd known him, she couldn't dredge up one single memory of Gaspard changing his mind. Not once. Still, his mention of *stipulations* niggled at her. Try as she might, she couldn't imagine what they would be.

He couldn't back out now, could he? Not after letting her hopes soar so high. Gaining possession of the Domaine was forefront in her mind—of course it was—but behind that there was something else that she didn't want to prod too closely, not when she was already feeling raw from the events of the past few weeks.

One thing was certain—it had been a relief to have Gaspard around. Whenever she'd needed him the most, he'd been there. It made her wonder what a life with his unequivocal support would feel like … but there was no point in that. They had destroyed it once before, after all.

She got out of bed with an unpleasant rolling sensation in her stomach. It didn't go away as she said good-bye to Éloise and picked up her car keys from the front table.

She was out in the courtyard, blinking in the bright morning sunlight, when Jean-Marc's flashy Mercedes SUV sped in and stopped abruptly next to her.

Bile rose in her throat. *Not him. Not now.*

He got out of the car, and she couldn't help but notice his face was red and puffy. He'd been drinking too much. She knew the signs. She bit back the urge to say something to encourage him to stop such self-destruction. Even though she'd come to hate him, there was still a tiny corner of her that cared for the brother he used to be. How destroyed would he be if she managed to beat him to the altar? No, she couldn't think about that. Her resolve couldn't waver by even a flicker.

"I'm just leaving," she said. "This isn't a good time to talk."

"Talk?" He let out a hoot of disbelief. "I just came by to pick up some bottles to drop off at the BIVB for testing."

"What?" Jean-Marc shouldn't be taking any of the wine bottles for testing. He would undoubtably take bottles of wine that he had made which were barely drinkable. The Domaine could lose its appellation status which would ruin its chances once and for all. Even if Jean-Marc was to inherit it, she would never wish for that.

She thought fast. "I'm going to Beaune. I'll take care of that."

"Why?" he jeered. "You worried I'll pick some of mine?"

"Yes."

He slapped his thigh. "Honestly, Amandine, when are you going to give up? I'm marrying Julie in a few weeks. Papa is dead. According to the terms of the will, all of this is going to be mine." He swept his arm around to encompass the whole Domaine. "Why can't you just give up?"

She was tempted to mention her agreement with Gaspard, just for the satisfaction of seeing what that morsel of information did to her brother's face, but she swallowed it back down. It would be short-sighted to reveal her cards to the enemy for only a split-second of revenge.

He hadn't always been the enemy. The winter before her mother died there had been a huge snowstorm and they'd gone sledding, just the two of them. Éloise was just a newborn.

They'd laughed and whistled down the snowy slope of the village hill all afternoon, until they were so exhausted they flopped on their backs on their sleds at the top of the hill. They gnawed at the icy snow on their mittens and stared up at the clouds scudding through the metal winter sky above them. Where had *that* brother gone?

"It's not in me to give up," she said, finally.

"Amandine." He shook his head, and she detected something that looked almost like regret in his eyes—but it couldn't be. "I beat you. It's done."

But Gaspard agreed to marry her, so it wasn't done. Not at all. "The will hasn't been read yet," she said instead, covering her tracks. "We don't know everything. You told me you didn't read the whole thing, just that clause."

Jean-Marc looked discomfited, probably regretting telling her that at all.

"When did you say the notary will be back for the will reading?" she asked.

"Four weeks from now," he said. "A week after Julie and I get married. The notary has left on a vacation in the South until then."

So she and Gaspard needed to get married in less than three weeks. Would he agree to that rush? She didn't know yet what terms Gaspard was going to require, but not agreeing to a quick wedding would defeat the whole purpose. She checked her watch. *Merde.* She was going to be late meeting him. If only he could be beside her now. He steadied her in a way that she desperately needed when talking to Jean-Marc.

"I've got to go, Jean-Marc," she said. "But please don't take your bottles to the BIVB."

"Do you think you could stop me?" he said, with a defiant tilt of his chin.

She threw up her arms in frustration. *Why was he like this?* "I just can't understand why you want this Domaine at all. Wouldn't you and Julie be happier if I just bought your shares over time? You probably wouldn't have to work at all after a while. It's clear to everyone that you don't enjoy winemaking."

"Julie wants to be married to a winemaker," Jean-Marc said, but averted his gaze so he was looking beyond her to the *cuverie* doors.

"I think she'd still want to be with you even if you weren't. She loves you, *tu sais.*"

He just glowered. There was no point in arguing with him when he was like this and she needed to leave. "I know one thing for certain, Jean-Marc—I love winemaking and you don't."

"I used to love winemaking," Jean-Marc said, his voice breaking in the middle of the last word.

Something about the melancholy note in his voice made her eyes snap to his face, curious. He was right.

When they were young they both liked nothing better than tripping off with their parents to work in the vineyards or in the vat room.

"Maybe you did, but somewhere along the line you just stopped caring. To this day I can't figure out why. Was it Maman's death? Was it that ski accident?"

He broke her gaze and stared at his work boots. "That's none of your business," he muttered. "You have no idea."

She growled with frustration. He was impossible and she had to leave, but she couldn't let him take his bottles to the BIVB and destroy the Domaine before she even had the chance to save it. "It's clear to everyone that winemaking is in my blood and it's not in yours."

His breathing became heavier. "It's in my blood just as much as it's in yours, Amandine. Maybe it's your turn to learn that even if something is in your blood, it doesn't necessarily mean life will let you have it. Maybe you'll get an idea of what hell I've been living all these years."

What was he talking about? She knew there was something important behind his words, but she couldn't quite access it.

"Forget it!" He threw up his hands. "You pick the bottles for the BIVB. I don't care."

He got in his car and sped off, but Amandine didn't miss the despair in his eyes. Maybe there was more to Jean-Marc's antagonism than she'd always assumed, but she couldn't figure out what, or why.

Thanks to Jean-Marc's visit, Amandine was late. She double-parked her Renault on the Place Carnot and sent up a quick prayer that the owner of the car she'd blocked would be on a long errand.

She rushed into the Café Vingt-et-Un, a place she'd never been before. Her and her friends and the other locals had their favorite haunts in Beaune, but they were well off the tourist circuit.

She froze when she caught sight of Gaspard, sitting alone at a booth near the back.

She registered two things—he was going to be her husband, and he was wearing his glasses. They were ivy green and she knew for a fact that Margaux had gone to the optical store with him and picked them out. He was far-sighted so usually only wore his glasses when he needed to read things up close or take notes. He just looked so serious in them—she was always overwhelmed with the desire to mess him up.

Why the glasses now? Was he going to take notes about their marriage?

Everything else about his face was strong and un-compromising—a proud nose, knife-blade cheekbones, black eyes under straight black brows. The glasses were a chink in his perfect armor. That and his mouth ... it was softer than his other features, and only when he smiled, which was a rare event. Maybe that was why his smiles felt so much more valuable than anyone else's.

This was the man she was going to marry. Eagerness and fear and gratitude and guilt warred under her breastbone.

Gaspard checked his watch. As she got closer, she noticed that his face was far paler than usual and a there was a telltale crease between his brows. Did he think she had changed her mind and stood him up? If so, she would have expected to see relief in his face, not anxiety.

Whichever, she couldn't leave him wondering one second longer. She rushed over and leaned down to give him *les bises* ... sniffing that familiar scent of coffee and licorice that would soon be a constant in her life ... until they got divorced, she reminded herself.

"You're late," he said, pushing his glasses up the bridge of his nose. That was another feature on his face that had always fascinated her. It was slightly off center and had not only one, but two little bumps on its bridge. One was just the way he was made, and the other was from Bertille whacking her head against it when she was an obstreperous toddler.

A memory of idly running her finger down it and resting in the spot between the two bumps made the hairs rise on her forearms. Her stomach dipped suddenly. What exactly did Gaspard want this marriage to involve? What were the stipulations he'd mentioned?

"Don't you even have an excuse?" he asked with his most forbidding look.

"I had an encounter with Jean-Marc on my way out the door."

He took a deep breath and nodded. "Ah. Not a good encounter, I imagine."

She shook her head. "He was going to take bottles of his wine down to the BIVB for testing."

Gaspard scrubbed his face with his hand. "I can see why you needed to put a quick stop to that. You didn't ...?" He lifted his shoulders in an unspoken question.

"Tell him about us getting married? No! I'm not an idiot. He'd have Julie to the mayor's office within minutes. By the way, that's something we need to talk about. The will reading is going to be delayed until four weeks from now. Jean-Marc and Julie are getting married in three."

Before Gaspard could say anything, the garçon came by and they each ordered an espresso.

"So … you haven't changed your mind?" she asked when they were alone again.

He didn't answer right away. She swallowed hard against the nausea rising up in her again. It would be worse to have the marriage offered and snatched back than if he'd never offered it at all. "No," he said, reaching up to rub the bridge of his nose. "Have you?"

She shook her head, vehement in case she hadn't quite conveyed her desperation. "No. *Bien sûr que non.*"

"Good." He nodded once, short and sharp.

"Yesterday you mentioned stipulations?" she asked. "I want to hear more about those. I didn't sleep much last night."

Gaspard raised his left brow. "You think I did?" That tug of shared humor made her let out a long breath.

"I have no idea what was going through your mind, to be honest."

The garçon set their coffees in front of them then, and Gaspard unwrapped his sugar and dropped one of the cubes in his espresso cup, whereas Amandine reached out and took the other and added it to her two full sugar cubes, as was her habit.

"Does this marriage mean you're going to be stealing a lot more sugar cubes from me for the foreseeable future?" There it was, one of Gaspard's smiles. It warmed her like a ray of sunlight shining down between a break in the clouds.

"I hate to break it to you, but yes," Amandine said, buoyed up. "Unless your stipulations have something to do with sugar cubes?"

Gaspard's smile vanished as quickly as it appeared. "Ah. My stipulations. All right. I suppose I'd best plunge right in."

Yet he didn't, which was out of character for him. Instead, he frowned down at his hands.

"I'm listening," Amandine prompted.

"Like I said before, I refuse to be my father." He looked up, capturing her gaze with his. "If we are going to do this, I want to give our marriage a full year."

He wanted a real marriage then?

"So we would both agree to try to see once and for all if we could make this … us … work." He started to rip apart the napkin sitting beside the espresso saucer, not meeting her gaze. Wait, was he nervous?

Amandine nodded, even though her mind was in a tangle. When she'd considered his stipulations, trying to make their fake marriage real was not something she'd anticipated. Not for a second. Was Bertille right after all, or was he simply digging in his heels about not repeating his father's mistakes?

"We will have a proper wedding," he continued. "Even though I realize it needs to happen discreetly to keep Jean-Marc in the dark. It can happen in an out-of-the-way place and be small, but it needs to be legitimate. My sisters would make my life miserable if we didn't."

Amandine nodded again. He'd given this a lot of thought, and from a completely different angle than she'd expected.

"And if we're going to give it a real try, it would be a real marriage in every sense of the term … do you understand what I'm getting at?"

She looked up from her coffee to meet his eyes, and something hot and unexpected flared between them. Heat ran through Amandine's limbs, making them heavy.

"You mean we'll be sleeping together," she clarified.

"Yes," he said. "I mean … only if you agree. I would never force you—"

She held up her hand. Gaspard had far too much respect for the women in his life for Amandine ever to assume he would impose anything physical on her. "I know."

After all, she was the one forcing things. It was only fair that he could ask for whatever he wanted. It would be strange, but maybe it could also be better than it was before? Things in that department with Gaspard had always been fine, but she often suspected that it was just the tip of the iceberg of what they *could* be together. Would it be different this time? Amandine was not averse to his suggestion. The electricity crackling in her veins at the mere idea of a wedding night was proof of that.

"Those are my conditions." Gaspard looked down again at his tiny espresso spoon and bit his lip. Wait a second … was he unsure she would agree? She resisted the urge to whip those studious glasses off his face and kiss him so hard that he understood just how sure she was. "So," he said finally. "Considering all that, I'll ask again. Will you marry me, Amandine?"

"Yes," she said. "I will."

And then he smiled again—a true, wide smile this time. She stayed absolutely still as she let his question and her answer fill her with bright joy. Her mother's vines, and her legacy, would be saved. That was the most important thing. She was prepared to give Gaspard anything he wanted in exchange for that.

Chapter Eleven

After their coffee, they agreed to go for a walk in the nearby park La Bouzaise to discuss the details of their wedding—Amandine felt a little current of shock run through her every time either of them said the word. It was a glorious July morning, and the small lake in the middle of the park was as smooth as glass.

"I have an idea," Gaspard said, as they entered the park gates. "I'll rent a rowboat so we can talk privately."

Amandine stared at the cluster of white rowboats tied to a little jetty on the side of the lake. "You know how to row a boat?"

"As it happens, I know how to do a lot of things, Amandine," he said.

"Huh," she said, trying to cover up for the stab of lust she'd just felt. She found herself really, really wanting to learn all the things he could do that he hadn't shown her yet. No, she realized, she was not against the 'real marriage' stipulation at all. "You know," she mused. "I've been to this park hundreds of times, but I've never once been out in one of the boats."

He winked at her. "There's a first time for everything."

She felt another stab of wanting him in a way that

had nothing to do with the inheritance. "So there is."

With no apparent difficulty, Gaspard managed to get Amandine into the boat without tipping it over and toppling them into the murky water of the lake.

When she was safely seated on the little wooden bench at the back of the boat, it dawned on her that rowboats were perfectly designed for admiring the person doing the rowing in the front.

Gaspard grasped an oar in each hand and rowed confidently towards a spot where the water was shaded by the branches of a massive, and extremely old, weeping willow.

He was wearing a white T-shirt, and Amandine caught herself staring at the bulge and flex of his biceps as he pulled the oars through the water. She'd always had a weakness for Gaspard's arms—he had particularly well-defined and capable ones.

He drifted their boat to a stop under the tree, so they were secluded by the branches around them that grew down so far they touched the lake. Beams of sunlight shone down all around them through gaps in the leaves.

She fought with an absurd desire to lean forward and kiss Gaspard. Two swans paddled under the tree branches to join them, creating such an absurdly romantic scene that she wanted to laugh in disbelief. Why not start the 'real' marriage right then? Who said they had to wait until they said their vows? It had never been in her nature to wait around for anything to begin, and she was not going to change her instincts with something so important. She started to shift her weight to get up without toppling the boat over, but the rowboat lurched to the side.

Gaspard looked at her in alarm. "What are you do-ing? You're not going to jump ship are you? Whatever you do, don't stand up or we'll both end up in the lake." He surveyed the water. "Incidentally, I think there's a lot of swan and goose poop in there."

Deflated and embarrassed, Amandine sat back down again, hard enough that the boat lunged to one side before Gaspard stuck an oar in the water to stabilize it, sending her an accusing look. "What is going on with you?"

Oh, I don't know. You just told me that you wanted to have a true marriage with me including having sex and the rest of it and then you bring me to the most romantic place I can think of, goose poop notwithstanding, and then you let me make a fool of myself for getting the wrong idea?

"Calf cramp," she muttered instead.

"Oh," he said. "Does it feel better now?"

"Yup. Much better." She clapped her hands together. "So, let's talk about logistics." If he was going to be pragmatic, then so be it. She could play that game.

"Right. The challenge is how to have a wedding that is proper enough that it will satisfy my sisters and be unequivocally legitimate but secret enough that it won't tip off Jean-Marc or anyone that could tell him." Gaspard's voice was brisk and businesslike.

A major roadblock popped into her head. *Éloise.* How was Amandine going to convince her sister to keep this secret from their brother? She hated the necessity of putting her in that position. Besides, she wasn't even certain Éloise would agree to go along with the subterfuge.

"What is it?" Gaspard asked. His posture was more relaxed now, although occasionally he dipped in one or the other oar to straighten their boat. "Are you having second thoughts?"

Amandine stared at him, incredulous. *No, you idiot.*

Up until you got all pragmatic I'd been about to kiss you. She had a moment of déjà vu from when they broke up—sometimes it was like they spoke two different languages. "I was thinking about how to get Éloise to keep our secret."

"Ah." His mouth softened.

She was momentarily distracted by his mouth but yanked herself back to the problem at hand. "Éloise won't like keeping it a secret from Jean-Marc. I hate to ask it of her. There's nothing she loathes more than choosing sides. I'm not at all certain she'll agree."

"What if I get my sisters to talk to her?"

"Doesn't that seem a little underhanded?"

Gaspard shrugged. "Maybe, but also effective."

Amandine nodded. Gaspard's idea was probably their best chance at bringing her over to their side. "Okay. I'll talk to her today, then I'll drop her off at your house to hang out with Bertille and the rest of your gang. I'd bet you're right—they'll manage to whip up some excitement in her for the wedding, despite her qualms."

"Excellent." Gaspard tapped his fingers on the side of the boat. "I stopped by at Clovis's—or Cerise's, more accurately—on the way here. They were discharged from the hospital last night. We're welcome to have the reception at Domaine du Cerisier."

Wasn't that just like Gaspard, doing the work himself before she even had time to help. "But they have a newborn," she said. "They won't be in any shape for hosting a wedding."

Gaspard tilted his head, accepting her point. "Yes, I thought of that too."

Of course he had.

"I considered asking Luc, but Savigny and Pernand are so close to each other. There's no way the news would not get to Jean-Marc's ears. Domaine du Cerisier is far enough out of the way in the Hautes-Côtes."

He had a point. Savigny-les-Beaune, where Luc's family Domaine was located, and Pernand-Vergelesses, where Amandine lived, were so close by that they were interconnected not only by vineyards but by families and friends. Still, she didn't like the officious way that Gaspard was making these decisions for her. At the same time, maybe it was his way of exerting some control over something that had never been his choosing. She could understand that. Besides, she owed him so much. How could she possibly complain?

"I suppose you've already picked a date?" she said, trying her darndest but still unable to conceal an edge of archness in her voice.

Gaspard leaned forward. "What's wrong with that? You seem to be forgetting that I'm the one doing you a favor, not the other way around."

It was exactly what she'd just been reminding herself, yet somehow hearing him talk about the marriage in those terms ignited sparks of anger in her chest. What did he want, exactly? A real marriage or a fake marriage? He was all over the place. Anger crackled within her but she had to put a lid on it. She had too much to lose if she let it burst into flame like she normally did with Gaspard. She couldn't afford to burn everything down in her path … not when her mother's vineyards were in jeopardy.

"True," she managed to get out.

Gaspard gave a little clap. "Bravo. I didn't think that would go down so well."

She couldn't help but give him a black look.

He sighed, his dark eyes looking even darker in the shade of the branches. "To tell you the truth, I regretted it almost as soon as it popped out of my mouth. It's wrong of me to bait you right now—you're under enough stress as it is. But you have to realize … this is all very strange for me and not at all what I'd planned. Taking action by organizing things is my way of coping, I suppose."

Just like that, her temper was extinguished. Of course he was as unsettled as she was—more so, even. He had nothing to gain from their marriage like she did, and he had everything to lose. Ever since they were in elementary school together he'd had an innate bias for action … how could she expect him to change now? Her throat felt thick with guilt. He was sacrificing his beliefs to help her. "You sure you want to do this?" Her sense of honor obliged her to ask.

He didn't answer right away, and the rustle of the wind through the willow branches didn't soothe the coil of tension in her chest while she waited for his verdict.

"Yes," he said. Relief poured through her. "Like you, I don't see any other options. You've been placed in an extremely unfair predicament through no fault of your own. I can get you out of it. My first reaction … when I refused and got angry … I apologize for that. It's just that this has completely turned my plans for my life on their head, but how could I leave you to suffer when I can help?"

"There's no need to apologize," she said in a soft voice that she almost never used, and certainly never around Gaspard. "And thank you." She realized then the magnitude of Gaspard's sacrifice. She was taking away his chance to find someone and fall in love and get married in the traditional way, the way he'd always wanted. She tried to breathe in but couldn't seem to fill her lungs. How could she be so selfish? Yet … her mother's legacy … it was the only way.

His gaze on her became more intent and she was aware of a sudden sensation that he was trying to probe what was in her heart, but finally he cleared his throat. "So! Our marriage. We have a location, and yes, we even have a date two weeks from now, a solid week before Jean-Marc is due to get married. Not such a dummy, your future husband, *n'est-ce pas?*"

Now they were on familiar ground, but Amandine's breathing was still much shallower than usual. "As much as it grieves me to give you a compliment, you are very clever, but I'm still uncomfortable with imposing on Clovis and Cerise with Myrtille so little."

"Yet oddly you seem to have no issue imposing on me."

If only he knew how heavy that was weighing on her, but she still didn't see any other solutions. She tried to make light of it and forced out a chuckle. "That's different."

He smiled at her, and she realized what lengths she would go to to see that smile appear more often. "I assured them that we would keep it extremely casual and do all the work."

"Do you think we can manage that?" Amandine asked. Two weeks was not a long time and they both had their vineyard work—

"Amandine," Gaspard interrupted her thoughts. "You clearly haven't thought this through. We have five incredibly industrious, brilliant, creative sisters with a far better esthetic sense than either of us. Do you truly think there's anything they couldn't pull off?"

He was right. Besides that, she adored hearing him talk about his sisters and how capable and smart they were.

"Sophie, Louise, and Margaux can drive now, so if we just give them a budget, they would be delighted to pull things together as our wedding gift."

"You've already talked to them," Amandine guessed. What hadn't he organized? She bit her tongue. The vineyards were the important thing, she reminded herself, not the wedding. She couldn't lose sight of that.

"Of course."

"So?"

"So what?" Gaspard asked.

Amandine tapped her foot on the bottom of the boat. *Honestly ... men.* "How did they react?"

"Oh! That. They were overjoyed. Margaux got out the bottles of *crémant* and insisted on a toast."

Amandine smiled to herself. Gaspard's sisters had always liked her and being Éloise's sister was a tick in her column, but they were protective of Gaspard in the same way he was protective of them. She hadn't been entirely certain how they'd react, especially Bertille. Then she had an unwelcome thought. "Did you give them the specifics on *why* we're getting married?"

Gaspard sighed. "I mulled over this at length last night. There's no way that we can do this and not let our inner circle in on our motivations. It's all too sudden."

Amandine nodded. "I came to that conclusion too. I mean, otherwise how would we explain that Jean-Marc and Julie aren't invited or explain why we have to keep a tight lid on the ceremony? You're right, it would also seem too sudden to be believable, even for us." Their first engagement had taken their friends and families by surprise, but a second one out of the blue just wouldn't be credible.

"Precisely."

"But then ... what you were saying about it being a

real marriage … if we act like a real couple in public people are going to get confused." Heck, she was still confounded by the implications of Gaspard's request.

"I thought about that too," Gaspard said. "It was hard, last time, having everyone involved in our relationship and weighing in with their opinions, *n'est-ce pas?*"

Amandine nodded. Their friend group, not to mention their sisters, had strong ideas about everything and couldn't help but meddle.

"We need to tell people about the inheritance and our motivations for getting married for the whole secrecy thing to work, right?" He rubbed that enticing bridge of his nose again.

"Right."

"But as far as it being a real marriage … maybe it would be nice this time to actually have some space and privacy to see what we can make of this without everyone looking over our shoulders."

She realized then the seriousness of his intention to make their fake marriage something real and lasting. She should have known. Gaspard never did anything halfway.

She had that same giddiness in her stomach as when she ventured too close to the edge of the cliffs above the nearby village of Bouilland. "You have a point." This was Gaspard. She'd known Gaspard forever yet somehow this step … it felt different.

"Amandine," he said, in that rough, commanding tone of his. "Do you feel the same way?"

She thought she did, but this was all so new. The words caught in her throat. Was there a way to say yes without making herself totally vulnerable? She knew she should be able to trust Gaspard, now more than ever, but her father and Jean-Marc had broken the ability for her to trust men when it mattered most.

Gaspard glowered at Amandine. "Do you?"

Amandine knew immediately that she'd mis-stepped. She couldn't have Gaspard back-tracking. Not now. Then, the solution came to her—acquiescence without enthusiasm. That was how she could protect herself.

"I'll do whatever you want," she said. "As you re-minded me, you're the one doing me a favor. I'm hardly in a position to negotiate."

Gaspard flinched and lowered his eyes to the bottom of the boat. "I'm not going to force your hand at anything, Amandine."

"You're not forcing my hand," she clarified. "I asked you."

He spoke to his feet instead of her. "If we're going to give it a year, which I would like, wouldn't it be more pleasant if we had some basic affection between us?"

"We have affection."

He rubbed his nose. "I think you confuse affection with fighting."

Amandine smiled, despite herself. "Sometimes it's hard to tell the difference with us."

"That's true," he admitted, still not looking up.

"How about we deal with the logistics first, and ac-tually get married without Jean-Marc finding out, then we can figure out the rest later. Deal?"

He sighed and then grasped the oars to begin rowing back to the dock. "Deal."

Chapter Twelve

The next week was filled coordinating with their sisters and late-night phone calls with each other to hammer out last minute details. It was all happening so quickly, and the vines were growing so fast things were crazy in the vineyards as well. Amandine barely had time to wrap her mind around the fact that she and Gaspard were going to be married in a week's time.

She had started to dream of him though—every single night since their rowboat ride at La Bouzaise. She would wake up in the middle of the night with her sheets twisted and damp after dreaming about sharing the same bed with Gaspard, and finally unleashing that fire they both tended to bottle up.

She began to worry she was confusing real-life Gaspard and the man who came to her at night, full of need and passion. Next time she saw him in person instead of just talking to him over the phone and exchanging texts, her face was probably going to burst into flame.

It was Saturday, and she'd bribed Éloise and Bertille to help her serve wine at her stand for the Ballade Gourmande.

This, an annual event in the villages around Pernand, was a hugely popular and important date on the winemaking calendar in her neck of the woods. People paid for tickets to wander through a designated route in the vineyards, stopping at stands to taste the local wine. If it was merely an event for tourists, Amandine wouldn't bother, especially not a week before her covert wedding, but tons of locals participated and many of the wine pros came from all over the world.

Being asked to have a stand to give out her wine to taste was an honor, and not an opportunity that any local winemaker could afford to waste.

As Bertille and Éloise helped her set up the stand on the vineyard path halfway between Pernand and Aloxe-Corton, Amandine thanked God that she had seen neither hide nor hair of her brother since their fight in the courtyard. She could only assume that Julie was keeping him busy with wedding preparations. The last thing she needed was him hanging around telling everyone he was going to inherit the Domaine on a day when she needed to make a good impression.

Éloise and Bertille were in a buoyant mood and could barely contain their excitement about the wedding. Gaspard had been right—his redoubtable sisters had talked Éloise around her initial reservations.

Amandine shushed them. "You guys have to play it cool, remember? It'll wreck everything if anyone clues into what's going on."

They both nodded obediently but couldn't resist whispering in each other's ears.

They were about two hours into the morning when Amandine looked out to the crest of the hill beyond to see how many people were making their slow, meandering way to her stand. There were at least half a dozen stands before hers and the combination of the bright sun and wine meant that people were not necessarily walking in a straight line by the time they reached her. She spotted a familiar figure walking briskly in stark contrast to everybody else, and her entire body froze like a fox encountering a wild boar in the forest. A fizzle of anticipation ran through Amandine.

Gaspard overtook the laughing groups of tipsy strollers.

He wasn't directly involved in the event because it was only on her section of the Côte, not his. Was he there because of her?

"*Salut frèro*!" Bertille waved at him.

He waved back, that right side of his lips tugging up.

Even though his sisters challenged him all the time and tormented him to no end, the love between them was plain to see. As would be expected, his sisters rebelled against Gaspard's dictates at every turn—and he was the first to admit he was bossy by nature—but Amandine sensed they also realized how lucky they were to have a solid parental influence in their life to butt up against. Gaspard gave them a sense of security that they never got from their neglectful father or wayward mothers.

He reached the stand, all dark and ... *Gaspard*. Amandine's stomach lurched so violently she covered it with her hand. Her heart pounded and the thought that in a week she was going to be sleeping in the same bed as him could not be dislodged from her mind.

He greeted Éloise and Bertille first with *les bises*.

"I didn't know you were planning on coming," Bertille said accusingly. "Why didn't you tell me?"

Gaspard tilted his head, his eyes ripe with humor. "I didn't know I was obligated to inform you of my movements."

Amandine couldn't wait to kiss him. *Wait ... what*?

Bertille put her hands on her hips. "Well ... I think

you are. I'm only sixteen you know."

"I'll remind you of that next time you want to go up to Paris with friends to see a concert at the Bataclan."

Bertille waved her hands at him. "Forget it. What can I get you to drink?"

"Bonjour Amandine," he said, leaning in to give her *les bises*. Was it just her imagination, or did he linger longer than usual, his lips warm and soft on her face? She shivered at the feel of his breath in the shell of her ear. "What do you suggest?"

When he pulled back, his face held an expression meant only for her—it was their shared secret that they were going to give this marriage a real try. Amandine wondered if Gaspard was becoming as intrigued by that prospect as she was.

"Ummm …" Normally Amandine would be able to select a wine for Gaspard in a split second, but he had thrown her decidedly off her game. "Let me see."

"Preferably something Jean-Marc had no hand in," Gaspard added with a wink.

She snorted. "That goes without saying."

Finally, she selected a bottle she had hidden underneath the stand for people she really needed to impress.

Gaspard's eyes widened. "Corton Grand Cru?"

Luckily the meanderers were still a fair distance from the stand, and Bertille and Éloise were off to the side whispering about something. "Only the best for my husband-to-be," Amandine said in a low voice meant only for him.

Gaspard's mouth dropped open. He stared at Amandine, his skin flushed.

"Don't look so surprised. I intend to take this seriously too."

He cleared his throat. "I'm glad to hear that." Something she wanted to see more of flared in his eyes.

"Taste what you are saving." She passed him his glass and hid the bottle under the stand again.

It was just in time too, as the group finally approached the stand and Éloise and Bertille resumed their posts. "What did she give you?" Éloise asked Gaspard, nodding at his glass.

"Corton Grand Cru," Amandine said to Éloise out of the corner of her mouth. "But don't offer it to anyone else. I've hidden it again."

Éloise's eyes went wide. "Consider yourself honored," she said to Gaspard. "Amandine almost never pours that."

"Oh." His dark eyes connected with Amandine's and a current of highly promising energy ran between them. "I do."

The new group was bearing down on Amandine's stand now, and more appeared behind the hill. "Brace yourselves," Amandine said. "Incoming."

"You know what?" Gaspard said, coming around the back of the stand to join them there. "I'd like to stay and help for a while if you don't mind."

"But Gaspard," Bertille protested. "You hate this sort of thing."

"What do you mean?" he said, indignant.

"You hate people."

"I don't hate *all* people, Bertille," Gaspard said. "In fact, I like some people very much. Is it all right with you if I stay, Amandine?" he cast her a questioning look.

Her stomach fluttered, but in the best possible way. "Yes. Absolutely."

Gaspard never could have imagined in a thousand years that he could enjoy himself this much at an event that involved making small talk with strangers.

Working alongside Amandine felt right and, better yet, there were indications she was open to his suggestion … okay … his stipulation—even though he regretted calling it that—to at least try to make their fake marriage real. He'd initially asked because he wanted a chance to be different than his father, but there were deeper reasons emerging—reasons involving the yearning heat he felt when he thought of Amandine as his wife.

Bertille and Éloise made a team and Gaspard and Amandine made another. Was it just him or were he and his fiancée bumping up against each other more than was absolutely necessary? When she passed him a glass or took a bottle from him to uncork, their fingers kept touching, and lingering for a second or two longer than usual. Every time, a bolt of lust shot through his entire body, unmistakably concentrating in some spots in particular.

Could it be different between them this time? Gaspard's hopes were gathering steam—frighteningly so. Not that there was anything precisely *wrong* with last time. It was just that she hadn't been willing to let down her guard enough for them to truly connect and, if he was going to be honest, it wasn't just her. He was so unused to being able to have something he wanted—and he had wanted Amandine more desperately than he'd ever wanted anything. He'd been terrified to fully indulge his desires, convinced that if he did he would eventually have to pay a price.

He'd learned the lesson that only disappointment came from asking for what he wanted when he was ten.

Bertille and Margaux's mother had just flitted off to Tahiti, without her daughters, where she'd taken up with a world-famous yachtsman. His father had taken refuge in the study of their house. Bertille was just a baby, and his other sisters were still small, and overwhelmingly busy.

He'd been looking forward to going to his friend Luc's birthday party for weeks. It was going to be a sleepover in the harvester's rooms at Luc's family Domaine in Savigny.

Gaspard wasn't usually invited to such things. Most of the other children in his class either disliked him or were scared by his brusque manners. Thank God he always had his buddies, Luc and Clovis and even Amandine, who formed an essential corner of their quartet.

All the work he had done looking after his sisters, feeding bottles, making meals, changing diapers, wiping tears … all of that he could tolerate if he could just do something for himself. After all, he was their brother, not their parent. It wasn't fair that his father stayed in his study, and thought he was doing his part by arranging for daycare and hiring a woman from the village to come by and do some cooking, cleaning, and laundry for a few hours every morning.

The evening arrived when it was time to go to Luc's party. Gaspard knew better than to ask his father to drive him, so he'd already planned to take his bike. He'd carefully packed his backpack days before, and now it sat in the front hall as he held Bertille in his arms and went to the forbidden lair of his father's study. It was where his father poured over manuscripts in medieval French for hours on end—that was his true passion. He should have been a professor.

Bertille had terrible colic, far worse than her older sisters. To Gaspard, it sounded like Bertille was being slowly stabbed to death, and he often wondered if the colic was not the final straw that made Bertille and Margaux's mother decamp to Tahiti. The crying was so bad that a little part of Gaspard didn't even blame her.

It would have been much better if Bertille wasn't crying when he knocked on his father's study door, because if she'd been quiet, he might have accepted her to sleep beside him while he worked. She was wailing worse than ever, but he couldn't put it off any longer. He was already late as it was.

"Gaspard!" His father bellowed when Gaspard took a step into the room and on to the dusty carpet on the wooden floor, a wailing Bertille in his arms. "What is that infernal racket?"

"It's Bertille. I have to go to Luc's sleepover now, so I need to give her to you."

His father looked at Bertille, her face red like a tomato and her mouth wide open mid-scream. He shook his head. "I can't take her while she's crying like that."

"But remember, Papa? You promised. I already told Luc I could go."

"But I need to finish this page of translation. I didn't expect her to be crying like *that*."

She always cries like that. "You promised."

"No, I'm sorry, Gaspard. You'll just have to take a rain check on tonight."

A white-hot spurt of anger flared in Gaspard's narrow chest. "But you're not even getting paid for whatever it is your reading!" Gaspard dared say. The medieval stuff was a hobby. How could that be more important than being a father? Gaspard was just Bertille's brother. She wasn't his baby. It wasn't fair.

His father sat back in his chair and eyed him coldly over the tops of his glasses. "Since when have you become so mercenary, *mon fils*?"

"I'm not," Luc said. "It's just … I want to go to this party. I'm just asking you … please … can I go?"

His father examined him for a moment longer. Bertille continued to shriek.

Please let him say yes. Please. Wasn't Gaspard allowed to want things too?

"This is an excellent opportunity for a life lesson." Gaspard's father steepled his fingers together. "Do you happen to know the root cause of unhappiness in the world?"

There was no right answer to such a question—Gaspard knew that in his gut. It was just like his father to speak in parables.

"You don't know?" his father said. "I thought not. The root of unhappiness is, quite simply, wanting things. Did you realize that?"

"Uh … no." Better to agree than disagree.

"And do you know what creates even more unhappiness than wanting things?"

"No."

"*Asking* for things you want." He laughed bitterly. "Toughen up, Gaspard. Life is not a candy store. Plans change and tonight you are needed here, with Bertille and your sisters. That will help you remember such an important lesson."

His father turned back to his manuscript. The bitter taste of resentment filled his mouth. Bertille was still screaming, so he put her down in her crib for a few minutes. He was too angry to be safe right then and was terrified that he would squeeze her too tightly without meaning to.

He paced back and forth in her bedroom, not knowing what to do with this white-hot anger that ran through him like bolts of lightning. He turned to the closest wall and imagined his father's face there, smug and uncaring. Before he realized what he was doing, his fist flew out and he punched a dent into the plaster wall. *Putain de merde* that hurt. It rained down little plaster pieces as he clutched his throbbing knuckles with the other.

The pain made him realize Bertille had stopped crying and was now looking over at him with her big eyes, black like his.

He lifted her out of the crib gently and sat down in the rocking chair in the corner of her bedroom. "What are we going to do?" he murmured into her shell of an ear. "What are we going to do with a pair of bad-tempered souls like us?"

Bertille blinked up at him, giving him the impression that she understood. Her mouth began to move and she smiled. Gaspard realized right then and there that he'd been mistaken back in his father's study. Bertille wasn't his father's baby … not really. Bertille was his baby to look after.

Bertille grinned so widely she was showing off her gums. Despite everything he laughed back at her and dropped a kiss on her forehead. Maybe there were silver linings in a life of looking after others. Besides, perhaps Luc's overnight wouldn't be that fun after all.

Amandine probably thought that the fact he didn't even argue when she dumped him last time was proof he didn't love her. She couldn't be more wrong. Sure, his pride was a barrier, but more than that, he was still unable to ask for what he wanted, and he'd never wanted anything like he'd wanted Amandine.

He'd ignored his doubts with that quick proposal after they'd slept together for the first time, and the fact that she'd broken his heart shortly after had confirmed all his fears.

But life, and ironically Amandine's perfidious father, had handed him a second chance.

Amandine brushed past him. His arms ached to pull her against him right then and there. She had no idea how stunning he found her. Her features were elfin and magical in the way of the fairies his grandmother had always told him lived in the forests in the Morvan. The way she relentlessly challenged him left him wanting to prove himself in every way—he could never be with someone who wasn't a match in temper and obstinacy.

He took a sip of her wine. It was as breathtaking as she was. Deep color, powerful nose, and ripe with the notes of candied fruits and spices. Tasting her talent and hard work was a powerful type of foreplay for him.

She raised her hand in greeting at someone approaching. He had to stop staring at her—he couldn't give them away. More importantly, he had to keep his expectations in check.

Chapter Thirteen

The wedding was in four days, and Amandine realized belatedly that perhaps she should buy a dress for the occasion.

The only ones she owned were black, and even though the circumstances of their wedding were odd, she was not wearing a funeral dress. Her mind and heart were both a tangle of conflicting emotions about her imminent nuptials but there was growing happiness inside her that—while she didn't completely trust it—surely merited a cream dress at least?

The mere idea of wedding dress shopping filled Amandine with fear. She had no idea where to begin. Luckily, Cerise and Sadie came to her rescue by proposing a daytrip down to Lyon to go dress shopping. That was how she found herself on a train heading due south with them and baby Myrtille. The best thing about this excursion was that they were all going to look at wedding dresses. Well, except baby Myrtille of course.

Clovis had proposed to Cerise at Christmas. They were still in no huge rush, but they had been talking about a winter wedding. Luc had proposed to Sadie a few days before. Sadie didn't give out many details— Amandine got the impression it had been a private moment strictly for the two of them—but Amandine did know it had been in a little stone *cabotte* Sadie and Luc had spent hours playing in as children.

Even though everyone loved Luc, Amandine was realizing there was a part of him that he kept for Sadie and only Sadie.

Amandine stared out the window of the TGV, wondering if despite the convoluted beginnings of this marriage, she and Gaspard could ever be that for each other.

"So, how are we feeling about this whole shopping for dresses thing?" Sadie asked. Like Cerise, she wasn't in a rush either. Her and Luc were still deciding on a date when her dig partner, Frederick, and her sister, Stella, could join them from England, as well as her mother and brother from the U.S.

"I'm far more comfortable in the vineyards than a bridal shop," Amandine said.

"I get it." Sadie blew an errant curl out of her eyes, impatient. "I'm happiest in a big mud pit digging for treasures. We'll be each other's emotional support." She twirled a different curl around her index finger. "I wonder how many girls actually like the whole meringue wedding dress thing?"

"Not many, I would think," Cerise said, wincing as Myrtille latched on. "I cannot believe this child was born with a tooth."

"Is that supposed to be good luck or bad luck?" Sadie asked.

"I actually did an internet search, if you can believe it." Cerise laughed at herself. "Depending on the culture, both are believed."

"Excellent. You can choose," Amandine said.

"*Oui*. I'm choosing good luck, obviously. Trust me,

we'll need it today. Taking a newborn shopping is not for the faint of heart."

They all laughed.

"I guess all the dresses aren't meringues these days," Sadie admitted, but didn't sound convinced. "Hopefully there will be some simpler ones."

"You could always go back to New York to shop," Cerise said. "They must have everything there."

Sadie shrugged. "It's honestly not worth that much effort to me. I just want Luc. I could care less about the dress."

"I guess we're all trying to make ourselves care about the dress part," Amandine said, relief making her limbs weak. "You don't realize how much better that makes me feel."

"We're here to help." Cerise winked at her over Myrtille's perfectly shaped head, covered with a shiny cap of dark hair.

"Don't worry, Amandine." Sadie sighed. "We'll all get through today and find you something nice but not too—"

"Poufy," Cerise supplied.

Sadie gasped. "How dare you? We would never inflict poufy on Amandine." She sat back in her seat, a playful smile on her animated face and her red curls highlighted by the sun shining behind her through the train window. Amandine wasn't used to having female friends, but somehow it was easy with Cerise and Sadie.

Amandine had always liked Sadie when she'd gone to elementary school in Beaune with them for a few years when her father was on sabbatical in Burgundy, but they'd never been close like Sadie and Luc had been. Now though, Sadie fitted right in.

"How are you feeling?" Cerise asked. "Yours are

rather unusual circumstances for a wedding."

Amandine hesitated. Usually she wouldn't confide, but she felt like she could with these two. She'd witnessed the beginnings of their relationships with her closest friends, and neither Cerise or Sadie had ridden a smooth path to get where they were now.

She knotted her hands together. "Confused." It was the truth.

"Understandable," Cerise said, as she patted little Myrtille's back. "Clovis and I were confused too. The way Gaspard explained it ... well, he said it was just so you could inherit the vineyards, but then sometimes I get the impression that maybe there's more to it than that?"

Amandine shrugged. Part of her wanted to tell them everything. It would be so wonderful to have help in unravelling her thoughts, but she would never betray Gaspard's trust in such a way. He wanted them to try in private and his logic made sense. "It all happened so fast and we've barely had any time together to discuss it."

"I would generally recommend talking *before* the wedding, but I guess this is a peculiar set of circumstances." Sadie raised an auburn brow.

"Hmmm," Amandine said, noncommittal.

"At least you and Gaspard are such good friends," Sadie continued. "Surely if anyone can talk about awkward things, it's you two."

How to explain that even though they could talk about most things, neither of them were in the habit of discussing what was closest to their hearts? Maybe that had been the deal breaker last time, she realized only now. They both carved out moats around their souls and neither of them had ever attempted to cross.

Amandine tapped her fingers against the train window. "Slight problem. Whenever we stray into personal topics it tends to degenerate.”

“You mean fight?” Cerise clarified.

“Yes.”

Sadie regarded Amandine with shrewd eyes. “Yet it seems to me that the two of you enjoy your arguing. It’s the oddest thing.”

Amandine bit her lip, trying not to smile. “That’s not completely wrong. We’re both so intense that we need a steam release valve in our lives. I guess fighting provides that.”

Cerise arched a fine black eyebrow. “You know, there are other ways to let off steam.”

“Such as?” Amandine stared back, feigning wide-eyed innocence.

Cerise rolled her eyes. “You’re going to make me say it, aren’t you?”

“Yes.”

“Okay, you brat. The bedroom.”

“Hmmm,” Amandine said, turning the whole conver-sation into a joke to cover up the fact they were straying on to painful ground. “I never thought of that.”

It had been convenient for her to blame their lack of passion in bed on Gaspard, but deep down she mostly blamed herself. Her father and brother had broken her trust so many times—how could that not break her ability to trust a man with her heart? At times she was struck with an unshakeable panic that she was going to mess everything up this time as well.

Yet a dangerous hope had started to take root in her—maybe this time would be different. Finding the right dress probably wouldn’t make any difference, but she was becoming superstitious in her desperation. Maybe it would.

At the bridal store they played pass-the-baby with Myrtille as they took turns trying on dresses. The owner of the small and *trés* elegant boutique passed them each flutes of Veuve-Cliquot. The whole place smelled of vanilla cake. Even Cerise took a few sips out of her tiny glass.

"A sip or two of champagne makes babies more beautiful!" the tiny shopkeeper declared after admiring Myrtille's dark hair and cherubic legs.

"I thought that old saying was for when women were pregnant," Cerise said. "Not breastfeeding."

The woman straightened her impeccable pencil skirt and let out a tinkling laugh. "Aren't you droll! We're going to have so much fun."

Amandine offered to hold Myrtille first while Cerise tried on a few dresses, before her daughter got fussy and needed to breastfeed yet again.

When Cerise passed her over, she was surprised at the solid weight of the baby in her arms. It was an inexplicably satisfying weight—like a bucket of freshly cut grape clusters during the harvest. Myrtille was also deliciously warm, and breathed in soft, fast little breaths. Amandine quickly felt her own breathing softening to match the baby's rhythm.

Her eyes were changing color, losing some of that baby gray and turning a deeper blue like her father's. Drawn over them, though, were two little fine black eyebrows, just like Cerise.

Amandine had never thought much about babies

before, beyond the fact that they were apparently a ton of work. Now, though, something she didn't even know she had inside her began to loosen as she gazed down at Myrtille.

Also, Cerise was managing to continue blazing her brilliant path as one of Burgundy's most innovative and talented winemakers with three children—four including Clovis's daughter, Emily, who came over from England to stay at Domaine du Cerisier more and more frequently.

Myrtille began to squirm and fuss again, so Amandine stood up from the elegant Louis XVI sofa and began pacing back and forth across the lush carpet of the store, patting Myrtille's tiny, rounded back. The way Myrtille had shaped herself against Amandine's torso— like one of the little limpets she collected once on vacation in Brittany—left her feeling uncharacteristically sentimental.

If they were able to make this a real marriage, as Gaspard wanted, maybe they could have babies too. For the first time in … well, ever … a desire for that ignited inside her.

"How are you finding juggling winemaking and a newborn?" Amandine asked her friend through the curtain of Cerise's dressing room. Cerise's feet shuffled below the curtain as she shimmied into a simple, non-meringue oyster-color dress she'd chosen from the rack.

"I'm not going to tell you it's easy, because it's not," she said. "But Myrtille is not only my responsibility." She swore quietly under her breath. "God, my boobs are huge right now with the breastfeeding."

Amandine didn't know quite how to respond to that.

Luckily, Cerise continued. "Clovis and I are sharing all the care. As a matter of fact, he's frustrated he can't help with feeding her yet. Trust me, this time around it's a completely different experience than with my first husband, Antoine. He was very much of that old-school 'women are the main caretaker of the children' philosophy."

"Ugh."

"*Je sais,* but in his defense, it was the way he was brought up. It wasn't in his nature to question that sort of thing. Besides, we were so young when we had Yves and Marc—practically kids ourselves."

Amandine paid close attention. Cerise didn't talk about Antoine very often and generally only to keep his memory alive for her sons.

"So … you've been able to continue winemaking?" Amandine said.

Cerise snorted. "As if anything could stop me! I'm not going to sugar coat it—it's challenging finding the focus and the time right now, but I'm managing. One advantage to Myrtille being my third is I know from experience this baby stage isn't going to last forever, so I'm just trying to accept the exhaustion and enjoy it as much as I can."

Cerise pushed her curtain aside and came out to show them. The oyster silk was beautiful with her black hair and ivory complexion, but she wasn't wrong—it was definitely strained around the chest area.

She passed a hand over her tummy. "I still have a bit of a pregnancy belly, and … you know, breastfeeding boobs, but this one has potential."

"It's beautiful," said Sadie, who had been busy thumbing through the racks and now had a dress in her arms.

"It will be." Cerise smoothed down the silk and smiled at her reflection. "Now, let me get out of this and take Myrtille so you two can have your turns."

Sadie's prowling around the store had unearthed a gorgeous cream gown with tiny shimmering beads. "You haven't picked anything out, Amandine." She frowned.

Amandine nodded down to Myrtille. "My arms were full."

"Can I pick something out for you?" Sadie asked. "Please, please? I'm not exactly known for my style like my twin sister, Stella, but being in this store I feel like maybe some of her fashion sense did rub off on me after all."

"Sure." Amandine felt a rush of gratitude. The idea of her imminent wedding felt so surreal and full of uncertainty that it seemed almost too loaded a thing to pick out a wedding dress for herself.

What if her choice sent Gaspard the wrong message? Too fancy and he might think that she wanted something from him that he couldn't give. Too simple and he might think that she didn't care about him at all and was just using him.

Ten minutes later Amandine had passed off Myrtille to Cerise and was in the dressing room beside Sadie's.

Her heart pounded as she surveyed Sadie's three dress selections for her, all hanging on a brass hook mounted on the wall beside the curtain. No meringue poufs to be seen, *merci dieu.*

Amandine picked her favorite of the three—a pure white silk column with an incredibly simple cut and a halter style top that attached behind her neck. She slipped it on, buttoning up the halter straps around the nape of her neck. It fit well if she wasn't mistaken, although she was hardly a good judge of such things.

She took a deep breath and stepped outside her dressing room. Cerise was sitting on the couch, nursing

Myrtille again. That little girl had a true Burgundian appetite.

Cerise glanced up, then sucked in air. Oh no. Was it bad?

"Oh my God, Amandine," she said. "It's perfect."

Amandine turned and stared at herself in the mirror, disbelieving the reflection that she saw. How could such a thing as a simple dress be so transformative? It made her spare frame look willowy instead of skinny, and her chopped blunt cut look intentionally chic instead of just low maintenance. This was no longer Amandine who stared back at her. This was a *bride*.

Sadie's curtain was pushed back with a clatter of curtain rings, and she joined them in front of the mirror, looking every bit a magical garden creature with her curling red hair and the creamy richness of the dress setting off her skin and the freckles on her nose. Bell sleeves and sparkling beads interwoven in the delicate lace made her look like the perfect woodland bride. It suited her perfectly. Luc was going to *die*.

Sadie and Amandine examined one another.

"You look ... magical," Amandine said finally.

"And you!" Sadie exclaimed. "Oh my God, Amandine, it's so perfect and unadorned and stunning ... I have such *excellent* taste." She mock preened herself a bit.

They all laughed.

"You know what?" Cerise said. "I think you both just found your wedding dresses."

"Really?" they both said in unison, Sadie turning to Amandine with her gold eyes wide.

Myrtille made a funny little noise, almost a shout.

"Even Myrtille agrees." Cerise leaned down to give her daughter a kiss.

The difference was, Amandine remembered as she undid the back of her dress once she was back in her changing room and let the silk pool at her feet, Sadie was marrying the love of her life for all the right reasons. Her reasons were wrong, but could she and Gaspard make something right out of it?

Chapter Fourteen

It was the day before the wedding, and with all the doubts and conflicting emotions warring within him, Gaspard was glad that he and Louise had scheduled to aerate the roots of the vines in the Champans vines.

She wasn't as experienced as Gaspard was at the technique and it took her some practice to acquire the *coup de main* for the technique they referred to as *griffage*. They were both on their knees in the dirt, yet Louise seemed full of joy and pleasure at the task—certainly far more than Gaspard had ever been.

"So," Gaspard said, holding up his pronged trowel to show Louise. "You have yours?"

She waved hers with a flourish.

"This task involves scratching the surface of the land around the vines to remove weeds," he explained. "It also aerates the soil and helps the nutritious elements penetrate back in. I should tell you—it takes a certain attention to detail to ensure the root itself isn't damaged in the process."

Louise watched as Gaspard showed her how he did it, her sharp eyes missing nothing.

"Now you try." He nodded to the vine root one plant over. She did. After a few tries, and a tip of two from

Gaspard, Louise was doing it perfectly. They fell into a rhythm—Gaspard working on one side of the wire and stakes and Louise on the other. The June day was warm and cloudless ... and the next night he would be sleeping in the same bed as Amandine.

The marriage was one thing, but the idea of the marriage bed ... that was something that had been keeping him awake since they'd had their conversation—or was it a negotiation?—in the Café Vingt-et-Un. He was having second thoughts—not from any lack of desire—no, definitely not that.

It was dawning on him, however, that his requests to Amandine about a 'real' marriage had come directly from his heart, not his head. How could he have asked for such a promise from her? Even after they were married, she owed him nothing. To coerce her into sharing a physical intimacy that she had shown no desire for? His gut was increasingly shouting at him that no matter how many hours he lay in bed, hard and yearning for her, it was wrong of him.

"This weather is supposed to hold," Louise said. "It'll be perfect for tomorrow."

Having a hard time tearing himself out of his thoughts, Gaspard just grunted in agreement.

"How are you feeling?" she asked.

He wasn't in the habit of inflicting his moods or his doubts on his sisters, so he made another noncommittal noise.

"I'm going to need more than that." Louise finished her vine before him and moved over to the next one in line. "Slowpoke," she added.

Gaspard laughed at this. That was one thing about his sisters—they always managed to make him laugh. "I'm feeling rather overwhelmed to be honest," he admitted.

Louise considered this without her hands pausing. "I guess that is sort of normal, isn't it? Given the circumstances."

"Yeah."

"Do you love her?" Louise asked.

What a question—one he hadn't even dared to ask himself. It was just like Louise to go right for the jugular.

"I know the circumstances are strange," she continued. "But somehow I've always thought the two of you belonged together."

So had he at one time. In fact, he'd been so convinced of it he'd proposed to her. "Shame that Amandine didn't agree."

"I don't know about that," Louise said. "Just be patient. You might have to let her come to you."

Yes, why on earth hadn't he thought of doing that instead of demanding an intimacy she had never desired when she had no other options available to her. Maybe it wouldn't be a bad idea to get Louise's opinion in a roundabout way. Besides, there was something about her abrupt departure from Paris that had left him wondering.

"I'm curious," he said, not stopping his work. It was easier to have these difficult conversations when they were both busy with a task. "We haven't really had a chance to talk more about why you left school. I know it didn't interest you and you felt called to come back here, but was there ... was there anything else?"

"Are you trying to change the subject?" Her voice had lost all its humor and she didn't look at him—signs he was on to something important.

"Yes."

She sighed, and he caught up to the vine beside the one she had started on. "Fine," she said finally. "But I don't want you to get the wrong idea."

"I won't ... or at least I'll try not to."

She didn't answer right away, but when she did it was in a halting voice. "I'm telling you this as a brother, ok? Not as a de facto parent."

Something heavy and unpleasant settled in Gaspard's stomach.

"Even as my big brother," she added. "You don't have to protect me anymore or fight my battles. I can do both those things myself."

"I know, but sometimes I just can't help it."

"I know," she said. "But know in advance that in this case there is nothing you can do. It's over, and it's for the best. I could have stuck it out at the school, but I'd realized long before that I wanted to be a winemaker. My heart never truly left Volnay. I don't think it ever will."

"All right," Gaspard said, agreeing in words, but his hands already tightening into fists despite himself. *Who had dared mess with his sister?*

"Do you remember me talking about my friend, Alec?"

Gaspard searched his memory. Collectively his sisters talked so much that sometimes he tuned out. He wasn't proud of it, but there it was. He did vaguely remember Louise mentioning an Alec—her first friend in her program in Paris. "I think so. You two became close quickly, right?"

"Yes." Her head bowed. "He was interested in a romantic relationship but me ... not as much. I just loved him as a friend."

"Did he force himself on you?" Gaspard demanded.

Louise laughed. "No! This is exactly what I warned you not to do. Calm down."

Honestly, what did she expect? He was never going

to be accepting of anyone wronging his sisters. "Right," he grumbled, determined to keep her talking.

"Anyway, I liked him so much as a friend, and he was so persistent, that I thought maybe I should try ... so we did."

"And?"

"It only lasted a few months. He thought it was going great."

"What about you?" Gaspard asked, the weight in his stomach pushing bile up his throat. He didn't know exactly what was to come, but how could he not draw the parallel between Amandine—who from what he had to go on, only wanted friendship and help from him—and Louise?

"I tried, I truly tried, because I loved him so much in a platonic way. I had hoped that maybe it could become more, but it didn't work. I couldn't keep leading him on like that, so I split up with him as gently as I could."

"Let me guess what happened—"

"He stopped talking to me. He just dropped me like a hot potato, saying it was too hard for him to just go back to being friends. He was one of the only people that made my wrong choice of school and program survivable. Once he withdrew his friendship ... I had nothing tying me to Paris anymore."

"So he wanted love or nothing from you," Gaspard said between gritted teeth. He was no better than this Alec fellow.

"Exactly."

"He thought you owed him more than you wanted to give." It struck Gaspard like a body slam just how wrong, how *tyrannical* and lacking in respect, it had been to lay out his 'stipulation' for a real marriage with Amandine. She owed him nothing. She never had and she never would.

She'd never wanted more than his help to extract herself from an impossible dilemma. He'd made the mistake, yet again, of asking for what he wanted. Hadn't he learned his lesson that night of Luc's sleepover party and colicky Bertille so long ago?

"No, it isn't right," said Louise, but Gaspard was only half listening. "But it is human I suppose. After that … well, there was no reason not to come home and tell you what I really wanted to do. Thank you, by the way, thank you for taking me seriously."

He couldn't let this pass "Why wouldn't I take you seriously? It's clear to me that you'll be ten times the winemaker I am within a year or two. Besides, I enjoy your company … and, you know … I don't say that of many people."

Louise laughed. "You always try to convince people that you're so gruff and stand-offish, but we all know what a softy you truly are."

She wouldn't think that if she knew what he'd demanded of Amandine.

He'd never been so grateful it was a Tuesday. Gaspard could take his tortured thoughts to the weekly rendezvous at the bistro in Savigny. It was a far more palatable option then sitting at home, steeping in them.

Maybe Amandine would be there too, and he would have a small window before the wedding the next day to tell her about his change of heart. He couldn't impose a real marriage on her after his conversation with Louise. He also owed her a sincere apology—how could he have ever made such a mistake?

But when he went into the café he only found Luc nursing a glass of Pommard.

They shook hands and Gaspard sat down across from him, lulled into a slightly less tortured frame of mind by the clatter of the café and the familiar scents of spilled wine and old cigarette smoke.

"Where is everybody?" Gaspard asked.

Luc's eyes danced. "In case you've forgotten, you're getting married tomorrow."

Gaspard sent him a black look. "Keep your voice down *bétion*."

Luc just smiled. "Clovis is here."

Gaspard glanced around. "Has he added invisibility to his list of life changes this year?"

Luc gestured to the far corner of the bistro, where the oldest and most grizzled winemakers held court and spent their evenings complaining about the younger generation of winemakers and how they did everything wrong.

There, ensconced at the table with the old-timers, was Clovis. In the arms of the grizzliest of the grizzly old men—one with whiskers sprouting out everywhere on his face and clothes that looked narrowly salvaged from the rubbish bin—was Myrtille. The man's friends were all cooing over her.

Clovis's face was wreathed in smiles. He was clearly accepting their accolades over his daughter and glowed with pride. Gaspard chuckled to himself.

"A rare sight, *n'est-ce pas*?" Luc joined Gaspard's laughter. "I didn't think anything could unbend those *anciens*, but apparently all it takes is a baby."

They watched, entertained, until Clovis finally took possession of Myrtille, but only after she had been passed around and every man at the table got an equal amount of time to hold her in their arms. They clearly didn't want Clovis, and especially Myrtille, to leave but Clovis pointed over to his friends waiting for him. Gaspard and Luc waved, but as expected, the older winemakers just scowled at them. They, after all, didn't have babies to coo over.

When Clovis returned to them with Myrtille nestled against his left shoulder, Gaspard and Luc couldn't contain their mirth.

"I never thought I'd see the day you could unbend that crowd," said Gaspard.

"*Serieusement.*" Luc clapped. "*Bravo.*"

Clovis moved Myrtille so she was nested in his arms and he could gaze down properly at her little face. She *was* a beautiful baby. Her coloring was dramatic with her dark hair and pale skin, and her eyes were well on their way to being as blue as her father's.

Gaspard had never thought much about children of his own. He had done so much parenting already with his sisters that the idea of adding another child to the mix had always felt ludicrous. Now though, watching Myrtille's animated little features as she stared up at her father, he wasn't so sure.

Non. He checked himself. That was ridiculous. His marriage with Amandine wasn't going to be real and he was going to tell her as soon as he saw her, preferably *before* their wedding ceremony.

"You love showing her off, don't you?" Luc asked Clovis.

"Of course I do." She started to fuss a bit so Clovis returned her to his shoulder and began rubbing her back in small, regular circles. "I missed out on a lot of this with Emily, and of course I wasn't in the picture at all for Yves and Marc, so I'm soaking up every minute."

"Where is Cerise?" Gaspard asked. "And Sadie?"

Luc leaned forward and said in a whisper. "They're at a bridal party thing for Amandine."

Why had Gaspard heard nothing about this? Oh right ... because Amandine didn't have to tell him everything. He needed to get that into his thick head—she owed him nothing, just like Louise owed Alec nothing.

Still, a bridal party didn't sound like the sort of activity that Amandine usually enjoyed. She hated being the center of attention. "Did she know about it?"

Clovis shook his head. "Cerise told me it was a surprise."

"Sadie and Cerise will make it fun for her," Luc assured him. Gaspard's doubts must have been written on his face. "Don't worry. Hey ... does that make tonight your stag night?"

Gaspard rolled his eyes so hard it actually hurt. "No *merci*."

Luc sighed. "Sadly, that's the response I was expecting."

"Anyway, we need to keep it all on the down-low," Clovis added in a conspiratorial voice.

"Plus we have a baby with us," Luc added.

"What are you saying?" Clovis said. "Are you saying that Myrtille wouldn't be welcome at Gaspard's stag party?"

Gaspard patted Clovis's arm. "Yes, yes," he said, soothingly. "I can assure you Myrtille would be most welcome at my hypothetical bachelor party that is not actually happening."

"Good," grumbled Clovis.

They all exchanged glances and then started laughing.

Luc sat back in his chair and ran a hand through his sun-bleached hair. "I guess this makes you the first one of us to actually get married. That's huge."

Gaspard stared down at his hands. It was all so backwards. He was the only one of his friends who wasn't in a loving, committed relationship, yet he was the one getting married the very next day. He'd never wanted to take marriage lightly like his father had, but here he was. Of course doing this helped Amandine, but still … it all felt wrong.

"Gaspard?" Clovis prompted. "What's up? You have the oddest expression on your face."

Gaspard hesitated.

"Come on, man," Luc urged. "Don't bottle it up like you always do. You'll explode one of these days, *tu sais*."

Gaspard massaged his temples, which had started throbbing. "You guys know the circumstances around tomorrow … this is never what I wanted. I never wanted to become like my father with all his weddings and divorces."

"You're nothing like your father," Luc said, vehemently. "And this situation is nothing like anything he ever did. You're doing this to help Amandine. Your father has never spared a second thought for anyone else in his entire existence—he's a textbook narcissist. You have looked after others your entire life, Gaspard, often at the expense of yourself."

Gaspard made shushing motions with his hands, as Luc's voice had grown loud. From the flash in his eyes Gaspard could tell he was truly angry—a rare thing for his usually easy-going friend. "No need to get irate."

"I just never want to hear you compare yourself to your father again," Luc said, his voice still stony but, thankfully, quieter.

Gaspard wished they had found a more private place to hash out all these things. "Right, well the facts are I'm marrying Amandine because she needs my help and she'd been pushed into a corner. I'm the only one who can get her out. It's as simple as that."

"Is it?" Clovis cocked his head.

"Yes." Gaspard fixed him with a blighting look.

"Don't bother with that look on me," Clovis said. "I've simply known you for too long, *mon ami*. I think you love Amandine even if you're too frightened to admit it to yourself."

"This marriage is not about that," Gaspard growled. "She owes me nothing for helping her."

"Don't bother with the growly voice either." Clovis's lips twitched to the side. "Maybe the marriage is not starting on those terms, but who's to say it can't evolve and become something different than how it started?"

"Amandine does." The words hurt, but they were the truth. She'd agreed to his stipulation because she'd had no other choice. He could never hold her to that. "She's made it clear she's not interested in anything from me besides friendship."

Clovis looked annoyingly unconvinced. Gaspard looked to Luc for support, but his face held the same skeptical expression as Clovis.

"We'll see," said Luc.

Chapter Fifteen

It was her wedding day, but it still didn't feel real, and Amandine wondered at this point if it ever would.

She'd been out late the night before with Sadie and Cerise. When she'd arrived home in the wee hours of the morning, she'd found a note from Gaspard, telling her he'd come by to talk to her.

She hated that she'd missed him. More than anything she hoped they would get a chance to at least exchange a few words before they found themselves at the mayor's office exchanging their vows. The lead-up had been so rushed and secretive, and they'd both had to pretend like nothing was in the works, that here they were—about to get married—and they hadn't even had a private moment to discuss the ceremony and how they felt about it.

Her stomach fluttered at the thought of she and Gaspard sharing his bed that very night. Nerves mixed with anticipation. She remembered that spark she'd felt between them behind her stand at the Ballade Gourmande, leaving her knees strangely watery. She'd set this whole marriage ball rolling thinking only of her Domaine, but now it was more—more complicated, more exciting, more confusing.

Amandine was in Cerise and Clovis's bedroom—a

place she'd never set foot in before. It was shaping up to be another warm day, verging on hot, so Cerise had opened the shutters and windows wide to let in some of the cooler morning air before shutting them against the heat in the afternoon.

The breeze lifted the white linen curtains, making them look as though they were dancing. *Were they going to have dancing at the reception the sisters had been planning?* Surely a bride-to-be shouldn't be this ignorant about such things, yet Amandine had been quite happy to leave all of that up to the sisters.

That couldn't be a good sign, she mused as she went over to the window and gazed out at the gravel court-yard. Beyond it were the rolling vineyards of the Hautes-Côtes. She gave Gaspard silent credit for his choice of doing the wedding in Cerise's village. It was tucked away from all the gossip and machinations of the more prestigious winemaking *côte* below.

She was still wearing the cut-offs and T-shirt she'd thrown on that morning, but as she pushed herself from the windowsill she caught sight of her dress which hung on the slightly open door of the huge oak armoire.

What kind of alternative universe had she stepped into that she would be slipping that on shortly and be getting married to Gaspard?

She knew she should be feeling gratitude above all else. Gaspard was sacrificing himself to give her the Domaine she'd always dreamed of controlling. Her mother's vines would finally be hers to cherish and protect … but increasingly her thoughts stuck on the *man* she would also be agreeing to cherish and protect. If only her feelings around him were as clear cut as her love of the vineyards.

Would Gaspard resent her forever? It was a terrible

thing to ask him to betray his principles in such a way, not to mention his chance to fall in love with someone and marry them in the conventional way. Then again, that was muddled by his request to try and make their marriage real. She knew he'd never hold her to this if she resisted—Gaspard would never chase after someone who didn't want him. If only she knew whether his stipulation to make their marriage real stemmed from his values or his heart.

Sadie and Cerise were consulting over a collection of nail polish bottles spread out on Cerise's bedside table.

"Do you think I could grab a few minutes to talk to Gaspard before the ceremony?" Amandine asked them.

Both their heads whipped around. "Are you having second thoughts?" Sadie asked, her auburn brows pulling together.

"No." Amandine shook her head. "It's just we haven't had a chance to talk in the past few days."

Cerise frowned. "Nothing is impossible, but the plan was for us to drive you to the mayor's office in one car, and for Clovis and Luc to pick up Gaspard direct from Volnay and drive him to meet us there in another."

It would require a lot of rearranging then. She didn't want to make a scene and have everybody wondering. She waved her hand. "Don't worry about it."

They had to forgo a church ceremony, of course, because for that banns would have to be publicly read and posted. That would have undoubtably reached Jean-Marc's ears and he would whisk Julie off to the nearest *Mairie* and beat them to the punch.

"But we can," Sadie insisted. "I'm sure it can be arranged. Let me just call Luc. Of course you two should have a chance to talk."

She regretted asking the question. "Really, it's fine."

She made her voice as definite as she could. "We'll have plenty of time to talk afterwards. Just last-minute nerves … don't mind me."

Sadie examined Amandine closely with those amber eyes of hers. "Are you sure?"

"Certain. Now, which nail polish have you picked out?"

Sadie pushed her curls off her forehead with a rueful smile. "Cerise and I were just lamenting that as far as glam squads go, you could have done much better than us."

Amandine burst out laughing, grateful. It was true that Cerise was simple in her style and seemed most at ease, like Amandine, in jeans and a T-shirt in the vineyards. Sadie, on the other hand, was in her element on archaeological digs with mud splattered from her work boots to her red curls. They could both dress up, of course, but even when they did, they kept it simple.

"I wish Stella was here," Sadie sighed down at the nail polishes, as if they were a particularly thorny calculus equation. "She'd know exactly what to do."

Cerise stared forlornly at them as well, wrinkles of worry pleating her forehead. "Yeah."

There was a knock at the door.

"Boys?" Cerise called. That made sense—Yves and Marc would be the most likely candidates for knocking at their mother's bedroom door, especially because they'd been assigned to watch over their baby sister.

The door opened and Éloise poked her head around it. "Nope, no boys here."

Relief surged through Amandine at the sight of her sister's face—the only blood family she would have at her wedding day. The door opened and the room filled with not only Éloise, but Gaspard's four sisters as well.

They weren't empty-handed. They carried a stagger-ing collection of curling irons, hairbrushes, makeup bags and makeup brushes.

"I'm terrified," Amandine said, surveying their equipment.

Cerise and Sadie nodded. "You should be," Cerise said. "It's like they're preparing for a war."

"Nonsense!" Bertille tsk'ed. "We're your fairy god … sisters."

The other sisters all shouted their approval at this clever play on words.

"We can't leave you in the hands of these two ama-teurs." Louise pointed at Cerise and Sadie with a curling iron. "Too cruel."

Rather than be offended, Cerise and Sadie's shoulders sagged with relief.

"I'm not going to argue," Sadie said, while Cerise nodded in agreement. "Work your magic god-sisters."

Gaspard was right about their collective sisters being a formidable force of nature.

Within five minutes they had Amandine seated in an armchair in front of the floor-length mirror inset in the middle panel of the armoire.

They buzzed around her, picking up strands of her hair and debating styles. Margaux was pulling out make-up palettes and Bertille and Éloise were arguing over the merits of a brown and green eye palette versus a gold and green.

In her reflection, Amandine cast an alarmed look at Sadie, who was reclined on the bed with Cerise, looking vastly entertained.

"Soon this will be you two sitting here," Amandine said in her most menacing tone. "I plan on enjoying every minute."

"Oh yes!" Sophie crowed. "We'll do your weddings too."

Cerise cast Amandine a dirty look and Amandine felt a bubble of laughter rise up in her chest. Thank heavens for the sister tornado, as their chatter and questions didn't leave any space for the noise in her mind.

"I can't tell you how excited I am about having you as a sister," Margaux crowed, on her hands and knees searching for a plug socket to heat up the tongs she was wielding in her hand. "To think, Éloise and you will truly be part of the family now. We're going to have so much fun. Cerise, where is your closest socket? Will I need an extension cord?"

"There's one just above the baseboard." Cerise pointed to where she meant. "A tiny bit behind the left side of the armoire."

Éloise came up behind Amandine, her face glowing with happiness. Why had it never occurred to Amandine just how much having a boisterous family like Gaspard's would fill a huge gap in her sister's life? With their father's anger and Amandine's stalemate with Jean-Marc, family joy and solidarity had been in short supply since their mother died.

Being amongst the chatter of the sisters made everything feel lighter for Amandine too, but, she reminded herself, she couldn't know yet whether she and Gaspard could make their marriage work long-term without it culminating in a massive fight like last time.

Hope could be a dangerous thing, but Amandine let it spark under her breastbone anyway. Still, she had to make sure the girls didn't have any illusions. Privacy was definitely an issue with this lot, and the pressure of their expectations could only backfire.

"You *do* know why we're getting married, right?"

Amandine ventured, as Margaux applied several different 'test stripes' of foundation to her jawbone.

Bertille shrugged. "Gaspard explained it to us—about the Domaine and your father's will and Jean-Marc, but we decided none of that matters."

"It doesn't?"

Bertille shook her head. "Don't be silly, Amandine. *Bien sûr que non.*"

"Of course it does. That's why this wedding is happening in the first place—that messed up inheritance. I just don't want all of you to get carried away and then be disappointed."

"Too late," Louise said. "You two were meant to be together, so the why doesn't really matter."

Éloise nodded in agreement. "You'll figure it out."

But what if they didn't? Still, if the sisters were convinced, maybe that gave some justification to that flame of hope. "Do you really think so?" she asked in a rare moment of vulnerability.

The rest of the girls nodded. "We've discussed it," Margaux said. "At length."

Amandine was fascinated. Imagine having a family where you casually discussed such things. It would be so strange and kind of … wonderful.

"We know that you love each other," said Bertille. "Even if neither of you has realized it yet."

Amandine cast a glance over at her friends on the bed, who were looking equal parts riveted and awed.

"Did you say that to Gaspard?" Cerise asked.

"No," Margaux shook her head. "He wasn't ready to hear it yet."

Amandine couldn't extinguish a hope that maybe, one day soon, he would be.

Even though the mayor's office in Cerise's village was a mere five minutes away from Domaine du Cerisier, they didn't walk, but drove in Sophie's crappy old purple Renault.

It was less conspicuous that way, Gaspard had decided. He was right, as usual. Even though the ties between the Hautes-Côtes villages and those on the lower Côte weren't as tight, they were far from nonexistent. A bride walking down the street in a silk dress and a beautiful white calla lily clipped in her hair would inevitably draw attention.

Back in Cerise's bedroom Amandine didn't recognize herself in the mirror once the sisters were done with her. She'd been thrilled, but now her hands trembled with nerves. Maybe her dress was too much of a wedding dress … if only she had a second to talk to Gaspard before the ceremony.

She felt more beautiful than she ever had in her life, but she also felt like an imposter. Gaspard should be going through these motions with a woman who he truly loved—someone who wanted to marry him because she loved him heart and soul, not for mercenary reasons like inheriting the family vineyard. A good person didn't force anyone they truly cared about to get married under false pretences, but she was not, it was clear, a good person.

She had every intention of following through.

Éloise sat beside her in the backseat. The car smelled like spilled Orangina and Pétit Lu biscuits, but beggars couldn't be choosers. Éloise was staring out the window, her former exuberance nowhere to be seen.

Amandine touched her sister's wrist. "You okay?"

Éloise turned to Amandine and bit her lip. "It doesn't feel right that Jean-Marc isn't here."

"It had to be this way," Amandine said, trying to be gentle. "Anyway, he wouldn't want to be here. He loves you, but he and I don't really have much of a relationship anymore. He doesn't care about me, Éloise."

Éloise blinked. "You don't truly believe that, do you?"

"I do."

Her sister shook her head. "Have you ever considered that perhaps he's jealous of your talent and it's eating him up inside?"

Amandine tried to tamp down the spurt of fury inside her. "You don't need to make excuses for him."

"You're too blind to his faults to see that they come from a place of deep pain."

Amandine bit back a retort. They were going to arrive at the Mayor's office any second so she scanned outside the car windows to see if she could find Gaspard. "Can we just forget about him for the rest of the day and try to enjoy ourselves? Jean-Marc has ruined enough of my life; I don't need him ruining my wedding day. I need to find Gaspard."

Éloise looked out of the car as well. "Fine," she sighed. "I don't see your groom," she said. "He's probably already gone inside."

Chapter Sixteen

As the throng of sisters pushed her into the mayor's office, Amandine met Gaspard's eyes. This was happening. The time to talk had passed.

He was standing at the front, just across the large wooden desk from the mayor, who wore the tri-color sash around his torso to underline that this was a very official rite in the eyes of the *Rébublique*. The portrait of the Président and the flag of France didn't exactly detract from that impression.

When her eyes met Gaspard's she forgot how to breathe. Everything and everyone else around her faded out and there was only him. Her heart pounded as she absorbed how handsome he was. He wore a tailored dark-gray suit—its severe cut set off the jet-black hair rising off his forehead, his beautifully carved cheekbones, and that regal nose. Something about the suit sharpened his sharp edges and oh … how she longed to explore those. He looked like a truer version of himself—forbidding, intimidating, and blindingly sexy. He looked like a man, she realized from the thrum of something primal pulsing in her blood, who she wanted desperately in a way that had nothing to do with vineyards.

He was standing so still she could almost have

thought he was a carved statue if it wasn't for the heat in his eyes as they locked on hers.

Amandine couldn't break that gaze, even when Éloise pried open her fingers and shoved the long stems of a bouquet of calla lilies into her hands. She knew she needed to look elsewhere, but it was impossible.

They could make it work this time. Her breath came in staccato bursts as a wave of longing washed over her.

Gaspard. Her friend. Her soon-to-be husband. She knew what she was feeling for him in this moment would complicate everything, but resisting it was like resisting the sunrise.

She silently thanked God or the president up there on the wall or Gaspard's moral compass for his stipulation that they give this marriage an honest try.

Gaspard, she only noticed now, was looking as stunned as she felt. Was he having a moment of realization like her? *Please let it not be a moment of regret.*

She became aware of hands on her back, pushing her forward.

"Walk!" Éloise hissed in her ear.

On wobbly legs she walked towards Gaspard and, when she reached him, she made a wavering attempt at a smile.

His whole face softened. "Don't be scared," he murmured. "I don't bite."

How to explain to him that her shakiness wasn't reluctance, but rather the ache for him that was coursing through every fiber of her being? As for biting ... maybe she wouldn't mind under certain circumstances.

"You do." She searched his eyes. There were worlds there she couldn't wait to explore. He brushed her pinkie finger with his. The light contact sent a bolt of electricity up her arm.

"Maybe sometimes," he admitted. "But I won't today. Are you sure you're all right? I thought you were going to faint for a second there."

That made her straighten her spine. "I've never fainted in my life. This is just ... different than I was expecting."

He cast her a knowing look. "When I saw you ... well ... time stopped."

"Same."

The mayor began his speech, welcoming the crowd with no small amount of pomp and ceremony.

"Are you sure you want to do this?" Gaspard whispered to her.

Her eyes went wide. Did he want out? Her first thought wasn't losing the vineyards but losing him. "Are you?"

He didn't answer for a few seconds, during which she was certain her heart stopped beating. Finally, he nodded. "*Absolument.*"

"Thank God," she breathed.

Twenty minutes later they were married. It would have been even quicker than that if the mayor didn't love the sound of his own voice, but to be fair, Cerise had warned them about his notorious penchant for grandstanding.

They signed all the papers, then Gaspard led her outside the mayor's office to cheers and pats on the back and kisses from their family and friends. Normally the sisters would be throwing rice and confetti, but they had to make their way back to Domaine du Cerisier as quickly as possible.

She slid into the back of the car—every second they were outside the gates of the Domaine in their wedding finery was an added risk. Even though the papers were signed, Amandine didn't put it past Jean-Marc to try and figure out a way of invalidating the marriage, or arguing it wasn't legitimate for the sake of the will.

Whenever she fretted she was being overly paranoid in keeping her marriage a secret from him even after the knot was tied, she remembered the time her brother had switched the labels of the Grand Cru Corton she was entering in one of France's most prestigious wine competitions with the lowest quality passetoutgrain. He'd not only destroyed her chances of winning, but he'd severely damaged her reputation as well. He'd taught her not to trust him, and she had to heed that lesson.

Gaspard slid in beside her.

Much to her disappointment, he hadn't touched her yet, besides a brief peck on the lips during the ceremony. Amandine had wanted to howl in frustration, but reasoned Gaspard wasn't the type of man to show her how he truly felt until they were in private.

She admired the vintage square cut diamond on her hand. It was perfect—simple and unfussy and she was shocked at how natural it was. "I didn't know you had a ring," she said. "It's absolutely gorgeous."

Gaspard was gesturing at Luc who was signaling something to him from outside the car. "It was my grandmother's," he said, looking over his shoulder.

Guilt pressed down on her again. She didn't deserve to be wearing one of Gaspard's family heirlooms.

"I'll give it back." The words burst out of her, but as

Gaspard's head jerked back, she realized she'd said the absolute worst thing. The short drive was filled with tense silence after that. She spent the five minutes wanting to grab at the charged air between them and snatch her words back.

After they drove into the courtyard, the large wooden gates that were usually left open were securely locked behind them.

She was going to open her door and climb out when she felt Gaspard's fingers on her arm. "Wait," he said, and got around the car to open her door and reach down to help her out. She wasn't used to such gallantry, and she was shocked just how much she liked it. She slid her hand into his and concentrated on the warmth where their palms touched. He was an anchor. He'd always felt like her anchor, she realized now, whether they were kissing or arguing.

They walked a few steps from the car together until they were ambushed by the sisters and their friends and Marc and Yves, pelting them with rice and confetti.

They laughed and posed for photos until Gaspard turned to her with one of his rare smiles. Her heart caught as he lifted his hand and picked a piece of confetti out of her hair. *Attendez.* Was he going to—

"Kiss! Kiss! Kiss!" their rowdy audience cheered.

Gaspard raised his left brow. "Do you want to?" he asked, turning towards her so their bodies were only separated by a few centimeters. "We don't have to appease the noisy rabble, you know."

Amandine couldn't find words, so she just nodded.

Time slowed down as she waited for his lips to meet hers. When he did, his mouth felt hard at first, almost bruising, but then something extraordinary happened. His lips softened and hers followed, then they opened, and she flicked his tongue with hers … beckoning him to share more of himself. A instinctual need for him pulsed through every cell—they were magnets and she was powerless against his pull. Any remaining shred of resistance went out of her and she sunk into his arms, reveling in the difference. This time, she would let the fire between them rage, not caring if it incinerated the walls she'd built around herself. They were husband and wife now. That changed everything. She pulled him tighter against her and the crowd let out a *ban bourgignon.*

Gaspard stepped back suddenly. His breathing came in ragged bursts and the back of his hand flew up against his mouth. His eyes were dilated, inky black.

"Sorry," he said, breathless. "You … in that dress … I got carried away. I apologize."

Why was he apologizing? Wasn't it clear they were getting carried away together?

She tried to find the words to tell him this, but before she could they were being pushed into the barn.

The barn was slung out, perpendicular, to Cerise and Clovis's house. Nobody had been allowed to so much as peek in there while the sisters were performing their decorating magic. They were determined for it to be a surprise.

When Éloise and Bertille opened the two huge wooden doors with a flourish, Amandine stood rooted to the spot for a long time.

Gaspard stood beside her, his eyes as round as hers as

he took in the beauty their sisters had created. Calla lilies, matching Amandine's bouquet, stood in tall glass vases. Fairy lights hung in great swoops between the centuries old oak rafters that were at least twenty feet above the flagstone floor. The end result was stunning and wildly romantic.

"I think it's safe to say our sisters have high hopes for us," Amandine whispered to Gaspard.

She was expecting a chuckle or at least that quirk of his lips, but he just turned to her with a stricken expression. She was still holding his hand, she realized, and she squeezed it to get him to stop looking at her in such a bleak way.

He cleared his throat. "I told you they were capable of miracles." He tore his eyes from hers and scanned the room, leaving Amandine bewildered.

The long table was covered with white linen table-cloths and set with a mish mash of vintage silver they must have collected from their different houses. It was set with the purest white Limoges china that Amandine knew usually resided in an old armoire in her basement. It had belonged to her mother.

She blinked away tears. Had Éloise known that choice would bring the memories of her mother into the day? There was something magical—almost sacred—in the choices the girls had made. It would be perfect, if only she felt Gaspard caught up in it as well instead of holding himself back in that way she knew, and dreaded.

The only color was the moss green linen napkins and tendrils of new vine clippings artfully piled into the center of the table, interwoven with more fairy lights, creating a wild, untamed centerpiece. That tender green ... it was the color of new beginnings. She hoped it was an omen.

Gaspard squeezed her hand back then, and her heart

faltered.

"That green," he said, his voice scratchy. "It's the color of your eyes."

Amandine turned to him, desperate to communicate to him to just how much she wanted to make good on his plan to make their marriage something real, but Luc swooped in, squeezing them in one of his warm hugs.

Sadie was not far behind and soon after, a glass of *kir royale* was thrust in Amandine's hand by Cerise.

"*Félicitations*," Cerise said. "This deserves a toast."

"They did an incredible job," Amandine murmured. "I'm in shock."

"Right?" Cerise admired the space. "They love you and Gaspard so much."

"We all do," added Luc, with one of his heartfelt smiles. "We all want the same thing—for you two to be happy."

Gaspard had been right to suggest trying to make their marriage real without everyone's eyes riveted on them. Even if the interest was friendly and well-meaning, it still upped the pressure. They weren't strong enough to withstand that … not yet, anyway. She hoped they would be one day.

"This is so lovely," Amandine said, then thought of a way to create space between their friends and this brand-new dynamic between she and Gaspard, which felt as vulnerable and fragile as those new tendrils of vines in the centerpiece. "But don't get the wrong idea. This is still a pretend marriage."

Gaspard dropped her hand like it was on fire. *Couldn't he see she was just trying to divert attention, as they'd discussed?*

"It didn't look pretend to me when you were kissing just now in the courtyard," Luc said out of the corner of his mouth.

Sadie kicked him in the shin.

"Ow!" he said, mock hurt in his eyes.

"Don't meddle," she said, her face fierce. "Remember? We talked about this."

Cerise shook her head. "Don't even bother, Sadie. Meddling is in our Burgundian blood. We can't help it. *C'est plus fort que nous.*"

"*Ha! Exactement,*" crowed Luc. "You see *mon amour*? It's beyond my control."

Gaspard remained silent, a darkness in his eyes that brought questions but no answers and made her doubt everything.

"Let's give them some space to figure it out themselves." Sadie grabbed a reluctant Cerise and Luc and dragged them away from the newlyweds.

But before they could even begin to do that, they were shown by their proud sisters to the head of the table to be thoroughly fêted.

Chapter Seventeen

It was torture—sitting next to his wife who looked as exquisite as the calla lilies, after she had just publicly stated that their marriage was fake. He wanted to throw his morals to the wind and ravish her so badly that he couldn't think straight. But, if he ever wanted proof that she wanted nothing from him but friendship and help out of an impossible situation, there it was, clear and uncompromising.

She had always been beautiful to him, but never had he imagined she could look this otherworldly. His fingers itched with the need to run down the silk of her dress, tracing the lovely lines of her. He would do it so slowly, so reverently …

As he nibbled at a choux pastry stuffed with cream he felt himself go hard thinking of how he would go about removing her dress. He flushed in shame. He'd made his decision—he could not ask her for anything—but oh God, resisting her was pure agony.

He wanted so much more than he had any right to ask for. She turned to him and gave him an uncertain smile. *The things he imagined doing with her …*

It would take every ounce of willpower to do the right thing by Amandine, and he wouldn't keep her in suspense for a second longer than necessary once they were alone. He couldn't stand the idea of her thinking he still expected her to give him part of herself that she hadn't freely offered.

There was dancing, and Gaspard made sure it was not with each other except for that first dance. During that one, he wanted to gather her as tightly against him and claim her as his in front of everyone that mattered, but instead he held her loosely, every muscle in his arms twitching with the effort to resist pulling her closer.

It was dark outside when Gaspard and Amandine slipped into his Citroen, which had thankfully been left undecorated due to their continued need for subterfuge. At first he'd thought Amandine was being paranoid about Jean-Marc being able to do anything after they were officially married, but the more he thought about it, the less he wanted to risk it. He didn't trust Jean-Marc any more than Amandine did, and he suspected he would stop at nothing to wreck revenge on his sister as soon as he discovered how she'd outmaneuvered him.

They drove to Gaspard's place in charged silence. On the family Domaine, Gaspard didn't live in the main house. He'd renovated a separate outbuilding and made it his—close enough to be fully present for his sisters at meals and for ins and outs of their days, but far enough away that he had the privacy he needed.

Amandine, of course, had been inside his place many times before, but never as his bride. The idea of her in his house, alone with him, in that dress, made him want to waste not as much as a second before feeling the heat of her skin against the cool silk. Instead, he carried Amandine's bag in. It was small and compact.

He noticed her breathing had quickened as she walked before him to his front door. He was attuned to every tiny thing about her, whether he wanted to be or not. A lump of remorse stuck in his throat. She was probably dreading this. He couldn't bear this misunderstanding between them to last one minute more.

He closed the door behind him. The hush felt all the more crushing because of the joyous hubbub of the party they had just left—well, that and because his mind was teeming with ideas of what he would like to do with Amandine against that door.

He had to tell her. Instead, all he could manage to do was watch her, riveted, as she leaned her back against the kitchen counter, and began to slowly remove the pins from her hair. She was like a mirage in the midst of his home.

She pulled the lily from her hair and put it down, ever so gently, on the counter. She filled his whole house with the scent of flowers and herself. Her leaf-green eyes flicked up to him. They were filled with doubt.

He tried to swallow but couldn't. It was cruel to let her worry like this. "I changed my mind," he blurted out.

She pushed off the counter and stood up straight. Her head jerked back. "What do you mean? You changed your mind about what?"

"About my stupid 'stipulations'." The coiled frustration in him was too much for him to contain standing still, so he started to pace back and forth across the flagstone floor.

The elegant line of her throat curved as she became fixated on the lily on the counter. "You're going to have to explain better than that."

"I know." He raked a hand through his hair. "You remember what I said initially, about demanding a 'real' marriage from you, or at least that we try?"

"I think 'demand' is a strong word given the circum-

stances." She crossed her arms in front of her. "Especially when I consider the enormity of what I asked you to
do. I realized today that if I was a bigger person—*better*
person—I wouldn't have followed through with this
marriage. It wasn't fair to you."

Gaspard stopped pacing for a second and paused in
front of her. "Don't be ridiculous." His voice came out
more biting than he intended. How could she know that
the anger in it was meant for himself, not her? "You had
no choice," he said, managing to sound a bit gentler.
"What else could you have done?"

She traced the seam between the rough stone slabs
with the point of her silk shoe. Ah, how he would have
liked to slip those off her feet and make her toes curl. "I
could have accepted defeat."

Gaspard's mouth dropped open at such a notion. He
welcomed the absurdity of it—anything to break this
tension between them. "If you had, you wouldn't be
you."

She sighed. "I know."

"Don't think for a second *you* are the one who needs
to change."

She lifted her left shoulder—bare and so smooth he
knew it would feel like silk too under his fingertips.
"Maybe I should."

He could try to withstand the torture of resisting her,
but he could not bear seeing the fire within her snuffed
out. "Don't be ridiculous," he snapped … again.

Just like that, they were on familiar ground again.
This sniping dynamic—they knew how to do this like a
rehearsed script. Besides, being nettled by her was a
much-needed distraction from his need to make her
tremble and moan and come all around him.

"Fine," she countered. "I'll continue to be ruthless

and selfish."

"Glad to hear it." He snorted softly. "As if you could stop."

"Maybe I could!"

He cast her a look ripe with skepticism.

She shook her head. "Wait a second—we're getting way off topic here. What do you mean exactly about rethinking your stipulations?"

"I'm not going to ask anything of you beyond friendship, Amandine. It's decided."

Her green eyes went wide. Was that relief in there? Definitely annoyance. For a flash he thought he saw disappointment, but surely he'd just imagined that. *Wishful thinking.*

She cleared her throat. "Oh, it's *decided*, is it? Why?"

He tugged at his hair again and resumed his pacing. "When I started to think about what I was asking—no, demanding—of you, I felt terrible."

"Again ... why?"

"I can't and won't force you into something you don't want, Amandine. I realized how wrong it was of me to even suggest that, let alone demand it as a requirement of agreeing to help you."

She tilted her beautiful head to better study his face. "I think we can safely say that marrying me goes well beyond the realm of merely 'helping'."

He waved his hand, impatient with such details. His mind was made up. "That makes no difference. Demanding that was an ill-judged impulse of the moment, talking of the marriage bed and all that nonsense. I regret it, and I apologize." Those last words felt torn out of his chest. Apologies had never come easily to him.

She began to slow clap. "Bravo, Gaspard. That must have been hard."

"Yes," he flung back at her. He couldn't believe she was mocking him now, when he was aching for her more than he'd ever believed possible. "You know it was."

"All this self-flagellation is not necessary—" she began.

"But it is!" All this guilt bottled up inside him burst out. "I started thinking about how I would feel if someone forced one of my sisters into such an ignoble bargain. I offered to help you, but to demand anything else of you ... it was abhorrent of me. I talked to Louise about it—" He waved his hand again. "Anyway, that's neither here nor there."

"Isn't it?" Amandine said. "This about-face certainly feels sudden to me."

He raked his hand through his hair, uncaring if he looked as deranged as he felt. "I will never force myself on you. Please know I never would have followed through on that. I would despise any man who would take advantage of one of my sisters in such a way. The fact that I talked like I was that man ... it revolts me."

Amandine bit her lip. It was clear to him her mind was whirring, but it was impossible to know what she was thinking. "So you're retracting it?" she asked, at last.

She had to be relieved, but he couldn't know. Her expression remained frozen—her features strictly schooled.

"Of course I'm retracting it," he said. "You're my friend and you were in an impossible situation. I was the only one who could help you. I should have agreed right away, and I should never have asked anything of you in exchange. I'm ashamed to say I took advantage of you."

She put her hands on those narrow silk-sheathed hips of hers that he ached to grasp so he could feel her heat underneath his palms. "Gaspard," she said, impatiently. "You didn't *do* anything. Anyway, it was understandable. What I asked you was just so much. It went against so much of what you believe in and what you planned for your life. You should be angry with me, not yourself."

"The men in your family gave you no other choice, Amandine," he said.

"I could have done what you'd recommended long ago."

"What do you mean?"

"Buy another vineyard."

He couldn't believe the words coming out of her mouth. That suggestion, after all, had earned Gaspard wrath like he'd never experienced before in his existence and their hideous break-up.

"Give up on my family Domaine," she continued. "Go out on my own."

He realized with a startling clarity that he wanted her to have everything she'd ever dreamed of, even if it meant he stood forever on the sidelines. Hearing her talk of compromise made him recoil. "Why are you talking like that, Amandine? You don't really mean that, do you?"

She twisted her fingers together. "I guess not."

"We can't have that," Gaspard said, his voice gruff. "*I* can't have that."

Silence descended on them again. Goddamn if her scent of lilies wasn't everywhere he turned, taunting him.

"So what do we do now?" Amandine finally said in an odd voice.

This, at least, Gaspard had planned for. "I've concluded it's still best if you stay here with me, in case Jean-Marc ever questions the validity of our marriage."

A muscle in her jaw jumped. "That's not really what I was getting at."

He sighed. "As for the rest, there's no way anybody could know what does or doesn't happen between us. I made up the second bedroom for you to stay in. You can sleep there and rest assured, I won't bother you."

Her mouth opened as if she was going to say something, then she shut it again.

Gaspard sighed. "Look, it's been a long day. You should find everything you need in there. I left you some towels and fresh soap and a hanger for your dress in the armoire."

She bit her lip and nodded. How he wished he was taking her to bed.

"You looked so beautiful today," he said, his voice strained and rough. "I'm sure I didn't tell you that enough. You took my breath away, Amandine. The dress … your face … you need to know that I could never in my wildest dreams have imagined a more perfect bride."

"*Merci.*" Her voice was barely a whisper.

He leaned over and gave her a quick kiss. Then, untying his tie as he stalked to his bedroom, he slammed his bedroom door behind him. Gaspard leaned against it, breathing hard under the weight all the things he wanted but couldn't ask for.

Chapter Eighteen

Amandine, like most winemakers, generally rose with the roosters. A night tossing and turning in the guest bed, acutely aware that Gaspard was just on the other side of the thick stone wall that separated them, meant that she was wide-awake before the roosters had even stirred.

She'd been completely caught off guard by his rejection of her. How long had he been stewing over that?

For the first few seconds, she'd tried to find the words to explain that she'd actually been eager for them to try. She quickly chickened out, however, too scared by the idea of broaching that vulnerable flame of hope that had grown steadily every day inside her. Squabbling had come as a relief—comfortable ground—at a moment when she'd been utterly confused … and yes, shocked.

Amandine stared up at a crack in the plaster of the ceiling. It splintered off in several different directions, making it look like a shattered heart—not far off what that same organ felt like in her chest.

Maybe she should have let out the words she'd almost spoken last night when Gaspard had promised he wouldn't bother her. *What if I want you to bother me?*

She let out a strangled sound of frustration and got out of bed. She pulled up the white linen duvet Gaspard had made up the bed with. The house was quiet. It wasn't near light outside and she was surely the first one up. Thank God, because she needed to collect her thoughts before she saw him again. She had a quick shower and pulled on some jeans and a T-Shirt—vineyard clothes—from her bag, trying her best to push away the hurt that kept collecting under her sternum.

There was work to be done in her vineyards, after all. Vineyards, she suddenly realized with a novel thrill that ran through her, that were hers now. Brushing her hair in front of the mirror, her diamond flashed in the light. She examined it more closely, trying to find fault with it, but Gaspard had chosen perfectly.

It was simple, clear, and perfect. With some reluctance, she slipped it off and tucked it away in her toiletry bag. She couldn't wear it of course—that would be a dead giveaway to people who could tell Jean-Marc. She knew he would stop at nothing to inherit. The fact that she and Gaspard hadn't consummated their marriage, and didn't look likely to, made her even more anxious.

There was another reason though—one that cut deeper. Gaspard had decided he didn't want her as a real wife, so her ring made her feel like a fraud.

She frowned at her reflection in the mirror. The bride of the day before was gone but the Amandine who was reflected back at her didn't look quite right either. *Coffee.* She needed coffee to feel like herself again. Black, strong, and copious.

She went into the kitchen and began opening cupboards, looking for some filters and coffee grounds. Gaspard didn't seem to have any. What was this fresh hell? How dare Gaspard not have coffee after leaving her wanting and confused the night before. She didn't care about nice towels, which he had provided. They were even scented with lavender, but who cared about towels?

Maybe it was the sexual frustration, or how Gaspard had misread her so badly, but she started banging the cupboard doors harder as her search became more frenzied.

It took less than a minute until Gaspard's bedroom door flew open and he stormed out, his hair sticking up all over the place and some rather fascinating stubble on his face. He was wearing only a pair of black boxer briefs and … well … nothing else.

Amandine reached behind her to grab on to the counter for support as she took in the sharp cut muscles in his torso and shoulders. How she'd missed those. They made him look as though he was a Greek statue carved out of marble, but one that was alive and crackling with energy. Her eyes shifted down to another sight she had desperately missed—Gaspard's morning erection. Good God, it was glorious.

Heat rushed through every part of her body. She wanted desperately to be bothered by him, and by that …

He followed her eyes down, then hastily covered himself with his hands, or tried to anyway. "It's morning!" he barked. "It doesn't mean anything." He went back into his bedroom and slammed the door behind him.

How she wished it did.

He came back a few seconds later, still buttoning up his jeans and with a T-shirt covering up that beautiful chest. "Now," he said, his eyes flashing. "Why are you banging around like a wild boar near a chestnut tree?"

"Coffee, of course. I need it and I can't find any." Her voice was ripe with spleen. If they couldn't sleep together, at least they could fight.

He took a deep breath, trying to gain mastery over his temper. She took a perverse pleasure in seeing his struggle. "I don't bother keeping those here because I always make a point of having breakfast with my sisters. It's important I check in with them before they start their day."

"Oh," she said, hating that he had such a good excuse.

"You know, you're welcome at breakfast too," he said. "In fact, it will seem strange if you don't come. The girls would think we're fighting."

She scoffed. "Aren't we?"

"That? A fight? Come on, Amandine. You underestimate us. We can do far better than that."

She wished she had a good comeback to that, but she was coming up with nothing … he'd scrambled her brain with his naked chest and his morning … magnificence.

"You should go and scream into a pillow or something if you're going to explode," he said. "I'll wait and then we can go over to the main house together."

"Shut up."

He pressed his lips tightly together, but after a few seconds, a telltale twitch at the corner of his lips quivered.

She tried to stay angry with him, but a chuckle finally escaped her too. "Fine. Let's go."

Amandine had rarely been in a room so full of estrogen.

They could hear the noise of Gaspard's sisters talking—or yelling, judging by the decibel level of their voices—the minute they stepped into the main house.

When they arrived in the kitchen, she spotted Éloise sitting at the table beside Bertille. In the middle of all the chaos, her sister looked happier than Amandine could remember. It was going to be terrible for Éloise when she and Gaspard went their separate ways.

When the sisters caught sight of the newlyweds, the table erupted into a *ban bourgignon*—the ubiquitous Burgundian drinking song that was sung liberally for any celebration.

Amandine felt the warmth of a blush creeping up her neck—all the more vexing because nothing had happened between she and Gaspard worth blushing about.

Gaspard made hushing motions with his hands.

"Did you stay over, Éloise?" she asked her sister, leaning down to start her round of obligatory morning *bisous* to everyone at the table.

"*Oui*. I'll be doing that a lot in the future."

"Maybe you should go home to Pernand-Vergelesses today just so Jean-Marc doesn't get suspicious," she suggested, not quite sure how to manage that.

Éloise shot her a mutinous look, but Gaspard nodded.

"Amandine's right," he said.

"Jean-Marc has all but moved in to Julie's house from what I can tell," Éloise said.

"Anyway, what's the point of keeping it a secret now?" Louise leaned back in her chair. She was dressed just like Amandine and Gaspard—ready for the vineyard. "I don't get it. If Jean-Marc finds out about your wedding now, so what? He can't unmarry you."

Amandine sighed. "First, it's for Julie. Jean-Marc

might cancel their wedding and that would be cruel to her. She's done nothing wrong."

"And?"

"Second, to prevent Jean-Marc trying to wheedle his way back into the will."

"But what could he possibly do? Your father is dead," said Margaux, blunt like Gaspard but truthful. "You two are married now."

"If you knew my brother, you wouldn't be asking that," Amandine retorted. "He has no limits when it comes to thwarting me."

"Amandine!" Éloise's eyes grew round with shock. "He's still our brother."

"I'm sorry, but it's true. He's shown me time and time in the past just how cruel and devious he can be. I don't trust him. In fact, I think he's destroyed my ability to trust men."

"Well … not Gaspard, surely." Margaux got up and went to the sink to rinse her coffee bowl.

Gaspard and Amandine exchanged a look.

Gaspard cleared his throat. "Listen up, sisters," he said. "One thing you are all going to have to become familiar with now that Amandine and I are married is—"

"What?" Bertille interrupted.

"Boundaries," Gaspard finished.

His sisters all groaned, but quickly recovered. "So how did last night go?" Sophie asked with a pointed wink.

Mortification washed over Amandine. Gaspard had made it clear he didn't want her in his bed. What was she supposed to do with that? It was yet another vindication of her reluctance to trust men, but somehow that didn't feel nearly as good as it should.

"Remember … boundaries?" Gaspard raised a finger,

getting all of their attention. "So you want to know how last night went?"

All the sisters nodded, eager for any gossip.

"Last night went like it was none of your business, that's how." He ignored the groans, did a quick round of *les bises*, poured a coffee for himself and Amandine, and sat down.

He took a paper wrapped sugar cube out of the ceramic bowl in the middle of the table. He unwrapped it, lost in thought, then dropped half of it in his coffee. He looked up at Amandine then, and his brow cleared. He passed her the other half of sugar. "Here you go," he said.

"How did you know I wanted your extra sugar cube?" Her tone was playful, but her heart squeezed in her chest. If only she wasn't attracted to him, this situation would be so much easier.

"Because you always steal mine." Gaspard winked at her. "Wife."

He meant it as a joke, but that word stung. If only Gaspard had followed through on his original intentions.

"By the way, thank you again for yesterday." Gaspard smiled at his sisters as he stirred the sugar in his coffee. "You are all a force to be reckoned with, and you pulled it off with beauty and panache. *Chapeau.*"

The girls looked at each other and grinned. It was clear that whatever people outside his home thought of Gaspard's abrupt ways, his sisters adored him.

"We do love you, you know," Margaux said. Gaspard's eyes started to grow decidedly watery. "And Amandine too."

Now hers were doing the same. Éloise had been right about missing out on having a big, supportive family.

Gaspard took a sip of his coffee. "All right. Morning

check in! What has everyone got going on today? Margaux, did you study for that practice bac test for chemistry?"

Margaux rolled her eyes. *"Oui, Papa,"*

Calling him Papa was of course, a jibe, but Amandine sensed his sisters secretly liked the fact their brother kept an eye on their lives.

"Bertille, how about that project we did together on Egypt? Did you get a grade back yet?"

"Fourteen out of twenty," she said, still blowing on her bowl of hot chocolate, which her and Éloise preferred in the morning to coffee.

"Fourteen!" Gaspard tapped the table with his palm. "That's it? What a travesty. We deserved a far better grade than that. Eighteen out of twenty at least."

Bertille's eyes danced behind the rim of her bowl. "Well, my prof is a hard marker."

"Still! Our model of the great pyramid was perfect. It was some of the best work I've ever done."

Bertille patted his hand. "Don't feel badly. We got the second to best grade in the whole class."

Gaspard made a noise of disdain.

Bertille shrugged at Amandine. "He's so hard on himself about our projects. A fourteen in that class is actually really good."

Amandine had seen Gaspard with his sisters, but never this up-close. This side of him was so easy to love. Was this what he would be like with his own children? Anyway, it didn't matter, because he didn't want her like that. Last night he had made that abundantly clear. She hated how much that hurt.

"What work are you doing today besides pruning?" she asked him, to move the conversation onto safer ground.

"More pruning." His shoulders fell and he looked uncharacteristically defeated.

"Me too!" Louise said, with the enthusiasm Gaspard was lacking. "I'm so thrilled to have another winemaker in the family to learn from, especially a woman."

"It sounds like you've been bitten by the winemaking bug," Amandine observed. Louise reminded her of herself and Cerise—part of an exclusive club.

She nodded. Oh yes, there was that fervent look in her eyes. "Absolutely."

"Welcome to the club."

But Gaspard still looked beleaguered at the prospect of his day of work in the vines, rather than passionate. It was true that Gaspard had been given little choice in the matter, but surely he loved his work in the vineyards just as much as her and Louise? How could anyone not?

"It's a shame you both have to work today," Margaux said. "You should be on a honeymoon somewhere gorgeous."

"*Oui*," Sophie added. "On a tropical beach somewhere, like the Maldives or Tahiti."

Gaspard raised a brow at his sister. "Honestly Sophie, can you picture Amandine and me lolling on a beach?"

"You always say it's important to try new things," Louise quipped.

If only he'd tried a new thing on their wedding night. Amandine was struck with a thought. Maybe he considered being with her something they'd already tried and failed. Was he going to wait for their divorce and then find a woman he could actually love?

The pain of this made Amandine hunch over and clutch her stomach. She realized two things. By deciding not to sleep with her, Gaspard had repudiated any hope of making their marriage real. Also, she didn't know what she would do if she couldn't win Gaspard's heart as well as his betrothal—she wanted all of him.

"My words always come back to haunt me, don't they?" Gaspard said.

Chapter Nineteen

For the next week, Gaspard was acutely aware both he and Amandine—or rather, his wife—were keeping as busy as possible to avoid the awkwardness at home. It wasn't that they'd been fighting—the most unsettling thing was they hadn't fought since that first morning over Gaspard's unforgiveable lack of coffee. Their usual sparring would have come as a welcome relief. The formal, distant politeness between them was intolerable.

It would be convenient to place the blame at his wife's door, but his behavior was just as guarded as hers.

It was easy in June to work late on their respective Domaines thanks to the long evenings and the overabundance of tasks to do with the vines growing so fast. Breakfasts and dinners with their sisters in the noisy kitchen meant they barely had to talk to one another.

The only time they had alone was at night when they walked back to Gaspard's outbuilding together. Gaspard had felt many things around Amandine, but he'd never felt awkward the way he did now when he was alone with her.

There were times when it seemed like she was almost going to say something to him, but then she didn't. It was possible he was just imagining it anyway.

He had given his speech to her on their wedding night about not requiring anything from her beyond friendship, yet he wondered whether they even had that between them anymore.

It was all the more agonizing because even in those short moments when they saw each other during the day, it struck him just how much he wanted to be more than her friend. God, so much more.

There was little point denying it to himself, he wanted to be her husband in every sense of the word. He wanted to spend a weekend with her in bed, serving her every need, getting lost with her in a place beyond time and day-to-day life … but she gave him no indication of wanting any more than what they had. If she didn't tell him she needed him in the most unequivocal of ways, he could never ask.

If there was an upside, it was that Jean-Marc appeared to have remained ignorant of their marriage. He wondered when exactly Amandine was planning on breaking the news to her brother. After all, Jean-Marc and Julie were getting married the next day and Amandine, of course, was invited. Gaspard was coming along as her 'date' rather than her husband.

"Amandine!" Gaspard called, when he arrived home after quickly checking on a leaking wine barrel in the cellar. He tried not to work too much on Saturdays, and Amandine had said she wouldn't either. He hoped she made good on her word, because they were due at Sadie and Luc's cottage in Savigny for a casual lunch between friends.

It was the perfect way, really, for both of them to gather strength before Jean-Marc's ceremony and their marriage going public the next day. When they'd both headed out after an early breakfast, eager to get away from one another, they'd promised to meet back at Gaspard's house at eleven o'clock, ready to go.

Amandine, of course, wasn't there. Of course she was still working in her vineyards. He hated knowing that she would never care for anything or anyone as much as she loved those plants. Gaspard took the opportunity to hop in the shower. Only when he stepped out of the shower did he realize that there were no towels hanging on the rack like there usually were. *Merde.*

He'd also forgotten to get his clean clothes before showering. He was still not used to Amandine being around and hampering his ability to walk from room to room naked if he chose. He eyed the dirty, sweaty clothes in the corner of the bathroom. Disgusting. He was not going to put those back on.

He leaned closer to the door and listened. Nothing. He hadn't heard her come in, and even if the water had been running in the shower, his front door creaked loudly.

He would make the dash between the bathroom and his bedroom, like he always used to before getting married. He opened the door and made his way across the floor when his feet lost traction. He slipped and hurtled backwards onto his tailbone.

It took a few seconds before he could breathe again. Those flagstones were unforgiving. *Putain de merde* it hurt. Pain ricocheted up his spine. He clutched his back and surveyed the soaking wet flagstones around him. *So this is where getting a wife had landed him.*

He tried to get up but the daggers of pain as his back spasmed forced him to regroup on the floor. Even his legs were locked up and his entire body was protesting. He let out an impressive string of swear words without stopping for a breath.

Then, absolutely capping his misery, the door opened and Amandine came in. She stood frozen to the spot, letting the door slam shut behind her.

Gaspard swore again and tried to cover himself up with his hands. "I was trying to get up. I didn't want you to see me like this."

Amandine's chartreuse eyes had gone round as saucers. Something he wanted to study further flashed briefly in them. He must be quite a sight, he thought ruefully. At such a moment, he didn't find it at all surprising that she didn't want to be anything more than friends.

She jerked out of her daze. "Are you hurt?" she asked, stepping towards him. "Can you get up?"

He stopped trying to struggle to get up on the slippery stones, and instead just lay there, flat on his back and cupping himself. Might as well just give himself over to the humiliation.

"I don't want you to see me like this," he said again. Really though, it was too late for that, wasn't it?

"Don't be ridiculous," she said. He couldn't see her face from where he lay, but he could hear the chuckle in her voice. "Tell me what hurts?"

"My dignity," he groaned.

Now she laughed for real. It was a sound that instantly made things feel lighter, even if she was laughing at him. "I'm serious *bétion*. Is it your back? Can I help you stand up?"

Gaspard gave this serious consideration. He didn't know how his back would react if he tried to get up again. Right now, it was rippling with spasms, but it wasn't exactly like he could stay here sprawled out on the floor either.

"I slipped and fell on my tailbone. I'll try to get up if

you can lend me a steady arm." He glanced down at where his hands were. "I don't think I could keep myself covered though. It hurts too much and I'm just not that coordinated."

"Gaspard." Her was voice matter-of-fact. "It's not anything I haven't seen. Besides, I'm your wife, remember?"

He sighed. He racked his brain but couldn't really find another way out of his predicament. At least the formality between them had eased a bit—not enough to make his predicament acceptable, but still. "Fine," he agreed.

"You could be a little more gracious about it."

"I'm in agony here!"

She leaned down and took his arm with a firm grip. "I'm going to put your arm over my shoulder."

Even though he was heavy with solid muscle, Amandine was strong too. It wasn't obvious from looking at her, but all her physical work in the vineyards meant that she could win her fair share of arm wrestles with the men of the region.

The spasms robbed Gaspard of his breath as she half-pulled, half-supported him as he got upright. She started trying to move towards his bedroom and he yelped in protest.

"What?" She turned to him, her eyes so luminous and green that he couldn't form words for a moment.

He put up his hand. "Just … just give me a minute for the spasms to subside," he gasped. "All right?"

She examined his face. "*D'accord.*"

"Distract me," he hissed through clenched teeth.

"Ummm … What I was going to talk to you about when I walked in the door is that I decided I'm going to tell Jean-Marc and Julie before their wedding ceremony tomorrow."

"Tell them about us being married?" Gaspard wheezed. She was distracting him, at least. "Why then?"

"I can't in all good conscience let Julie marry him if she doesn't know all of it, even if she has dreamed of the big poufy wedding all her life. I'll let them know, then … well, they can decide what they want to do with all the information. It's only a week until the will reading now. I honestly don't think Jean-Marc could do much in such a short period of time."

"It sounds like you've given this some thought," Gaspard choked out. "I agree about Julie. It's only fair."

"Yes," Amandine agreed. "If it wasn't for her, I wouldn't tell him until the will reading but I can't do that … I can't be as bad as him."

"Just for the record, I don't think she'll change her mind. I think she loves him," Gaspard said, then yelped as his foot slipped slightly on the tile and jarred him again. "*Putain de merde de bordel de merde.*"

"That bad, huh?" Amandine tried, but failed, not to look amused at his plight. "Come on, we're half-way there. I have some muscle relaxers I'll give you after we get you on your bed. *Courage!*"

He braced himself, trying to ignore the fact that he was as naked as the day he was born. Slowly, the spasms were easing, but in the space where pain had been, grew an awareness of the warmth of Amandine's body pressed up against his side, and the delicate curve of her breast against his torso.

Now he had another problem. "*D'accord,*" he said, his voice unnaturally shrill. "We can move now." He began to shuffle forward.

Amandine did, but when they were almost to his bedroom she happened to glance down. Her breath caught for a moment.

Oh God. The humiliation. "Please don't look," he begged through his clenched jaw.

"How can I not?" she asked.

Gaspard bit off a bark of laughter. "I'm sorry, it's just … well, I'm sorry."

"We *are* married." Amandine maneuvered him onto his bed. "I think that makes it okay for me to see you naked and … well." She waved her hand down south and swallowed reflexively. "Honestly, if it has anything to do with me, I'm flattered."

The room filled with unspoken things as they stared at each other. *Did she?* Could she want what he wanted? He needed her to be absolutely clear about that before he tried anything. Confusion could ruin everything.

She crossed her arms in front of her, preoccupied. He would have paid anything to know what she was thinking. Finally, she said, "I'll go get those muscle relaxers for you and a glass of water. Do you need help getting dressed?"

That was that then. Gaspard's head buzzed with frustration. Why couldn't they get it right?

"No, I'll be fine," he said finally. "Slow, but fine."

They were going to be late, and he had humiliated himself enough for one day.

Chapter Twenty

The lunch at the cottage on Luc's family Domaine in Savigny was delicious, and the perfect way to forget the weirdness between them, especially given the scene before they had left Volnay.

The past week had been pretty much sheer torture for Amandine. The war of civility that had broken out between she and Gaspard was unbearable. She was immensely thankful that Gaspard's little mishap had given them a temporary cessation of hostilities.

As she ate the tabouleh salad Luc had prepared as their first course, filled with freshly cut mint and parsley from the garden, she reveled in the summer breeze that flowed in the French doors. The conversation of her friends flowed over her, as well as the occasional squawks of Myrtille who Clovis held with one hand, his fork in the other.

Gaspard was sitting across from her and squirming uncomfortably in his chair despite the fact that she'd dosed him up with pain killers and muscle relaxants before they'd left, and Sadie and Luc had brought him a selection of cushions and pillows and ice packs to make him as comfortable as possible.

Seeing him naked and vulnerable like that was …

well, it was completely different but just as appealing as experiencing him strait-laced and forbidding like at the marriage ceremony. She realized as she looked down at him on the floor that she wanted to know every facet of her husband.

Then he had … well … it had … anyway. She couldn't quite explain the whoosh of relief she'd felt when she'd seen visual evidence that she didn't leave him entirely cold. Up until that, she'd been starting to feel rather pathetic that the lust she felt wasn't reciprocated.

Did he just want that though—sex? She knew she should just come out and ask, but the men in her life had destroyed her willingness to make any confessions that would leave her exposed.

She was scared at just how much she wanted all of Gaspard—every tiny millimeter of his body and soul. It would be different this time between them if he said yes. *She* would be different.

"How about you, Amandine?" Cerise was asking her.

Amandine had just popped a shiny black niçoise olive from the salad into her mouth. She took her time eating the soft flesh around the pit, then removing the pit from her mouth and placing it on the side of her plate, hoping someone would tell her what the question was. She hadn't been listening.

"Sorry," she said, finally. "I was daydreaming."

Luc nodded sagely. "Newlywed life will do that to you."

Gaspard sent him a warning look, to which Luc merely grinned like a naughty boy.

"Can you repeat the question?" Amandine asked.

"We were talking about our dream jobs when we were children. What was yours?"

Amandine thought back. Those years before her

mother died were hazy. The few times she'd gone to a therapist it was suggested to her that her memories were that way due to the trauma of losing her mother and then … well … everything after that. She couldn't remember a time when she hadn't wanted to be a winemaker though, and she'd never loved anything as much as her vineyards. The memories of working with her mother were the ones that remained crystal clear in her mind, like they'd just happened.

"I remember going out in the vineyards and working with my mother. She was always the better winemaker of my parents—I guess I just always wanted to be like her."

"You never even considered anything else?" Clovis asked.

Amandine shook her head. "Nope."

"I guess that explains why you'd go to such lengths to keep the Domaine," said Sadie, her ginger eyebrows drawn together in thought. "No offense," she added to Gaspard.

Gaspard squirmed a bit in his chair and waved his hand. "None taken. Marrying me *is* going to extreme lengths. How about you?" he asked Sadie. "Was it always archeology?"

She shook her head. "No, believe it or not there was an era in my life before I saw my first dinosaur bone."

Luc laid his hand over hers on the table. "That's almost impossible for me to imagine. I must have met you after the dinosaur exposure, because that's ninety per cent of what you wanted to talk about."

Sadie chuckled. "I did have a bit of an … er … obsessive personality."

"Did?" Luc stared at her.

"All right. Still do."

"Join the club," Amandine said.

Cerise raised her hand. "Hear, hear!"

"So what was it you wanted to do before dinosaurs?" Amandine asked Sadie.

"Drive the school bus." When everyone laughed, Sadie just shrugged. "It's yellow and the driver gets long breaks during the day. Not such a bad deal, when you think about it. How about you?" she asked Luc.

"A pilot with the Air Force," he said.

"Ah!" Clovis said. "Was it those ultrasonic jets that flew over from the base in Dijon?"

Luc nodded. "Yup. I think most of us kids living underneath their flight paths dreamed of piloting those when they were older."

Clovis jiggled Myrtille, who had begun to fuss a bit. "I know I did, but I know someone who didn't."

"Who?" Amandine asked.

"Gaspard," Clovis said. "All Gaspard ever dreamed about was being a firefighter."

"Really?" Amandine said. She looked at Gaspard, but he was frowning at his friend. Maybe there was a reason he hadn't confided this to her.

"Oh yes," Luc answered for him. "Gaspard was obsessed with becoming a fireman. I think the happiest I've ever seen him was the day we visited the fire station in Beaune on a school field trip. Surely you remember?" he said to Amandine. "You were there too."

Amandine shook her head. Maybe that was a time when her memory went murky. "Sorry, I don't."

"I only shared that burning ambition with Luc and Clovis," Gaspard said. "And it was a *secret*." He sent them a black look, which just increased their mirth.

Luc and Sadie cleared away the tabouleh and replaced it with a beautiful looking tomato tart and a huge green salad studded with shallots in the vinaigrette dressing.

Something about this new information left Amandine feeling like she needed to know more. "Just how obsessed were you?" she asked Gaspard.

"Big time obsessed," Luc answered for him, ignoring Gaspard's obvious displeasure. "You know Gaspard. By the time he was eight he'd already studied what physical tests he needed to do to pass the exams and had set up a training course in his own back yard. You should have applied, Gaspard, just to see if you could have passed it."

"Of course he would pass it," Clovis said. "I would stake any amount of money on it."

"Did you?" Sadie asked him. "Apply I mean?"

Gaspard sighed and shook his head. "No. My mother went off to Martinque with her new lover to open an eco-lodge."

"What!" Sadie said. "I thought your mother was dead!"

Gaspard laughed. "No! Why would you think that?"

"Because nobody ever mentions her, like … ever."

Gaspard shook his head. "No, No. She's perfectly alive and quite healthy I believe, thanks to those tropical smoothies she drinks all day long. She phones me once a month and sends me the occasional postcard."

"Does she ever come back to Burgundy?" Sadie asked, patently fascinated.

Gaspard shook his head. "Never. Anyway, my father married again, and then came Sophie and Louise, then their mother left as well; then he married again and had Margaux and Bertille, then their mother took off, so I had to stop thinking of firefighting. I had more or less started to take over the Domaine by then too.

"Wait a second … you never really wanted to be a winemaker?" Cerise asked, reaching for Myrtille whose fussing had been growing in volume.

Gaspard shrugged. "My life was defined by things I needed to do. What was the point of becoming fixated on things I wanted?"

He said the words as lightly as possible, but they struck a chill in Amandine's heart.

She always just assumed that everyone felt the way she did about winemaking. She'd had to fight so hard for her vineyard that along the way she'd forgotten to consider there might be people who didn't want theirs.

The conversation drifted on to other things, and eventually when they were eating panna cotta with *caramel au beurre sale sauce* poured over top, Luc shifted his gaze back to she and Gaspard. "So ... Jean-Marc and Julie's wedding tomorrow ... how are you feeling about that?"

Amandine laughed bitterly. "Remember what Gaspard said about winemaking? We have no choice but to go, so what's the point in overthinking it?"

"When are you going to tell them about your wedding?" Cerise asked, eating her panna cotta with one hand as she jiggled Myrtille with the other. Her and Clovis had passed their baby back and forth like a rugby ball during the meal.

"Before the ceremony, so Julie can have an informed choice. I might even slide my ring on at the reception."

"I wonder how your brother is going to react?" Sadie mused.

"I have no idea," Amandine answered honestly. "Not well, I would bet. Jean-Marc gets particularly nasty when he's been thwarted."

"You won't be doing it alone," Gaspard said. "I'll be there."

Amandine shook her head. "I don't need you. I can handle Jean-Marc."

A loaded silence fell around the table. She realized only after the words were out of her mouth how abrupt they must have sounded. She only felt that he needn't feel obliged … he'd done so much for her already, how could she ask him for one more thing?

Gaspard winced for a second, which gave her a sickening sensation in her stomach that had nothing to do with the big meal.

"You know," Clovis said. "Sometimes it's a relief not to have to deal with everything alone."

Clovis was right, it would be a relief, if only it wasn't so difficult for her.

Back at Gaspard's house, they both collapsed on the comfy couch set up right across from the massive stone fireplace instead of retreating quickly to their respective bedrooms. It was only seven o'clock and Amandine knew she owed him an apology.

"A little *digéstif* before heading to bed?" Gaspard asked, with an arch to his brow. "We have a big day tomorrow."

As always, their lunch extended into a walk through the vineyards, Clovis steering Myrtille's stroller adeptly over the occasional stone the plowing had thrown on the path, and then a snack of leftovers before everyone said their *au revoirs*.

Amandine was struggling with a restlessness that kept her mind hopping from one thing to the next and her body unable to find a comfortable position on the couch.

It was not unsurprising. She'd hurt Gaspard, she had to tell her brother the next day that she'd beat him, and she was married to a man who left her feeling as confused as she was attracted to him.

Besides, the conversation about their childhood career aspirations still niggled at her, although she couldn't put her finger on exactly why. A *digéstif* would be most welcome.

"Do you have any Chartreuse?" Amandine asked.

"Need you ask?" Gaspard answered, getting up from the couch and heading over to the old cheese cupboard carved into the rock in his wall that housed his bottles of stronger alcohol.

"I guess not."

Both Amandine and Gaspard had a deep and abiding love for the bright green liqueur made by the monks at the Chartreuse monastery in the mountains near Grenoble. It was concocted like a magical potion from a secret recipe of mountain herbs and tasted just as fresh as its color. It was purported to have medicinal qualities—helping digestion, relieving mental trauma, lubricating joints, and pretty much everything else. The older generation in Burgundy swore by it, and Amandine figured it couldn't hurt to take the edge off.

She watched Gaspard as he unscrewed the bottle, took two tiny etched crystal glasses from the cupboard, and poured them each a bright green glass. His movements were always so precise and perfectly calibrated. That's why finding him sprawled on the floor earlier had been such a shock. She thought back to how he'd hardened when he was pressed up against her ... she shook her head ... no, that was not going to help her restlessness.

Gaspard had wanted to be a firefighter? She'd come

into this marriage thinking she knew him backwards and forwards—after all, they'd been in a relationship before and had known each other since they were children—but it was dawning on her that perhaps she only knew what he chose to reveal to her.

As he settled down on the couch beside her with his glass, she was struck by how the dim lamp in the corner of the room softened the lines of his face. The curve of his lips was soft now where often it was tight. His eyes were contemplative instead of hard as flint.

How little room he must have had in his life for day-dreams and desires of his own. He'd had such overwhelming responsibility thrust on him at such an early age in the form of his sisters … she was struck by a yearning to help him explore his wants and desires instead of just his obligations. She wanted to make him shout with pleasure and break free from the chains of his inhibitions. She wanted to show him just how good she could make him feel.

She squirmed. That line of thought wasn't helping the restlessness either.

"So … a fireman?" she said instead. "I thought we had no secrets from each other."

He looked at her narrowly. "No secrets? Why on earth would you think that?"

She shook her head. He was right. She wasn't in any rush to reveal how she felt about him, but up until then she'd always believed Gaspard to be more or less what he showed her. How incredibly shortsighted. "*Touché.* So … winemaking … how do you really feel about that?"

He shrugged.

"You're just so good at it that I never thought to question whether that was what you truly wanted to be doing," she admitted.

The lines around Gaspard's eyes crinkled with sympathy. "Given what you had to fight against, nobody could blame you for thinking everyone dreams of being a winemaker."

"But did you?"

"No. I never wanted to be a winemaker."

Why was this the first time she was hearing this? This was crucial information. "And now?"

He lifted one shoulder in an expressive movement. "I never had a choice, so what's the point of torturing myself over what might have been?"

There was something so sad in his words that Amandine was bereft of speech for a while. "So you became incredibly skilled at what you needed to do," she said, finally. "And turned your thoughts away from what you wanted to do."

Gaspard examined her now, his dark eyes bottomless. "That's it," he said in a gentle voice. "That's it exactly."

Their eyes were locked, and Amandine was overcome with the desire to take him in her arms and to make him want something that she could give him right away.

This vulnerable side he was showing her—it was new, and it was irresistible. He was showing her an empty part of himself that she could help fill—if only he'd let her. He'd never been helped in his life; he'd only ever done the helping. This was why he'd finally agreed to marry her. The desire to change that for him burst to life in every one of Amandine's cells.

It was so quiet she could hear the clock on the mantle tick away the seconds.

He cleared his throat, but no words came out.

She couldn't kiss him, not when he had made it clear he didn't want her to. That invisible thread she'd always felt between then was becoming shorter, reeling her closer to him, but no … he didn't want a real marriage. He'd made that crystal clear.

"Has your fireman dream lasted?" she asked instead.

He took a sip of his Chartreuse, then bit his lip.

"*Allez*," she chided. "I saw you naked this morning, *tu souviens*? You can tell me."

His lips quirked. "Thank you for reminding me. I'd actually managed to forget about that humiliation for a few minutes."

She wanted to make another joke—to tease him like she always did—but he would never let her in if they relied on their old dynamic. "You truly can let me see you, you know. I mean it." She hoped he heard the sincerity in her words.

"Can I?" She watched as his eyes morphed from contemplation to rapier-sharp focus.

"You can trust me." He could too, with his deepest secrets and wildest dreams and naked body and soul and everything else between. Why couldn't he just show himself to her? What was stopping him?

He ran his fingertip over the cuts in the crystal glass he held, tracing them. "*Oui*, I still dream of it. I take the long route in and out of Beaune to drive by the fire station and I slow down and indulge in a few moments of daydreaming."

For a second there she'd forgotten that they'd originally been talking about Gaspard wanting to be a firefighter, but now her mind snapped back to the point at hand. "What is it about that job that you think you'd like?"

Gaspard mulled over this for a few moments. "I suppose I have a strong desire to help people," he began. "Also, I think I function well in a crisis—I've always been like that. When other people get confused and frightened, my mind sharpens. I'm able to decide the best thing to do and to do it."

Amandine nodded. Every word he was saying was true. "You're strong and physically capable," she said. "That's a huge asset."

She tried to push memories of the firm, beautifully knitted muscles of his back out of her mind. He hadn't given her access to those.

Gaspard stared at her with a certain touch of disbelief in his eyes. Had she been so awful before that he was shocked she wasn't trampling on his dreams with judgement or criticism? *She had to do better.*

"I always loved the idea of intervening to help when help was truly needed," he continued. "I operate at my best when it's a crisis. It's the maintenance and the day-to-day work aspect of winemaking that …" He shook his head, hesitant to continue.

"That what?" Her voice lowered to a whisper. It felt as though this was a confession of sorts, and she wanted to treat it with the reverence it deserved.

"It kills my soul a bit more every year. I appreciate good wine and fine winemaking as much as any other Burgundian, but the cyclical nature of it … I struggle with that. I can rarely turn around and look at my work and say, 'I did well there,' with a sense of contentment."

How could he think that? Each vintage or each appellation was like a separate painting, or … no, she had to try and look at it from Gaspard's perspective. It was true that as soon as the grapes were in, the vinification began, and then the wine needed to be transferred to barrels and then the aging—she could see how someone who didn't share her obsession might view it as constant and tireless work that never ended. She was cut out for it, but perhaps Gaspard wasn't, despite what she'd always assumed.

"The winemaking just … it never ends, you know?" He frowned.

How she wanted to lean over and kiss away that crease between his eyebrows.

She took another burning sip of Chartreuse and the thread between them tightened again. Somehow, they'd moved closer together on the couch. She could feel the warmth of Gaspard's breath on her face. All it would take would be to lean forward—

"You couldn't understand." Gaspard's words were a bath of ice water over the heat between them. He sighed. "All you've ever wanted to do was winemaking, Amandine, and you've had to fight so hard just to do that."

"I'm trying to understand," she said, and searched for ways to show him she really was, for once. "Maybe with Louise helping, you could volunteer at the fire station or something?"

He shook his head. "Louise doesn't know about the firefighting thing."

"Why don't you just tell her?"

Gaspard shook his head, emphatically. "Absolutely not. She must never know, and the same goes for the rest of my sisters."

"Why not?" She truly didn't understand.

"I can't have them thinking I sacrificed my dreams for them."

But he had. She managed not to let those words slip out. "Don't worry," she said instead. "I would never say anything."

"*Merci.*" Gaspard chewed the inside of his cheek.

His sacrifices troubled her—both the ones he'd had to make in the past and the ones he continued to make every day and, most of all, the one he'd made for her. "I want you to have everything you've ever dreamed about," she burst out. It was terrifying because it had come directly from her heart. Her eyes raised slowly to his face.

He squeezed his eyes shut for a second and then opened them again, reeling, as if the concept alone was something he'd never considered before.

He reached out then and took her hand in his. Their fingers intertwined the way they used to, but the electricity of his touch shocked Amandine in a way it never had before. A surge of joy flowed through her … of belonging.

She leaned forward, expecting him to meet her half-way. Instead, he stayed exactly where he was, his eyes growing more and more inscrutable. He looked al-most … terrified.

He leapt up from the couch then and downed the rest of his Chartreuse so quickly that he spluttered.

"Time for bed," he said, and was already walking to his bedroom. "Tomorrow is going to be a long day. *Bonne nuit,* Amandine." He slammed his door shut, leaving her alone and bereft, and none too happy about it, on the couch.

Chapter Twenty-One

Gaspard was up the next morning, dressed and ready to go to Jean-Marc and Julie's wedding before Amandine had even emerged from her bedroom.

It was a beautiful June morning and he'd had a wretched night sleep.

He wanted to give Amandine some time and space to get ready for what would surely be a difficult day, so he decided to go and inspect his vineyards closest to his house. It was just through a doorway built several centuries before into the stone wall that led from his courtyard right into the vineyards.

This Clos-des-Ducs was one of his favorite plots of grapes, and one of his favorite vines as well. He strode through the rows of vineyards, inspecting the leaves and training a few vines as he moved along the rows.

He'd made such a mess of things and he'd had the whole night alone in his bed to regret his decision to leap up from the couch when he did. Had she really been about to kiss him or had that just been his overactive imagination? He'd been so unnerved by her understanding reaction to the whole firefighting business that he hadn't known up from down.

She'd truly listened, and he could tell she was trying

so hard to see things from his perspective, even though that had never come easily to her. Did that mean they could really talk about the important things … the things that he could talk about to no one else?

He'd resigned himself to pretty much living in a state of wanting to kiss Amandine every second of every day since their wedding day. He felt wrong to take advantage of their forced proximity—he wanted her to come to him freely. He needed to feel that she needed him.

Maybe he'd simply chickened out. The connection he'd felt between them the night before was new … different. He sensed it could lead to something deeper between them—something they'd never been able to access before. The prospect was as terrifying as it was enticing.

The church bell chimed out over the vineyards. Ten o'clock. He needed to go and wake up Amandine if she was still asleep—although that was highly unlikely. Julie had delivered her bridesmaid's dress yesterday to Amandine's house when they were at Luc's and they'd picked it up on their way back to Volnay. As a member of the wedding party, Amandine needed to be there early. Besides, she had to find a moment to break the news to them before everything at the church got underway.

Amandine had informed Gaspard with disgust that Julie had decided to have a wedding *à l'Americain* with bridesmaids wearing matching dresses and flower girls and all the hoopla that the French generally eschewed.

Would Julie and Jean-Marc still want to go ahead with their marriage after Amandine made her revelation? Gaspard was fairly certain that Julie would, but he entertained serious doubts about Jean-Marc. He wasn't even sure Amandine's brother was capable of love.

Regardless, Julie could never possibly look as beautiful as Amandine had on their wedding day. That image of her would be burned on his retinas until he drew his last breath. More than anything, he wanted to see her in that dress again, but of course he couldn't ask that of her.

He opened the door of the cottage. It was quiet, until a wail of despair coming from Amandine's bedroom shattered the still air.

Gaspard didn't waste a second. *Was she hurt?* He crashed through her bedroom door, then froze at the sight of her.

She stood in front of the floor to ceiling mirror propped up in the corner of her room, staring at her reflection, her top lip curled with disgust.

"You poor thing," Gaspard said, from the heart.

The dress was hideous. It was a travesty, truly, to dress such an exquisite woman in something so heinous.

Amandine turned around. "Go ahead. Laugh. I know how bad it is. I mean, seriously, we all knew Julie had bad taste, but this surpasses my worst nightmares."

Gaspard could barely take it all in. The dress was made of stiff taffeta in such a lurid bright pink that Gaspard's retinas ached from looking directly at it. "It's …" He frantically searched for something reassuring he could say but came up empty-handed. "It's bad," he finally admitted.

It had a strapless bodice and layers of fluffy, poufy fabric that stopped just below the knee. The skirt length made Amandine's strong, capable legs look spindly. Gaspard was certain the fuchsia shade did no-one any favors, but it washed out the color of Amandine's face. Normally she looked as though her features had been tinted by the hand of a master watercolorist, now she just looked stricken with a nasty stomach flu.

"Do all the women in the wedding party have to wear those?" Gaspard asked, trying, and failing to image the collective horror.

Amandine nodded, grim. "Yes, and the men have to wear bow ties in this color." She pointed down to her dress, then looked despairingly up at Gaspard.

"*Purée*. It's going to be hideous," he said and meant it.

"What are you going to wear?" she asked.

"My wedding suit."

"Oh no," she groaned.

He was struck by insecurity. He had adored how she'd looked at the wedding. Had the admiration not been mutual? "Don't you like it?"

"No! The opposite. You're going to look so handsome. I wouldn't blame you at all if you didn't want to be seen with me, you know." The disgust was so patent on her face that he started laughing. She was adorable. He went over and stood in front of her, her upper arms in his hands. "I'm always proud to be seen with you."

She glanced down again at her dress. "Even in this?"

"Even in that travesty."

Amandine gave him a tiny, shy smile. "If that isn't a proof of loyalty today, I don't know what is."

Even the fuchsia couldn't detract from the brilliance of her eyes. Want he wanted to do most of all was whip that dress off her and show her just how much he adored the way she looked with no clothes on at all.

"I don't know how I'm going to be able to talk to Jean-Marc and Julie with a straight face wearing this," she said, her fine blonde brows knitted.

"Are you having second thoughts about doing it today?"

She shook her head. "No, he's going to find out

sooner rather than later. I have to give Julie a real choice. Besides, these weeks of waiting to break the news ... it's been harder than I thought. I want to get it over with. I hate being in this strange limbo."

He was overcome with pain, but also relief that he hadn't succumbed to his baser instincts. She probably couldn't wait to begin the divorce proceedings and get on with her life.

"Right," he said. *"Bien sûr.* Just so you know, I'm not planning on hindering you in any way, you know, us splitting up when it's time and all that."

Her head snapped up. "No. Wait, Gaspard. That's not what—"

But he was already on his way out of the room. "I should get dressed or we'll be late."

Her words had pierced him like spikes, but it was his own fault for wanting her so badly.

She had no idea where Jean-Marc was waiting the hour before he was meant to be at the mayor's office, so she had to break the news by phone. She'd said her piece and he'd responded by hanging up on her. She confided in Gaspard that she had no idea what he was going to do with the information.

Gaspard just took her hand and squeezed it before dropping her off at Julie's house, where the entire hideously fuchsia bridal party was assembling. He told Amandine he would just park by the Maire and he would come and pick her up if she needed him at any point. If

Julie attacked her for example, or … well, both of them had leant their mind to it and they couldn't think of many fates worse than having to wear that bridesmaid dress.

At Julie's house, Amandine managed to pry her away from her friends, mother, and aunts by asking Julie to help her with something in the bathroom.

All of Julie's hair and make-up had been done, but she had wrapped her body in a white silk robe and was waiting to pull on her dress at the last moment.

"What is it, Amandine?" Julie asked, understandably impatient. "I don't have a lot of time before I have to put my dress on, you know."

"I know," Amandine. "And I'm sorry. I'll also be quick. There's something I must tell you that you need to know before you decide to get married to my brother."

"Decide to get married?" Julie let out a little choke of laughter. "We *are* getting married Amandine, in about an hour."

"We'll see."

"Amandine," Julie said in a firm tone of voice that made Amandine think there was more to her than she'd assumed. "What is this about?"

"My father's inheritance."

Julie rolled her heavily eyelined eyes. "That stupid thing? I've heard enough about it, thank you very much. I couldn't care less."

Amandine decided to take the rest in a rush. "Gaspard and I got married over a week ago. It's official. That means I will inherit the Domaine."

Julie put her hands on her hips and shrugged. "So?"

"So Jean-Marc's going to be furious and he might decide not to marry you and you might not want to marry him and—"

Julie grabbed on to Amandine's forearm to stop her. "This doesn't change anything," she said. "Stop being ridiculous."

"But … but it's the vineyards—"

"I've heard quite enough about the pesky vineyards," Julie declared. "And I am more than happy to be rid of them. Maybe now Jean-Marc and I can get on with our lives. Come now, my soon-to-be-sister-in-law. You're all riled up. I need to pour you a flute of *crémant*."

The tedium of the ceremonies—one at the mayor's office like he'd had with Amandine and one at the beautiful little medieval church in the center of Pernand-Vergelesses—was alleviated by Amandine's whispered confession that Julie hadn't cared about their news, and Jean-Marc had just hung up.

They had both held their breath until Jean-Marc arrived at the mairie, looking shockingly calm.

"Now I feel like an idiot for keeping it a secret," Amandine had hissed in Gaspard's ear, but he didn't think so. The bridal couple's complete lack of reaction—especially on the part of Jean-Marc—was both perplexing and oddly stressful. Was he going to snap at some point? Gaspard mulled this over as he sat in the hard wooden pew of the church, watching his wife up at the front, pale and uncomfortable.

She was miserable. Besides her understandable confusion it was not hard to see that her dress itched terribly.

At first, during the mayor's ceremony, she'd tried to

scratch discreetly, but by the time they got to the church she'd given up on discretion and clawed at the fabric and her skin like a caged animal.

Gaspard waited until Jean-Marc and Julie had gone into the antechamber with the priest to sign the required paperwork before he got up and moved to the front near Amandine. "Are you all right?" he asked.

"No," Amandine hissed. "I'm not all right. This material feels like it's made of fire ants." She nodded over to Éloise, who was standing on the opposite side of the altar and was also scratching herself with a pained expression. "Also, what am I to think of Jean-Marc? He followed through on the wedding. Do you think maybe he didn't hear what I said on the phone."

Gaspard considered this, then shook his head. "Knowing you, I imagine you were quite clear."

"I was."

Éloise noticed them whispering, and Amandine beckoned her over to where they stood. "Are you itchy too?" Éloise asked when she reached their side.

Amandine nodded. "Dying."

Éloise grimaced. "It's torture, and don't even get me started on these heels. I have a blister the size of Greenland."

"Do you want me to run and get you both a change of clothes for the reception?" Gaspard asked.

"Yes!" Amandine yelped, and some elderly relatives cast her a dirty look.

Éloise shook her head. "Julie would be so upset. We can't, Amandine. It's her wedding day."

Amandine made a funny little "hmph" sound of annoyance but didn't protest. Éloise had a point and Julie had been remarkably sanguine about her news. Surely she deserved the wedding day she wanted, down to every last detail.

An elderly aunt wearing a hideous yellow hat shhh'd them very angrily.

Amandine rolled her eyes but stayed silent.

At long last, the paperwork was finished and Jean-Marc and Julie walked down the center aisle of the church, over flagstones with people buried underneath in 1246 who surely never had to contend with itchy neon taffeta.

In the tumult of people at the exit of the church, Gaspard stuck close to Amandine. Leaving her around Jean-Marc would be like leaving her beside an unexploded bomb.

After several minutes of being congratulated outside the church, Jean-Marc moved closer to Gaspard and Amandine. Gaspard braced himself and flung out a protective arm in front of his wife.

"So!" Jean-Marc grinned at them. "What did you think?"

Gaspard was shocked by the change in him. His round face was glowing with pride—maybe this rush to the altar had been a good thing for Jean-Marc. He might be happier as a married man, Gaspard thought, and even though Julie might have terrible taste in fashion, she had proven to be loyal and loving—she very clearly hadn't married him for any inheritance. Maybe this was a new beginning for Jean-Marc.

"*Félicitations?*" Amandine said in the most questioning tone Gaspard had ever heard.

"Are you going to wish us happiness?" Jean-Marc said.

"Of course," Amandine said. "I wish you lots of happiness."

Gaspard wanted to keep an eye on them but his arm was grabbed by someone behind him, and he turned to look into the eyes of the bride herself. Julie kissed both his cheeks warmly.

He was surprised, as they'd never been close. "*Félicitations,* Julie," he said. "You look so happy. Are you … all right?"

"So you and Amandine?" she asked, smiling cheek to cheek. "Aren't you sneaky."

"I'm sure you must have been—"

"I've never been happier," she said decisively. "And good riddance to that stupid inheritance. That piece of news made my day."

He was aware his mouth was hanging open yet couldn't seem to shut it.

"I thought you two were on the outs." Julie nodded towards Amandine, who was now saying something to Éloise.

Gaspard shrugged. "We always are, more or less. It's just our way."

Julie shook her head. "Well, I don't understand that, but I wanted to give you my congratulations."

Maybe he should have suspected that Julie was more than what she seemed on the surface. He reached out and squeezed her hand in true appreciation.

The joy in Julie's eyes was unmistakable. "You're truly happy aren't you?" Gaspard asked her.

Julie blinked away tears of emotion. "This is the happiest day of my life. Can I tell you a secret?"

Somehow the crowd had thinned a bit around them, and Amandine was a few feet away whispering with Éloise. He smiled, amused and touched. "Of course. I'm a vault. What is it?"

"I'm pregnant."

His eyes opened wide. The more he thought about it, the more he thought that could be wonderful for them—

a lovely diversion from the inheritance and the vineyards and the rest of it.

"That's wonderful, Julie. And you really love him … I mean, Jean-Marc?"

"I know he's not perfect," she said simply. "But I do."

"I'm truly happy for you then. You deserve the very best."

Julie surprised him again with an enveloping hug and clung on to him. "I so hope that you find this happiness too with Amandine. Don't tell anyone about the baby though, okay? It's still early days."

"It's our secret," Gaspard said.

"Thank you," she said.

"For what?"

"I was going to explode if I didn't tell anyone."

"Well then," said Gaspard. "You're most welcome."

Chapter Twenty-Two

After the massive four-course meal, the pièce montée, and dancing, Amandine still didn't feel at ease. She needed to find Jean-Marc and talk to him. She couldn't just leave it in this weird, unprecedented place the week before the will reading. She opened her purse and the small velvet bag inside and slipped on the beautiful ring Gaspard had given her. It was amazing how it fit perfectly.

She explained her plans to Gaspard, who nodded with understanding. "Next time he leaves the room I'm going to follow him," she said. Her husband had stuck close to her the entire day and it was easy to get used to his steady, unspoken strength beside her. She tried not to think about how it would feel when he took it away.

"Do you know what you're going to say?" Gaspard asked.

"Yes … no … I don't know." Uncertainty made her feel scattered.

He squeezed her hand. "Have you ever considered maybe you did your brother a favor?"

That was certainly a generous interpretation of her actions. "How is that?"

"You taking over the vineyards will leave him to

concentrate on his family life with Julie."

Now she understood Gaspard better, she could see that maybe this is how he would feel, but not her, and probably not her brother. "Jean-Marc isn't you," she reminded him.

"Thank God for that," he said, and out of the corner of Amandine's eye she saw Jean-Marc duck out of the room.

She nodded in his direction. "I'll find you after."

He put a reassuring hand in the middle of her back and it was so warm and solid it made her want to stay right where she was. "I'll be nearby. Just say my name if you need me."

As she followed Jean-Marc, she found herself mulling over Gaspard's promise to be there for her. He always was when it counted, wasn't he? He was perhaps the only man in her experience that she could depend on, yet he asked for almost nothing from her in return. If she could settle things with Jean-Marc once and for all, maybe she would create enough space in her life to fix that imbalance.

Jean-Marc didn't head towards the bathroom as she presumed he would. He headed in the opposite direction, to a door that led outside to the village Salle des Fêtes where the reception was being held. The door was propped open to let in the fresh night air, and she watched as he went outside, then dug out a package of cigarettes from the back pocket of his suit.

Amandine took a deep breath, and joined him outside, her chest tight with the odd combination of trepidation and determination to come to some sort of resolution that he'd denied her earlier.

He was standing still, cupping his hand around the tip of his cigarette as he lit it, when she came up behind him. The night sky was clear and spangled with stars. She cleared her throat.

He whipped around. He'd drunk quite a bit—she'd watched him do it—and now was definitely a bit the worse for wear, like most of the guests inside the reception dancing to Claude Francois's *Cette Année-La* she could hear faintly in the distance.

She braced herself, waiting for him to say something cutting, but instead he sat down on an old-fashioned wooden bench set up against the stone wall of the salle des fêtes, and patted the seat beside him. "Come, Amandine," he said. "Sit with me."

"I'm good." There was no way she could sit still. She began to pace back and forth, her arms crossed across her torso.

"Suit yourself," he stared at her, curious, for a while, then gazed up to the stars. "I wish *Maman* was here tonight," he said, his voice cracking. "I miss her so much."

Amandine stopped and stared at him in amazement. Since the day their mother had died, she could count the number of times Jean-Marc had mentioned her on one hand. Was the wine making him maudlin? Stranger still, he was echoing the exact same thought Amandine had had on her wedding day, although she'd mentioned it to no-one.

"Of course I miss her," she admitted with some difficulty. "I miss her all the time. I thought that it would get better, but—"

"It doesn't."

Amandine stopped in her tracks and studied him. "No," she said. "It doesn't."

Jean-Marc cracked his knuckles. "We have no choice but to just continue living, I guess, even though sometimes it feels like the hardest thing in the world."

"Yeah." Amandine was so stunned to see this side of Jean-Marc again that she struggled to find the right words. She didn't want him to vanish right away. "Are you happy?" she asked. "I mean … with Julie?"

Jean-Marc smiled at that—a real smile, not the usual mocking or sneering one she'd grown to expect. "*Oui.* I should have married her years ago, but I don't know … ever since Maman died, I couldn't seem to make any decisions. It … it froze me somehow."

Amandine often had this same impression, that things had been locked in the same dynamic for too long—her animosity with Jean-Marc, her fights with her father, even her frequent clashes with Gaspard. "I get that," she said.

"I love Julie." Jean-Marc touched the center of his chest, something she'd never seen him do before. "I still can't understand why she loves me back, but I'm too selfish to refuse it."

"I'm … glad." The most astonishing thing of all was that Amandine truly was glad for her brother.

"In a way I should thank you and Papa for that stupid provision in his will. It pushed me to do something I should have done years ago."

Amandine hated to break up this first civil conversation she'd had with her brother in well over a decade, but a suspicious voice in her head wondered how much of Jean-Marc's serenity was the fact that maybe he'd misunderstood her. "About that," she said. "When you just hung up on me, but showed up at the wedding … well, I didn't know what to think. You understood what I said to you on the phone, right?"

He nodded.

"Are you angry I won?" she asked, then bit her lip.

"Sorry. That's a dumb question. Of course you are. I would be in your place."

He merely shrugged.

"What I don't understand is you're acting like you don't care so why did you want to win in the first place?" Amandine blew out a gust of a breath. She truly wanted to know. "Now that Papa is gone and he's not around to pit one of us against the other, I'd like to understand. Truly. didn't you see how much I love the Domaine and how much it's a part of me? Didn't you realize that if I inherited, I'd pay you a salary. I would never leave you in the lurch, despite—"

Jean-Marc let out a bark of laughter. "Yes, despite …"

"So … why?"

"I'm the only boy." He took a long drag on his cigarette. "If I didn't at least fight for it, people would wonder what was wrong with me." He broke eye contact then and studied his dress shoes instead.

That wasn't any explanation. Who cared what people thought? "Come on, there's more and more daughters taking over Domaines these days."

Jean-Marc shook his head. "Maybe, but that only happens when there isn't a son to take over."

"Some siblings are partnering up."

"Could you really see us working together, Amandine? Really?"

"Maybe …" But she was just stalling. Of course she couldn't.

He waved that suggestion away. "You know as well as I do just how much of a disaster that would be. You need to be in control all the time. There's no way you would treat me like an equal partner."

She sighed. "You're probably right."

"What I want to know is … where did you get married? When?"

She hesitated, but then realized no harm could come from sharing the details now. "We married quietly up at Domaine du Cerisier, well away from the avid eyes and ears and the gossips around here."

"Just the two of you?" Jean-Marc asked. His normally ruddy skin had gone ghostly pale in the streetlamp. It was an odd question, but then again it had been an odd day.

"No. Our friends were there, and Gaspard's sisters, and Éloise."

"You didn't invite me?"

Amandine huffed with disbelief. "Is that what's bothering you? I never even imagined … If I'd invited you, you would have created a scene at my wedding. Besides, it's not like we're close."

Jean-Marc dropped his head into his hands. "I can't believe it," he said, after a long while. "You got married and I wasn't even there to walk you down the aisle."

Amandine stood above him, baffled. She honestly had no idea how to respond. "Stop gaslighting me, Jean-Marc. Of course, I didn't ask you to walk me down the aisle. We were at war."

"Don't you realize I never wanted to be at war? I think I hated it as much as you."

"Are you only realizing this now? It sure looked to me as though you were enjoying yourself."

"I just—" He shook his head. "I can't believe I missed your wedding. I can't believe you didn't invite me."

This was becoming downright absurd. "Come on, Jean-Marc, you're being ridiculous. I honestly … I don't know what to do with you like this. I thought you'd be angry about me tricking you. *That* I can deal with."

Jean-Marc just shrugged.

"What's come over you? I thought you'd be so furious you'd get violent."

"I've never done that to you, have I?"

"No …" said Amandine. "But there are ways to strike a person without using hands."

He just shook his head again. "To think I missed your wedding day—"

"Look," Amandine sat beside him, disconcerted by the hurt on Jean-Marc's features. "I'm not just going to leave you and Julie high and dry." She reminded herself that even if Jean-Marc might be hurt, at least he couldn't hurt *her* anymore.

"Thank you, I guess," he said, still lost in his thoughts.

"I expected you to be much, much angrier," she admitted. "Is this the calm before the storm? You seem almost … resigned. I was not expecting that."

He shrugged. "Knowing you I'm sure you didn't make any mistakes with the legalities of the whole thing."

"No. I made sure of that, but still—"

He smiled—a tremulous, hopeful smile that she had never seen on his face before. "I think maybe I'll look back on this and realize you just did me a favor."

That unexpected sentiment robbed her of words. He was relieved?

"Are you happy?" he asked, his face tilting up to hers. "I know you and Gaspard were engaged and broke up pretty spectacularly before. Tell me the truth for once, Amandine. It's not like I can do anything about it now anyway, but did you fake this wedding just so you can inherit the vineyards?"

Amandine studied his face. Should she be honest, or was he just trying to extract information from her that he could use against her in a surprise attack? "We're not close enough for me to talk to you about that," she said finally.

He bowed his head again. There on the bench, slumped and sad, he looked … defeated. She didn't know what to do with that either.

"Well, I've said what I came here to say, so I'm going to go," she said finally. "I guess I'll see you at the will reading."

Jean-Marc caught her off guard by standing up and grasping her hands in his. "I wish you all the best in your marriage. Please believe me when I say that, because it's sincere. Gaspard and I didn't exactly get along, but I respect him. I'll move my things out of the Domaine and into Julie's. I've been staying there all the time anyway. It's so … free of memories there."

Amandine just nodded, dumbly.

Jean-Marc ground his cigarette butt on the ground with the toe of his dress shoe and made his way back into the hall, leaving her alone in the dark, trying—and failing—to make sense of what just happened.

Chapter Twenty-Three

Amandine was still standing there when Gaspard slipped out from behind the door.

"How long have you been there for?" she asked, inexplicably disconcerted by Jean-Marc's reaction of sadness instead of anger. She knew what to do with his animosity, but not his grief.

He shrugged. "I wasn't sure how things would go with him—I wanted to stay close by in case you needed me."

Amandine could tell by the seriousness in Gaspard's eyes and the way he was scanning her, as if checking for both external and internal injury, that he was trying to figure out what she needed. The answer to that flashed through her like lightening. *Him.* She needed him.

"How are you?" he asked.

She shook her head. She had to tread carefully. He was so precious to her … so indispensable, she couldn't get this wrong—not again. She pressed her palm to her chest to stem the mix of sorrow and vulnerability pushing at her from the inside, but it wasn't working. "Bewildered," she admitted. "He didn't even seem angry. If I didn't know better, I would say he was relieved. He was mostly upset about me not inviting him to our wedding. Can you believe that?"

Gaspard whistled long and low. "I never did understand your brother."

That connection between them tugged, and then tugged stronger, insistent. She wanted him to hold her so she could find her bearings again.

"What do you need from me?" Gaspard asked.

There he was. Solid. Gorgeous in his wedding suit. Giving and never taking. *Hers.* She knew what she needed, but was she brave enough to say it?

She must have stayed silent for longer than she realized, because finally Gaspard prompted.

"Are you all right?"

"You," she said, and the word came out as clear and definite as a bell. "I need you, Gaspard."

His jaw dropped, and with some effort he mastered himself and closed it again. "You have me," he said, his voice guarded. "I'm right here."

She took a step towards him, close enough to see him blink. "Not like that. What I meant was I was disappointed when you decided for both of us that you didn't want to make our marriage real. I've been wanting to tell you, but I was a coward."

His breath caught. "You were?"

She nodded, biting the inside of her cheek. She could just reach out and—

"It wasn't that I didn't want to," he said, taking a step closer to her. His breathing had sped up. "It's that I realized I could never ask that of you."

"You didn't ask for it." Amandine moved closer still, so there were only a few centimeters separating them. "But I want it ... I want *you,* Gaspard. I need you. Badly."

He pulled her against him then. All those scattered pieces of her came together again and she let out a sigh that seemed to originate in the deepest part of her soul. *This*.

He tightened his arms and his lips touched hers. What began as a gentle, tentative kiss quickly became desperate. The need to get closer to Gaspard, to give him everything, and take everything as well, fizzed through Amandine's veins. She raked her hand up through his hair, drawing his lips harder down on hers.

"I need you in bed," Amandine gasped. "With me." She'd never been one to equivocate—why start now?

Gaspard reached down and fumbled in his pocket, extracting his car keys. "Did you have a purse or—"

"I can pick it up tomorrow. I don't want to go back in there." She grabbed his hand and, snickering like a couple of school children, they ran across the street to where his Citroen was parked. They were both racing to a place that, Amandine was quite sure, neither of them had ever been before.

The drive to Volnay had never felt so long. At first, they continued to stroke and kiss each other as Gaspard attempted to drive, but then he almost veered off the road near Nuits-Saint-Georges and came a hair's breadth from landing his car in a ditch. With considerable effort he picked up Amandine's hand where it had been exploring and placed it firmly back on her lap.

"We have to wait," he said. "Or I'm definitely going to cause a traffic accident and what a waste that would be."

Amandine arched her head up against the seat rest and groaned in frustration.

"You think it's bad for you?" Gaspard nodded down at his lap, where the moonlight revealed a large bulge against his zipper.

Amandine reached out again to touch him and then he closed his eyes for a second, overcome, and narrowly avoided an old stone statue of Jesus nailed to the cross.

She pulled her hand away, now convinced about their need for restraint.

The next few minutes were spent in charged silence, until Gaspard spoke. "Can you say it again?" he asked.

"Say what again?"

"That you need me."

"I need you, Gaspard," she said, her voice low and rough with desire. She'd been denying it to herself, but that void in her life and her heart that only Gaspard could fill had been steadily growing since he'd agreed to marry her, maybe even before that. Had it ever really gone away?

Gaspard turned and smiled at her—a heartbreakingly open smile of tenderness and love that she'd never seen before. "That is the most beautiful thing I ever heard," he said, turning into his courtyard in Volnay.

The girls weren't back from the wedding yet, so Gaspard and Amandine scrambled out of the car and dashed towards his house. Halfway there, Gaspard ducked behind Amandine and swung her up in his arms. Fuchsia taffeta stuck out in all directions, but he ran with her anyway. Amandine started to laugh. "When I fantasized about us doing this, I hadn't envisioned wearing this dress."

"I'll have it off you soon enough." Gaspard tightened his grip on her. "But you were right. This thing does itch like hell."

"Told you so!"

"So you did." He somehow managed the trick of unlocking and opening the door of his place while still carrying her. She loved how strong he was.

He took her right into her bedroom. Amandine kicked the door shut behind them with her foot and slammed her husband up against it.

They kissed, and then kissed and kissed again. Exploring. Sharing. Deeper, and deeper still. Amandine closed her eyes to better savor him—acutely aware of the hard muscle and warm skin under his suit. She could do this forever, except that there were too many layers of fabric between them.

"Get this dress off me," she whispered in his ear, and he unzipped it and yanked it off in record speed. He threw it over his shoulder, not even bothering to look where it landed.

"That thing was a travesty," he said into her mouth. "But this ..." Gaspard's hands ran down the length of her spine and flared out over her hips. She shivered under his touch. *More.* He ran his rough palms up over her stomach and then he reached the undersides of her breasts. Every nerve flared in response to his touch. *This was new.*

"Yes," she moaned.

"*Parfait,*" he murmured, as he cupped her breasts in his warm hands. "So perfect to me." She could feel the urgent stiffness of him as he pushed up against her and that matching throb between her legs drove her wild.

"You're wearing too many clothes," she said, as she pulled off his jacket, then began to unbutton his dress shirt with trembling fingers. "I need them off."

A tiny corner of her mind watched for that reserve

that had marked their encounters before to kick in. She felt like it might kill her now if, all of a sudden, Gaspard threw up barriers between that part of himself she so desperately wanted to access—but most of her was consumed with a frantic need to take his clothes off.

She pushed off his shirt and her hands ran over the beautiful muscles she had admired the morning before as he lay on the flagstones. They were hard yet warm and knit together with stunning perfection. She wanted him. All of him.

This time, she wasn't going to allow for any misunderstandings—she was going to tell him exactly what was on her mind.

"I need you in me," she whispered into the whorl of his ear as she unzipped his pants and curled her fingers around the hard length of him in his boxer briefs.

From the movement under her fingers, she sensed her words electrified him. "You do?" he asked, and the words sounded as if they were ripped right from his heart.

"Yes," she said. "I need to feel you inside me, as close as we can possibly be. I've been longing for you for weeks. I want it to be different this time … *more*."

He gave her a curt nod, and his pants dropped to the floor as well as his briefs. All that was left was Gaspard—her gorgeous, loyal, short-tempered husband.

He swept her up in his arms and half-threw, half-lay her back on the bed, and in one swift movement pulled off her underwear and lobbed it over his shoulder.

She gazed up at him, looming over her, dangerous and familiar and … *hers*.

"I have to warn you," he said. "I don't think I have much restraint left."

The intensity in his eyes made her heart trip with

need. "Good," she said. "Because neither do I."

He fell on her then, pinning her to the bed with his body as though she was going to escape. She loved the scent of him—aftershave and his minty shampoo and something else that was ineffably *him*—and how it surrounded her. But she wanted more … so much more.

"I need you *now*," she murmured into his ear. She darted out her tongue and bit his earlobe, just because she could. "I need all of you. Everything."

He pushed himself up on his arms above her and stared down at her, his eyes blacker than she'd ever seen them before. "I can do something about that," he said, and plunged into her in one definitive movement that made Amandine gasp as the shock of him went everywhere. She'd never felt this pleasure before—the wild ecstasy of Gaspard holding nothing back.

All of a sudden, she knew why women in old stories would swoon during lovemaking. It was *this*. This is what they'd been missing before—this absolute abandon. She bucked her hips in response.

Curling his arm around her head with exquisite gentleness, he was ruthless in giving her what she'd asked for. She lost herself in ecstasy as he drove her forward, clutching at his body to bring him closer still, even though he filled her up so completely.

Before, she'd been quiet when they'd made love … they'd both been, but now Gaspard was ripping noises from Amandine's throat that she hadn't even known she could make. His name popped up on a gasp, and then "*oui, oui, oui,*" urging him on. He joined her, whispering her name on an ecstatic sigh, telling her he loved her on the tail of a moan, and that he always had, and that it had been torture to have her in the next bedroom and not do this with her. The fire between them grew even hotter.

Amandine held it back for as long as she could, but

then suddenly the pinnacle was right in front of them. She yelled out his name and he understood exactly what she meant.

"I love you," he groaned and began to explode inside her, but she was already exploding around him, reaching a crest of bliss she never could have imagined in her wildest dreams.

Finally, he collapsed beside her. After a few minutes, he pushed back the stray hairs that had fallen over her face and lifted the duvet and tucked her in. He kissed her on the cheekbone, then on the tip of her nose, then on her lips … as gentle as the wings of a butterfly.

"Go to sleep," he said, smiling down at her. "It's been a day."

She found his hand under the duvet and grabbed it. "Don't leave."

He chuckled. "Trust me, I couldn't move now even if you wanted me to."

She was overcome with a delicious heaviness that stole over all her limbs. Gaspard curled behind her and crossed his arms around her front, pulling her against his warm, firm torso. She felt completely protected, supported, and cherished.

"*Bonne nuit*," she said. "My husband."

Amandine woke up to blinding sunlight. They'd slept in—hardly surprising as they'd fallen asleep, made love a few hours later when she'd stirred awake, then made love again in the early hours of the morning when the ortolans were singing as the sun rose.

She searched inside herself for any feelings of regret or fear but in their place was just … happiness. The Domaine would soon become officially hers. Gaspard and her were married and in a far better version of the love than what they'd had before, and it was Monday. She was going to be late to the vineyards, but for perhaps the first time in her life she didn't care.

She turned over and watched Gaspard. He slept with deep, even breaths, as spent as she was. She finally felt as though she'd seen him the night before—truly seen him in a way that was an immense privilege and a gift. Had it always been that simple? Just … asking him? Telling Gaspard she needed him had unlocked something essential in her husband—a part of him he'd never allowed her to access before.

One of Gaspard's thick, long lashes had fallen and lay on his jawbone. She pressed the pad of her thumb against it, relishing the warmth of him, and then blew the lash towards the window with a wish—that she be brave enough to continue trusting him. Gaspard had never deserved to be punished for all the times her father and brother had let her down.

She focused in on that wonderful nose of his and she couldn't resist reaching up and running her finger over the bridge, lingering in the dip between his two bumps. She'd missed that.

His eyes flew open, and she watched his eyes as he saw her, then remembered where he was, and what had happened. It didn't disappoint. A large, lazy smile grew on his lips.

He leaned forward and kissed her, his lips savoring hers. "Bonjour my love. My wife."

"My husband," she replied and settled her head in the crook of his neck. They both sighed deeply, staring at the ceiling, running their hands over one another—not to any end, just because it felt good.

"Aren't you glad I asked you to marry me?" Amandine asked after she didn't know how long.

He glanced down at her finger as it trailed down his torso. "The happiest I've ever been about anything."

She gazed up at the cracks in the ceiling that she'd seen her first night in her bedroom … their wedding night, even though it certainly hadn't felt like it at the time.

He must have been doing the same thing, because he said, "I never noticed those cracks before. This is the first time I've ever slept in this room."

Amandine stretched to move closer to his hand, which was tracing the curve of her breast. "The first night I was here I decided it looks like a shattered heart … you know … breaking up into pieces."

Gaspard stared up at it, narrowing his eyes as he considered this. Finally, he shook his head against the pillow. "No."

"No what?" She pressed closer to him.

"It's not a broken heart."

"It's not?"

"No, it's an exploding heart."

"Exploding? That doesn't sound good."

"Oh but it is," he rolled her on top so she straddled him. Oh! That felt …. Mmmm … "It's a heart that's exploding from happiness and pleasure and belonging. It's how mine felt last night, and how it's starting to feel right now if you keep doing that—"

Amandine did keep doing it, because her heart was exploding too. She never wanted it to stop.

Chapter Twenty-Four

The days that followed were probably the happiest of Gaspard's life. He and Amandine continued their work during the day, but when they met at night they accessed a world that was completely their own.

It was a world where they explored each other and yet somehow never got to the end of wanting more. Gaspard discovered that his wife had a sensitive spot behind her earlobes, and at the back of each knee, and on the silky skin between her thighs. When he was inside her, every cell in his body was filled with a visceral sense of rightness that he'd never suspected existed.

He'd let her know that he adored hearing she needed him—it was like the green light that gave him permission to enjoy her and enjoy *them*. He also loved it when she trailed a chain of light, torturous kisses down his torso before taking him in her mouth. After that, his thoughts disintegrated entirely.

They were noisy and wild and tender, and it was everything he'd ever dreamed of. The thought that she was his *wife* … well, it made him feel both as fragile as a bubble and like he could conquer the world.

One thing was certain though, what they had between them now felt so completely different from the start of their marriage that he wanted to consecrate this new beginning somehow—maybe have a proper religious ceremony, even though the church aspect wasn't highly important to either of them. He wanted to do something though—something that felt sacred, to make amends for how they'd gone into their wedding for all the wrong reasons. He wanted to do right by her ... his Amandine.

That morning, they'd woken up in each other's arms, as usual, after a busy night love-making.

"I knew it," Amandine murmured in his ear. How he loved to feel her close—her warm breath, her scent of wildflowers and milk soap. The early morning sun was slanting into his bedroom, where they'd decamped because it had the bigger bed for their nocturnal activities.

"Knew what?" His finger traced the soft curve of her hip underneath the duvet.

"I knew that it could be like this between us."

He just leaned down and kissed her, cupping her face in the curve of his palm.

"I've come to an unpleasant conclusion," she said, but the laughter in her voice belied her words.

"Oh? And what's that?"

"You were holding out on me before ... you know, when we were engaged the first time."

He chuckled. "Maybe, but so were you."

He felt her lovely shoulder lift up in a tiny shrug. "I guess. I just can't figure out exactly why. I mean, just consider what we were missing out on."

She gave him a kiss on his chest that filled something essential inside himself. He loved nothing better than feeling her satisfied, and loved, and taken care of. There was nothing to lose by telling her the truth, not when he'd been revealing the truth about himself in so many ways since the night of Jean-Marc's wedding.

"I was scared," he admitted.

"Can you tell me why?" She propped herself up on his chest to better study his face.

His mind flashed back to the sleepover at Luc's that he couldn't go to because he had to look after baby Bertille. "I'm not used to … I'm not used to taking things for myself."

Amandine thought about this for a while and then she gave a funny nod against him. "Seeing how much you've given your whole life, I can see how that could become your default."

He was suddenly weak with relief that they could talk about their barriers, and in that way knock them down one by one, together. "Yes," he murmured, letting his fingers run over the delicious curve of her bottom. "I think that's why … or at least part of the why."

She propped herself up on an elbow then, and stared down at him, her fine blonde eyebrows pulled together. "But don't you see that—in our case anyway—taking also means giving?"

Gaspard just stared at his beautiful wife, stunned. That was it—that was what was different between them this time, and what made it so very, very good. "You're right," he said, his voice ripe with awe. "I never thought of it that way."

"Maybe you can start now," she said, lying back down again and sneaking her hand below the duvet to find him hard and ready. "And we can practice a bit. Do you want me to help?"

He looked down at her, and that tiny self-satisfied grin of hers made him feel as if his heart might burst. Well, that and her delicate fingers wrapped tightly around his length. "Please," he urged in a ragged voice.

She pushed him on his back, and dove beneath the duvet, replacing her hand with her mouth.

"Marry me," he gasped, after a few minutes of exquisite torture. He flipped her over and, plunged deep into that absolutely perfect place of connection.

"I already have," she said, her voice caught on a moan as he stroked her there, at her very core.

"Marry me again." His voice was ripped straight from his soul.

She took her pleasure from him, but in taking it gave it back to him tenfold. She was *such* a good teacher.

"Yes," she cried, but about the marriage or their lovemaking, he couldn't be sure.

They were over at Amandine's Domaine picking up more of her things. Though he preferred her wearing nothing at all, she had started to get sick of the small amount of clothes and such that she had brought in her 'wedding night bag'. How things had changed since then, and Gaspard still had to pinch himself from time to time to convince himself that this was real—that the universe was letting him have this happiness.

He wanted to be able to trust it completely—this thing they had between them—but pasts weren't healed in a day. He felt as though he was making progress though, and his confidence in life giving him something this good without whipping it away again was growing slowly but steadily, like something green and new.

"Are you sure you're okay not living here?" Gaspard

asked Amandine for the umpteenth time. Now that this Domaine was all hers—or would be in three days' time at the will reading when the notary got back from vacation—he felt guilty about asking her to move to his Domaine.

It wasn't nearly as convenient for a winemaker to live away from the main production site and Volnay and Pernand-Vergelesses were on opposite sides of Beaune—a good fifteen-minute drive or more depending on the amount of impatient drivers around the ring road. He wanted to give Amandine everything, and the fact he couldn't come up with a way to give her this was driving him around the bend.

"Yes, I'm sure," she said, leaning over and kissing him to underline it. "I mean, we both know it's not ideal for me but you have more sisters than me and we need to be around for them. Anyway, I was solidly outvoted by Éloise—she's already living at your place and has no intention of coming back here."

Gaspard grinned to himself. Éloise had been overjoyed when, after they'd discussed it over themselves, they decided to ask her which living set-up she preferred. When she discovered that she could stay with Bertille and become a true part of her best friend's crazy, raucous, loving sisterhood, with Amandine and Gaspard in the cottage right next door ... well ... she had leapt around the room hugging everyone. There was little risk of her changing her mind.

Gaspard gathered Amandine in his arms, despite the fact that she'd been in the middle of folding a sweater. He gave her a kiss and balanced his chin on the top of her blonde head. "When Bertille and Éloise graduate and decide what they want to do, then we'll be free to move in here."

"You wouldn't mind?"

Gaspard shook his head. "Not at all."

"You wouldn't care about being so far away from your vineyards?" Amandine asked, a pucker between her brows illustrating that she was genuinely perplexed.

"The people I care about have always been more important to me than my vineyards."

She stepped back from his embrace and cast him a hurt look. "Was that a dig meant for me?"

Well … the vineyards had always been of the utmost importance for Amandine in a way he'd never been able to comprehend, but he hadn't meant to criticize her. Panic froze him for a few seconds, terrified that this misunderstanding could lead to another break-up … was this life snatching back what he didn't deserve?

But no. He had to try to do it differently this time. To talk. To explain. To speak. "I'm so sorry," he said. "That came out completely wrong. It was not what I meant at all." Really, he'd been trying to share his frustrations with winemaking with her. He knew her views were completely different, but somehow that tether of connection they had forged between them convinced him that he could trust Amandine to try to understand. "I've been thinking about our conversation about volunteering at the fire station. I can't get it out of my mind, and now there's Louise helping me …"

Indeed, Gaspard's first impressions had been correct. Louise was picking up speed, and she had begun to bring a few of her own ideas forward. They were—and he was sure it wasn't just brotherly bias—brilliant. She would surpass him as a winemaker eventually and that left him with only one emotion—that of immense relief. Well, that and pride.

Amandine was still considering. He could see the

tension in her capable, strong limbs. He had tried to change their pattern and now all he could do was wait for her to decide what to do. After what felt like a long while, she took a deep breath and gave him a radiant smile. "I see what you did there," she said. "And I appreciate it."

"I don't want to mess this up," he said, gesturing with his hand back and forth in the space between them. "I don't want to make the same mistake we did last time."

She stepped back into his arms. *Ah.* No, he couldn't lose her. "I don't want to mess it up either," she said. "It's just too good."

He kissed the top of her head and just held her against him. He could stay like this for an eternity.

"If Louise is doing well in the vineyards, I really think you should try volunteering for the auxiliary fire force," she said. "Or at least look into it. I got what I wanted. I want the same for you."

He looked down into those leaf-green eyes of hers. For the first time, she was trying, truly trying, to understand things from a perspective that wasn't her own. He knew how much that must be counterintuitive for her, because her thinking had always veered between black and white, but she was making the effort for him.

"*Merci,*" he said softly.

"So, are you going to look into it?" she demanded.

"Are you going to keep harassing me if I don't?"

"Definitely," she said.

"Glad to hear it. I will look into it, and do you know what?"

"What?"

"*Je t'aime.*"

She kissed him. "I love you too. Now, please let me

fold my sweaters so we can go back home and jump into your huge bed."

He laughed and grabbed a sweater from the pile she'd dumped on the floor and began folding it too. "I'm keen on that plan. I'm going to help so it goes faster."

As they folded Gaspard tried to get used to the unfamiliar sensation of somebody helping and supporting him rather than the other way around. It definitely didn't feel natural, and he was still niggled by guilt. Maybe if he could find a way to help her with something—besides folding sweaters that was.

Then he thought of something—it wasn't much, but it was a thing he just sensed was bothering Amandine. If he was honest, it was bothering him too.

"How are you feeling about how things were left between you and Jean-Marc?" he asked.

She stared down at the sweater she held in her hands. "Weird," she said. "Sort of … unfinished, I guess."

He waited. There was more. He wished he could tell her about Julie's pregnancy, but she'd sworn him to secrecy. The idea of betraying the trust of a pregnant woman didn't sit well with him, even for Amandine. Besides, what difference did it make? Amandine had won the Domaine. She'd beaten Jean-Marc once and for all.

After a minute or two, she found more words. "The whole conversation with him left me feeling so uneasy. He reacted so differently than I'd expected. I just can't figure out what to make of it."

"Do you think maybe … maybe he really was hurt by you not inviting him to our wedding?"

She shook her head at first, then it morphed into a nod. "Normally, I would scoff at that, but I got the impression he was truly sad. He was just in such a strange mood that night. I can't figure it out."

"It does sound out-of-character for him."

"And now … I haven't seen him once since the wedding and you know I've been coming here almost every day to check up on the place and work in the *cuverie*—there's no sign of him," she continued. "He seems to have accepted his defeat without a protest. He hasn't even questioned our marriage or tried to challenge it. I want to just be grateful but instead it makes me suspicious … I keep asking myself, what is he up to?"

"Maybe nothing," Gaspard thought back to that unexpected note of relief in Jean-Marc's voice when he realized Amandine had beat him. Gaspard had recognized it and understood it. He would feel something similar if someone lifted the responsibility for his own vineyard entirely from his shoulders.

She frowned. "I wish I could believe that. I *want* to believe that, but I can't let myself. I can't trust him. I'm just waiting for the other shoe to drop."

Gaspard thought then of how he could help put Amandine's mind at ease and help build back the shaky foundations of a new relationship with her brother. He wouldn't tell her right away though, he needed to plan first.

"Maybe getting married was the best thing we ever did," he said instead. "And maybe everything is going to work out. Can you just try believing that for a little while?"

She chuckled. "And maybe you're lulling me into a false sense of security."

"Maybe."

Chapter Twenty-Five

Two days after Amandine moved into his house for good, Gaspard found himself driving past the fire station on his way back home from Beaune.

Amandine's words flashed into his head and he was shocked anew that the dream of firefighting hadn't been extinguished by all the years and responsibilities he'd taken on. It had been stifled by that heavy weight, definitely, but judging from the excited leap in his chest it had not been snuffed out.

Trying not to think too hard about what he was doing, Gaspard parked his Citroen and walked in, resolutely shoving away his doubts. Why would they ever want a winemaker like him? He had no experience in firefighting. He had no training. He'd never been able to join the young firefighters clubs when he was younger like Luc, because he had far too many responsibilities at home between his sisters and the vines.

He felt his hands shake and shoved them into the pockets of his jeans. Why did it feel so terrifying to do something for himself for no other reason than he wanted to? Well … he knew why, but it still didn't stop the panic gnawing at him.

He would never had taken this step, he realized now,

if Amandine hadn't suggested it. In trying to understand him, she'd given him more strength than she realized.

It was thinking of her that allowed him to take one step, and then another, past a gleaming firetruck being washed outside in the sun and a few firefighters laying out their equipment of oxygen tanks and ropes and consulting with each other as they checked them over.

He couldn't put his finger on why he'd always longed for this career, but maybe everything in his life didn't need to have a reason behind it.

His heart stuck in his throat with excitement when he thought of wearing one of those blue uniforms himself, or climbing up a ladder to help someone, or best of all, saving a life that would otherwise be lost.

He found himself in the fire station office, where people both in and out of uniform buzzed around, looking busy ... surely too busy with important things to deal with someone trying to realize his boyhood dream of being a fireman.

"*Puisse-je vous aider?*" A man in dark-blue pants with a red stripe down the side of each leg and a lighter-blue polo shirt with red epaulettes—the off-duty uniform—asked him from the other side of the plexiglass.

"Ah ..." Gaspard began, but found himself tongue-tied. He couldn't truly ask for this ... could he?"

The man raised his eyebrows.

It all came out in a rush. "I wondered if you were recruiting any volunteer firefighters right now?" Gaspard said. "If so, I would like to apply. I'm strong, and not afraid of heights—"

"Wait." The fireman pointed his ballpoint pen at him. "Aren't you a winemaker?"

"*Oui,*" Gaspard admitted. No point in lying about that.

"Thought so. I'm from Pommard."

The villages of Pommard and Volnay lay so closely together, and were so interlinked by families and bloodlines that it was pretty much guaranteed this stranger and him were somehow connected.

"I'm Gaspard, from Domaine Arnoux."

"Of course!" The man nodded and shook his pen at Gaspard with more enthusiasm. "You're the one with all those stunning sisters."

First impressions be damned, Gaspard glowered at the man.

The man laughed. "Don't worry—I don't have designs on any of them. Just sincere admiration. Wait there." He lifted a finger and asked a man behind him to mind the desk. He walked around the plexiglass and put his hand out for Gaspard to shake.

Gaspard hesitated for a second, but the man's face was so clearly good-natured that he ended up shaking it.

"My name's Bastien Lafarge," he said, shaking Gaspard's hand heartily.

Suddenly, the name shuffled through Gaspard's mind, and he made the connection. "Wait … are you related to Alec Lafarge?" Alec was a fine winemaker, a year or two younger than Gaspard, who was based in Pommard and had taken over the family Domaine. He and Gaspard had a few plots that abutted each other and knew each other well enough to wave and stop for brief chats about the local winemaking scuttlebutt.

Bastien nodded. "He's my younger brother."

"Oh … but … wait—"

"I know what you're thinking," Bastien grinned. "Why didn't I take over the Domaine if I was the oldest?"

"Yeah," Gaspard said, fascinated despite himself.

Bastien shrugged. "To put it bluntly, I didn't want to."

"And your family?" Gaspard asked. This was not the sort of statement that tended to go over well in dynastic Burgundian winemaking families.

Bastien laughed. "They were horrified. Absolutely horrified, not to mention extremely angry with me, but Alec always wanted to be a winemaker. He's far better at it than I'd ever be. It was the most pragmatic solution, even though it took my parents almost a year to come around."

"So … how long have you been doing this?" Gaspard asked.

"Three years," Bastien said.

"And?"

"I love it," he said, and the contented expression on his face told its own story. "I made the right choice. Winemaking is great for Alec, but I never wanted a job that was twenty-four hours of responsibility. I had no desire to manage employees. I wanted to be part of a team, not the boss of one."

"I know what you mean." Something about Bastien, who was hardly a stranger after all—Gaspard was certain they were probably loosely related by blood in the not-too-distant past like everyone from Pommard and Volnay—made Gaspard feel, after many years, that he was truly understood. *Enfin*, here was someone who spoke the same language as him—a far cry from the slavish devotion to the vineyards he'd always been surrounded by.

Gaspard began confessing far more than he'd planned on. "The winemaking … well, I had no choice about that, but I've always wanted to do this." He waved his hand in an uncharacteristically dramatic gesture, encompassing the whole fire station and everything in it.

"Same with me," Bastien said. "I've always had a cool head in a crisis so I can contribute something valuable here. The best thing is—well, that's hard to say actually as there are so many good things about my job—I do my hours in the station, do my absolute best to help people, then I go home and sleep well. I don't have to worry about rot on the vines or clouds that might bring hail or a barrel of wine turning to vinegar."

Gaspard nodded, relating to all of this deep in his bones.

"Firefighting is not for everyone, but for me, it's the right choice."

"I'm jealous," Gaspard admitted. He truly was.

"Don't be jealous." Bastien put his hands on his hips. "It's never too late to change things. How would you like a tour?"

Gaspard truly felt like a young boy again—before his mother had left and his father had remarried. He was reminded how it felt to be excited by life and all its possibilities as Bastien showed him around the fire station.

Bastien was remarkably thorough as a tour guide and his visit included climbing up into the trucks, sliding down the pole, and explaining every minute detail of the active-duty firefighting uniforms.

It was clear that Bastien's enthusiasm for his chosen profession had not waned one iota in his three years on the job. His eyes were bright, and he seemed thrilled to take time out of his day to show Gaspard around. He even took Gaspard up to the bunk house where the firefighters slept when they were on duty. There was a women's wing and a men's wing, with shared spaces in between.

Bastien told Gaspard proudly that they had six female firefighters on staff who could best many of the men in arm wrestles and had bravery and cleverness to spare. Gaspard heard that with no small amount of relief, as he would never fit in a place that didn't treat women equally.

When they finally found themselves back at the front of the station, they chatted for so long that the slant of the sun made Gaspard realize he'd completely lost track of time. This had gone so much better than he ever could have imagined. He felt a wave of gratitude for his wife, who had encouraged him to look into it.

"So … have you got any volunteer positions open?" Gaspard asked.

Bastien shook his head slowly. Gaspard's heart sunk. He hadn't realized how much he wanted this until now.

"But," Bastien said. "One of our squad just got transferred to Paris. His wife was offered a huge promotion at work."

"What does that mean?" Gaspard asked, sensing from the dramatic pause in Bastien's speech that the next words out of his mouth were important.

"It means we have a regular position to fill. We were going to start taking applications next week but—"

"But what?" Gaspard asked.

Bastien put his hands on his hips and studied Gaspard. Finally, he shrugged. "I see myself in you, I guess. I'm fairly certain that if you don't at least try to do this, it will nag you for a long time to come."

Gaspard felt this parallel between their lives too, but then again, Bastien had his brother waiting in the wings, eager to take over, and he didn't have a flock of sisters to care for either.

"But the vineyards." Gaspard bit his lip.

Bastien crossed his arms across his chest. "Is there no one in your family who would be interested in taking over?"

"There's my sister, Louise. She recently changed career direction and started helping me, but she's a fast learner and she tells me that winemaking is what she wants to do. However, partnering with her brother and running the place herself are two very different things."

Bastien's face lit up. "Louise? I went to school with Louise. She was always the smartest person in the class. She's back from Paris?"

Gaspard nodded, not quite sure what to do with Bastien's enthusiasm about his sister.

"I would bet that Louise is capable of anything she decides to do."

Bastien's assessment, while maybe a little too *interested*, also happened to be perfectly true. "I agree," he said.

Bastien nodded. "Well, there you go."

"But—"

"Look … firefighting positions don't come up very often. Sometimes years go by between new posts. I don't know you that well, Gaspard, and I know our situations are different, but I sense that you were cornered into winemaking like I was. Even though nobody in Burgundy believes it, not all of us are cut out to do that, despite what other people's expectations of us might be."

Gaspard was thinking too hard to answer.

"Besides," Bastien continued. "Let me explain something to you about fireman's hours. Because it's four days on, five days off, many of us have second jobs—often in the vineyards. The two aren't as incompatible as you might initially think."

Gaspard squinted up at the sun. Besides Amandine,

he'd never wanted anything quite this much. Did he dare take it? Louise had made it clear she was willing and able to assume more responsibility in the vineyards. Amandine had given him hope that maybe he could start going after things he wanted now. Maybe, like Amandine said, taking could also be a form of giving.

"Look," Bastien said, finally. "This job has given a meaning to my days that I'd been looking for my whole life. Do you want to see the photos of the people I saved?"

Gaspard nodded. He did. He really did.

Bastien reached into his back pocket and took out his wallet, removing a bunch of newspaper clippings, some so worn that they could barely be read, but the photos were still visible. A family stood in front of their charred house in St. Romain; an elderly man and his wife clung to each other under emergency blankets in Dezize-les-Maranges, and several more of the same.

"You saved all these people?" Gaspard asked. That would be something—a truly concrete way to help.

Bastien nodded. "They're out there, living their lives, because I got them out. I'm not saying I don't appreciate a wonderful bottle of wine as much as the next person, but saving these people ... it gives me something in here." He touched his sternum with his fist. "That winemaking never could."

"I get it," Gaspard said, and he absolutely did. This was what he had always wanted.

"You'll have to pass the tests still, and qualify and everything but what I'm asking you is, are you in?"

Gaspard thought of Amandine. She had freed something in him, given him faith that life wasn't out to take from him and never give.

"I'm in," he said.

Chapter Twenty-Six

He'd been planning on telling Amandine all about his conversation with Bastien on his way back from the station—as well as about the application tucked away in his bag on the passenger seat of his car—but he'd found her in her vineyards. She was pruning, her face glowing with exertion and with a streak of vineyard mud across her right cheekbone.

She had always been happy in the vineyards, but now with the knowledge that they were hers, she was unstoppable.

"*Bonjour toi*!" She stopped her work and opened her arms wide. He walked right into them and planted a bruising kiss on her lips. Things between them were so perfect … he felt an odd and not entirely pleasant mix of elation and fear that somehow, without meaning to, he would make a mistake and screw everything up. It was easier to kiss her than think about that.

"*Ca promet,*" she murmured against his mouth after things started to get a little too rowdy for plain daylight, especially with several other winemakers dotting the plots around where they kissed.

"Were you just in Beaune?" she asked. It was the perfect opening. He opened his mouth to tell her he was thinking about applying for the full-time position—that was the sort of thing one was supposed to talk about with their spouse, wasn't it? Probably, but he was such a novice at this relationship stuff, not to mention the marriage stuff. It all felt very, very fragile.

"Yes," he said simply, his mind hampered by anxiety.

What if she felt it was too fast to apply for the full-time position? What if they fought about it like they did about the vineyards last time? He had barely survived losing her the first time around. Now he'd glimpsed the life he could have with her, and he knew with absolute certainty that losing Amandine a second time would destroy him.

"What were you there for?" She had gone back to pruning off errant shoots while they chatted. She was nothing if not efficient.

He should tell her … but tell her what exactly? Nothing was certain yet. What was the point of telling her anything before he actually got the job? There might be nothing to tell. Bastien had given Gaspard a blunt warning that the qualification process was grueling and difficult. Only a few of the candidates even made it through.

If he didn't get the job, he knew he'd be embarrassed and disappointed. Those were the kinds of emotions he preferred to deal with alone—he wasn't in the habit of inflicting his pain on others, and he had no inclination to start, especially on his wife when this thing between them was so new. If he failed, the less she knew about it, the better.

"Cat got your tongue?" she asked him, but she was intent on inspecting a shoot to decide to snip it or not. She didn't seem overly concerned.

No, he wasn't going to say anything. Going after his

dreams was such a new and terrifying thing for Gaspard—he needed to keep it as small as possible to start with. There would be plenty of time to celebrate with her if he was offered the position but that was still a long way off, and most likely would never happen.

"Are you up to something?" she asked, but without looking up, and with laughter in her voice. That was when he caught a flash of her diamond under the sun.

He caught her left hand. "Just blinded by that diamond," he joked to cover his tracks. Also, to cover up the squeeze of his heart. How incredible it was to see his grandmother's ring on the hand of the woman he loved. *No, he could not screw this up again.* "When did you start wearing it?"

She stood up then to meet his eyes and rested her secateurs carefully down on top of the nearest post.

"I put it on at Jean-Marc's wedding. I took it off because I wasn't sure I wanted to wear it to work in the vineyards, but I put it on this morning before leaving the house," she said, turning the ring this way and that on her finger with her other hand. "It just felt right. Besides, I reasoned that diamonds are tough, right? I love it you know … did I ever get the chance to tell you that? It's perfect."

He took her left hand again and pressed it, fingers splayed, across his chest. "How do you get me right here?" he asked her. "Every time. Straight to my heart."

She smiled and kissed him, with her hand still between them.

Eventually they had to stop themselves yet again, as they were pushing the bounds of public decency. She sighed, understanding the necessity. "I should get this pruning done," she admitted. "I'll be angry with myself if I don't."

"I'll stop ravishing you while you're trying to work," Gaspard grinned. "I need to go to Volnay and check in with Louise anyway. "I'll see you tonight," he said. "I'll have dinner ready. What do you feel like eating?"

She answered by taking a playful nip of his earlobe.

"That's dessert," he said. "I meant before that."

She winked at him. "That's the course I'm most looking forward to."

He left her with a final kiss, feeling happier than he had any right to be.

At his Domaine, Louise was busy in the vineyards, like Amandine. She was pruning too and looking just as happy as his wife had. They were both completely in their elements in the vines in a way he had never been.

They hadn't seen each other that morning at breakfast so they gave each other the quick *bises* and Louise promptly launched into a status update of what she'd been doing and what she thought their priorities were. Every word out of her mouth illustrated to Gaspard just how capable she would be at taking on more responsibilities.

The thing was that Gaspard refused to have those responsibilities imposed on her like they'd been imposed on him. He would not make the mistake of assuming she wanted to do this long term just because she was so good at it.

Just as he was formulating that question, she jumped in with her plans for the next few days in the vineyards and how they should most efficiently split up their tasks.

"I'm ready to work for a couple of hours this afternoon," he said. "But tomorrow I have some errands to run in the morning and on Friday I want to go with Amandine to the notary's office for the reading of her father's will."

Louise turned to him, squinting into the sun. "Ah! The notary's finally coming back from the Côte D'Azur?"

"*Oui.* I'm not sure how Amandine is going to feel afterwards—if she's going to feel like celebrating or crying or going back to work, but whichever way it lands, I need to be there for her."

Louise studied his face. "You're a good husband, you know."

He smiled to himself. They had kept their recent closeness to themselves, and as far as he knew neither his sisters nor their friends were aware of the change. It wasn't that he and Amandine were hiding it. It just felt right to keep it to themselves for a bit. "I try to be."

Louise crossed her arms, resting the shears on her hip. "I can't put my finger on it, but I get the impression that something fundamental has changed between you and Amandine ever since Jean-Marc's wedding. Am I completely off-base?"

Damn his sisters for being so eerily perceptive. He should be used to that by now. Well, they were going to find out sooner rather than later, and it wasn't exactly a state secret. Besides, a growing part of him was so happy and proud to claim Amandine as his that he wanted to climb on top of the hill above Pernand-Vergelesses and shout it out for all to hear. "No, you're not entirely off-base."

"So am I right that your marriage is now ... well, not

just about the inheritance anymore?"

Gaspard nodded. "You are."

She bounced on the balls of her feet and grasped her brother in a huge hug. "I'm so happy for you," she said. "You were meant to be together and seeing you two now … well, it gives me hope for myself."

Gaspard laughed. "There's no rush, Louise, you have plenty of time. You have to figure out who you are first before adding anyone else to the equation."

"Yes, Father." She rolled her eyes.

"Sorry, I swear I don't mean to sound paternalistic."

She waved her hand in a dismissive gesture. "It's fine. Anyway, back to work. I was wondering about these shoots—"

Gaspard lifted up his palm to her. "That's what I actually came to talk about. I was wondering … if I were ever to take a slight step back from the Domaine, how would you feel about taking a step forward? I'll always be here to help if you need me, but the Domaine has taken up so much of my life these past several years … I would like a bit more breathing room. I'd like to see what you would do if you were to take charge for a bit."

Louise stared at him, her mouth slightly open and her blue eyes wide.

Gaspard didn't want to mention the job application a few meters away in his car to Louise any more than he did to Amandine. It was still such early days—what was the point? Besides, Bastien had mentioned four days on and five days off—in which case if he was lucky enough to get the job he could still help.

"Why do you look so shocked?" he asked, then it occurred to him in a blinding flash. Maybe, like him, she never wanted such a burden but didn't know how to tell him. "If you're not interested, just say the word—"

"No! I'm interested," she assured him, hastily. "I'm just having a hard time imagining anyone not wanting to do this."

Gaspard laughed. "Amandine is the same as you, she's trying, but I know deep down she just doesn't understand it—but we're all different you know. As hard as it may be for people in Burgundy to believe, not everybody is born to be a winemaker."

Louise considered this, and from the surprise written over her features it was clear this novel idea had never occurred to her. "I guess that makes sense," she said finally. "You know, law of averages and all that, but I just assumed because you were always so competent at it that you loved it too."

Gaspard shook his head. "I wish I did, but I don't." Something in him that had been trapped down by all his years of pretending soared free. It felt wonderful … liberating.

"Is it wrong of me that I'm glad you don't?" Louise asked, with a wince.

"No," Gaspard assured her.

"Good, because that leaves more room for me to make my mark, doesn't it? Not that I won't be asking for your help, because I will, but I like the idea of being in charge. Does that shock you?"

"Does your ambition shock me?" How could she possibly think that when he had always encouraged that trait in all his sisters? "I wouldn't have it any other way, Louise. I'm hoping it also means that, along the way, I maybe did something right."

Louise fixed him with that penetrating gaze of hers. "Gaspard, you did everything right, by all of us. If you want to take some distance from this, I may not understand it, but you have earned it one-hundredfold."

Gaspard leaned over and kissed her cheek. "Thank you *ma soeurette*," he said. "Now, let's begin as we mean to continue, for the next little while, at least. You're the boss. Where do you need me?"

The next morning, Gaspard and Amandine kissed then went their separate ways.

Gaspard found himself sitting on a molded plastic chair in the medical laboratory on the Rue de Lorraine In Beaune, waiting his turn to get a blood test that was required to go along with the physical health portion of his fireman's application.

He was just going to fill out and submit the application as quickly as possible, he'd decided, before his mind started to question what he was doing, or, worse yet, why he hadn't told his wife about it?

He'd again considered telling her the night before, after they'd made love for a second time in the shower and lay, damp and entangled, in his bed, but he couldn't quite bring himself to take the risk.

"Gaspard?" A voice snapped him out of his reverie. He looked up, and there was Julie, with a bright-pink requisition in her hand. Of all the coincidences. What a coincidence. He'd been planning on asking Julie and Jean-Marc to dinner to try and ease the tension between them and Amandine—that, at least, was something he could help her with in the same way she'd helped him with the firefighting thing. He knew a meal would be far less awkward in the raucous, noisy atmosphere of family dinners at his house. His sisters left no time for tense silences.

Then he remembered about the pregnancy. He honestly hadn't thought much about it since she confided her secret to him—his mind had been too full of firefighting and Amandine for much else. He couldn't help but notice the number of boxes ticked on her requisition. He leapt up to give her *les bises*, then offered her his chair.

She smiled and took it gratefully.

He leaned down to her. "How are you feeling?" he asked. "Is everything … all right?"

She shrugged her shoulders. "I have my first ultrasound soon," she said. "But because of some … concerning symptoms they need to check a bunch of things."

He could tell from the strain around her eyes that she was worried. He put his hand on her shoulder. "I'm sorry," he said simply. "I hope everything ends up being fine."

She sighed. "Thank you. It's been stressful. We both want this baby so much." She ducked her head and blinked rapidly before taking a deep breath and looking up at him as brightly as she could manage. "Anyway, what's new with you? Please distract me from this horrible waiting game I'm in."

Gaspard nodded, his heart going out to Julie and even surprisingly, to Jean-Marc. "How is Jean-Marc? I don't believe he and Amandine have crossed paths since your wedding."

"Well, they will the day after tomorrow." Julie took a deep breath. "At the will reading."

"Right." Gaspard nodded, aware of an odd alliance between him and Julie. "I know we can't sit in on it, but I was planning on taking Amandine and waiting around … you know, just in case …"

Julie smiled a knowing smile. She was savvy, Gaspard realized, in her own unique way—not someone to be underestimated, terrible fashion choices withstanding. "I was thinking the exact same thing."

They shared a complicit smile. "How is Jean-Marc though?" Gaspard asked again.

Julie thought about this for a moment. "You know what … he is actually, surprisingly good. He went to the job center and has been poring over the course catalogue for the technical school. I think somehow he's relieved to have the vineyards taken away from him."

Gaspard nodded. He, perhaps more than anyone, could understand that. "I'm glad. Also, you know that Amandine said she has every intention of giving him a monthly salary from the Domaine, even when she inherits the whole thing. She's a very fair person."

Julie tilted her head. "I never doubted it. Funnily enough, neither did Jean-Marc from what I could tell. I think maybe they just both needed a bit of space from each other. I'm hoping finalizing things at the will reading will be a new start, not just for the Domaine but much more importantly for them as siblings."

"I have been thinking about that," Gaspard said. "Would you and Jean-Marc like to come over for a family dinner? Why don't you come tomorrow night so they can see each other before the notary's office? My sisters will be there, and Éloise of course, so even if there is some initial tension, I don't see how it won't be drowned by the sheer chaos that reigns."

Julie considered this. "That is a brilliant idea," she said finally. "It will give them a chance to see each other in a non-confrontational way before the will reading. I love it."

"Will you be feeling up to it?" Gaspard nodded down at the requisition in Julie's hand.

"I'm sure I'll be fine," she said. "I'd rather keep busy while waiting for results anyway."

"Good," Gaspard said. "Seven o'clock then?"

"Perfect. I'll get Jean-Marc there, and you and I will force our spouses to behave for once."

"All I can promise is that I'll try with Amandine," said Gaspard, with a wink. "I have no doubt that with you as his wife, Jean-Marc will be toeing the line in no time."

She placed her hand on her belly and sighed. "And our baby, God willing."

Gaspard reached down again and squeezed her shoulder.

She looked up suddenly with alarm. "You didn't tell anyone, did you?"

"About the pregnancy?"

She nodded.

"Of course not, although now that we've bumped into each other, I wanted to ask you, can I tell Amandine at least?"

She shook her head wildly. "Please don't. If the ultrasound ... well, if things don't work out, I don't want to have to deal with everyone's sympathy. Neither would Jean-Marc, I'm certain. In that case, I would want it to stay private—I know not everyone is like that but it's just what I'd prefer. We'll tell everyone when we get the all-clear, but not before. It helped me to confide in you at the wedding though," she said. "Please know I'm grateful for that. I would have burst if I didn't tell someone, and I knew I could trust you. Now, with all these tests ... well, I'm glad I kept it a secret."

Gaspard nodded, understanding her reasoning. "I

won't tell a soul," he said. "Promise."

"I didn't think to ask why you're here." Julie's eyes widened in alarm. "Is everything all right with you?"

He smiled down at her. "I'm thriving," he said. "I'm just here for routine bloodwork. Nothing to worry about."

Just then, the woman in a white lab coat behind the desk shouted out, "Gaspard Arnoux. Here for blood-work to be sent to the applications department at the fire station?"

He slid a rueful glance at Julie, who was looking up at him like she'd never seen him before. The cat was out of the bag.

"A fireman?" Julie said. "You kept that well-hidden."

"Now it seems I have a favor to ask you," he said. "Can you keep it a secret? I'm just applying. It's more likely than not that I won't get the job. I figured what's the point of telling people if—"

"Don't worry," Julie said. "Your secret is safe with me—just as safe as my secret is with you. You know what? It's lovely to have a brother-in-law. I feel like someone is on my side ... besides Jean-Marc, of course."

He reached out and squeezed her shoulder. "I'm always on your side." He followed the white-coated lady to one of the rooms.

Chapter Twenty-Seven

The next day, Amandine didn't stay late in the vineyards, even though the days had reached their peak of daylight and she could work until almost nine o'clock if she chose.

For the first time in her life, she was eager to finish her workday, get back to her new home, and feast her eyes on her husband.

It was frightening how much she loved him now that she let herself, and how much that love grew with every interaction they had—every shared look that made them feel alone in a room full of their sisters, every noise that escaped their lips as they fought to get as close to each other as possible, the hushed laughter as they talked about everything and nothing as they lay in their bed, sated and connected, after their lovemaking.

Amandine didn't recognize herself and couldn't exactly trust this new, fragile happiness either, but she was trying … she was really trying.

This could last, she would tell herself. This could get just better and better. What they had discovered between them had been far more intense and wonderful than Amandine ever could have fantasized about in her wildest daydreams, but she was realizing that sometimes getting what you've been wishing for was the scariest thing of all. She was trying to be brave and let herself trust her husband. It was hard though, not letting all the times she'd been let down in the past color her present.

As she drove back through Beaune towards Volnay, she wondered what Gaspard had made for dinner. He was an incredible cook and had been used to preparing meals for his sisters for years. He was just so attractively *competent* and generous. What had she done, she wondered often, to deserve the love of a man such as him?

She was always ravenous when she got back to his place. It was a good thing their meals were very much family style as she had no patience to shower beforehand.

She shouted *bonjour* as she came in the front door and headed towards the comforting noise in the kitchen. Gaspard's big, crazy family was so easy to love. She tried very hard not to think about how awful it would be if it was ever taken away from her. There was no reason why it would be, she told herself. Trust was a muscle and she had to work every moment of every day to strengthen it.

She walked into the kitchen but stopped halfway to the table when she saw who was sitting there. Jean-Marc and Julie were ensconced beside Éloise, participating animatedly in the conversation.

Jean-Marc looked up. "Amandine!" he said, a warmth in his voice that she didn't recognize. "Surprise!"

What was this ambush? Her lungs felt like they'd been filled with concrete, and she flashed back to all the other times her brother and father had played nasty tricks on her.

Her husband turned then. He'd been taking something out of the oven and was clutching a casserole in his hands. He placed it on the table, then came over to her, his eyes guarded.

"Did you know about this?" she hissed to him.

He studied her face. "Yes. I bumped into Julie yesterday and I invited them."

"Why didn't you tell me?" Indeed, there had been ample opportunity the night before. They'd made love on the couch, and then with Amandine perched on the kitchen counter with her legs wrapped around Gaspard's waist and her head thrown back. All that time, he was keeping this from her?

He bit his lip. "Maybe I should have, but Julie and I thought maybe it would be nice for you and Jean-Marc to see each other before tomorrow in a completely non-confrontational setting. Besides, look at how happy Éloise is." He gestured with his oven mitt over to Éloise who was laughing with Julie and Bertille, her face full of joy. Jean-Marc, on the other hand, was looking worriedly at Gaspard and Amandine conferring in the corner.

"I just wish you'd asked me first," Amandine said, trying very hard to keep her voice even. Every instinct was telling her to get angry at him and then retreat, like she'd always done with the men in her family. It was the only way to protect herself. How dare he spring this on her?

"I guess I was afraid you would say no," he admitted. "I thought it was for the best."

"I know you did," she said through clenched teeth. It took every ounce of self-control not to show him just how wrong he'd been. "But *I* know what's best for me, and you have to trust me on that."

Gaspard considered this. "You're right. Old habits … you know … I apologize."

This was one of those times when she needed to prac-

tice trust. She hated this type of surprise, but she searched deep in herself to conclude that Gaspard had done it for the right, if misguided, reasons.

It smells delicious," she said, stiffly. "What are we having?"

"Endives in béchamel sauce." He leaned forward and kissed her while sighing in relief. "Your favorite."

Her sense of humor, and her husband's charm, got the better of her, despite everything. She cocked a brow. "Peace offering?"

He tapped his temple. "Crazy like a fox."

She kissed him, pushing down all those voices in her head screaming at her to protect herself. "I love you."

He kissed her back, and suddenly the whole room erupted into a *ban bourgignon.* They'd let the cat out of the bag.

"So you do love each other!" Margaux crowed as Amandine finally took her place at the table. She regretted their carelessness, but not the kiss itself. Never the kiss itself.

When she met Jean-Marc's eye, he was, much to her shock, grinning at her. "I'm happy for you," he said in a voice meant only for her. The table was noisy with chatter all around them. "You two seem perfect for each other."

Maybe Gaspard had a point, she thought, in his officiousness. It was easier to do this with the constant cacophony of his sisters around.

"Thank you." She cleared her throat, not quite sure how to handle the sheer incongruity of her current situation. "How have you been?"

"I'm good." He smiled at her, coming across as a different person than he'd been in so, so long. She tried to push down her knee-jerk reaction of distrust. "Great actually. I've been looking at a bunch of courses, trying to think about what interests me."

If he was going to be civil … well, she might as well try too. "Has anything struck you?"

"Lots of things actually. I can't stop thinking about horses."

"Horses?" She took a bite of the endives Gaspard had prepared and suppressed a groan of pleasure. His béchamel was thick and creamy and perfectly spiced with nutmeg. The ham was a bit caramelized on the edges and the endive wrapped inside perfectly braised and seasoned and silky against her tongue. His cooking was really the best possible foreplay.

"Yeah." Jean-Marc ducked his head. "You've seen how more and more of the most valuable appellations are using horses to plow the vines, right?"

Amandine had noticed that too and had been considering it herself. "I have actually."

"Well, I've always liked working with animals and I like working outside … I don't know. It's probably a crazy idea, but I just can't stop thinking about it."

"You'd be great at that," Amandine said, and, much to her surprise, she meant it.

"*Merci,*" he said shyly. "That means a lot, actually."

Who was this stranger who had come and taken over the body of her brother?

"Can you drop by the Domaine sometime next week?" she asked. "We need to discuss your shares in the Domaine and how I can compensate you for them."

Jean-Marc's top lip lengthened. "But Amandine, it's going to be all yours, as of tomorrow anyway. You don't need to transfer anything. You won."

She shook her head. "I don't care what the notary says tomorrow. I'm not going to leave you with nothing—the way Papa set it up was unfair and I plan to correct that. I'll retain ownership but we'll figure out the best way for you to continue deriving an income from it in the way you are due."

"But you don't need to do that."

"I do," she said. "I think we'll both be better off if we decided not to repeat our father's mistakes."

His brows pulled together and he blinked away something that looked suspiciously like tears. "Thank you," he whispered.

She didn't know quite what to make of Jean-Marc's sudden vulnerability after so many years of bracing herself against his bullying, but she added with a shrug, "Maybe we can ... be different too?"

"I'm hoping that," he said.

"Hey Jean-Marc!" Éloise grabbed his arm. "Back me up here. Bertille says there's no such thing as coq au vin made with white wine ... there is, isn't there?"

And just like that, they were both swept into the chaos around the table.

When Gaspard and Amandine found themselves back at his place after Jean-Marc and Julie took their cheery departure and the dishes had been washed and the leftovers put away, Gaspard took her in his arms.

"I'm sorry if I ambushed you," he said. "Like I said, old habits die hard. That managing side to me is unfortunately well-engrained. I'll work on it."

She smiled, a bit tired, despite herself. "It was a good

idea actually, but just for future reference, I'd rather you talked to me first. We have to start discussing things like that."

Something odd flashed across Gaspard's face, and she wondered … She rubbed her shoulder as she watched him.

"Are you sore?" he asked.

"Yeah, I've been going at it pretty hard these past few days."

Gaspard arched a roguish eyebrow, and she laughed. "Yes, I have a sex fiend for a husband, and we've been going at it hard too."

Gaspard's mouth was a study in male smugness. "I have an idea," he said.

"Oh?"

"How about I run us a bath, and you go into the bedroom and take your clothes off and join me in the bathroom."

She chuckled. "That sounds like a lot of effort—will you make it worth my while?"

"*Eh oui,*" he said. "And then some."

"Like I said, sex fiend. Should I leave my ring on?"

"Oh definitely," he said. "Always that."

Chapter Twenty-Eight

The old Amandine would have been exasperated that Gaspard insisted on driving her to the notary's office and sticking around during the meeting. She would have protested that she could do it on her own … that she could do *everything* on her own.

The new Amandine enjoyed being with her husband whenever and wherever, and she appreciated he was there for her with his strong, steady support. At this rate, she might actually become a trusting person one day … well, maybe that was taking it too far, but she would be able to trust her husband in any case.

Jean-Marc at the dinner table had been a bit of a shock, but once she'd convinced herself that Gaspard had set it up for the right reasons and wouldn't keep something like that from her again, she was able to see the logic behind his reasoning. It was nice that she and Jean-Marc could see each other in a neutral setting before the stilted nature of a will reading. She tried her very best to remember that.

This new existence felt very raw, and very exposed, but she was trying to be brave. She had to be brave for this to work. It was impossible for her to stop the old tracks of suspicion her brain was used to running on, but at least she could reason with herself … so far, anyway. The fear that she would trip up was always with her, but she hoped that would fade with time.

Gaspard gave her a kiss when the secretary ushered her into the office. Part of her was hoping that Jean-Marc would also arrive a few minutes early so they could chat again before they sat down in front of the notary, but he was clearly running late.

She sat across from the notary, in awkward silence. Maybe she could try some small talk? That was not her nature, but she was changing, wasn't she? Anyway, she needed a distraction from the ambient scent of fountain pen ink and musty papers that made her want to flee outside and take a deep gulp of fresh air.

"How was your vacation?" she asked him. His normally pale skin had taken on the burnished look of oiled oak.

"Too short," he said. "Have you been to Cassis?"

She shook her head. "No, I don't go on vacation very much."

"You should," he sighed. "It's paradise. I'm just counting the days until my retirement."

Well, that was a sad sort of existence. She tapped her foot against her chair leg, impatient. Where was Jean-Marc? The sooner this was over with, the sooner she could walk out of here with the Domaine in her possession and get on with the rest of her life. That included trying to mend the relationship with Jean-Marc if he was willing to meet her half-way.

Finally, Jean-Marc blew into the room. "Sorry," he said. "Family emergency."

"Is Éloise okay?" Amandine snapped to attention.

Jean-Marc smiled at her—that was new—and waved his hand. "Oh, she's fine. Nothing to do with her.

Everything's fine. Julie was just waiting for some lab results but they're good—fantastic, in fact!"

Again, Jean-Marc was surprising her. Instead of resentful and angry, he seemed the lightest and happiest she had seen him in … well … since she could remember. It was like the light that had been extinguished around the time her mother died had been relit.

"I'm relieved to hear that," she said, and was surprised that she truly meant it. She would try not to hold that pink dress against Julie.

Jean-Marc sat down, his eyes wide. "You really mean that, don't you?"

She nodded. "Of course I do, Jean-Marc."

"Thank you."

The notary cleared his throat and, when they were both facing him again, launched into the reading of their father's will. There seemed to be endless caveats and 'heretofores' and 'wherethatares'.

Jean-Marc quickly slumped down in his chair and at a certain point when the tedium had been dragging out for several minutes already, Jean-Marc met Amandine's eyes and rolled his. That was something they used to do with each other when they were little—a secret language of exasperation and impatience. She'd thought the brother she'd known before he changed had gone forever, yet here he was. Her heart clenched with relief at finding him again, but where had he been all this time, and why?

Finally, the notary reached the juicier stuff. "The rest of the will isn't long as the only asset your father possessed, which even though solitary, is certainly valuable, is the wine Domaine. This includes all the vineyards, the house and all of the attached buildings and all the contents.

The notary then went on to outline each of these vineyards using the land survey information—a hugely tedious process. Good God, how the notaries liked to get into technicalities.

Not long? Amandine was terrified to contemplate sitting in for the reading of a will the notary *did* consider long.

"So, as to who inherits all of this," the notary said. "It is the first one of you who is married."

"Yes, our father informed us of that before he died," Amandine said. "And that's me." She took out the marriage documents and *livret de famille* out of the bag she'd brought with her and pushed them across the desk to the notary.

At the time she'd signed them, the marriage paperwork just seemed like documentation to back up her claim for the Domaine, but now … she almost got misty-eyed looking at them on the notary's huge wooden desk. They meant so much more than she'd initially intended. What she and Gaspard had between them; it was so much more than convenience or even their mind-blowing physical connection—they'd found a home for their souls in each other. Their marriage documents had become precious over the weeks since her wedding to Gaspard. She shook her head in disbelief at this new sentimentality in herself.

The notary held up his hand. "That's not all."

Amandine's head jerked back. "What do you mean? Of course that's all. Our father told us himself from his hospital bed just before he died."

The notary lowered his eyeglasses down his nose and peered over them. "Well, he was very ill, if you remember. He must have forgotten to tell you the whole thing."

What 'whole thing'? The blood froze in her veins.

Amandine whipped her head to Jean-Marc. Was this all part of some elaborate trick? Had they all been lulling her into complacency?

Jean-Marc's face mirrored the incomprehension Amandine was experiencing. "He never told me about anything else but the marriage thing," he said. "I swear."

"Yes, well … as I said, he was not a healthy man." The notary shrugged. "But this will was drawn up two years ago, before his downturn in health."

"What is it?" Amandine snapped, her heart pounding in her chest. "What else is there?"

Jean-Marc nodded. His normally ruddy complexion had gone pale as a sheet. "Tell us."

The notary looked down at the will. "Your father had one other stipulation of the person who inherits the Domaine."

Oh no. That wave of dread Amandine had been trying to hold at bay since deciding to change her ways crashed over her. The floor tilted and chills ran in sickening waves over her limbs, despite the stuffy room.

"What?" Jean-Marc and Amandine said, for once united by their impatience.

"It says here that your father says the person who inherits will be the child who is the first to get married and give birth to a baby in the family bloodline."

What sort of dynastic sick joke was this? Amandine sat back in her chair, feeling like all the blood was draining out of her.

"But what if one of us got married after the other, but has a child first?" Jean-Marc demanded.

Amandine's head snapped to him. She should have maintained her high level of alert. *She should have seen this coming.* This is what she deserved for letting down her defenses—she couldn't bear it.

"Well, the way this is worded it's the first child to be married *and* have a baby, so the baby is the true tie-breaker if you're both married. The baby trumps who got married first."

"This is … this is ridiculous," Jean-Marc spluttered.

"I agree, it does seem very old-fashioned." The notary clicked his tongue. "What if one of you couldn't have natural born children?"

"Our father was not a kind man," Jean-Marc said through gritted teeth, and for once Amandine felt like he was on her side. Could she trust that? Every survival instinct was yelling at her not to. Her mind revved into frantic thinking of how she could regain control over the situation.

Was she and Gaspard having children completely beyond the realm of possibility? She would hate to rush things because of her stupid father, but at the same time, her marriage had turned out far better than she ever could have expected. Still … could she be sure Jean-Marc hadn't been in on this?

"Did you know this?" she turned to him.

His eyes were haunted. "No. I swear to you, Amandine, I'm just as surprised as you are. Papa never mentioned it to me. I had no idea."

"Okay, well … we need to talk about it then." She shot a glance at the notary. "Can we get rid of that provision?"

"I wouldn't advise it." The notary peered down his glasses at them. "You would be caught up in courts for years and it would cost a fortune."

She nodded, disappointed but resigned. "We'll talk," she said to Jean-Marc. "After this, privately—just the two of us."

Jean-Marc opened and shut his mouth a few times, as

if he wanted to say something but couldn't quite get it out.

"Yes," she prompted. "What is it?"

He dropped his head in his hands. "You should know … Julie is pregnant."

Amandine sprung up from her chair, despair fueling her wrath. "What!?!" she seethed. She'd been so stupid, so … pathetic and in love and caught up in her marriage when Jean-Marc had been using that time to plot behind her back.

"Julie's pregnant. She got pregnant before the wedding, well before I even proposed, actually. I swear to you that it had nothing to do with the will, or the Domaine, or any of that."

"I don't believe you," she snapped back. She'd lost the vines … her mother's vines … how stupid to have trusted anything—the will, her father, her brother, Julie, even Gaspard with the peace-making dinner he'd sprung on her. *She'd been so naïve.*

Incandescent with rage, and with nausea rising in her throat, she stormed out of the office. She couldn't bear a second longer in the stifling air of her own gullibility.

When she opened the door out to the parking lot she saw Julie and Gaspard, sitting on a bench against the wall, chatting companionably.

Amandine pointed her finger at Julie. "You! You knew, didn't you? Just like he did!?"

Jean-Marc rushed up behind Amandine then, and grabbed her arm. "Nothing gives you the right to berate my wife!" he said, in a stern voice. *Ah, the old Jean-Marc returns with a vengeance.*

"Hey!" Gaspard leapt up and inserted his body between the seething siblings. "What the hell happened in there?"

Neither of them answered, but instead stared at each other like fighting roosters ready to attack.

"Do you know what's going on?" he asked Julie.

Julie shook her head. "No idea, but it doesn't seem good. What is this about, Jean-Marc?" she demanded.

Amandine's mind spun in wild circles. Of course they'd known, both Jean-Marc and Julie. They'd tricked her, they'd stripped her of everything she held dear, without remorse. Worse, they were pretending to be innocent of their Machiavellian manipulations now. How dare they take her for a fool. Yet, she was ashamed she'd been acting like one—a wide-eyed, trusting, lovesick fool. *Well, that was over.*

"The notary read another stipulation in the will that our father didn't tell us about when he talked about the marriage thing," Jean-Marc said to Julie. "The Domaine will go to the first one of us who is married and has a baby."

"What!?" Gaspard demanded.

"They knew it!" Amandine flailed against Gaspard, frustrated at his immovable strength. "They had to know!"

"We didn't," Julie said. "I swear it."

"But Julie's pregnant," Jean-Marc told Gaspard.

Julie wrapped her hand around Jean-Marc's forearm. "Gaspard has known about the baby since our wedding." Her eyes darted up to Gaspard's face. "The blood tests came back this morning. They were all fine."

Amandine watched the blood drain from Gaspard's face with a sick sense of premonition. *He'd known too.* Amandine staggered backward. The pieces of the most awful puzzle were slowly coming together. Gaspard had known, and he hadn't told her.

"I'm glad," Gaspard said to Julie, but without tearing

his eyes away from Amandine. "Back to this inheritance thing though … this is a major issue."

Jean-Marc nodded and slipped his arm around Julie. "Julie and I need to discuss this," he said. "And Amandine and I can talk when she calms down."

Calm down? Never. She would never calm down again. Look where it had gotten her! "You bastard," Amandine hissed through clenched teeth.

Jean-Marc just tilted his head and let out a long breath. "Look, Amandine, I need to discuss this with my wife before I discuss it with you, but right now I need to get her home so that she can rest. It hasn't been an easy first trimester for her. We can discuss this later when you're not ripe for blood."

"Don't bother," she spat. "I'll move out and you can have the Domaine to drive the thing into the ground you incompetent, useless man."

"Amandine," Gaspard said, a warning in his tone, but this only stoked the rage that scorched her from the inside out. Gaspard's betrayal hurt more than anything, even more than losing her vineyards. He'd known about Julie's pregnancy and even though they'd made love every night and whispered their deepest secrets to one another into the wee hours of the morning, he hadn't even deemed it worth mentioning. He'd invited them over to dinner without telling her, and now to discover he'd been keeping the secret of Julie's pregnancy from her the whole time … how could she trust Gaspard ever again?

Jean-Marc put his arm around Julie and began to lead her away.

"I hate you!" Amandine yelled at his retreating back. "I never want to talk to you again."

Julie turned around and frowned. "Don't say things

like that, Amandine," she said. "This might all turn out okay after all."

"Yes, for you!" Amandine hollered and she slammed her body against Gaspard's as he held her back.

Julie shook her head and then sent a grimace of sympathy at Gaspard. Since when had the two of them become confidants? Nothing made sense anymore, and the reality of her life had suddenly become far worse than her worst nightmare.

"Best of luck on the firefighting job application!" Julie said to Gaspard with a wave. "I'll be keeping my fingers crossed for you. You'd make a great firefighter."

Amandine's head had been pounding with her heartbeat and rage burning white hot inside her, but hearing that, she suddenly went icily calm.

She turned and ran away from Gaspard, her father's will, from all of it. She kept running through the narrow alleys and obscure pathways through Nuit-Saint-Georges until she stopped thinking altogether.

Chapter Twenty-Nine

Gaspard was frantic to find her. He called Éloise on her cell phone to tell her what had happened and put the rest of his sisters on alert to call him immediately if she returned back to Volnay. He'd thought he'd seen Amandine in all her moods, but never before had he seen her like she'd been at the notary's office. She'd been like an injured animal, wild with despair and desperate to go off to suffer alone.

His heart had stalled seeing her in that state, but at the same time he could hardly blame her. Life had told her to constantly be on guard and to trust no-one, and when she finally had … well, he'd made some mistakes … big mistakes.

He swallowed the bile that kept burning his throat ever since he saw her face—pale and wretched—as she stormed out of the notary's office. He had to find her—she was in no state to be by herself.

He tried to put himself in her position—she'd lost the vineyards, she thought Jean-Marc and Julie had been planning this all along, and she thought that Gaspard was in on it. It was all wrong, of course, but he had a lot of explaining to do.

He drove for hours, often getting out of his car to

retrace paths through the forest she might have taken, and which weren't suitable for cars. He called his sisters every twenty minutes or so, but she hadn't shown up there, and he keep looping back to Pernand-Vergelesses to check her house, but there was no sign of her.

When he had tried everything, he resorted to the one thing that almost anyone who had been brought up in the Catholic Church would turn to if they had exhausted all other options—he decided to pray.

He'd just swung by Amandine's Domaine for the fourth time so he wasn't far from the Virgin Mary on top of Pernand. It was getting late—nine-thirty at night—but the dusk was long and there was still light enough to see. He couldn't bear the thought of her being outside at night though. *Where was she?*

He parked the car at the top of the hill and half ran, half staggered to the statue, a sob pressing against his ribs. Why hadn't he just told Amandine about the firefighting job when he'd had the chance? Why did he keep that a secret?

He got to the base of the statue and looked out to the valley which had turned to molten gold in the setting sun. He began to pray to the Virgin, and to Saint Vincent, and Saint Anthony of Padua—the Patron Saint of Lost Things—while he was at it. He would do anything to find her ... anything. The crickets had begun to chirp their nighttime song, projecting his prayer out to the four corners of the sky.

A movement in the vineyards below caught his eye. He looked down, and there, crouched between the rows of vineyards that had been her mother's was his wife. He'd checked there an hour earlier, but she hadn't been there, or maybe she'd just been between the vineyards and he hadn't seen her.

He scrambled down the rock slope, heedless of a sharp pain in his ankle and a deep scratch across the palm of his hand, to where the plot of vineyards begun and then he ran down the hill until he reached her.

"Amandine," he said, but she didn't even turn around. He sat down beside her.

She was too still. The need to take her in his arms, to assure himself that he had really found her, pulsed in every muscle. There was something … suspended … about her, though, that told him he needed to proceed with the utmost caution.

"Amandine," he said again, keeping his voice gentle. "You scared me … you scared all of us."

She just picked up a handful of soil and watched it run between her fingers.

"What are you doing here?" he asked.

"Apologizing to my mother," she said, staring at the dirt running through her fingers. "I tried *Maman*. I tried as hard as I could but I still lost your vines."

The absolute despair in her voice made Gaspard's heart ache for her. She had scratches on her face and leaves in her hair. He needed to help … he needed to fix this.

"Amandine," he said, carefully modulating his voice. "All Jean-Marc said was that he needed to talk to Julie. Neither of us knows what he's going to decide to do."

Amandine rested her head against her knees and shook it. "I know exactly what he's going to do. He's going to take over the Domaine, lord it over me for as long as he can to inflict the maximum amount of pain, then destroy it in front of my eyes."

"Amandine—" Gaspard tried to reach for her hand but she shook it away and instead wrapped her arms around her knees.

"You knew," she murmured. "You knew about Julie being pregnant, and you didn't tell me." It wasn't a question. Gaspard tried to imagine how such a secret would appear to Amandine, who had been lied to and betrayed by the men in her life for years.

"She swore me to secrecy," Gaspard tried to explain. As he'd searched for Amandine he'd had plenty of time to ask himself if he should have broken Julie's trust, and he honestly didn't know the answer to that. "I had no idea about this new requirement in the will, I swear."

"I'm having a hard time believing that," she said. "I'm having a hard time believing that you weren't all in on it."

"That's ridiculous, Amandine," Gaspard said, getting frustrated despite himself. "I know you're devastated, but even you cannot suspect me of that, not with what we've had between us recently."

She just leaned her forehead against her knees. "I'm your wife. You should have told me." Her voice was stripped of all emotion in a way that sent warning signals up his spine.

Despite it all, he still wasn't sure about that. "Julie had her reasons for keeping her pregnancy under wraps ... health reasons. Not knowing about the will, I didn't see it made a difference when you found out."

"I still think you should have told me," she said. "I haven't hidden anything from you, and it hasn't been easy for me ... being that unprotected. I can't stand to think you are keeping secrets from me. Maybe some women could, but I'm different." She choked on that last word. "I'm broken."

That last word robbed him of breath. How could she think that? "You may be injured and scarred," he said. "But not broken ... never that, Amandine." Every nerve needed to reach out and touch her, but at the same time, he couldn't ... not until she'd given him a sign she would welcome it. "I'm still learning to be a good husband. Please ... *je t'aime*."

Silence blanketed them, but not the comfortable silence that he loved. Instead it was bleak and frigid.

"What was that about the firefighting job?" Amandine demanded, finally. "Why didn't you tell me about that?"

He sighed, twisting his hands together in front of him. How he regretted keeping that from her—it had been so stupid to revert to his old habits of protecting those close to him by keeping everything to himself. In contrast to Julie's pregnancy, he didn't even have a leg to stand on. "I wish you hadn't found out that way." Even as he said it, he realized just how lame it sounded.

"It was almost worse than finding out about Julie's pregnancy. Not only did you keep the biggest thing from me, but something minor, something so ... innocuous." She shook her head, staring out straight in front of her. She still hadn't so much as glanced in his direction. Her hands began to tremble. Was she cold? Was she in shock? He wanted to warm her up, stroke her pain away. "Can I at least put my arms around you while I explain?" he said. "You're shaking."

"Don't touch me." Her voice was low and vibrated with anguish. It made his heart plummet in his chest. She sounded like she was somewhere far away, and he was struck with fear that maybe she couldn't find her way back.

"But, Amandine—"

"Explain."

Gaspard bowed his head. "I took your advice about maybe volunteering for a job at the fire station. That dream still haunted me, like I told you. Anyway, I stopped in there one day on my way back from Beaune, just intending to pick up an application for the auxiliary volunteer force, but I met this firefighter there, Bastien."

Now he said it, he realized there was a lot more to his firefighting application that he's glossed over—a lot of important components that he'd decided to keep from her. *So stupid.* They'd been together every night. Why had he kept something like that from her, from his wife?

Amandine maintained a stony silence.

"We began talking and he took me on a tour of the station. He was in a similar situation as me. He's from a winemaking family from Pommard. I sort of know his younger brother."

Amandine remained silent, but he could tell from that prickle of awareness beside him that she was listening.

"Anyway, Bastien was the oldest son too, and expected to take over the Domaine but like me ... and unlike you ... he just didn't have the desire. He didn't want to be maintaining something as huge and constant as vineyards, and he wanted to help people in a more concrete and direct way. It was like he was speaking to a part of me that I'd been quashing since Bertille was born."

Yes, he'd been denying even to himself how important that meeting was to him.

"Go on," she said, when he'd paused.

"I went in to apply to volunteer, but Bastien encouraged me to apply for a full-time position that had become available. That doesn't happen very often, apparently."

All this ... and not a word to her. He was such an idiot. "So, you applied?"

"Yes," he said. "I'm still going through the qualifying

process. That's how Julie found out. We bumped into each other at the medical lab when I was getting blood-work done for my application and her for her pregnancy."

She didn't respond and he was possessed with a need to make her understand. "I was terrified of what you would think of me if I didn't get the job," he said. "Bastien made it clear that it was a long shot, and I just couldn't bear seeing myself as a failure in your eyes, Amandine. Not telling you was a way to circumvent that ... a terrible, misguided way ... but I did it because I care so deeply for what you think of me."

"And the vineyards?" she asked, after a while. Of course she would ask about that.

"The day I picked up the application I went directly to talk to Louise. I didn't tell her why either." A stupid mistake as well, in retrospect. "I asked her if I took a step back if she would be willing to step into the breach."

That terrible silence fell again. "Isn't it ironic?" Amandine said, still not looking at him. "You don't want the vineyards you have, and I can never have the vineyards I want."

There was a resignation ... a bitterness in her voice that was entirely new. He hated it, and he hated even more that he could have caused any part of it. "Look," he said, leaning towards her. "We'll figure out a solution. We love each other. Maybe you can work with Louise on our vines, or maybe we can go back to the plan of finding some new parcels to buy for you or—"

"You never understood me, did you?" Amandine said, her voice like flint.

"What do you mean?"

"I don't want just any vineyards. I don't want to be

thrust onto your sister's dreams just because we're married. I wanted this vineyard, Gaspard." She picked up another handful of dirt, stuck together with limestone and fragrant as it released the heat it had absorbed during the day. "This was my mother's dirt, this was her terroir, this is *my* terroir. I cannot stand by and watch my brother destroy it. I cannot just stand by while the men in my life lie to me and betray me."

Indignation flared in him like a bright, guiding light. "Amandine! I know I screwed up … badly, but you cannot possibly lump me in with your father and Jean-Marc!"

"Why not? You've lied to me about significant and insignificant things. Where's the difference?"

"Amandine," he sputtered. "Like I said—"

"Today I realized I can't trust you, Gaspard," she said. "And it's destroyed me. You should have figured out by now that trust is everything for me."

"But—"

"You actively chose not to tell me things," she said. "Exciting things, new things, things that would affect not only your life but that of your wife, yet I didn't hear a word about it. We were together every night, Gaspard. I can't live like this, wondering what else you're not sharing with me."

"Nothing!" he said. "I swear it."

She shook her head. "I thought I could trust you, but I can't. A breach of trust that might not be a big deal for another woman is intolerable for me … unlivable."

"Don't say that," he said, low and urging. "I was wrong not to tell you about the firefighting thing, but if I didn't get it—and there's a high chance of that—I didn't want to inflict my disappointment on to you."

"Isn't that what married couples are supposed to

do?" She turned to him finally, and his heart broke to see the tears gathering in the corner of her beautiful eyes. "Share the good and the bad and the highs and the lows? There is nothing I haven't shared with you, Gaspard. Nothing."

"I know," he said. "But like I said, I'm learning. We have to accept that we're going to make mistakes at this marriage thing, don't we?"

Amandine stood up, and sliced her hand through the air, as if cutting their conversation off at the roots. "No," she said. "Not mistakes around trust. Like I said, my father and Jean-Marc … they did damage to me that cannot, I realize now, be undone."

"Amandine, you can't mean—?" Gaspard stood up as well, his breathing hitched and painful.

"I'm ending this now," Amandine said, her voice stony and detached. "I just can't do this."

"*Non*!" The protest was ripped from Gaspard's soul. She couldn't possibly be—

"I'll be walking back to my house now. Please send Éloise back home. I'll have to make arrangements for me and my sister—find myself a place to live and a job."

"Don't do this, Amandine," Gaspard breathed.

"It's done," Amandine said. "I will be applying for a divorce. If you have any remaining feelings for me, please don't make this difficult."

"Remaining feelings!" he exploded. "Amandine, don't be ridiculous! I'm in love with you."

Amandine's cat-like eyes narrowed then. "Gaspard," she said. "As it turns out, I don't need you after all. I don't think I ever needed you. I too made a mistake."

Gaspard could feel all the blood draining from his face. "Don't say that."

"Why not?" Amandine said. "It's the truth." She

turned and walked down the row of vineyards towards the road to her house, leaving him there with the certainty that he deserved this. He knew it had been coming … dreading it. This was life's punishment for finally getting what he wanted.

Chapter Thirty

Éloise didn't return that night, so Amandine slept by herself in the empty house that was no longer hers, in her old bedroom that was stripped of her favorite clothes and things that were still at Gaspard's house.

The next day, she still didn't think she could face going over to pick them up, so she sent Éloise a text asking her to pack them up and bring them with her.

But at the same time, what did it matter? This wouldn't be home for very much longer anyway. Amandine felt an anvil of loss on her chest every single waking hour, but one thing was certain—she would move out before Jean-Marc and Julie moved in and she would get as far away from Burgundy as humanly possible.

Gaspard hadn't tried to call her and hadn't tried to follow her home. His absence was a hole punched through her heart, but she'd said those words—that she didn't need him anymore—fully knowing they would cut that tether between them.

Telling him she needed him had been the magic that allowed them to come together on the night of Jean-Marc's wedding. Everything about their dynamic had changed the moment those words had left her mouth—

they were the only way to flick a switch inside of Gaspard.

She'd turned off that switch just as effectively. She'd known it would be the only way to rip herself from him, and she'd been right.

How stupid she'd been to actually believe, even for a second, that her happiness with Gaspard could be something that could last. She was damaged goods. The sooner she built her life around that fact, the better.

She ran through various ideas for her survival. It would literally kill her to watch Jean-Marc drive her mother's legacy into the ground. The farther away she could be, the better. They always wanted French winemakers in the New World, places like Australia and California, didn't they?

Being cut off from her land would be like being cut off from water, but that was still a better alternative to staying. There were, quite simply, no good alternatives anymore.

It took three days for Éloise to come back. She'd probably thought Amandine would change her mind, but Éloise should have known better.

Jean-Marc had been trying to reach her on the phone, but Amandine couldn't bring herself to answer or listen to any of his multiple messages—it would simply hurt more than she could bear.

She'd been standing at the counter, trying to force down a bit of coffee when Éloise had appeared in the kitchen. Doing the most basic things for survival—eating, sleeping, breathing, had become an ordeal.

She turned around and tried to manage a smile for her sister, but she could tell as she was doing it that it looked like some grotesque grimace.

"You look like shit," Éloise informed her.

"I know," Amandine said. "I own a mirror."

"You look just as bad as Gaspard," she said, "I didn't think that was possible."

"I don't want to hear about him," Amandine said in a tight voice. It wasn't anger as much as she just couldn't bear being reminded of what she'd had and lost.

"Don't be stupid." Éloise put her hands on her hips. "We were waiting for you to come to your senses, but this morning at breakfast we decided an intervention was clearly required."

"We?"

"The sisters."

Amandine fully realized in that moment how difficult, if not impossible, it would be to lure Éloise from her life at Gaspard's to travel across the world.

"The idyll is over, Éloise," Amandine said. "The sooner we accept that, the better. I've lost the vineyards. It can never work with Gaspard, and we need to get as far away from Burgundy as possible."

"We?" Éloise demanded.

"*Oui*. You'll need to come with me, of course. I was thinking somewhere warm with beaches and palm trees that also has a wine industry. How about California? Australia? You can choose if you'd like."

Éloise stamped her foot. "You're being ridiculous, Amandine."

"No, I'm not. I've finally come to my senses. I've given up trying to make a life for myself here. I know I can get a job in the wine industry in both of those places, and a work visa wouldn't be a problem with my specialized skills—"

"Shut up!" Éloise put her hands over her ears. "Just shut up!"

"Is there somewhere else you want to go?" Amandine asked, feeling so exhausted she had to clutch on to the kitchen counter for support.

"Sit down, *idiote*," Éloise jerked her head towards the kitchen table and chairs.

Amandine was too drained to do anything but take a seat.

"For once in your godforsaken life, you're going to listen to me, *d'accord*?"

Amandine didn't agree. She hadn't become *that* pathetic, but she remained silent all the same.

Éloise began to pace around the kitchen.

"I know you," Éloise said finally. "And you're no coward. How could you possibly be thinking of running away right now?"

"I'm not running away … well, I'm leaving, but I'm accepting things as they are for the first time in my life. It's not the same."

"Don't delude yourself. You're running away from this situation at the Domaine with Jean-Marc, but way more importantly than that, you're running away from Gaspard and what you could have together. No vineyard can be worth that."

Amandine shook her head. How could she make Éloise understand that her ability to trust, which was an essential part of any successful relationship, had been irreparably broken? "You're sad about us not all being one big happy family anymore. Look, I'm sorry about that, I truly am—"

"Stop it." Éloise held up her hand. "Just stop it, Amandine. You're missing the point of what I'm telling you. Do you know Jean-Marc has been trying like a madman to reach you?"

"I have nothing to say to him," Amandine said. "He won. I lost. End of story."

"I wouldn't be so sure about that. How about you have faith in him for a change?"

Amandine exploded in disbelief. "Do you have any idea what he's put me through this last decade?" Amandine said. "Him and Papa? How dare you stand there and tell me I have to give him the benefit of the doubt. You have *no idea*."

"No," Éloise said, placing her hands on the table in front of Amandine and leaning in. "I don't know the extent of it. How could I? You never shared anything with me. When are you going to realize I'm no longer a child and don't need to be protected? I'm not asking you to forgive him or be nice to him—punch him for all I care! I'm asking you to listen to him for your benefit, not for his. He's changed, Amandine. Marrying Julie has changed him and now this baby ... he wants to talk and come to a solution that will work for you both."

Amandine shook her head vehemently. "I refuse to work for him."

"I don't think that's what he has in mind at all," Éloise said. "How can you know what he's thinking when you haven't even talked to him?"

But how could Éloise want her to expect something helpful from anyone who had hurt her that much in the past? *Unthinkable.*

"I know maybe things with Jean-Marc might take a bit of time and may never be fixed if you don't want it, but all I'm saying is don't think the Domaine is a lost cause quite yet."

An unruly flare of hope went up in Amandine's chest, but she snuffed it out immediately. No, she'd been down that road of optimism before, and look where it had gotten her.

"And what about Gaspard?" Éloise demanded.

Even his name pierced her … it was so cruel of life to give her something so good and then snatch it away. "What about him?"

"He won't … he won't tell us what happened exactly," Éloise said in a more tentative voice. "Although we've been trying to get it out of him. Can you tell me?"

Amandine hesitated.

"Please … stop treating me as your baby sister."

Amandine swallowed hard. "It's not just that … it just …" She gasped and pressed her fingers against her chest, right over her heart—right where it felt like a hole had been punched through her chest. "It hurts."

Éloise rushed to her side, pulled out a chair and wrapped her arms around Amandine. "I'm so sorry you're in pain," Éloise said. "I hate to see you like this. If you tell me, maybe I can help make it better?"

Amandine shook her head. "I'll tell you, but only if you promise you're not going to try to use this information to get us back together."

Éloise clamped her lips together. "I don't think I can promise you that."

Amandine sighed. "I guess you'll find out eventually anyway. I know how tenacious you are. Gaspard has been keeping secrets from me."

"Other women?" Éloise said, then shook her head. "No, I don't believe that for a second."

"Of course not," Amandine said. "In a way, this was worse. He kept things from me that he had no objective reason to keep from me … it's his default behavior."

"Like what?"

"Like the fact he's known about Julie's pregnancy since her wedding with Jean-Marc."

Éloise's eyes widened. "And he didn't tell you?"

"No, Julie swore him to secrecy."

"Did he know about that thing in the will?"

Amandine shook her head. "He swears he didn't."

"Then I don't really see that as a betrayal, Amandine." Éloise crossed her arms in front of her and chewed her lip. "Sure, he might have told you, but if Julie specifically asked him to keep it a secret … shouldn't you be glad that your husband—"

"Don't call him that," Amandine choked.

"Okay … *Gaspard* … is a man of his word. Would you want it any other way?"

That stung, but if it had just been that mistruth from Gaspard, Amandine rather thought she might have been able to accept it.

"There's more," Amandine said.

"What?"

It was so odd how this stupid firefighting thing hurt one hundred times more than the pregnancy thing. No-one had so much as asked Gaspard to keep his application a secret, yet he had opted to just not tell her about something important going on in his life for several days. A relationship couldn't be supported on that sort of foundation, especially not a relationship involving someone so essentially damaged as herself. "He applied to become a firefighter—a full-time job, no less—and he'd been doing all these tests and meetings and things. He never said one word to me about it. There were so many opportunities, Éloise, and I would have been so happy for him. He chose not to share it."

"He did what?" Amandine was gratified to see that at least Éloise was shocked by Gaspard's pivot as well. "But what about his vineyards?"

"He even had a discussion with Louise about taking over management of them so he could step back—"

"And he mentioned nothing to you?"

Amandine shook her head. "Not a word. You have to imagine how that feels. We were together every night, as close as a couple can be, yet he never let on, not once. He took away the chance for me to be happy for him, to be proud, to celebrate with him."

Éloise's brows drew together. "That is pretty shitty, I have to admit it."

Amandine nodded. "I'll always wonder … if he can keep a secret that well, what else is he hiding from me? After Jean-Marc and Papa it was such a welcome thing to be able to be in a relationship with someone who I thought I could learn, despite my past, to trust. To find out that wasn't the case … well, it was devastating."

Éloise continued to chew her bottom lip, deep in thought. "He should have told you," she said, at last. "It seems strange that he didn't. I can't know what his reasons were, but knowing Gaspard and how much he loves you, I just can't believe there is any malevolence behind it, Amandine. Don't take the pain that Jean-Marc and Papa inflicted on you and put it on Gaspard."

"It's not like that," Amandine said, dully. Of course Éloise couldn't understand.

"I think it is," Éloise said. "You deserve something better than that. So does Gaspard."

Amandine shook her head. "I'd rather leave than be with someone I'm constantly doubting. That wouldn't be fair to me, or to them."

Éloise shook her head. "Look, you need to talk to

Gaspard and Jean-Marc, in that order. I'm going back to Gaspard's house. I just came here to drop off some of your stuff like you asked and get the full story. Now, I need to think."

"But you can't stay there," Amandine protested. "You're *my* sister."

"I love you, Amandine," Éloise said with the stretched patience of a long-suffering parent. "But I refuse to be caught up in this ridiculousness just because you and Jean-Marc and Gaspard are tearing yourselves apart. I found a family I feel a part of, and they are just waiting to welcome you back with open arms."

Amandine snorted. "Given Gaspard's temper, and what I said to him, I doubt that."

"You'd be wrong. People change. Gaspard has, and I believe Jean-Marc has too. As for you … well, that's up to you."

With that, Éloise turned on her heel and left.

Chapter Thirty-One

Gaspard was in the *cuverie* helping Louise when Éloise came back from seeing Amandine and told him that her sister was planning on fleeing the region and moving to somewhere sunny and far-away.

He stopped what he was doing and knew he wouldn't get any more work done that day. Who was he kidding? He was doing a pathetic attempt at it in the first place. He hadn't been able to accomplish anything—his mind was consumed of Amandine's final words to him which still rang in his ears. She didn't need him. She never had.

He tried to tell himself that she'd been upset and in pain and he shouldn't take those words at face value. Still, there had been something so set in her features ... so decided ... how could he not? He'd finally been brave enough to reach for something he wanted in life and everything had gone to pieces.

A strong part of him, that part that had long before given up on anything but duty and sacrifice when he had to look after baby Bertille as well as his other sisters, told him that the pain that lay over him ever since Amandine's rejection was no less than he deserved.

Louise had been trying to poke and prod to get answers from him, and she continued to offer vague morsels of advice she thought might help, but he didn't even know what to say or how to explain why he had kept the firefighting application a secret from his wife. He'd already felt like he wasn't good enough to deserve his wife, to deserve what they'd had together—the idea of her seeing him fail had been unbearable. Now though, all his reasons shriveled up to nothing in the face of losing her. His heart felt like it had turned to lead.

After Éloise had left to go and find Bertille in the house, he asked Louise, "What day of the week is it?"

"Tuesday," she said. "How come?"

It was bistro night. From what Éloise had told him he knew that Amandine wouldn't be there. Of course more than anything he wanted to go and see her, but she'd made her feelings clear. Not respecting them would be not respecting her, or what life was so clearly trying to teach him.

Second best would be to talk to his friends. They'd all been through impossible-seeming hurdles in their own relationships and somehow managed to clear them. Besides, he was going crazy, spinning within the circles of his own recriminations.

Without even bothering to change from his vineyard clothes—half the people that went to the bistro in Savigny didn't—Gaspard only stopped briefly at the house to tell his sisters where he was going.

Éloise and Bertille were alone in the kitchen, whispering to each other in a way that set off Gaspard's fraternal alarms.

"What are you two concocting?" he asked.

"Oh, nothing," Bertille answered, far too airily for his comfort.

He just crossed his arms and waited, favoring her with one of his stares.

She blew out her breath. "Fine," she said. "Éloise and I have been invited to a party this Friday night. We want to go."

He cocked his brow. He hated this part of pseudo-parenting more than anything. He lived in fear of his sisters being exposed to situations that were dangerous, or more than they could handle. At the same time, he knew they needed freedom to develop confidence and life skills that they would need.

"Who's throwing the party?" he asked.

"Just some friends of ours in Beaune?" It was never a good sign when Bertille answered a question with something that sounded like another question.

"Do they go to school with you?" As a rule of thumb, he'd found parties that stayed within the same age group were fairly harmless.

But Bertille and Éloise's eyes darted around the kitchen, landing everywhere except Gaspard's vicinity.

He cleared his throat.

"Not exactly," Bertille admitted, finally. "They are students, though."

"Where?"

"At the winemaking school."

"*Non!*" Gaspard said, without equivocation. He'd gone through the prestigious École Viticole himself and had not forgotten how the guys there liked to throw parties to lure in younger local girls. Éloise and Bertille had no place there.

"But you don't even know them!" Bertille protested.

"I would very much like to meet them," Gaspard said. "In fact, I think I might have quite a few choice words to say to them. What are they about anyway, inviting girls five years younger than themselves to parties out of the blue?"

"We're going to talk winemaking!" protested Éloise.

Gaspard opened his eyes wide in disbelief at this. Éloise had never shown any interest with winemaking whatsoever. She actually seemed to have developed an acute aversion to it, which, with her family history, made complete sense. "Is that so? Well, you are more than welcome to do that here when I'm in the vicinity or perhaps meet them at a café in Beaune?"

"But what's the difference?" Bertille asked.

"You'll figure it out," Gaspard said. "You're smart girls."

"I wish you were still with Amandine," Éloise grumbled. "You would have let us go then. You and Amandine were so much nicer when you were a couple."

Pain sliced through Gaspard's heart, but that didn't deter him from the truth. "Neither of us has ever been *that* nice. Maybe Amandine and I are no longer talking, but I know her well enough to know that she would not be on board with this idea. She went to the winemaking school as well, if you recall. Have you asked her?" He was desperate to hear anyone talk about her, no matter how peripheral.

Éloise became fascinated by the scarred wooden tabletop. "No," she grumbled.

"You cannot go to the party. Absolutely not. Now, I'm going to Savigny."

"Will Amandine be there?" Éloise asked with a hopeful voice.

"I doubt it. From what you said she has enough on her plate right now. Say, have you seen Jean-Marc since the will reading?"

"Yes," Éloise said. "He's desperately trying to reach Amandine, but she's not picking up any of his calls."

"Do you know why exactly he's trying to reach her?"

Maybe Jean-Marc and Amandine could come to some kind of *entente*, and then maybe—no, he was getting ahead of himself.

She shrugged. "He wouldn't tell me, but I know he and Julie were having their first ultrasound in Beaune today."

Gaspard remembered the stress on Julie's features at the medical lab. "I hope everything went well."

"Me too," Éloise said in a quiet voice.

"Gaspard," Bertille began again in a pleading voice. She had clearly regrouped and thought up a different angle to plead her case. He had to make his getaway before she did.

He waved his car keys at them and bid them an *au revoir* over his shoulder. "I won't be too late!" he shouted from the hallway.

Clovis and Cerise were already at the bistro enjoying what looked like a romantic glass of wine *tête-à-tête* despite the clatter and loud voices all around them.

Gaspard hesitated a few feet from the table, not wanting to interrupt them. As he watched them his ribs felt like they were being squeezed with an iron band around his torso. He and Amandine had been that happy. How could they have blown it up again so spectacularly?

Before he could turn around and leave to allow Clovis and Cerise their night alone, Xavier the bartender shouted his name in greeting. Clovis and Cerise whipped around in their seats.

By the time Gaspard reached them, Clovis had already pulled out a chair for him but Gaspard remained standing. "I feel like I may be interrupting a precious night out," he said.

Cerise shook her head. "Don't be ridiculous, Luc and Sadie will be here any moment."

"Where's Myrtille?" Gaspard asked.

"Geneviève and my uncle came over to spend the evening with her and the boys. I honestly don't know who is more thrilled. Cerise is pumping now and I've got a bottle, so I have a few hours."

Gaspard cast an uncertain glance at the chair Clovis pulled out.

"Sit," Cerise said in a tone that brooked no opposition.

One should never try to argue with a mother, Gaspard reminded himself. It was a loser's game.

Shortly after, Sadie and Luc came swinging in the door, Luc's arms snugly around Sadie's waist, the two of them grinning at each other and the world. Why wouldn't they?

He and Amandine had been like that. He should be getting used to that hollowness inside him that expanded every day but he still wasn't.

It was mere seconds after Sadie and Luc sat down and ordered that his friends got right down to it.

"What's this about the extra provision of Amandine's father's will and you two breaking up ... again?" Luc demanded, lowering his brows at Gaspard. It wasn't often that Luc got angry, but he was now.

Gaspard sighed, but honestly, it felt good to get the whole story—from beginning to end—off his chest. He hated having to tell them about how he'd kept things from her and messed it all up, but he did. It hurt in a good way, like confessing to the priest after shooting Clovis with a BB gun by accident when they were little.

When he was done, his friends all sat back in their chairs and, Gaspard took note, wore defeated looks on their faces.

"I can understand why you didn't mention anything about Julie's pregnancy," Sadie said. "I mean, she did ask you to keep it a secret and you had no idea that provision was hiding in her father's will."

"Exactly!" Gaspard said, realizing for the first time that he didn't only feel hurt, he was *angry* with Amandine. Yes, he'd screwed up badly, but a person couldn't change in a day as much as they might want to. She'd jumped to the worst possible conclusion and cut him off again, like what they had together was nothing. *It was not nothing.* It was the furthest thing from nothing.

"But the firefighting thing." Cerise cleared her throat. "You should have told her about that."

"I know that," Gaspard said. "I made a mistake, but who doesn't make mistakes?"

"Good on you for the firefighting thing, though," Luc said, grudgingly.

Gaspard held up his hand. "Woah. They haven't given me the position yet, and they may not."

"Sure they will." Clovis had become a lot more like Luc in his unequivocal support since getting together with Cerise. "You'll be perfect. I'm sorry I never realized how deeply you held that dream. Maybe you tried to talk about it to us in the past, but—"

"No," Gaspard interrupted. "I didn't share that with anyone since I was a child. Well, until the lunch we had together at Luc and Sadie's. That night Amandine and I chatted about it when we got back home, and she was the one who encouraged me to apply for a volunteer position."

"But you applied for an actual position?" Sadie clarified.

Gaspard nodded.

"So why didn't you tell Amandine if she was the one who had encouraged you to go down that road in the first place?" Luc asked. "I've known her forever too, and she's always been supportive of all of us."

Gaspard spun his wine glass around in circles. How to explain that at the time it had seemed to make complete sense?

"For one thing," he said. "If I didn't get the position—which is still a definite possibility by the way—I didn't want her to have to deal with disappointment on my behalf, and I didn't want to disappoint her."

Cerise leaned forward and put her hand on Gaspard's. "But that's what being in a couple is," she said. "Going through the good and the bad as a team. I had to learn that lesson the hard way too when I kept my pregnancy a secret from Clovis."

"To be fair," Clovis said, "We were split up at that point."

Cerise nodded. "Yes, but I had no intention of telling you if I hadn't collapsed at the wine auction."

Clovis nodded, then turned to Gaspard. "So you see? Sometimes that lesson isn't easy to learn, and we make mistakes along the way, but it's a crucial one."

"I think that's hit home now," said Gaspard. "But it's too late. One mistake and she wants a divorce ... she cast me off, just like the last time. She's even talking about leaving Burgundy."

Sadie shook her head. "I don't believe in too late,"

she said. "She hasn't left yet, has she? I was on a train on my way to London with another man, if you recall, when I changed *my* mind."

Gaspard's head pounded. How could he possibly be finding himself back here again? "She doesn't want to have anything to do with me. She says she can't trust me. Besides, the way she threw me away so easily when I was trying to explain and apologize … it hurt … it's still hurting. As much as I love her, I can't have a wife who threatens divorce every time I screw up. How is that supposed to work?"

"I know," said Clovis. "And I can see your side of it, but Amandine has past trauma that makes her throw everything off to protect herself. It's a matter of survival, I believe."

Gaspard sighed. "Yeah, I know … and the trust thing … it's very much her Achilles heel. That doesn't change that she was unequivocal about her desire for a divorce."

Luc snorted. "You have met Amandine, haven't you? What does she do that isn't unequivocal?"

"I bet she's regretting it now," Sadie was nodding, deep in thought. "I know I was after leaving Luc."

Luc reached out and pressed her tight against his chest. "Never do *that* to me again, please."

Gaspard shook his head. "Don't be so sure Sadie. Besides … I'm not comfortable with going after her again. There's too much hurt. I can't keep bothering her when she says she doesn't need me anymore."

Luc shook his head. "Good God, Gaspard, where did you ever get the idea that love was *comfortable*? It's wonderful, but not comfortable, especially the putting yourself out on a limb part. That part is downright terrifying."

Everyone around the table nodded.

Gaspard frowned. "I have my pride, you know."

They all stared at him, incredulous, then burst into gales of laughter.

"What?" Gaspard demanded, hating that they all seemed in on a joke that he was excluded from.

"Let me tell you," Cerise wiped her eyes. "Pride is a cold bedfellow, and pride and love … well, the two don't speak the same language."

Gaspard was mulling this over when the café door opened with a bang and Jean-Marc came rushing in. He looked around wildly, clutching something in his hand, and made a beeline over to their table.

"Gaspard!" he said without preamble. "Have you seen my sister?"

Gaspard shook his head. "No, she broke up with me."

Jean-Marc's large head snapped back. "She did? Why?"

Gaspard's hand twitched with the need to punch him. "She was devastated about the will and has a hard time trusting the men in her life … I wonder why?" he gave Jean-Marc a pointed look.

Jean-Marc's shoulders dropped, and a defeated look came over his face. "I'm to blame for that, I know, and I'm sorry. I'm trying to make amends … I promise you I am. I don't know if she'll ever understand but I have to try. I've been calling her day in and day out but she's not picking up."

"Have you been to the Domaine?"

Jean-Marc shook his head. "No, I didn't want to give her the wrong impression that I was there to take possession or kick her out or anything like that. I know her, and she would run a mile … I don't want that."

"Neither do I," Gaspard said, panic at the mere idea freezing his blood. In his gut he realized Jean-Marc wasn't completely off-base.

"I want to talk to her in a calm, non-threatening way," Jean-Marc said.

"What do you want to tell her?"

Jean-Marc surveyed Gaspard, but then shook his head. "No, I can't get this wrong. I need to tell her first if I have any hope of gaining even the smallest iota of her trust back."

"Is it good for her?" Gaspard demanded. Maybe they were split up, but he couldn't have Jean-Marc going and hurting her again.

"Yes!" Jean-Marc said. "It's very good. You don't need to worry yourself about that."

Gaspard raised a damning brow. "You can hardly blame me for having my doubts."

"This time is different. This time things are going to change."

With that, he sped off, leaving everyone at the table confused.

"Maybe you should go and check on your wife," Luc said to Gaspard.

Every nerve in Gaspard's body was screaming to run to her, but no … she'd made her wishes clear. "I can't go over there if she doesn't ask me to come." She didn't need him. She'd told him that distinctly … unequivocally.

And with that final thought still reverberating, he picked up his jacket and left.

Chapter Thirty-Two

She'd gone to bed early. The crush of heartache and regret pressing down on her shoulders drained her of her usual boundless energy.

She still couldn't believe Éloise didn't want to leave with her. She'd been texting and calling, but Éloise was digging her heels in and was refusing to budge from Gaspard's house.

She was still right in telling Gaspard she wanted a divorce, she told herself. Her initial reason had been that she could never trust him again, but that had morphed to something different since their final fight in her mother's vineyard. Now, she realized what truly forced her to break it off with him was the conviction that she was irretrievably broken—too broken to have a normal relationship, especially with someone she loved so deeply. Gaspard was too good a man to have to put up with that. Even though he might not realize it, she was divorcing him for his own good.

The loneliness saturated every cell in her body, made it ache and protest, but she just lay there in bed, trying to get it to sink in that this was her life now.

She was going to start packing in the morning. Leaving was the only thing left for her to do now that her past had been well and truly torched. She fell into an exhausted sleep.

She woke up to somebody sitting down on the edge of her bed. *Gaspard*! Half-asleep, her heart leapt with hope.

But she opened her eyes and yelped. *Jean-Marc*. The room was dark and full of shadows. What was he doing in her bedroom, on her bed in the middle of the night? She realized with encroaching shame that there was technically no justification for the fact that she had not already moved out.

"I know I shouldn't be here." She forced herself to sound as alert as possible. The idea of being anything less in the company of Jean-Marc was humiliating. "But I've left Gaspard's and I had nowhere else to go and—" She hated that she sounded like she was pleading.

Jean-Marc shifted his hand closer to her head. She wasn't sure what he was doing, but there was nothing in his movement that was threatening. He'd never laid a hand on her anyway, she reminded herself. His pain had been inflicted with words.

"Amandine, please look at this," he said. His voice sounded odd … muffled. Wait, was her brother crying?

He was holding out something in his hand. She sat up and took it from him, leaning over to switch on her bedside-table lamp.

She peered down at the funny strip of paper. It was a black and white print out of what looked like an ultrasound. She studied it, then looked back up at her brother. His shoulders were shaking with some sort of herculean effort. If she didn't know better, she would say he was trying not to utterly break down in front of her.

"I see it's an ultrasound," she said. "Wait, is it of the baby?" Goddamn him. She knew she should feel happy for them, but how could she be when this baby, as innocent as it was, symbolized the loss of everything she cared about in her life?

"Yes!" He pointed down to the strip of four ultrasound pictures, and to what looked like a glowing bean in each one.

"Are you here to rub it in?" she asked quietly.

His mouth dropped open in shock. "Good God no! Please don't think that."

"How could I think anything else?"

He shook his head wildly. "We went to our first obstetrician appointment and I heard the baby's heartbeat, Amandine! Things with Julie's pregnancy have been a bit touch and go for the past few weeks, but everything is great. It is so *great*. The baby's heartbeat was so loud. It filled up the entire room. It was the most amazing moment of my life."

He was clearly moved, and part of her was moved for him, but did he truly think that she could just forget what he'd taken from her and give her congratulations? Because of him she'd lost her work, she'd lost her vineyards, she'd lost her reason for living, she'd lost their sister and she'd lost her husband. That last one, she realized with a shock, was the one that hurt the most.

"That's great, but I should leave. You'll want to move in here with your family-to-be without wasting any time." She moved towards the edge of the bed.

"No! Wait!" He put his arm on Amandine's with a gentleness that was completely unlike him. "This changes everything, don't you see?"

"Yes, I believe I'm quite clear on that point," she said through clenched teeth. "Because you're going to be the first one to get married and have a child, you inherit everything. I'm homeless, and jobless, and ... well, everything-less."

"No." He shook his head, vehemently. "No, that's where you're wrong. You're not."

"What are you talking about? Are you drunk?" She eyed him narrowly, but if he was drunk, it was only on happiness.

"This baby," he continued. "Hearing our baby's heartbeat … I understood why I was put on this earth. It was to be this baby's father and a happy person for my child. That means I will not be taking over the vineyards. You can have them."

"What?" She breathed. It felt as sudden as having the rug pulled out from underneath her at the notary's office.

He nodded. "You can have them. All of them. All of it. You were right this whole time—you're the only one who can make a success of this place. That's what made me so angry all this time—I knew how right you were, and it killed me."

Amandine didn't dare say anything, for fear of breaking this spell. She pinched herself. Please let this not be a dream.

"I've been awful to you." He bowed his head. "I know it and please know I am so, so sorry. I was angry and sad and bitter, and the way Papa pitted me against you, making me always feel lesser … well, I took it out on you for so many years. I'll be working the rest of my life to make up for that."

"But …" Amandine couldn't even find the words. "I'm so confused right now," she said finally.

How could a person change so much in a day? But then, she thought back to when she'd told him she'd been married without him there, and how upset he'd been.

"I guess I should start at the beginning," he said.

"Please."

"You remember how I went on that ski trip and hit my head on a tree, just after Maman died?"

"Yes."

He blinked. "We were all still grieving and in shock, but it all started with that accident."

Amandine didn't say anything. Instead, she listened with every ounce of attention in her body.

"At first I thought it was just a concussion. At my age, I'd had a few of those before and after a day or two of rest I was always fine. I really didn't think it was such a big deal even though I'd hit my head harder than I ever had before. I was out cold for several minutes, according to my friends."

"I didn't know," she whispered.

"I didn't tell anyone. When I got home, you had made *coq au vin* for dinner, remember?"

Amandine remembered. She'd taken over much of the cooking when her mother was ill, even though she wasn't naturally gifted at it and it made her remember her loss all over again. *That coq au vin* had been the first recipe that she hadn't completely botched. She was excited for Jean-Marc to try it when he got home from his ski trip, and proud too.

"Well, I don't know if you made it because it's my favorite dish or not—"

"As a matter of fact, I did." Now she was the one blinking back tears, remembering how close they'd been before everything changed.

He reached over and squeezed her hand. "I never thanked you for that but thank you. Anyway, one of the things I loved most about *coq au vin* was the smell as I walked into the kitchen. I remember you telling me that you had made it, and I walked into the kitchen full of anticipation and saw it bubbling on the stove, but something was wrong ... I didn't smell anything—no wine sauce, no onions, no garlic ... nothing."

Amandine clapped a hand to her mouth. For a winemaker, the loss of one's *odorat*, or sense of smell, which was always linked to the loss of taste, was one of the worst possible things that could happen. Some winemakers she knew had even taken out specialized insurance on it.

Her heart surged in sympathy for her brother, for the first time since she could remember. "That must have been terrifying."

He nodded. "At first, I wasn't too worried ... disappointed, for sure, because everything tasted the same, but I figured it would pass."

"Most of the time it does."

He grimaced. "Yeah. And then, two months after the accident, do you remember how Papa forced us both to do a tasting competition?"

Amandine looked down to realize she was twisting the duvet between her fingers. "I remember him saying it was to take our minds off Maman's death, but I doubt his intentions were that pure. I didn't mind though, because I liked that sort of thing. I was good at it, and it was a way to prove myself to Papa that I wasn't just some girl he could underestimate."

Jean-Marc pursed his lips, thinking back. "That's when it began, if you remember? Him pitting us against each other. Now I realize just how screwed up it was. Why did he make us feel like we constantly needed to prove ourselves to him? Why couldn't he just love us?"

Amandine nodded, her mind shifting and rearranging so many memories. Looking back, she realized that it hadn't been any fairer to Jean-Marc than it had been for her. If only she'd known about his injury.

He blinked. "Can you imagine? A blind tasting when I had no sense of taste or smell?"

"You must have been terrified."

"I was. I was supposed to be the heir because I was the only boy, but unless my *odorat* came back, I knew better than anyone I was incapable."

"Which isn't fair," Amandine said mutinously. "The 'only boy as heir' thing."

"No," Jean-Marc, much to her surprise, agreed, "But you have to admit that it was the way things were done at the time."

It was an unpalatable truth, but the truth all the same.

"You got all three wines right, right down to the parcel." His eyes took on a haunted look of a scared little boy. "While I mistook white wine for red wine."

"I remember." Amandine was quickly revising what had been in her memory a moment of pure triumph. "You got everything wrong, and I mocked you. I mocked you mercilessly. I had no idea."

He squeezed her hand. "You couldn't have known. I worked so hard to make sure that nobody did. I was far too scared of what Papa would do and say if he knew. I did everything I could to hide it, including going along with Papa's nastiness."

"I was so angry that it was just assumed that you would take over. Can you understand that?"

"Yes," he said. "I do now."

"Anyway, I'm still sorry. If I recall correctly, I was so cruel about it."

"Yes, but I know why now. Still, can you understand why I was so furious with you then? Not that I'm asking for you to excuse me, because how I acted was inexcusable, no matter what."

The old clock on Amandine's bedside table ticked past the seconds as something in Amandine's heart loosened. "I think I need to hear it from you," Amandine said, softly.

"I was so mad because you had all the talent that had been taken away from me with that accident. Your mere presence was provoking, and then your sheer brilliance on top of that … I realized that even if I hadn't hit my head that day, I probably still never would have come anywhere close to your skill and accomplishments. At the time, though, I knew I could no longer do the job, and the grief of that plus the grief about *Maman* … well, it was far easier to be angry than to let myself feel everything else."

Was that what she'd done with Gaspard—fallen back on her old habits of anger and rejection instead of just facing up to the grief of losing her mother's vineyards? The truth of that began to reshuffle everything in her mind.

"Amandine?" Jean-Marc prompted.

Amandine rested her chin on her fist. "Papa did nothing but egg us on," she said finally.

Jean-Marc nodded. "He did. And maybe … maybe it was easier for you to be in a feud with me than grieve *Maman* too? Maybe it was easier for all of us to just be angry people?"

"I did grieve *Maman* in the vineyards … it was where I connected with her. Keeping them alive was … is … a way of keeping her alive."

Jean-Marc just stared at her for a long time, his eyes watery, and then he swallowed hard. "Really? I didn't know that."

"We didn't exactly have a relationship conducive to talking about such things."

He studied the ultrasound photos again. "The damage I'd done truly hit me when you told me you'd gotten married and that I hadn't been invited. I could understand why, but I was confronted with just how completely I'd destroyed our relationship. I should have been the one to walk you down the aisle, to grill Gaspard and make sure he would treat you properly."

"Why not negotiate a dowry while you were at it?" Amandine said with some asperity. "We don't live in the eighteenth century anymore, Jean-Marc. I'm my own person. I don't need looking after by anyone."

"But that's wrong," Jean-Marc said. "We all need looking after by someone, Amandine. Every one of us. Julie does that for me, she always has, and I owe her my life for it. She always loved me unconditionally and she has never cared less about prestige or winemaking or anything like that."

"Neither did Gaspard," Amandine said, marveling as she said it. Gaspard loved her for herself—completely, unequivocally, despite all her shortcomings. It was nothing short of miraculous.

"Now I'm becoming a father," Jean-Marc continued. "I have to stop this nonsense and do better. I have to make amends. I have to become a better person to be the father I want to be."

She could tell from the sincerity etched in his features that he meant every word.

"Amandine, when I was in that ultrasound room, I was overcome with the certainty that I did not want to be our father. I no longer wanted to be the kind of brother that I'd been to you for too long."

"But ... what does that mean exactly?"

"My sense of taste never came back," he said. "I have to make peace with the fact that I cannot be a winemaker in this lifetime, but this baby … this baby inspires me to find something else I want to do and follow that, to be a whole person again. I'm still interested in the horse plowing thing, like I mentioned at that dinner before—"

"I remember. Before the will reading."

He nodded. "I want to sign over the Domaine to you, Amandine, and watch you make a roaring success of it. I know you will. Will you … will you do it for both of us and for Maman, and Éloise too?"

Amandine blinked away tears. This little baby, the seed of her destruction, was in fact a miracle. This baby was their salvation.

"Of course I will. And you can be sure that you will get an income from the Domaine too, as is your birth-right, injury or no."

He smiled … the smile of the brother she remembered from before his accident. "I trust you. You're fair. I'm going to make an appointment with the notary for tomorrow to sign over everything to you. The sooner the better. Can you come?"

She nodded, but still … the past and its doubts tugged at her, trying to drag her under again. "Yes, but to be completely honest, I'm struggling a bit to trust this change of heart."

"Of course you are." He patted her knee under the duvet. "But you'll understand when you have a child of your own. They make us want to be the best version of ourselves, Amandine, even before they are born."

She snorted, thinking of her fight with Gaspard. "That's not about to happen anytime soon. I asked Gaspard for a divorce."

"I saw him at the café before coming here. He looked wretched."

She nodded, intrigued despite herself. She wanted to

know more. What did he say? Did they talk about her?

"Should I go back and talk with him?" Jean-Marc asked.

She rolled her eyes. "Now is a little late to start being *that* kind of big brother."

He laughed and he opened his arms. "All right, all right. Can I give you a hug?"

She sighed, unsure. "Look, this is a lot to take in. Maybe tomorrow?"

He nodded. "You wait until you're ready. *À demain.* I'll text you the time for the notary."

When he reached the door, he turned. "*Bonne nuit, soeurette,*" he called out, softer than she'd heard him say almost anything for the past ten years.

Chapter Thirty-Three

The next day, after Amandine returned from the paper signings with the notary, and Jean-Marc—true to his word, had signed the entire Domaine over to her in the matter of an hour or so—Éloise was waiting for her in the living room.

She was still reeling from the sudden turn of events, and especially from the warm hug she'd given Jean-Marc as they bid each other good-bye. She'd found him again—she'd found her brother. This pressure building up behind her ribcage was far more than happy—it was disbelief and uncertainty and regret about Gaspard and relief … it was just so many things.

Éloise was drumming her fingers on the arm of the couch, with what looked like a newly packed duffle bag of her things at her feet. She greeted Amandine with an exasperated breath. "Where were you? I thought you'd gone and moved out or something!"

"No!" Amandine said, then shook her head, checking if it had sunk in that she fully, unequivocally, owned the Domaine now. No, not yet.

"Where were you?"

Amandine flopped down beside her sister, surveying the somewhat shabby but comfortable living room.

"You're not going to believe this."

"Try me."

"I just got back from the notary's office. Last night Jean-Marc came here and told me that he's been thinking, and he wanted to sign over the whole Domaine to me." She wasn't sure whether she should share the part about Jean-Marc's injury, or whether he preferred to talk to Éloise about that himself.

"I told you!" Éloise sat up and pointed an accusing finger at Amandine. "I told you not to assume the worst when he was trying to reach you."

Amandine tilted her head. "You did tell me, but given my past history with Jean-Marc, I hardly think I could have thought otherwise."

"Amandine," Éloise said, warningly.

"Okay, point to Éloise."

"Ah-hah!" Éloise shouted in triumph. "And now you'll get back together with Gaspard and—"

Amandine shook her head. "I just threw him away again … I've done that twice now. Why would he want me back?" He was so good. He deserved to be with someone who wasn't so screwed up.

"Oh, come on … he's moping around like somebody died. He looks like death warmed over."

"Is he in a bad mood?" That would be something. A tiny thing … but something.

"It's worse than that. He doesn't seem to care about anything anymore. Bertille loaded the dishwasher all wrong just to get a reaction from him … any reaction … and he didn't even comment."

She shook her head again. "I was awful. I hurt him too much." She'd rejected him so soundly, even going as far as to tell him she didn't need him any longer. The guilt had never left her since those fateful words flew out of her mouth. She'd been wrong to say it, in the same way that Jean-Marc had been wrong to lash out at her when he was in pain. She'd spent years damning her brother, but really, she was no better.

"What obstacles are you constructing in that brain of yours?" Éloise gave her a hard look.

"I'm not—" Amandine began, but seeing Éloise's expression of exasperated skepticism, she shut her mouth. That was exactly what she had been doing, wasn't it?

"You'll never know if he'll take you back unless you try," Éloise said.

Amandine let out a big sigh. Having Gaspard back in her life, even if they only had a smidgen of what they'd had together, would be the best possible thing she could imagine. At the same time, it was terrifying. She would have to trust him and give him the benefit of the doubt, even when he screwed up. She honestly didn't know if she was capable of that.

"I don't know if I can change," she said, finally. "I think maybe I'm broken."

Éloise examined her face with avid curiosity.

"What?" Amandine demanded finally.

"I know you're many things," Éloise said to her. "But I never took you for a coward. I'm revising that opinion."

Amandine shook her head. "You don't understand."

"I think I do," Éloise said. "You're not broken, you're flawed like pretty much everyone else. Flaws can be healed over time, you know, especially with the help of people who love you."

This piece of wisdom struck Amandine so forcibly she remained motionless on the couch, pushed down by the centrifugal force of its truth.

"Yeah," Éloise said, nodding. "Take some time to reflect on that. Anyway, that isn't why I came."

It took Amandine several moments to snap out of her trance. "Why did you come?"

"Bertille and I are going to a party tomorrow night in Beaune, so I came to get some clothes, then you weren't here so I started to worry you'd left."

There was something in the nonchalant manner Éloise used to announce this that set Amandine's suspicions firing, despite the revelations she needed to take and mull over further. "A party where?"

"In Beaune."

"Who with?"

"Oh, just some guys we met."

"How old are the guys? Do they go to school with you?"

Éloise cast Amandine a furtive glance. "Not exactly."

"How old are they, Éloise?" Amandine asked. "This wasn't the first time Éloise and Bertille had tried to pull such a thing over on Gaspard and Amandine. Even though they still hadn't talked, Amandine welcomed even the small sensation of alliance with Gaspard.

"A few years older. They go to the wine school."

"Out of the question!" Amandine made a cutting motion in the air with her hand. "Even though Gaspard and I are not together, I know there's no way in hell he would have agreed to this."

"He did," Éloise insisted. "He said it was fine."

Amandine frowned. "Maybe he doesn't care how Bertille loads the dishwasher at the moment, but that I don't believe."

"You can call him or, better yet, visit him to ask him yourself."

Amandine was sorely tempted to do just that, but ...

she just needed to *think*. Was Éloise right about the possibility of healing her flaws? How could she make herself worthy of Gaspard's forgiveness? Besides, she had a sneaking suspicion that perhaps the party was merely a trick to get her to speak to Gaspard. She couldn't take it quite as seriously as she normally would—heaven knew these two loved to conspire. "Gaspard isn't your father," Amandine said. "Even if you are staying at his house for the moment."

"But Amand—"

"No. You listen to me. Even if Bertille is going to that party, which I don't believe, you are not allowed to go under any circumstances, do you understand?" *Voilà.* That would put a lid on their matchmaking schemes.

Éloise blew out a frustrated huff. "Aren't you going to contact Gaspard?" she demanded.

Ah ha. "No," Amandine said.

Éloise made a noise of contempt.

"Will you promise me you won't go?" Amandine demanded.

"Fine," Éloise spat out standing up, picking up her duffel bag, and stalking towards the door. "But you made a promise too, if you remember, when you married Gaspard. For better or for worse? That ring a bell?"

There had been one bright light in the unrelenting bleakness of Gaspard's days, and that was a phone call from Bastien letting him know he had made it to the next selection round for the firefighters position.

"The next step," Bastien said over the phone, "Is to come and do a shadow shift at the station with us tomorrow night. Well, it's not actually a shift, per se. You're strictly there to observe from the sidelines. The point is for you to get a feel of what a shift is like, and to see if you mix in well with the crew. Can you come?"

"I'm game," Gaspard said. He'd tried to sound overjoyed, but he wasn't certain Bastien bought it. The truth was that Éloise had come from her home earlier that day with a new duffle bag full of clothes and the news that Jean-Marc had experienced a change of heart and had signed the entire Domaine over to Amandine.

He'd spent the rest of the day, not to mention the night, in a state of readiness. Surely she would come and see him? Or at least call him? How could she not give him a second chance?

But … nothing. No sign of her. She hadn't budged an inch, and he refused to—not until she took the first step. Maybe his friends said pride had no place in love, but goddammit, he was not going to serve himself up on a platter for her to hurt again.

His body didn't agree with his mind, unfortunately, and he'd spent the entire night so rigid and yearning for her that it was all he could do to not leap out of his bed and drive directly down to Pernand and hop into hers. But no … she didn't want him and, more than that, she didn't need him. As such, she was strictly off limits.

Spending a night shift at the station was the perfect distraction, really. He said a quick good-bye to his sisters, including a final admonishment to Bertille and Éloise to not even think for so much as a millisecond of sneaking off to the forbidden party, even though he wouldn't be there to enforce it.

Once at the station, he tried to lose himself in the

easy camaraderie of the team. Thankfully, he was kept busy. There were so many introductions made and so many new names to remember and information to process that it wasn't until hours after dinner that he actually had a chance to think about Amandine going to bed, without him, for one more day. He hoped the station might get called out that night so he didn't have to spend several more hours mulling over her stubbornness.

An alarm sounded then, and Gaspard jumped.

Bastien grinned at him. "You're in luck! Sounds like someone may need us. Don't get your hopes up though. We get a lot of false alarms."

"I'm ready," Gaspard said. He didn't have a uniform yet, so was just in his jeans and T-shirt. "Any last-minute instructions?"

"Just watch unless we ask you to do anything," Bastien said. "That might be harder than you think. Let us do the job and observe. *D'accord*?"

"*D'accord*," Gaspard agreed, and slid down the pole after the rest of them.

Chapter Thirty-Four

It was one o'clock in the morning, Gaspard saw when he checked his watch in the fire truck.

"Any details about the call?" he asked Bastien, who was all suited up and sitting beside him.

"Looks like an actual fire," Bastien said. "We don't know too many details so far, but it's in a house on the north side of Beaune."

Gaspard nodded, trying to push down the unease that crept up his spine. Up until this moment he hadn't thought about what it would be like to do this job when he didn't know the exact whereabouts of his family and friends at any given moment. That was going to be a definite challenge. Still, there was no way Bertille and Éloise would have dared go to that party … would they?

As the siren wailed through the empty streets of Beaune, Gaspard furtively took his phone out of his pocket and dialed Bertille's number. It rang and rang but she didn't answer. Of course, the explanation could be completely innocent—she and Éloise had most likely fallen asleep, but somehow … He just wished she would pick up the phone so he could reassure himself she was at home, in bed.

"Do they know how the fire started?" Gaspard asked.

Bastien shook his head. "Not exactly, but from what the dispatcher could tell it's a house party scenario. We'll find out soon enough."

They roared down a gravel driveway, and the headlights and flashing red siren light illuminated a stately, bourgeois stone house with black smoke belching out one side of the lower windows.

Gaspard swore under his breath. Please God let none of his sisters—including Éloise—be in there. If only Bertille would call him back or answer her phone …

There was a knot of young men standing outside, smoking cigarettes and conferring with each other, their shoulders hitched up by anxiety. The acrid smell of smoke filled the air, making Gaspard's eyes burn and his lungs feel clogged.

As Gaspard followed the firemen over to the house, his phone rang. Thank God, It had to be Bertille … but then he recognized Amandine's home number immediately.

His heart leapt, even though this was neither the time nor the place to be taking the call. "Amandine?" he picked up. If she was tentatively reaching out to him, how could he tell her he needed to call her back without putting her off for good?

"Just listen!" she commanded "I just got a call from Éloise and Bertille. They went to that goddamn house party."

"With the guys from the wine school?" Gaspard demanded, his voice thin and his eyes raising up in horror at the house in front of him. No, there couldn't be such a horrible coincidence. There were probably numerous house parties in and around Beaune on any given night.

"There's a fire, and they're trapped on the second

floor. They gave me the address." Amandine, in a jagged, breathless voice, read out the address of the house that Gaspard was currently standing in front of. "I'm going down there right now, but—"

Fear like he'd never felt before pressed down on him. "I'm here," he said.

"What?" she demanded, clearly confused.

"I'll get them," he said. "I promise you, Amandine."

A hesitation, then, "I know you will. I trust you."

Amandine ran outside to the car. This wouldn't have happened if only she could have put her pride aside and called him when Éloise asked her about the party. She owed him an apology, and she thanked God he was somehow, miraculously, already there. There was no one else she trusted to save her sister and Bertille, but Gaspard ... Gaspard was everything that she wanted, everything that was pure and true, she realized. So what if he made mistakes—who was she to reproach him for that?

The thought of her sister and Bertille caught in a fire though ... her chest felt like a boulder was sitting on it.

She raced down the hill and into Beaune. She didn't understand why Gaspard was already there, or how exactly he was going to rescue Bertille and Éloise—did it have something to do with this firefighting thing?

She knew he would save them. She didn't trust anyone else to fix this situation like Gaspard. She made a mental note of that. *She trusted him when it counted most.* That certainty inhabited her as surely as her own heart.

She madly bargained with God, life, fate, as she screeched around the ring road. *Please let nothing happen to the girls. Please let nothing happen to Gaspard.* Whereas twenty minutes before she was mired in uncertainty, now everything became crystal clear.

But Bertille and Éloise needed to be okay. They could be so happy. The thought of living without either of them crushed her soul.

Trust was hard … trust might always be hard for her … but she had to be courageous enough to take that leap. Flawed, not broken, as Éloise had argued. She had to be brave for herself, and she had to be brave enough for him.

But would he take her back? She shook her head. Right now, that was the least of her concerns.

Bastien and the other firefighters ran around the side of the house where the most smoke was coming from, and Gaspard followed them, his mind spinning wildly with how he could get Éloise and Bertille out of there. The firefighters were rushing a hose over and talking to the men outside about the closest water supply.

Gaspard ran over to them and had to yell for Bastien to hear him over the noise of shouting and the fire and crack of splintering wood. He'd never known how noisy fires were before. "My sister," he gasped. "And her best friend. They're trapped inside."

"What?" Bastien's eyes went wide. "Here?"

"Yes, I just got a phone call from … that doesn't matter. They're on the second floor, in one of the bedrooms in the back. The man Bastien had been talking to, who Gaspard suspected was one of the party organizers, was standing right here. Gaspard grabbed him by the collar.

"Where are the two young girls you lured here?"

The guy threw up his hands. "I have no idea. They just disappeared. That's what I was trying to tell that other fireman."

"Is this your house?" Gaspard demanded. "Can you tell me the floorplan?"

"I just borrowed it from a friend for the weekend. I haven't even been upstairs myself!"

Putain de merde.

Bastien stuck his arm out between Gaspard and the man, who Gaspard was ready to murder. "You can't attack him, Gaspard, and you definitely can't go in. You'll lose any chance at this job."

Try and stop me. There was no way he wasn't going to do everything humanly in his power to get them out, even if it meant losing this dream job of his and returning to the vineyards.

Bastien ran around the back of the house and yelled for a ladder to be brought around. Gaspard ran ahead. He tried to see if he caught a glimpse of the girls through the windows, but … nothing … Even though there was a light on inside, the windows were becoming increasingly opaque with smoke.

"The ladder?" he demanded to Bastien.

"It's coming," Bastien said. "I'll go check on it, but just to reiterate—you're not going up it."

Gaspard's priorities crystalized as they always did in

a crisis. But this crisis had the sickly quality of true fear … he and Amandine could not lose Bertille and Éloise … not on his watch.

The ladder was taking too long. There was no time to waste. If the girls had passed out from smoke inhalation somebody needed to find them and get them to the window and pass them down the ladder. The idea of doing nothing was not an option.

He spotted a door that nobody was paying attention to. The fire hadn't reached this section of the house, but the smoke had. Gaspard knew he had to move fast to find the girls in time.

He tried the door. Locked. He backed up and gave it a mighty kick. His entire leg throbbed, but he'd made enough of a hole in the wood to reach in and unlock the door from the inside. He crashed through. He was going to save Éloise and Bertille, or die trying.

Inside, he tried to hold his breath as long as he could as he found the stairs through the stifling smoke, but when he had to suck in more air when he reached the second floor, he fell to his knees. That was a mistake. His lungs burned in agony, and he was completely blinded. Reality started to take on the flickering quality of an old film. *Hold your breath. Do not pass out. You cannot pass out.*

He felt his way down a hallway and began opening each door, one by one. It probably wasn't the best thing to do, and he didn't know enough yet about firefighting technique, but Bertille and Éloise were inside one of the rooms. That outweighed any other logic. There were so very many doors.

Amandine screeched to a stop in the driveway with a spurt of gravel and ran around the back of the house where the girls had said they were. The firefighters she saw—two men and two women—were far too busy to pay any attention to her. Gaspard was nowhere to be seen.

"Are they out?" she shouted at the firefighter who was holding a ladder up to one of the second-floor windows.

The other one who had just begun to climb shook his head grimly. "The two girls? No. Who are you?"

She ignored that. "Where's Gaspard?" she demanded.

The guy didn't look at her as his face was tilted up to watch the firefighter at the top of the ladder get ready to bash the window in with a bright orange, strangely shaped hammer.

"Stand back!" he ordered her. "There's going to be broken glass everywhere."

She took a few steps back. "But Gaspard?" she yelled over the noise.

Another one of the firefighters came over to her. "Gaspard? You mean the new guy?"

Amandine nodded, her stomach a ball of ice. She needed to find him. She had been worried about losing Bertille and Éloise, and that thought still made her heart stop, but oh God, she never considered the possibility of losing Gaspard. *Non*! She had to find him.

"I haven't seen him in the past few minutes," she said. "He must have gone around the house."

Things slotted into place in Amandine's head. Gaspard wouldn't wait around for someone else to save their sisters. As long as she'd known him, if someone needed him, he was there. Period. End of story. Why would a raging fire make any difference?

She ran around the side of the house and saw a door ajar with a massive, ragged hole at its center. She knew then exactly what Gaspard had done. Her heart began tripping in an erratic rhythm—she'd never been so terrified and scared in her life.

Gaspard had to use every ounce of his sheer will not to succumb to the unconsciousness creeping in on him from all directions. The dizziness had become so overwhelming he'd been forced to drop to his knees and was now crawling from room to room. The smoke should theoretically be thinner at this level, but it was still thick enough to overwhelm every one of his senses.

Past the fourth door and into the fourth room, he crawled towards the window where he could see the light from one of the huge floodlights the firefighters had set up, when his knee bumped against something soft on the floor. He felt around, frantic, not knowing how much longer he had before he passed out. His lungs had begun to crackle now, even though he was doing his best to hold his breath. His fingers reached out, distraught. It was somebody ... it was one of the girls ... Éloise or Bertille he wasn't certain, but all he knew was that he had to get them out. He felt around some more and found the other girl.

He crawled towards the floodlight in the window and tried to open it from his kneeling position, but it felt jammed, or maybe painted, shut. He yanked his T-shirt over his head, wrapped it around his fist, and punched the windowpane. *Please let them be okay. Please God please.* He no longer cared about not asking for things. *Enough of that.* He would ask, beg, demand … and fate could do what it bloody well wanted.

He heard shouts outside and the clanging of the ladder. *Putain de merde.* They'd put the ladder at the wrong window. Gaspard cleared out the jagged edges of the panes of glass with his hand as best he could, taking a gulp of the bit of air that came in the room, but it was full of smoke, and again his vision started to blacken on the edges.

No. He was not going to pass out. Using every last ounce of strength in him, he lifted the first inert shape off the ground and threw her over his shoulder. The ladder had collapsed again by accident—he could make sense of the shouts from outside. *It was going to take them too long.* He had to get the girls out of there. Every second counted. He threw the other girl over his shoulder and after taking one last gulp of air from the window, ran both of them down the stairs, hanging on to them tighter than he'd ever held on to anything before.

As he burst out the back door, he tripped over something and flew, sprawling to the grass, twisting his body so he landed on neither of the girls.

He rolled over and tried to check the girls, but he couldn't see a thing. His eyeballs felt like they'd sustained a thousand razor cuts each. *Cough. Please cough.* He demanded God, fate, whatever, as he flung his hand over the torso of one of the girls.

Then one of them did, but dammit … he couldn't make out any shapes, and he couldn't seem to get any air into his lungs either. His throat felt like it had gone through a meat grinder and his blood turned to ice at the sound of a terrible, rasping breath … *please no, not one of the girls.* Then he realized that horrible, rattling sound was coming from him.

There was Amandine's voice—was she there already?—yelling for help and the flashing lights of an ambulance. He was trying to ask about the girls but couldn't get out any sound except a wheeze. He loved her. Dammit. He didn't care if she didn't need him … he wanted her more than anything he'd ever wanted in his life, and he was going to tell her.

Bastien stuck an oxygen mask over his face, then everything went black.

Chapter Thirty-Five

When Gaspard opened his eyes again, he found himself in a hospital room absolutely full of flowers and cards and balloons and what looked like drawings from Marc and Yves.

But he was alone.

It rushed back—Bertille? Éloise? He began to frantically search for a button to call the nurse and, at the same time, opened his mouth to yell out for help, but only a croak came out. The hiss of oxygen from the mask that was still on his face was louder. He ripped off the mask and started coughing. *Maybe not such a good idea.*

Just when he was going to launch himself out of the bed, he caught sight of a bright yellow piece of paper with writing on it—huge and black in capital letters. He recognized Amandine's hand.

BEFORE YOU TRY AND GET OUT OF BED READ THIS—I MEAN IT!!!

1. *Bertille and Éloise suffered smoke inhalation but are going to be fine.*

2. *Bastien told me to tell you that you still have the job if you want it—even though you didn't listen to him you showed excellent instincts.*

3. *You have quite severe smoke inhalation too but if you rest, you'll recover. <u>IF YOU REST</u>. I hope your eyes are working now so you can read this— the doctors assured me they would be.*

4. *Everyone has been here to visit you. Geneviève left crémant in the fridge down the hall for when you wake up.*

5. *The drawings are from Marc and Yves and they want to go for a ride in the fire truck.*

6. *You are a hero.*

7. *I love you.*

8. *I realized I'm flawed but I'm desperately hoping that you can be patient with me while I try to heal myself. I want our marriage to work more than anything—even more, I realized, than my vineyards.*

9. *Stay in bed. If you are up when I return, I will whip you. I just popped out for a coffee or some food. I'll be back very soon.*

She loved him?

Just then, the door opened. *Amandine.*

She swallowed when she saw him and tried to smile. She let out a strange gulp instead, half laugh and half sob. She ran towards him, put down her coffee cup on his bedside tray, and threw herself in his arms—not an easy feat with the tubes from his oxygen mask and IV.

He reached up and patted her back as she shook against him. This felt so … right. "I read your list," he murmured in her silky hair.

"Including number seven?" she sniffled back to him.

"*Oui.* That was my favorite."

She pulled back from him. "Really? I couldn't blame you if you didn't want to give me another chance. I was so terrible to you, and I want to apologize for that. I am damaged, like I said. When I said all those horrible things to you the night of the will reading, I honestly thought I could never be fixed, but now … I think maybe I can … with a lot of love, and help.

"Hmmm," Gaspard pretended to consider this, entertained despite himself by the pucker between her brows.

"More than anything," she said in a rush. "I want to make this work between us … it is so *good* with you, Gaspard. When I realized you were inside that burning house, I knew I can't live without you."

"You probably could." He smiled, soaking in the fresh green of her eyes. The color of new beginnings.

"Maybe," she admitted, "But I don't want to, don't you see?" Her voice cracked. "Needing you is irrelevant. The thing is I *want* you … more than my mother's vines or anything else."

Gaspard didn't say anything for a second, then he thought back to the revelation he'd had at the fire. "I want you too," he said. "And It has nothing to do with needing. I'm no longer scared to say that. In fact, I should warn you—I may become *quite* demanding as a husband."

"I can't imagine anything better," Amandine smiled, but then grimaced. "Are you okay with being patient with me? I promise I'll try my hardest."

Gaspard squeezed her hand. "How about we are both patient, and how about we both try to fix not only ourselves, but each other, with lots of love, and kisses, and late night chats under the duvet, and laughter and …"

"I love that idea." Amandine grinned. "And we'll never fight again."

Gaspard burst out laughing so much that he had to

take off his oxygen mask again, then started coughing.

"What?" she demanded.

"Oh, we're going to fight," he said. "We will yell and dig our heels in and send each other black looks and you will probably kick my shins under the table—"

"I will not!" She shook her adorable head, her eyes wide with shock. "I'll try so hard—"

"We're not going to become two completely different people overnight, Amandine," he chuckled. "And I'd never want that even if we could. The broken bits are all what makes this uniquely ours, and what makes it perfectly imperfect."

"You think?" That pucker was back. He leaned forward and kissed it, the silk of her skin welcome under his lips.

"I'm certain of it. We'll fight like the two headstrong, mulish people we are, then we'll make up, and it will be glorious. Do you like the sound of that?"

It was a good thing that Gaspard had already taken off his oxygen mask, because Amandine answered with a kiss that eventually required him to put it back on again.

Epilogue

Mid-October

The grapes were safely harvested and squeezed, and the vineyard leaves had turned fiery crimson, orange, and saffron as if to celebrate. It had all gone quite beautifully. Even though it was halfway through October and cooler at night, the days were still unseasonably warm.

Gaspard had taken the week off his new firefighting job to help Louise for the harvest, but he'd confessed to Amandine late at night in their bed that what once was a chore had become…fun. Amandine could see the difference in him now that some of the responsibility had been lifted from his shoulders. He smiled more, he was constantly catching her off guard with his touches and kisses, and the sound of his laughter became something she could rely on hearing every day. The night before they had fallen asleep chuckling over just how firmly Louise had everything under control at Domaine Arnoux.

Amandine, of course, had been working herself hard, but since taking ownership of the vineyards, a new sense of purpose flowed through everything she did. True to her word, she and Jean-Marc had agreed on a financial arrangement to compensate him for the shares he'd given to her, and they'd even begun to discuss him plowing the vineyards with his new plow horse for the next vintage.

Her chest filled with so much joy rediscovering the brother she'd lost all those years ago that sometimes she wondered how her ribs could contain it all. It was clear that fatherhood was going to suit her brother down to the ground.

Despite the rocky start to her pregnancy, Julie was thriving in her second trimester and Jean-Marc brought every piece of news and every ultrasound photo to show Amandine. Amandine didn't even have to fake enthusiasm. Nobody was more shocked than her at just how thrilled she was about becoming an aunt. She'd even found herself ruminating after Jean-Marc's visits about what timing would be the best for her to get pregnant in regard to the winemaking calendar.

Even though Amandine was tired when she got back home every night of the harvest, she was never too tired to make love to her husband.

His firefighting uniform—a dark blue jersey shirt with red stripes down the side and tight-fitting blue trousers, was a surprising aphrodisiac. It showcased his muscles and tendency towards heroism, and resonated in a primal part of her that she didn't even know she possessed. He looked so impossibly attractive she sometimes had to take matters into her own hands before he left for work, and Gaspard had learned from experience to give himself a fifteen-minute window between getting dressed and having to leave the house.

Their lovemaking was glorious and varied— sometimes quick and fevered, sometimes exquisitely slow, sometimes it was in Gaspard's big bed, and sometimes it was on the couch, or with her perched on the kitchen counter, or in the bath, or, one particularly memorable time, on top of a barrel in her wine cellar. Amandine continued to be in awe of how her love for Gaspard kept getting bigger and deeper, expanding into every corner of her being and her life. She was grateful for him every day and did her utmost to show him.

He'd been right about them fighting. They argued still…their shared love had not, as Gaspard had predicted, transformed them into Saints. However, they always made up. That was, hands down, the best part.

One Sunday morning after the harvest they lay in bed. The vineyards were at the height of their glory, and they'd just made love to welcome in their day of rest. Amandine had finally agreed to take Sundays off—most of the time anyway, although she did work when Gaspard was on a firefighting shift. His deft fingers smoothed her hair off her forehead as she lay, catching her breath, with her head against his shoulder.

"I have a surprise for you today," he said.

She pushed herself up on her forearms to better look at him, frowning. "You know how I feel about surprises. I'm trying but…well, they're still not my favorite thing."

The corner of his lips twitched, mischievous. "We're supposed to be working on our hang-ups, right? Together? I feel surprises are an important part of the whole trust thing for you."

Amandine was trying her best, but she couldn't completely banish her uneasiness.

When she didn't respond right away, he leaned over and kissed her collarbone. "I've been working hard on telling you how much I want you…like, every second of very day."

Her heart thrummed at the truth of that. Gaspard had been making *remarkable* progress. She bit her lip, innate caution warring in her with a determination not to back down. "What kind of surprise is it?"

He shook his head, his dark eyes dancing. "If I told you that, *mon amour*, it would hardly be a surprise, now would it?"

Merde. He had her there. "Can you give me any clues?"

"Well," he said. "I'm going to have a shower and leave after lunch, and then the sisters are going to come over and…do things…"

"Do you realize how ominous that sounds?"

He chuckled. "I only did after I said it. Knowing our sisters as we do, that *does* sound ominous, *n'est-ce pas?*"

She half laughed, half groaned, and flopped back over his chest. "What are you doing to me Gaspard? What is this torture?"

He stroked her spine, reading each one of her vertebrae with his fingertips as if deciphering an intriguing new language. "I promise you, it won't be, but now that you mention it, torturing you a bit sounds rather…intriguing."

He dove under the covers. His impossibly skilled lips traced a trail over her breast and then down to stomach to her navel and then…she yelped once, then she didn't say anything else for a while, except for her husband's name on the tail of a gasp.

It was three o'clock, and Amandine had been ordered back to their bedroom after the family lunch which Jean-Marc and Julie had joined. That was becoming a common thing on Sundays, and Amandine was amazed at how much she enjoyed seeing both of them, not to mention the smile that never left Éloise's face. The surprise continued to niggle at Amandine's mind, but it was amazing what a morning of lovemaking could do to mellow one out.

She was to wait in their bedroom for the surprise, Gaspard told her as he abandoned her with a lingering kiss and a final promise that he was ninety…no ninety-five per cent sure she would like the surprise…he hoped.

Amandine waited on the bed, fingering the soft linen duvet, anxiety and love warring in her chest. There was a new feeling there too—a trust that whatever Gaspard had planned—even if she hated it—was done out of love. She savored this new certainty like a wonderful chocolate, enjoying all its facets and nuances.

The bedroom door flew open flew open and the sisters burst in, equipped with Amandine's wedding dress, which was wrapped in a plastic dry-cleaning bag, and armed with the same arsenal of beauty products and tools as her wedding day.

"What's going on?" Amandine asked, but a suspicion was growing in her mind.

"You, *chére* sister, are getting married again," said Éloise. "And we're here to get you ready."

The final thing the sisters did to Amandine after getting her bride-ready was tie a silk blindfold over her eyes. That wasn't something the old Amandine would have agreed to but buoyed by the sheer joy of the sisters and her love for Gaspard, she decided to just enjoy this ride Gaspard had planned for her.

In the past few months, she'd learned how important it was to give the people she loved space to change and, even more importantly, to extend that same grace to herself.

In the car, she couldn't see anything but the golden light of the October evening that seeped through the edges of her blindfold, but even that was diluted – the sisters had been as thorough at making sure she couldn't see as they were with everything else. She could tell when they got to Pernand Vergelesses. Her body knew the curve and climb of the road intimately, but instead of stopping half-way up at the church like she expected, the car kept climbing up towards the top of the hill above the village. Where exactly was this wedding going to take place?

The car stopped after climbing up for a bit. Surely they weren't at the top already? She was rather unceremoniously pulled out of the car, then led, with Éloise on her left and Bertille on her right—she would recognize their voices anywhere. The ground was soft under her feet—they were in the vineyards—and she took a sniff of the smoky air and the unique mix of the soil. They were in her *mother's* vineyards—Amandine's *terroir*.

Élosie and Bertille drew her to a stop and then turned her a bit to position her in the right place. Her heart pounded in her chest, and she didn't know quite whether she wanted to laugh from joy or sob from emotion and anticipation.

"*Prêt?*" Éloise called out and a chorus of "ready!" rang out around her. It sounded like there were a lot of people, and many voices she recognized. Getting married again? Yes, she didn't care how, or when, but she would marry Gaspard a hundred times over.

Éloise reached behind Amandine and untied the blindfold.

"You sure tied this tight enough," she muttered to Bertille. "I'm surprised my sister still has blood flowing to her brain."

"I didn't want her peeking." Bertille's voice came from Amandine's other side.

"No risk there," Amandine chuckled.

Éloise whipped it away. Amandine couldn't believe her eyes.

The central row of her mother's vineyards had been transformed with hundreds of fairy lights. Their friends lined the next row, dressed in their wedding finery and grinning at Amandine with happiness, and yes, a little bit of 'I-told-you-so' satisfaction in their eyes. They had been right all along about Gaspard and Amandine belonging together, and they never lost an opportunity to remind them of this.

At the end of the row, close to what looked like a priest in his robes—how Gaspard found a priest who was willing to marry them in such an unconventional setting was beyond Amandine's comprehension—was her husband.

Her pulse raced at the sight of him. Even at this distance, she could see the warmth in his eyes, and a bit of self-congratulatory pride in the way he straightened his spine. As she absorbed the magic he'd created with the sisters, she had to admit his pride was warranted. He was wearing his wedding suit and looked a hundred times more attractive than he had on their first wedding day, because now he was finally hers and she was his—there were no more doubts.

Before Gaspard, she'd never imagined that love, freed of fear, could feel infinite. A lifetime didn't feel long enough to appreciate this man, and the alchemy they had together.

There was a tap on her shoulder. She turned to see her brother, dressed in an impeccable suit, looking happier and healthier than he had in years. Outdoor work suited him, as well as leaving behind the bitterness and anger of the last decade.

He extended his arm. "If you let me—" His voice cracked on the words, so he started again. "I would be so honored if you let me walk you up the aisle." He looked doubtfully ahead of him. "Or, row of vineyards I should say, because it is you after all." He smiled, but it was a bit wobbly, and his eyes were shiny.

Amandine felt dampness gather in hers. Finally, she and her brother could begin again. There was no-one she would rather have walk her up the vineyards than him. "I would love that," she said sincerely. "It would make me very happy."

He linked his arm in hers and they made their way up the row to a Bach cello concerto that had been a favorite of her mother's, and which the sisters must have found some way to play on a speaker hidden somewhere behind a vine root.

Amandine took a deep breath, inhaling her happiness. She even spared a thought for her father. She didn't forgive him, but if it hadn't been for his mean-spirited maneuvering, she probably wouldn't be getting married to Gaspard a second time—this time for real. There was nowhere else she'd rather be.

Making her way up the aisle at Jean-Marc's side, she absorbed the love of her friends as she went—her real family and her found family all blended together. Clovis,

Cerise, Yves, Marc, Emily, Myrtille, Luc, Sadie, the sisters, Julie, Adèle, Raphael, Aunt Geneviève and Cerise's uncle (she would have to ask for his name one of these days) Gaspard's new firefighting friend Bastien…and her mother—the spirit of her mother was all around her.

Gaspard took her hand as she reached the front. His palm was warm and perfect against hers. *Home.* His eyes kindled with roguish admiration.

"Well done," she whispered to him.

"Do you like it?" he asked. "Was I right?"

"I don't like it," she said, and was dismayed to see his face fall.

"I love it," she clarified.

He put a hand over his heart and breathed deeply. "Have pity. Don't do that to me," he said. "You see what lengths I had to take to see you in that dress again?"

"You went to all this trouble just for that?"

He winked at her and squeezed her hand. "That, and because I love you."

"I love you too."

"Then let's continue," Gaspard said, and they turned to the priest.

La Fin

Would you like to read the bonus epilogue for Return to the Vineyards, with the continuation of the wedding night from Gaspard's point-of-view?

Just go here to get yours!
mailchi.mp/laurabradbury.com/bonus-epilogue-return-to-the-vineyards

If you enjoyed *Love in the Vineyards*, then you will love my bestselling, romantic, and escapist memoirs, the Grape Series. The first book in the (so far) eight books series is only 99 cents on Kindle and free in Kindle Unlimited. It's also available in paperback and audiobook.

Turn the page for an excerpt of *My Grape Year*, voted number one in Buzzfeed's "18 Feel-Good Books That Will Make You Believe in Love."

Sneak peek of
Chapter One
My Grape Year

At the age of seventeen in a last-minute twist of fate, Laura Bradbury is sent to Burgundy, France, for a year's exchange. She arrives knowing only a smattering of French and with no idea what to expect in her first foray out of North America. With a head full of dreams and a powerful desire to please, Laura quickly adapts to Burgundian life, learning crucial skills such as the fine art of winetasting and how to savor snails.

However, the charming young men of the region mean Laura soon runs afoul of the rules, particularly the no-dating edict. Romantic afternoons in Dijon, early morning *pain au chocolat* runs, and long walks in the vineyards are wondrous but also present Laura with a conundrum: How can she keep her hosts happy while still managing to follow her heart? Follow along on Laura's journey to *l'amour* in *My Grape Year*.

Chapter One

RULES FOR 1990–91

OUTBOUND EXCHANGE STUDENTS—THE
FOUR "D"s

1. No Drinking
2. No Drugs
3. No Driving
4. No Dating

By signing this contract, I hereby accept my role as Ursus Youth Ambassador for the 1990–91 exchange year abroad and agree to abide by all four of the "Rules for Exchange Students."

The other outbound exchange students around me were scribbling their signatures on the forms.

No Drinking. I knew I was heading to Europe, Switzerland, if everything went according to plan, and even though I was drawn by the history and beauty and exoticism, I was also hoping to be able to enjoy a nice glass of beer or wine from time to time. I was seventeen and would be graduating from high school in three short months, so I hoped they wouldn't take this rule too seriously in what my grandmother always referred to as "the old country."

No Drugs. I seriously doubted that marijuana was as ubiquitous in Europe as it was on Vancouver Island,

Canada, where it self-seeded in many people's back gardens. And since I had no intention of ever trying any other type of drug, this rule wasn't an issue.

No Driving. It would be weird to no longer be able to drive nor enjoy the independence that came with that. Still, like many Canadians, I knew how to drive only an automatic and didn't like traffic very much, so I could live with this rule.

No Dating. This rule bothered me the most. It had just been explained to us that as Ursus Youth Ambassadors we would have to be available and open to all people we encountered during our year abroad. Having an exclusive romantic relationship would interfere with that goal. Also, the Ursus Club hosting us would be responsible for our welfare during our year in its country, and that would be far simpler to ensure when we students remained single. I could see the logic of it all, but my romantic life during my high school years had been seriously disappointing, if not to say practically nonexistent. My heart longed for romance and love.

Still, I felt as if the whole world was out there waiting for me, and I needed to take the step to meet it. If that meant signing this contract, then I would do whatever it took.

I picked up my pen and signed my name.

The men's polyester pants were off-gassing in the stuffy hotel room. The scorched smell of synthetic fabric tickled my nostrils. March was generally a cool month in

Victoria, so the hotel staff hosting the annual Ursus District Convention hadn't anticipated the heat wave. The Rotary and Lions clubs, similar community service organizations, had recently begun to welcome female members, which I was sure had lessened the polyester quotient. Ursus, though, stubbornly remained a men-only group, aside from their female International Youth Exchange Ambassadors like me.

A makeshift fan had been unearthed and stuck in the corner of the room, but sweat trickled inside my navy wool blazer, which had already been festooned with at least forty pins. Pins were the currency of the incoming and outgoing exchange students and were traded with the fervor of stocks on Wall Street.

The interview was almost over, thank God. If they liked me, I would get the final confirmation that I would be spending the 1990–1991 academic year as an exchange student in what I hoped would be my first choice of host country, Switzerland. There was only one available spot in Switzerland, and it was contested hotly every year. Belgium, my second choice, was better than nothing. Germany was my third choice, but I knew I definitely didn't want to end up in Germany. I'd never found blond men attractive, and I vastly preferred wine to beer. It was a crime that Italy, France, and Spain weren't options. I could completely envision myself at some Spanish or Italian bar, dancing on the tables after a night fueled by sangria or Prosecco—though I'd apparently signed away my rights to drink either of these.

"I see Switzerland was your first choice, Laura," the head of the committee observed.

Was? Not is?

Every one of the ten or so men around the table had a copy of my application in front of him. "Can you explain your reasons for that?"

I had answered this question so many times in previous interviews that I could do it in my sleep. "One of my main motivations for going on a year abroad is to learn a foreign language," I said. "Switzerland has not one but *three* official languages—French, German, and Italian. I would love to be exposed to more than one language during my year as an Ursus Youth Ambassador." Actually, I was hell-bent on a year abroad because I sensed this huge, marvelous world waiting for me beyond the mossy shores of my island home, and I vibrated with the need to meet it.

The Ursunian who was chairing the interview cleared his throat. "That is an excellent answer, Miss Bradbury. However, we just received the news that the Switzerland spot was nabbed by another district." The men exchanged shocked looks at this breach of fair play.

What? What about my fantasies of racing up and down the Swiss hills like Maria from *The Sound of Music* and warming myself up with some lovely cheese fondue and wine in a wooden chalet afterward, preferably with an entourage of handsome Swiss men? I knew I would have to deal with my disappointment later; right then wasn't the time. I dug my nails into my palms and smiled brightly. "I'll go to Belgium, then."

"We do have several spots there. I just feel we should let you know, though, that more than half of them are in the Flemish-speaking part of Belgium."

Flemish? I had been so sure I was going to Switzerland that I hadn't even considered the possibility of being sent to Flemish-speaking purgatory.

I flashed another smile. "Of course, I would make the most out of any placement," I said. "However, French is Canada's second official language, and growing up here on the West Coast, I have always regretted the fact that I have never learned to speak it fluently. I hope to go to McGill University in Montreal, so obviously French would be a huge advantage for me."

There was no need to mention that French had actually been my worst subject all through high school, and that I'd had to drop it after Grade 11 because it was torpedoing my GPA. Or that I ran out to the quad after my Grade 11 provincial exam for French and yelled, "Thank God! I will *never* have to speak French again in my life!"

A slighter, bald man piped up. "You may not be aware of this, Miss Bradbury, but there is no way for us to guarantee where you will be placed. We send over the files for the incoming students, and it's up to our Belgian brothers to allocate them as they see fit."

I struggled to maintain my bright-eyed demeanor.

"There's always France, I suppose," mused the head man, as though thinking aloud.

My head snapped in his direction. "I understood there were no exchange spots available in France."

He cleared his throat. "That *was* the case, but there has been a…ah…development."

My heart began to somersault. *France?*

A tall man at the opposite end of the table, who had been picking something fascinating out from under his thumbnail, jerked his head up. "With good reason!" he said, paying attention now. "Every exchange we arranged in France has ended in disaster. The families didn't even bother to come and pick up our students from the airport, or they suddenly decided that they were sick of hosting and locked the child out of the house or left on vacation without them. We couldn't possibly jettison another student into—"

The chair cleared his throat meaningfully. "I have a letter here from the Ursus Club in Beaune, France." He waved the letter, which from what I could see was written in elaborate cursive with a fountain pen. I longed to get a closer look—it possessed a tantalizing whiff of the exotic. "They say that one of their students is being hosted this year by our district, so they would welcome one of our students. Just one student, you see. It would be on a trial basis. They sound sincere."

"Don't believe them," snarled the tall man. "I was president of our club the year our poor student was abandoned at the airport in Paris. He had to take a plane back to Seattle the next day. Try explaining *that* to his parents!"

"We must believe them," the chair insisted. "Ursus spirit demands we have good faith in our French brothers. Besides, Miss Bradbury here strikes me as a competent sort of person who can deal with extreme situations. I wouldn't even mention the possibility of France to most of our outgoing students."

"I—I..." I stuttered, wondering how I was going to disabuse him of this notion. I couldn't imagine any horror worse than leaving for a year abroad only to have to return to Canada the next day with my tail between my legs. Yet...France! I had always wanted to see Paris and the Eiffel Tower and learn how to drape scarves properly.

"George"—the tall man's voice was stiff with displeasure—"throwing this nice young lady here to the French would be like throwing a lamb to the wolves, and I for one—"

"Neil," the head man said in a quelling tone, "there is an open space for France, and it needs to be filled. Miss Bradbury has explained how urgently she wants to learn French. She is mature and full of positive energy. I have complete confidence in her."

What is the word for "shit" in French? Merde? My mind whirred as I tried to find a way to extract myself from this fix.

But then I thought about red wine. Little cafés. Baguettes. French men were supposed to be very charming, weren't they? In any case, they had to be an improvement on Canadian boys. It could be a disaster, or it could be even better than Switzerland. In any case, I decided, it was definitely better than spending a year learning Flemish.

"I'd be delighted to take that spot in France." I straightened my shoulders.

All the men except Neil nodded approvingly at me as though I had just performed a selfless and heroic act. Darn. Had I?

The chair erased Switzerland and Belgium from my application and wrote "FRANCE" on it in large capital letters. He scrawled something in his notes.

"That settles it, then! You'll be heading to France in August, Miss Bradbury. I hope you have an excellent year, or shall I say a *bon voyage*?" He chuckled at his own joke.

"Thank you," I said, "or shall I say *merci*?" This got a laugh out of all the men, and they stood up and stretched their polyester-clad legs to indicate that I was dismissed.

I must have missed the sound over the whir of the fan and the muffled scrape of chairs against the carpet, but when I think back to it now, I am convinced there must have been a mighty creak. There had to have been, because at that precise moment my entire life shifted on its axis.

To purchase
My Grape Year
http://mybook.to/MyGrapeYear

The Grapevine

Interested in receiving Laura's French recipes, sneak peeks at her new work, as well as exclusive contests and giveaways, insider news, plus countless other goodies? Sign up for Laura's Grapevine newsletter and join our fantastique community.

Go here
http://bit.ly/LauraBradburyNewsletter

Merci

I wrote **Love in the Vineyards** in the first part of the COVID lockdown in 2020. Little did I know it would *still* be the COVID lockdown when I wrote this sequel, **Return to the Vineyards**, from February to May 2021. This pandemic has lasted so much longer than any of us innocent grasshoppers could have imagined in Spring 2020 with all of our sourdough starters, learning how to play the ukulele, and getting used to this new thing called Zoom. We were adorable. Now we're like weary dystopian characters from the book Dune.

We're finally seeing a light at the end of the tunnel with vaccinations. I got jabbed about a month ago and Franck gets his next week. Bless the scientists.

One thing that this bizarro 12+ months has taught me is how valuable stories are to us. Whether they be in the form of binging your favorite TV series or movies, podcasts, books, or audiobooks, storytellers help pluck us out of our daily life and give us the ability to live another one. This has saved me so many times—in my years as an awkward adolescent, again when I was waiting for a life-saving organ transplant, and just every day as a I curl up on our couch with my read-of-the-moment and my after-lunch coffee (sacred).

I'm greedy that way. I love my life, but I want to live so many other lives, and stories allow me to do so. I hope that my storytelling, especially this tale of Gaspard and Amandine that I adored writing, has allowed you to do it too.

Thank you to my wonderful readers who always keep me writing. You give me so much encouragement and support every day—the least I can do in return is write you another uplifting, heart-warming book to read.

Thanks to mon Franckie. We still love each other after a solid year of lockdown, which is saying something. Laughing and cuddling…man, do those two things go a long way in a relationship. Charlotte, Camille, and Clémentine—living through a "unique" moment in history isn't always fun, but you did it.

A huge merci to my friends Charlotte Buffet in Burgundy, Pam in Montreal, and all my walking, kayaking, and kvetching friends here in Victoria. Thank you to Nyssa for, you know, saving my life with half of your liver. Four plus years and counting! You remain the Queen of Everything. Kathy Chung and Karen Dyer are wonderful friends and such integral parts of my writing life. It doesn't feel lonely with you by my side. Same goes for the Surrey International Writers Conference and all the wonderful people there.

To Tricia, my assistant—I'm so glad you came into my life. Your work ethic and attention to detail, as well as our overlapping sense of humor has made working with you an absolute joy.

Lastly, thank you to my Grapeviners community (you can join at www.bit.ly/LauraBradburyNewsletter) for helping me with this book at every stage—the cover, the title, the blurb…you are so incredibly awesome and smart. I am honored to do this writing thing with you.

Bestselling author Laura Bradbury published her first book—a heartfelt memoir about her leap away from a prestigious legal career in London to live in a tiny French village with her Burgundian husband in *My Grape Escape*—after being diagnosed with PSC, a rare autoimmune bile duct/liver disease. Since then, Laura has received a lifesaving living donor liver transplant from her friend Nyssa, published many more Grape Series books and the long-anticipated cookbook to accompany her memoirs, entitled *Bisous & Brioche*. She has also written *The Winemakers Trilogy*, romantic novels set in the Burgundy vineyards, and with renewed health, writes with even more passion than ever.

Now living and writing on the West Coast of Canada with a new liver and three Franco-Canuck daughters (collectively known as "the Bevy"), Laura runs three charming vacation rentals in Burgundy with her husband, has an enviable collection of beach glass, and does all she can to support PSC and organ donation awareness and research.

Author's Note

Just a few notes from *moi* about *Return to the Vineyards*.

Both Gaspard's village (Volnay) and Amandine's village (Pernand-Vergelesses) are ones I'm intimately familiar with, and they are both downright magical.

Volnay is where my dear friend Charlotte's husband runs his family wine Domaine (since, like, the year 1565 no less). I've spent a lot of time there and the idea of the stone doorway that leads direct from the Domaine to the vineyards is taken directly from their layout.

With our house in Villers-la-Faye, we drive through the steep, winding streets of Pernand-Vergelesses on our way to and from Beaune (a trip we take several times a day). I never get over the sheer beauty of this village, with its golden stone and tiled church steeple and the way it clings to the side of the hillside topped with that statue of Virgin Mary that has become such a touchstone for me and Franck and our own love story.

The whole idea of found family with Amandine, Gaspard, Clovis, Luc, Cerise, and Sadie, really came to fruition in this book. In our most recent five-year stint in Burgundy, we had two couples like that. The six of us, plus our many children, became a de facto family that came together almost every weekend. We adored each other, we shared inside jokes, we helped each other move and had each other's backs—no question. It gave me a sense of belonging that filled something essential in my soul.

I loved replicating that in these three books, and I have plans to extend the series … I have story ideas for Louise and Bastien, plus Luc's brother and sister, plus alll the other sisters. Let me know at laura@laurabradbury.com whose story you would love to read.

The French I use in *A Vineyard for Two*, *Love in the Vineyards*, and *Return to the Vineyards*, as well as my Grape Series of memoirs, is colloquial. While it may not be grammatically correct it's a reflection of how we truly speak in Burgundy, including words of local *patois* such as *"bétion"* (really draw out the 'e' if you want to pronounce this with a true Burgundian accent!).

If you enjoyed *Return to the Vineyards*, then you will love my bestselling, romantic, and escapist memoirs, the Grape Series.

Find Laura Online

The Grapevine Newsletter
bit.ly/LauraBradburyNewsletter

Facebook
facebook.com/AuthorLauraBradbury

Twitter
twitter.com/Author_LB

Instagram
instagram.com/laurabradburywriter

Pinterest
pinterest.ca/bradburywriter

BookBub
bookbub.com/authors/laura-bradbury

Books by
Laura Bradbury

Grape Series
My Grape Year
My Grape Québec
My Grape Christmas
My Grape Paris
My Grape Wedding
My Grape Escape
My Grape Village
My Grape Cellar

The cookbook based on the Grape Series memoirs that readers have been asking for!

Bisous & Brioche: Classic French Recipes and Family Favorites from a Life in France
by Laura Bradbury and Rebecca Wellman
Bisous & Brioche

The Winemakers Trilogy
A Vineyard for Two
Love in the Vineyards
Return to the Vineyards

Made in the USA
Monee, IL
25 May 2021